RUTHERFORD PUBLIC LIBRARY, NJ

P9-EMH-519

Southern Sass
and a
Crispy Corpse

DISCARD

Books by Kate Young

SOUTHERN SASS AND KILLER CRAVINGS

SOUTHERN SASS AND A CRISPY CORPSE

Published by Kensington Publishing Corporation

RUTHERFORD
FREE PUBLIC LIBRARY
RUTHERFORD, N. J.

Southern Sass and a Crispy Corpse

KATE YOUNG

KENSINGTON PUBLISHING
www.kensingtonbooks.com

KENSINGTON BOOKS are published by

Kensington Publishing Corp.
119 West 40th Street
New York, NY 10018

Copyright © 2020 by Kate Young

All rights reserved. No part of this book may be reproduced in any form or by any means without the prior written consent of the Publisher, excepting brief quotes used in reviews.

To the extent that the image or images on the cover of this book depict a person or persons, such person or persons are merely models, and are not intended to portray any character or characters featured in the book.

This book is a work of fiction. Names, characters, places, and incidents either are products of the author's imagination or are used fictitiously. Any resemblance to actual events or locales or persons living or dead is entirely coincidental.

If you purchased this book without a cover you should be aware that this book is stolen property. It was reported as "unsold and destroyed" to the Publisher and neither the Author nor the Publisher has received any payment for this "stripped book."

All Kensington titles, imprints, and distributed lines are available at special quantity discounts for bulk purchases for sales promotion, premiums, fund-raising, educational, or institutional use.

Special book excerpts or customized printings can also be created to fit specific needs. For details, write or phone the office of the Kensington Sales Manager: Attn.: Sales Department. Kensington Publishing Corp., 119 West 40th Street, New York, NY 10018. Phone: 1-800-221-2647.

Kensington and the K logo Reg. U.S. Pat. & TM Off.

First Printing: June 2020
ISBN-13: 978-1-4967-2147-1
ISBN-10: 1-4967-2147-0

ISBN-13: 978-1-4967-2148-8 (ebook)
ISBN-10: 1-4967-2148-9 (ebook)

10 9 8 7 6 5 4 3 2 1

Printed in the United States of America

CHAPTER 1

If someone had asked me yesterday how I envisioned a perfect day, I would have told them a morning swim in the ocean followed by a day on a lounge chair with a good book and an ice-cold drink. Now I sat on my beloved beach a few feet away from a dead body with my blissful notion spoiled.

The murky water, a product of last night's storm, had obstructed my view of the sandy floor as my toes plunged into the grainy depths. The current hadn't been too strong. Fine for my dawn swim. Our island used the flag method to notify its residents and tourists as to the ocean's safety conditions. Red flag meant high surf and strong currents. Yellow, which flew today, moderate surf. Green meant calm. And lastly, the purple flag indicated a hazard from dangerous marine life that lurked too close to the shore.

The waves had lapped against my bare skin as I waded out into the surf, pulled my goggles down over my eyes, and dove through a wave. Bliss enveloped me as I swam the morning's troubles away. Several strokes in, I took a hit to the foot. Unnerved, I hoped someone had simply lost their paddle or bodyboard. Marine life was also the ever-niggling worry in the back of my mind. Encounters happened. Usually harmless and simply curious, baby sharks ventured closer inland. I sped up my strokes.

A microsecond later, I took a major hit to the side. When I turned to investigate, striking out with both hands, something slimy slid between my fingertips, and I came face to face with a badly burned profile. I learned, in that moment, you could scream underwater. Bubbles flew from my lips as all the air left my lungs. During some untimed gasps, I gulped in salty water. My chest burned. My arms thrashed, instead of slicing through the water, as I fought to swim back to the shore.

Waves crashed over me, shoving me toward the ocean's floor. A spike of adrenaline shot through me, fight-or-flight engaged in battle. I fought the unforgiving current and scrambled toward the shoreline. Pain shot through the soles of my feet as they pounded against the half-buried and broken shells at the water's edge. Pain notwithstanding, I persevered and propelled myself forward with the aid of a crashing wave until I fell hard to my knees. I crawled and sputtered before I collapsed on the beach. Sand stuck to my body in all the uncomfortable crevices where sand didn't belong. When I finally managed to crack open my lids, I came to the knowledge that the same wave that had flung me toward the shore had also flung the body. A half scream, half sob left my lips, and I scurried like a crab away from the corpse.

Of all the mornings to come out here and be daring. Now, with my robe fastened tightly, I watched as the Peach Cove Sheriff's Department did their thing. My deceased mother sat next to me, chastising me, of course.

"Child, I can't believe you're out here in your birthday suit. What on earth possessed you to do such a thing?" My mama, Clara Brown, had been tied to the island since the day she passed. She wasn't what you'd call a pure heart in life, and now the powers that be forced her to remain in limbo until she made amends in order to cross through the pearly gates. At least that was how I understood it. Betsy's meemaw knew all about island folklore and passed her knowledge on to my friend, who then passed it on to me. Mama hadn't denied the claim, deeming it accurate in my mind. The distinct possibility that Mama could be a hallucination and I had yet to be diagnosed with a mental disorder lurked in the back of my mind often. Either way, here she sat in her favorite yellow dress with white daisies on it. The same dress she'd been buried in.

"I find the experience freeing." I secured my bathrobe tighter. At least it covered me to below my knees. For all anyone knew, I could be wearing a swimsuit underneath. "Besides, this far down, the beach is usually empty."

Some investors had come in last year and bought most of the properties on the west side of the island and developed it for tourism. If it did well, you could bet your bottom dollar they'd come for the other beaches Peach Cove offered, including this one.

"That's no excuse, you ridiculous girl." Mama's face puckered as if she had sucked on a lemon.

I fought an eye roll. "Not like it's any of your business anyway. I just needed to get out this morning. To take some time for myself. In hindsight, and taking into account the amount of discomfort I'm in, I should have worn a bathing suit." I stared down toward the water, longing to rinse off.

"You had another fight with that Myers boy." She'd never liked Alex.

I didn't reply, determined to withhold the satisfaction she'd feel from clearly intuiting this morning's events. We'd indeed had a fight and it had been a doozy. After finding the body, the problems in my complicated love life felt minute.

"I told you that boy wasn't good enough for you. Consummate flirts aren't the settling-down type. They can't seem to help themselves. Their heads turn toward any pretty face that bats a mascaraed eyelash in their direction."

After last night's fight—well, technically, early morning fight—I couldn't exactly argue in his defense. Not that I should have been surprised, with our history. He'd had a thing with my arch enemy, Rainy Lane Ledbetter, when we were young. Still, I'd been shocked when my brother called me with the news that he'd caught Alex at a bar with a tourist. I had no idea where this left us. Even if we couldn't make it work, I didn't want to lose our friendship. Take the romance away and we were great friends. The best.

"Get your story together. Edward's coming over." Mama began fluffing her short brown curly hair as if Eddie would be able to see her. I struggled to my feet, while holding my robe together, in hopes of maintaining my modesty. Technically, Edward "Eddie" Carter was my father. Not knowing that fact for the first sixteen years of my life, I'd never gotten around to calling him anything other than his given name. Until that night when it all hit the fan and I found out about the affair that resulted in the conception of yours truly. I suppressed a shudder at the memory of a red-faced Eddie stomping out of the house when my half-brother Sam and I came home from the movies. Nothing was going on between Sam and me, *yuck* and *thank God*, but Eddie had feared it. Sam, as shocked as I was, had been livid not only for being kept in the dark but also because Eddie had still been married to his mama during the time of said affair.

Before that night, I'd believed that my sister, Jena Lynn, and I shared the same father. When he passed, Eddie and Mama had picked up where they left off. Needless to say, it had been a traumatic time in my life.

Eddie and I had worked on our relationship and, over the last year, we'd grown closer. And it had been a total blessing. Since moving back home after my painful marriage, followed by an equally painful divorce, having a good relationship with my family had been my salvation. My new life had been calm and pleasant up till now.

My father stalked toward me. His gaze trained on the sand in front of him until he reached me and gave me an odd glance before he cleared his throat.

Did he witness my conversation with Mama? I need to be more careful when speaking with her.

"Eddie?"

He averted his gray-blue gaze that was so much like my own. Not much made Eddie nervous or uncomfortable.

Oh no! "Someone saw me swimming." My face heated.

In confirmation, he pointed to the top of the dunes behind us. "Mrs. Foster likes to bird watch early in the mornings. She takes photographs of the morning feedings with her telephoto lens."

I knew I should have gotten that gym membership.

Mama clucked her tongue. "Shameful. Lord knows this is going to further taint your reputation."

I forced myself not to glare at her for longer than a second. And, of course, she still preened in Eddie's direction. She just couldn't help herself where her ex-lover was concerned. It was a shame she couldn't have shown him the love he deserved while she'd been alive.

"How many shots did she manage to get?" I was so thankful that my sunglasses hid my eyes.

"Enough. She said this activity of yours is a semi-regular thing. And if her husband were alive, she would have reported you for indecent exposure."

My face couldn't get any hotter. Since it was a scorcher today, maybe it could pass as sunburn.

My skin itched. The water had evaporated, leaving the salt behind. I rubbed my arm. "Next time I decide to go swimming, I'll wear a suit." Or go farther down the beach to where the old vacant fixer-uppers were. No chance of being spotted there.

"You certainly will, young lady." He raked his fingers through his graying blond hair wet with perspiration. "Lord, girl. Of all the things for a father to have to deal with."

I covered my face with my hands. "I'm sorry. And you don't have to worry. After today, I don't think I'll be swimming anytime soon." I shuddered at the thought of the body and dropped my hands. The idea of hiding was absurd now. "Any idea what happened to that woman? Besides the obvious, I mean." My assumption on gender was based on the small frame and length of hair. What was left of it, anyway. I almost gagged. The smell from the body was one I wouldn't soon forget. I hadn't eaten today and the idea of food completely turned my stomach. *Me*, the foodie queen.

"We have the coast guard on the lookout for a burned or burning boat. I'm sure we'll get an update from some of the fishing boats on the water as well. It stormed last night, so I'm not sure how many stayed out late. I hate to think this could be one of the party barges the tourists book a lot. This time of year the captains push the limits of safety for revenue. If that's the case, we could have more bodies on our hands." Eddie's phone chirped and he stepped aside to answer it.

Gulls glided above. I used their presence as a welcome distraction from the uncomfortable situation. We certainly didn't need to contend with a host of dead bodies.

"You being here isn't a coincidence. Remember what I told you last year." Mama faded from sight and I instantly recalled her words. *When one of us is forced to remain, it creates an energy around the person we're communicating with. An aura, if you will. The deceased will be drawn to you.*

Not again. I swallowed, my throat dry and scratchy. The corpse lay a few yards from the water's edge and was covered with a tarp. Teddy, the coroner, had been called in moments after Eddie's arrival. Teddy Gaskin and his father owned and operated the Gaskin Funeral Home. The only one of its kind on the island. Teddy had been elected coroner a few months back when Mayor Bill decided the island needed one. He was kneeling next to the body with his latex-covered hand up to his nose. Teddy had a wiry build and little beady brown eyes, with inky black hair and mocha skin. Today he wore little round glasses that sat at the end of his pointy nose.

A few yards from him stood the reason I ended up here on this awkward morning: Deputy Alex Myers. We made eye contact as he spoke to an elderly couple who had come down from their home to see what the commotion was about. I caught a bit of seaweed in my peripheral vision and pulled at it. It had dried and I had a hard time removing it from my hair. Oh well.

Alex was about five seven, a couple of inches taller than me, with a stocky build. He had dark, thick, wavy hair that always seemed to be in need of a trim. His skin was coppertoned from the sun and it complemented his deep brown eyes with flecks of green you could only spot when examining them up close. We'd always had a complicated relationship. One day I believed he was the love of my life and the next I wanted to murder him. I'd also go on record that he felt the same about me. From this distance, I could see the conflict on his face. He probably battled with regret for our earlier fight, where he'd proclaimed his innocence, but I could read anger there as well. He shifted his weight from foot to foot. A clear indicator that fury brewed below the surface, and it didn't take a rocket scientist to understand why. God, I hoped Mrs. Foster was a terrible photographer and the images wouldn't be clear.

Either way, Alex and I would be having words later. He started toward me, but I gave my head a small shake. A sigh left my lips when he stayed put. That he respected my wishes for space afforded me time to process. This certainly wasn't the time nor the place to have a battle of wills.

The man beside Alex, the new deputy, had come onto the force only a few weeks ago. What was his name again? I groped for it. When it didn't come to me, I asked Eddie when his call ended.

"Javier Reyes," Eddie said. Ah, that's right. "He's sharp." Javier was taller than Alex but shorter than Eddie, who stood at a little over six feet tall. Javier had a sharp military cut, salt-and-pepper in color, and olive skin. A handsome man. No doubt about that. The single ladies of the island would go gaga over him.

"You can go home now and get changed." Eddie put a hand on my shoulder. "Where's your beach bag?"

"Um—" I grimaced.

He held up his hand. "Never mind. Hopefully we won't have to speak of this again."

We walked up the beach toward the public entrance. The distance between the beach and my car never seemed so far.

"You'll need to come down to the station in"—he glanced at his watch—"an hour and a half. We'll need to get your statement on record. You'll give it to Javier." That made sense. No conflict of interest there.

"Of course. I'll call Jena Lynn and tell her I'll be in late today." Up the wooden steps toward the walkway we went. I wished Mama hadn't gone. Not that it mattered. I had no control over when she appeared and, most of the time, neither did she. The way she explained it, or at least as I understood it, was she had little control over the amount of time she was allowed to show herself. She would be notified if my life was in danger and be allotted more time. With her revelation this morning and how quickly she faded out, I supposed she showed up to see how I handled the discovery of the deceased. As much as I wanted this to be a coincidence or an odd mishap, something in my gut told me it wasn't.

Perhaps this was an accident. Maybe I could go on focusing on the average problems in life—men, diets, and my business. That sounded like a dream.

I slid into the driver's seat of my sea-mist-green Prius.

"Pumpkin." Eddie lowered his head to peer into the open window. "Let's not make a habit of this."

"The skinny-dipping or dead bodies?" I cracked a smile.

He gave me a stern look.

"Laughter is the best medicine."

"Laughter will do nothing for this splitting headache." He rubbed his forehead with his thumb and index finger. "Drive safe. I'll see you at the station." Eddie patted the hood of the car.

I sat there and watched him make his way back down to the beach. I waited until he was out of sight before I pulled away.

As I drove home, I wondered who the poor woman was. If she had a family. Was she a resident or a tourist? What had happened to her? One thing I was one hundred percent certain about: I should have turned Alex away last night and slept in this morning. If I hadn't been here, I could have saved myself and my father a lot of humiliation.

CHAPTER 2

I wiped the steam from the bathroom mirror in preparation for blowing dry and straightening my blond hair. I'd rallied since I'd showered and dressed. It was amazing how just getting clean made you feel better. This could all add up to be a horrible accident. Mama could be wrong. If not, people were going to start wondering about me. Well, those who didn't already. Since my divorce, I'd come to terms with the abuse I'd endured by my ex's hand. I'd been surprised by how much sharing with a group of others who'd had similar experiences helped me along my healing journey. That, combined with private therapy, gave me a healthier perspective on myself and life. There was still work to be done, but I could handle it. I'd learned that I possessed the strength to endure and grow.

Earlier this year, I began volunteering to help out by providing refreshments from the Peach Diner, our family business that my sister and I had inherited from our mother. When asked, I'd shared with reluctant newcomers my own journey. What I'd walked through and continued to walk through on a daily basis. Assured them they weren't alone and that together we were stronger.

The hardest part for me had been telling my family. Especially Eddie. He'd nearly burst a blood vessel in his forehead, and I truly thought he would drive to Atlanta and kill Peter. Thankfully, once he cooled down, he held me and we cried.

Now I hated for something to burden him further. If this island spirit nonsense continued, I feared he might grow to despise me. I wished Mama could hang around without the attachment of other deceased.

No. Stop it! This wasn't about me. Yes, it was horrifying. But that poor woman was the victim. Bless her heart. Time to accept the things I could not change and trust that everything would work itself out. One day at a time.

I brushed my lashes with mascara. My eyes were bloodshot. At least my skin had a nice summer glow. A little cover-up concealed the burn from the sand and, with a tad of lip gloss, I'd be set.

After I'd thrown on the Peach Diner–logoed polo and standard black work shorts, I slid into my Crocs, the perfect footwear for work, and snagged my purse.

Ten minutes later, Jena Lynn had been lightly informed and I sat across the desk from Deputy Reyes at the Peach Cove Sheriff's Department. Eddie had sectioned off the desk area of his two deputies with partitions, giving them each a cubicle of space within the small office. I'd been on him for as long as I could remember to update the drab wood-paneled walls and white tile flooring. Budget wouldn't allow it.

I'd already explained to the deputy how I came to discover the body this morning. That I'd not touched her other than by accident when she slammed into me. I gave him an exact account of my morning before arriving at the beach, including the argument with Alex. Hiding information easily discovered by law enforcement, I deemed a bad idea.

He was busy scribbling little notes on his yellow pad. I

wondered how many murder or accidental death cases this man had investigated. So, I asked.

The deputy's pen paused, poised to write, as he lifted his head. His deep-set eyes were full of intelligence. Something stirred within them that I couldn't read. Uncertainty, perhaps.

"I've investigated my fair share. Why do you ask?" His accent was slight but unmistakable. Alluringly exotic for our little Southern island inhabited with folks speaking in slow drawls mingled with twang.

I allowed my shoulders to rise and fall deliberately. "Just curious."

He went back to writing.

His desk was tidy and well organized. Alex's desk could be described as a typhoon of paperwork, manuals, and files. He rarely opened his laptop. I'd come in a couple of times and helped him type up reports. A task he detested. Most of the time he bribed the girl at the front desk to type them. Deputy Reyes, on the other hand, appeared to enjoy his data entry. There were neatly stacked files in organizers next to his open computer. He seemed meticulous about his work. I bet Eddie loved that about him.

"Did you call anyone other than the sheriff after you were, as you put it, accosted by the body?" He pierced me to my seat with a penetrating stare.

"Nope. Just Eddie." I sat in silence for a couple more beats, taking notice that his desk, void of family photos or personal paraphernalia, looked bland. No wedding band, so, single. Guessing, I'd say he could be about ten years older than me, making him around thirty-eight or thirty-nine. Divorced maybe. A consummate bachelor also a possibility.

"Do you make a habit of exposing yourself in public?" His tone came out so smooth and deliberate that it took a second to register the question.

When I did, I sputtered. "I . . . I beg your pardon?"

"You were nude on a public beach." His tone dripped with what I took as disdain.

Immediately on the defense, I groped for intelligible words. "No, I wasn't. Okay, I was, but not a single person uses that beach! There are only a few elderly people residing on that end of the beach. None of them swim." My shoulders curled forward, and I fought to keep them upright. He'd notice, of course.

"We've had complaints. If you weren't the sheriff's daughter, charges probably would've been filed." Eddie's words about Mrs. Foster came back.

"I didn't know the old woman could see." I fought to keep my emotions in check. "And, for your information, skinny-dipping on a deserted beach, with no one else around, isn't considered lewd conduct around here." For the second time today, my face burned. Here I'd attempted to be friendly, welcoming to the newcomer, and he insisted on being downright rude. I had no issue with the question; however, the tone in which he'd posed the question plus the expression on his face—his eyebrows raised and his lips pursed—had me discombobulated.

"Mrs. Foster begged to differ." He rocked back in his chair. His fingers tapping together in a trained fashion.

My mouth opened and closed several times as I sought an explanation.

My nails dug into my purse on my lap. "Am I being charged with indecent exposure?"

"No. I said you weren't going to be."

I regained the strength in my tone. "Are there any other *pertinent* questions pertaining to the actual case that you need me to answer?"

"Not at this time. That'll be all, Ms. Brown. You can go." With a wave of his hand, he dismissed me and bent back over his work.

"Fine." I rose and tossed my purse strap over my shoulder.

Still he kept his head bent. He didn't acknowledge that I'd stood. He didn't stand with me or shake my hand. Every Southern boy worth his salt would rise when a woman stood to leave. I expected him to do the same. Especially after what he'd just put me through. Would it kill him to afford me some dignity?

I folded my arms in defiance and waited, needing a win.

His head slowly rose and his eyebrows followed suit. "Was there something else?"

"Other than you being rude, no. I suppose a degenerate such as myself doesn't deserve a proper farewell."

"What type of farewell were you expecting? You've just been questioned regarding a serious crime."

Wow. Just wow.

"As a witness, not a suspect." I thought about shouting at him. Telling him that my poor judgment in the ocean this morning had nothing to do with this dead woman nor should it defame my character.

He regarded me with an emotionless expression as if I were insignificant—no, worse, childish. "Goodbye, Ms. Brown. I have a lot of work to do."

I swallowed the lump in my throat, along with my pride, and turned and left.

"Marygene." Alex caught my attention as I passed the front desk. "What were you thinking? Skinny-dipping? You should have seen Eddie's face. Now Javier knows about the pictures."

"I don't have to explain myself to you." I'd had about all the judgment and embarrassment I could take for one day.

"You don't?" Alex's eyes fired up.

"Look, it's been a rough morning." I pointed my finger at him. "And I'm in no mood to fight with you. We're not exclusive, remember?" I whipped his words from earlier this morning back at him.

He let out a bellowing sigh. "I explained what happened. She—"

I held up my hand. "Save it!"

"I swear it was nothing. How many times do you want me to apologize?" Alex sounded exasperated. We both were. "Besides, we agreed that neither one of us was ready for a serious commitment. So don't put it completely on me."

The truth in his words regarding the marriage talk we'd had recently resonated. Neither one of us had defined our relationship. We just sort of were a couple. At least I'd thought we were and, with what happened the other night, combined with our history, I wasn't sure if we should be in any sort of relationship.

Eddie stood in the doorway and called to Alex. I slid my sunglasses down from the top of my head to cover my eyes. A clear indicator as to where I planned to go. Outside and away from here.

"Everything okay?" Eddie asked and came to stand near me.

I said, "Just fine."

The exact second Alex said, "We just need a minute."

I shifted on my feet. "Sorry again about earlier."

Eddie cleared his throat and glanced away.

"Listen, I've got to go. I'm late and Yvonne has an event scheduled for tomorrow night that I'm catering. Lots to do."

Eddie's face held concern. "Are you sure you should be pushing yourself after this morning? I'm sure Jena Lynn can handle it."

I'm fine." I scrounged up a smile. "Promise."

"How'd it go with Javier?" Eddie rested a hand on the front desk.

I forced the corners of my mouth to remain up. "He's thorough. I see why you like him." Let that get back to the deputy. He hadn't rattled Marygene Brown. "Let me know if you need me to come down here again."

Alex gave me a long hard look before it was clear he'd given up on having it out with me here. Thank God. "I'll call you."

I nodded. A call could be safer than a visit.

Tonya, the department's receptionist, took her seat at the front desk as Alex and Eddie disappeared through the doorway. Tonya and Jena Lynn had graduated together. Both women were now in their early thirties. Jena Lynn had aged better. Tonya's dishwater hair fell lifelessly around her shoulders and over her floral scarf. She had been with the department for the past year or so, replacing the widow Mrs. Patty after her retirement. Tonya, a real sweetheart, hadn't always been the brightest bulb, but she was well-organized. Eddie had mentioned what a good job she was doing.

"Hey, Marygene." Tonya waved in my direction. "What's the special today?"

Knowing Tonya, the question wasn't out of place with the events surrounding the morning. She lived for food. I could relate. "Hey. You doing okay today?"

She made some adjustments to her scarf. "I'm all right, but poor Mr. Wrigley is under the weather. He's Persian and has respiratory issues. He requires lots of attention. I would have stayed home to care for him, but Eddie said I couldn't have the day off. Too much going on he said." She scowled.

That didn't sound like Eddie. I stepped toward the desk, a bit confused that she'd refer to her boyfriend so formally. "Oh well, Mr. Wrigley must be a special guy. Um, how long have you two been together?"

She stared at me, her round face filled with confusion. "Oh." The cobwebs seemed to clear and she laughed. "No. Mr. Wrigley is my fur baby. I adopted him at a rescue six months ago. You wouldn't believe how many people get rid of their pets once they outgrow the kitten phase."

Oh, she said Persian not Parisian. I chuckled, thankful to Tonya for adding a bit of humor to my day and helping me refocus. The phone rang and, after checking the time, I waved and made for the door.

She called after me, her hand over the receiver. "Wait! What did you say the special was?"

My shoulder held the door open. "Turkey meat loaf."

"I thought so. Thursday's special is usually turkey meat loaf, but since y'all have been changing up the menu, I wanted to make sure. Mr. Wrigley will be so pleased." She grinned.

The lunch rush would be in full swing, and I hurried to park closer to the diner. Rain had been forecasted for later this evening. Luckily, I'd made extra pastries and pies last night since we had loads of fruit that needed to be used up before it went bad. Otherwise, Jena Lynn might be in a mess. The wind whipped up and the leaves began to rustle in the trees as I waited at the crosswalk. We were nearing peak tourist season, where we'd see temperatures well into the high nineties. The sunrays danced on the giant shiny peach sign above the diner.

The square bustled with crowds, the influx of tourists both a positive and a negative, depending on who you asked. At first, Jena Lynn and I fought against the investors as our mama and nanny had done many times before us, but we'd lost and change came anyway. Surprisingly, and to our delight, it had been lucrative for our family business. We'd even been able to branch out and do some catering for a couple of weddings, one of which had been my sister's. Our wedding cakes were the talk of the island. Not only did we make beautiful cakes, but delicious ones as well. Something apparently other brides had found difficult to find elsewhere.

As I held the tinkling door open for some new arrivals in my packed-to-capacity diner, the chatter of happy diners, the clatter of silverware on plates and bowls, and the aroma of good ole Southern food lifted my spirits and delighted my senses. A few heads turned in my direction, and I hoped it had been out of idle curiosity and not that the news had already spread. I waved at Ms. Glenda and her sister, Ms. Sally, seated in the middle booth. I'd grown fond of the sisters since returning home. The ladies were part of Meemaw's widows' group, despite the fact that neither of them had ever been married. They'd been welcomed in with open arms. Which I thought was refreshingly nice. Our island needed to spread more kindness.

"Sorry I'm late." I scooted around the counter toward Jena Lynn and pivoted to keep from making Betsy drop the tray of food.

Her red mane flowing from her ponytail slapped me in the face as she passed. "Jena Lynn is about to have a coronary. We're almost out of peach rolls."

My sister's chestnut-colored hair bobbed around her chin as she spoke. "One of the ladies from the church came in and nearly cleaned us out for the seniors' luncheon they're hosting this afternoon. I told her next time she'd have to place an order in advance."

An emergency indeed. The peach rolls were one of our biggest sellers. I tied an apron around my waist and washed up. "I'm on it."

"Hey, wait." She grabbed my arm. "All okay?"

"Just fine," I lied. "Formalities. You know how Eddie's a stickler for them. It should all be cleared up soon. No worries."

Her name was called, rescuing me from lying to my sister further. In truth, I hoped it all would be cleared up soon and life could continue right along as it had for the past year. We had so much to be thankful for and look forward to with the expansion.

The yeasty dough was out of the walk-in refrigerator and dumped onto the lightly floured stainless steel surface in less than a minute. The first batch of rolls were cut and shoved into the proofing box in under ten minutes.

I'd just poured the confectioners' sugar into the mixer when Betsy stood in the doorway, hands on her hips. "You streaked down the beach buck-naked in front of Mrs. Foster?"

"Jeez. The rumor mill must have gone viral. Did you get a text?"

"No. Mrs. Foster told Mrs. Gentry who told Ms. Glenda who just now told me."

Figured. "Yes, I was skinny-dipping."

Her mouth dropped open but her eyes were laughing.

"I had a lapse in judgment." Several lapses, if I were to be honest.

"She said something about you get more like your mama every day."

I paused. "What's that supposed to mean?" If anyone favored Mama, it was Jena Lynn. Ms. Glenda must have been referring to my behavior. Odd.

Betsy shrugged and stepped farther into the room and lowered her tone. "Tell me you didn't actually find a dead body this morning?" She'd obviously been given a description of the corpse as well, by the crinkled expression on her face.

My shoulders sagged in response.

"Was it awful?"

"So awful." I added the vanilla extract to the mixer.

"Eddie thinks it could have been a horrible accident on one of those party barges."

"Betsy!" Sam, my half-brother and our line cook, yelled. "Your eggs are dying here."

"Coming!" She turned back toward me. "You don't think this has anything to do with your mama and the weird juju she put on you?"

I shrugged, not willing to share when we could be overheard.

"Betsy!" Sam yelled with more urgency.

She spun to leave. "We're not done talking about this. Oh, hey, did Tonya say if she planned on coming by for lunch? I saved Mr. Wrigley the end pieces of the meat loaf."

"She is, and Mr. Wrigley will be so pleased."

CHAPTER 3

Gulf Stream Street dead-ended at the Palmer house, as the family on my mother's side had referred to it. Generations of Palmers had lived in the old place for as long as I could remember. In my lifetime, I had never seen the estate look more beautiful. Yvonne bought the property last year, and she'd completely transformed it.

Arriving before Betsy and Jena Lynn, I had the time to fully take in the place. The large dining room was decorated beautifully. Her goal, as she'd described it to me, was to give the illusion of stepping inside an issue of *Georgia Coastal Magazine*. She'd succeeded. The lovely blues accented with taupe gave the room a calming, luxurious feel. Yvonne hung a large framed print of driftwood between the two large windows adorned with plantation shutters.

"Perfect," I breathed.

"It is, isn't it? I'm just thrilled it made it here in time for the showing." Yvonne wrapped her arms around herself.

"Don't worry." I looped my arm through hers. "You've done an amazing job. The house is breathtaking, the furnishings are ideal, plus you came in under budget." Yvonne had worked her butt off to showcase her skills. She'd sunk every last dime she had into her new business. A large chunk of it went into purchasing and renovating this old house. "One day, you'll be the interior designer to the stars."

"Thank you for that." She grinned a little and moved to straighten a picture for the third time, tension still visible in her posture.

"What is it?"

"What if the event is overshadowed by that awful accident yesterday? Or people might not show because they're afraid to attend." Her concern wasn't completely unfounded. The tragic way the victim had died would be a topic of conversation tonight. Fear, the ever-powerful motivator. I'd made up my mind not to indulge anyone seeking idle gossip.

With my hand, I began smoothing out the cream tablecloth on the large oblong table. "You can't worry about the things you have no control over. Besides, in my experience with people, which is vast, since I'm in food service, people like to gossip about other folks' troubles, but if any of those troubles could directly affect them on any level, they'll reason it away. They'll want to believe the victim to be a drunken tourist involved in a horrible accident until another explanation is presented."

"Well, don't you sound healthy."

"I'm trying. One day at a time, right?"

Her eyes were now downcast as her cheeks colored. "I'm sorry. It was insensitive of me to bring it up. You discovered the body, and that couldn't have been pleasant."

"No, it wasn't pleasant, but I'm perfectly fine." I straightened and smiled. "Enough about me. This is your night, and I insist we celebrate you and your success."

Her shoulders relaxed marginally.

"Betsy and Jena Lynn will be here in an hour with all the food." I steered the conversation toward cheery things. "And I'm glad we're doing this together. It's been ages since we've done anything."

A small smile began to crease her lips. "I know. Between Mama and the business, I've barely had time to breathe." Her tone shook. Before I could inquire further, she recovered. "Thank you again for doing this. I know the items on the menu aren't regular fare for the Peach. I can't believe you created lime cream puffs just for me." She moved to reposition the sea-green candles on the mantel above the fireplace. The color was a dead ringer for her dress. She certainly fit perfectly in this home. The old bones of this house, paired with Yvonne's ability to polish and bring out charm without losing the era, were simply sublime. Even Izzy seemed to fit in. The little white Chihuahua-poodle-terrier mix was lying in a little furry bed in the corner, napping. There was something special about Izzy.

"We were glad to do it." It had been the most fun I'd had in the kitchen in a long time. "You know I enjoy a change in routine."

She smiled and nodded.

"I must admit, the salmon mousse is to die for." It had taken me two attempts to get the texture perfect. Now I was eager to test it out on a crowd. Especially those who were accustomed to this type of cuisine. With the tourists came a wave of new palates that delighted in trying my new recipes. We had the snowbirds in the winter and families in the spring and summer. Some of our elderly island residents had even begun renting their homes out and downsizing. After Jena Lynn's wedding last fall, we'd discussed expanding again. With the memory still fresh that Mama would never entertain the notion when I suggested it, my sister made sure I understood she was on board with the idea. "Your talents are wasted with simple diner fare. You could be a pastry chef in a four-star restaurant." She'd flattered me.

I wouldn't go that far, but I did enjoy creating beautiful and tasty pastries. We were still undecided whether we'd simply expand the current location by building on to the back or purchase an additional storefront. Zach, my sister's husband, said he'd see what the county would allow us to do and draw up some plans.

"Do you think they'll choose to feature it?" Yvonne pulled me from my thoughts as we strolled out onto the front porch to flip on the strings of lantern lighting.

The pillow on one of the rocking chairs needed a fluff. I obliged it. "How could they not? The *Georgia Coastal* wouldn't be sending anyone if they believed it would be a waste of time. You've done a remarkable job. Enjoy it." I gazed down the beautifully elegant solar-lit driveway. The large oak, draped with Spanish moss, swayed in the warm breeze, a few branches dancing above the left side of the driveway.

Two lawn workers came from around the side of the building. "All done, Ms. Brooks. I just need you to sign off on the work order."

Yvonne met the man in old cargo pants and a white T-shirt on the porch steps. His coworker hauled a large ladder toward the work truck, his clunky tool belt hung low on his waist. They were both the color of burnt sugar, and pouring sweat. Working outside on the island could be rough on the skin if you didn't wear adequate protection.

"Yoo-hoo!" someone called from the far end of the yard.

As they approached the porch, we were able to make out the figures of Evelyn Gentry, Doc Tatum's receptionist, and her son, Junior.

"Are we early?" Mrs. Gentry tucked her hand in the crook of her son's arm.

Yvonne rushed down the steps to greet the mayor's wife and son. "Just a tad. Is the mayor with you?"

Mrs. Gentry shook her snow-white head. "He'll be along shortly. Government business, you know, always keeps him late."

Yvonne smiled politely. "Of course."

"How's Thelma doing today? I did get by to see her the other day." Mrs. Gentry's countenance softened into a pitying grimace. "Well, she just wasn't herself. Very confused, I'd say."

Concerned I was eavesdropping on what should be a private conversation, I started to leave. My thought pattern changed when Yvonne glanced back toward me. Something in her gaze told me she was glad I'd been in earshot. Her mama mustn't be doing well. My heart ached.

"Yes, she has good days and bad. So kind of you to remember and check in on her. Mama appreciates it, even if she is unable to express her gratitude. Please"—Yvonne stepped aside—"feel free to have a look around."

"Oh, an advance tour." She gave Yvonne a little pat on the arm and allowed her son to help her up the steps.

Junior was about a half a foot taller than me, with golden thinning hair and ruddy chubby cheeks. He and I were about the same age, though he hadn't gone to school with the rest of us. He'd been sent to a private school off island. We saw him mostly in the summer and on holidays.

Junior grinned and waved at me as the two passed by and went into the house.

Mrs. Gentry greeted me with a simple, "Marygene."

For some reason, this woman wasn't a fan of mine: Not that I cared for her either. She'd leaked information about me, or at least I had my suspicions that she had. Before I began my work with the support group and became open about my recovery, a few of her contemporaries had approached me expressing their sympathy before their nosy questions commenced. Nevertheless, I smiled and nodded pleasantly as Yvonne escorted the pair into the house.

With my face lifted toward the breeze, I caught the light scent of honeysuckle, a familiar fragrance, and my thoughts drifted to the dead woman. It seemed every time I found a moment where my mind wasn't completely occupied, the imagery came rushing back, along with a deep desire to know who she was and what brought her to such an awful fate. Alex had called a few times and left messages. With each message he progressively became more agitated. If I had been able to have a conversation with him without losing my cool, I would have called him back. If we had been on good terms, I could have inquired about the case.

Yvonne rejoined me on the porch and pulled me from my musings. "It's an hour and a half before the event. Why in the world would Mrs. Gentry show up so early?"

"Oh, you know her. She'll want to tell everyone she was the first to see what you've done here. If there's a scoop to be had, she'll want it."

"Yeah . . ."

"Listen, if you ever need to talk about or help with your mama, all you have to do is say the word." Shame that I hadn't been more of a shoulder for my friend overtook me.

"I appreciate it. Mama's in good hands and, as hard as it was to finally make the decision to move her into Sunset Hills, it's been good for her." She sighed. "I'd be lying if I said living in her house without her isn't tearing me apart."

Tears stung my eyes and I blinked them back.

"And when I'm with her, it's just as difficult sometimes. One day she seems her old self and the next she's accusing a caretaker of stealing her jewelry." She wiped at her eyes. "Tonight, though, isn't about my troubles. It can't be."

Understanding her need, I rushed to her rescue. "You're right." I beamed, pulling myself together. "Tonight is about your amazing talents and blossoming career. And look!" I pointed to the white van, with a large peach with the curly script *The Peach Diner* painted on the side, pulling into the driveway. The Peach delivery van was the newest addition to our business. When we did expand, perhaps we'd add several more to our inventory.

"They're early." Yvonne sounded relieved.

"Yes, and they'll have alcohol."

"Praise the Lord." Her mood had obviously lightened, and we both laughed.

"Hey y'all!" Betsy called as she hopped out of the van in her upgraded uniform. She wore her red hair up in a messy bun. Our uniforms for catering events were dressed-up versions of the usual ones we wore at the diner. Tonight the three of us dressed in black pants and short-sleeved classic white button-down chef coats with our logo embroidered on the left breast. Jena Lynn was the only one of us who didn't have to worry about her hair. The length was short enough not to be a problem. Mine, I'd pulled back in a red carpet–style ponytail. It had taken forever to get it right, even after several YouTube tutorials.

"Jena Lynn, could you drive around to the left side of the house, where the maids' entrance used to be? That leads directly into the kitchen."

My sister nodded and waved for Betsy to get back into the van. The second the van vanished around the corner, a black Lincoln Town Car pulled into the driveway. The man got out and pulled an expensive-looking camera from a case. We watched him take a couple of shots of the beautifully lit front lawn.

"Oh, he must be with the magazine." Yvonne began fidgeting with the white and green bangles on her arm.

I gave her hand a squeeze, and our blue gazes met. "Deep breath. The hard part is done. You'll be great. This place is stunning."

"Thank you, again." She took a couple deep breaths.

"Just stating facts. I'll go and get started setting up." My friend deserved to bask in her glorious achievement without concern for the setup.

Betsy and my sister were already unloading large trays of hors d'oeuvres when I made it to the kitchen. I preheated the oven and opened the French doors of the large stainless steel refrigerator.

"Marygene," Jena Lynn called from the side door as she struggled to keep the sheet-cake-sized box level. "The box got damaged during the drive over."

A couple seconds later, I had one side of the box and she the other, and we sort of maneuvered it through. "I hope the lime puffs aren't damaged," I said.

Jena Lynn's pursed lips told me she hoped the same thing. We set the box on the island and gingerly lifted the lid to peer inside.

"Oh, thank God."

They were all as they should be. Lovely little puffs filled with my lime custard and topped with a lime zest drizzle. They'd been a ton of work, and not something I'd want to do alone again anytime soon. I'd need to hire more help when we expanded.

"I just put the crab-stuffed mushrooms in the oven to keep them warm." Betsy motioned with potholder-covered hands. "I can fit four more trays in this oven." It was a real relief that this venue had adequate appliances. We had a couple of experiences on past jobs that hadn't. Not a big deal with some of our offerings, but one with all this seafood and poultry, it would have been a disaster.

Yvonne came rushing into the kitchen, Izzy tucked against her chest, just as Jena Lynn came in with a case of champagne. "How long will it be before y'all can set up the food? We're just under an hour from showtime."

Jena Lynn smiled at our friend and poured her a glass of champagne. "Don't you worry about a thing. Food service, we know. We're about to start setting out the food now. The food is always ready to serve thirty minutes ahead of schedule. Early arrivals are always expected."

Yvonne took a few deep sips from the glass. "I'm sorry,

y'all. It's just I need this to go off without a hitch. This showing could have a big impact on my career."

Her assistant came in and took Izzy from her. "I'll make sure she isn't underfoot."

"Thank you, Candi." Yvonne smiled at the young woman who appeared to be about twenty. She had toffee-colored hair styled in a spiky sort of haircut. She stood taller than Yvonne, who was about my height, only thinner. Candi appeared uneasy.

Her gaze darted around the room before it settled on Yvonne. "Did you know there's an old woman and a beefy weird guy skulking around inside the house?"

"You must mean Mrs. Gentry. The woman with hair like a dandelion puff?" Yvonne mimed a helmet. At the girl's nod of confirmation, Yvonne waved away her concern. "Don't worry about her. She's just nosy."

"Whatever you say." Candi shrugged. "The old lady seemed weird to me. Just thought you should know." She left with the little dog without a word to the rest of us.

"The girl's got good instincts." Betsy wasn't a fan of Mrs. Gentry either. She handed Yvonne one of the spicy mini chicken-and-waffles. "Eat this. It'll calm you down."

Yvonne did as commanded.

"Better?"

It didn't seem to have the effect she was hoping for. Yvonne's blond locks bounced around as she shook her head. Luckily, she had always been good at hiding her nerves. Once things got rolling, she'd be fine. I told her so.

"I know you're right. The photographer sounded polite and eager to get started. He said his colleagues should be arriving any minute." Yvonne placed the empty champagne flute on the counter.

"This is so exciting!" I grinned.

Yvonne beamed. "It is and I'm so grateful."

"We're all so happy for you. Um, didn't you say this house had a wine cellar?" Jena Lynn got us back on track. We had an event to cater. "Sam should be arriving shortly with more cases of champagne, and it would be great if we could utilize the counter space strictly for food prep."

"Oh yes." Yvonne put her hand over her mouth as she spoke. That she had gone back for seconds while stressed, I took as a huge compliment. She walked over and opened the small door off the back of the kitchen. I had believed that to be a pantry. She flipped on the light. "It's just down there. I've got to get back. The photographer is touring the yard. Be careful, though. I've only been down there once and recall the stairs are a bit steep. There should be an old light at the bottom. I think it's the kind you have to pull with the string."

"Great." Jena Lynn placed a chilled case on the counter to begin filling glasses as Yvonne left. "Sam better get here soon with the rest of the champagne or we're going to run out. Don't mention it to Yvonne, though. I don't want to cause her any unnecessary stress."

"Jena Lynn." Mrs. Gentry and Junior strolled into the kitchen. "I wonder if I could have a word with you before the event is underway."

"Of course." Jena Lynn handed me the bottle and I continued with the task. Jena Lynn and Mrs. Gentry stepped into the dining room, leaving Junior with Betsy and me.

"You want a mini chicken-and-waffle?" Betsy asked Junior.

He grinned wide. "Yeah. Can I have a few? I'm starving." He stared over at the platters Betsy had made up. "What's that?" He pointed to the mini cups.

"It's honey sriracha sauce. Marygene has it perfectly balanced."

His head bobbed up and down quickly. "Can I have some of that too?"

"Sure." She made him up an hors d'oeuvres–sized plate.

"Gee thanks, guys." He took the food from Betsy. "They're so little." His almond-shaped eyes lit up with a childish glint. "Let's see how many I can fit into my mouth at once." Before I could object, all five went into his mouth.

"Be careful. That sauce is a little spicy," I cautioned right before Junior dumped the contents of all three sauce cups into his mouth. Junior had a slight learning disability and had dealt with his fair share of teasing over the years. People could be so cruel. We'd stuck up for him when our group witnessed any bullying. He had a good heart and would do anything for his mama. He was a sweetie pie.

His face turned beet red a few seconds later. Tears began to stream down his cheeks as he choked down the mouthful. The sauce had a kick. A little went a long way.

Betsy giggled and handed him a glass of water.

After a few sips, Junior laughed along with her, while wiping his eyes with napkins. "You weren't kidding. Good but spicy. I'll see ya, Marygene. If you need anything, just holler."

"Thanks, Junior. Have a good time."

He waved to Betsy before he left the kitchen, still chuckling to himself.

Jena Lynn came back in a few minutes later. "Mrs. Gentry wants us to hire Junior as a busboy." She washed her hands in the sink.

"Junior's all right. It's his mama you've got to watch out for. She's a real busybody." Betsy pulled a couple of trays from the oven. She took the words right out of my mouth.

Jena Lynn said, "Junior's a hard worker, and we could use a second shift busboy. Besides, you can't judge a person based on who their parents are."

She had me there. "You're right. Hire Junior."

Betsy and I got busy.

Yvonne had popped in, overwhelmed with excitement

to inform us that cars were filling the driveway, lining the streets, and struggling to find places to park close to the property. We were ready, the food was beautifully presented on tall tiers and large platters and nestled in bread nests. Betsy was moving through the crowd, carrying a tray holding flutes of champagne. It was a self-serve buffet line. My sister and I were there to answer questions from interested parties. We were unaccustomed to answering questions regarding shellfish allergies. Not many of our usual clientele were sufferers.

"Yes, ma'am." Jena Lynn smiled at the elderly woman, whose neck was draped in rhinestone jewelry, as she answered her question regarding the mousse piped into puff pastry cups. At least I assumed they were rhinestones. "The salmon mousse is incredibly fresh, I assure you."

"That's good." The woman reached over and put a few on her plate with the silver tongs. "I sure don't want what comes next after eating old salmon."

Jena Lynn and I smothered snickers.

"My innards don't work like they used to." Her arm, adorned with too many bracelets to count, jingled as she put the tongs back on the holder.

My brother peeked his head into the dining room.

"Thank God," Jena Lynn breathed.

"I've got this. Excuse me for a moment." I scooted around the table.

"Hey," Sam greeted as I strolled into the kitchen. "Sorry I'm late. It took me ten minutes to find a place to park. It's a good thing I had the hand trucks with me. I would've had to carry those boxes two at a time and from all the way down the end of Orchard Street."

"Well, you should have gotten here earlier, then you could have parked where Jena Lynn did. I told you that we expected a huge crowd and parking could be difficult." I couldn't help but chastise him. He'd cut it way too close.

"I'll help you haul them into the cellar. The staircase is too narrow for the hand trucks."

Sam hefted three boxes to my one after I opened the door. "Sorry. I know how both you and Jena Lynn feel about setting up early. My fault and it won't happen again."

"It's fine. And I know it won't." I struggled for a good grip on the bottom of the case.

Sam hadn't had a bit of trouble. "You okay? Having nightmares about the body?"

"I'm okay and to the nightmares, thankfully, no, not yet anyway. It's the smell that's hung with me that's driving me the most crazy." I stepped aside for him to go down first. "Careful. I wasn't exaggerating about it being narrow."

He went ahead. "So, am I kicking the shit out of Alex or have you decided to forgive him?" Sam could switch subjects in a conversation so fast it could give a person whiplash.

A few days ago Sam and Poppy were out on a date at the Beach Bum Bar. He caught Alex chatting up a tourist. My brother confronted Alex and the two nearly came to blows. Poppy told me Alex had been wiping a bit of beer foam from the woman's lip. A tidbit that Sam had left out, probably wanting to spare my feelings. That was *the* incident that caused the fight that led me to the beach and then to the body. So, could I blame Alex for this? Yes. A resounding yes.

"Haven't decided yet."

I descended into the dark depths. The dampness and the musty odor accosted us.

"Well, you let me know when you do."

"Thank you, Brother." I tried to focus on where I placed my feet. The last thing I wanted to do was trip.

Sam thudded against what sounded like the wall when he reached the bottom. "We need more light down here." The light from the top of the stairs didn't make it past the midway point.

"Yeah, I know. This is dangerous. Yvonne said there was a ceiling light down here somewhere." When I reached the bottom, I stepped carefully to be sure it was indeed the basement floor, before setting the box down. My hands grasped the air in search of a string.

"Hurry, I think they might have a rodent problem."

I was having the exact same thought patterns.

"Or maybe a septic problem."

I surely hoped that wasn't the case. A backed-up septic tank during the showing would prove disastrous. "It's got to be here somewhere."

Sam stomped on my heel by mistake.

"Ouch!"

"Sorry. I can't see anything down here."

"Well, be more careful." The farther I made it into the room, the stronger the scent became. Now, the scent reminded me of my encounter on the beach. Almost like a combination of charred meat and ruined food. Bile rose in the back of my throat, and I froze.

"God, that smell is awful. Oh, here it is."

I heard a click, then the basement became poorly illuminated by the dim overhead lighting. A single bulb. I'd somehow ended up facing the stairs, with my brother a few inches from me, facing the opposite direction.

"Move out of the way."

I shook my head.

"I just can't find another body," I whispered hoarsely. If I found another body, there would be no way I could refute Mama's claim regarding the dead.

Sam looked over my head to view around the basement. "Marygene, move." He started to go around me. "Why would you think there was a—" Sam's jaw dropped.

"A dead rodent?"

He stood there gaping.

"Sam! It's a rat in a trap, right?"

He shook his head.

Slowly, I turned, following his line of sight, and gasped. I couldn't help myself. Now that my suspicion had been confirmed, something inside me forced me to lay eyes on the victim. Another body lay against the back wall next to the wine racks. This one, too, was charred to a crisp.

CHAPTER 4

"Who do you think it is?" Sam, now apparently over his initial shock, stooped closer to the victim, careful not to get too close to contaminate the crime scene. He examined the body with interest.

I stood there for a few heartbeats, pinching the bridge of my nose, trying to keep the headache at bay. I tried not to stare at the corpse. *The corpse.* The *second* corpse.

"How'd you know?" Sam glanced over his shoulder at me.

"The smell. The farther down I came, the more it reminded me of the other day."

"Ah." He focused back on the body.

"I'm sorry," Mama whispered.

This time I didn't jump. I could sense her now.

"I warned you that my presence had affected your molecular makeup. When the island's dead need help, they orchestrate the intercession."

"I'm so sick of dead bodies. God, can't people just refrain from killing each other!" I doubled over, putting my head between my knees.

"You'd think," Sam said with the obvious assumption I'd been talking to him.

Mama leaned down closer to me. "You're strong, my Marygene. You've walked through hell and back and remained whole. They can't break you, darling. No one can."

After a couple of deep breaths, I whispered a silent thank-you to my mama and stood. She'd vanished.

Sam whistled. "That had to hurt. Can you imagine burning to death?"

"I'd rather not." Time for practicality. If I didn't handle this properly, this could completely sabotage Yvonne's event. "Sweet baby Moses, I hate to be the one to break the news to her that we have to call this in." I knew that was insensitive of me, and I wasn't thinking ill of the dead, but there was absolutely nothing I could do for that poor soul on the floor right now. My friend had worked her tail off to make something of herself, and I'd be damned if I wouldn't try to keep this quiet for as long as possible. As ludicrous as it sounded, I considered waiting a few hours before calling this one in.

No, that wouldn't work. If it had just been me down here, then maybe, but Sam would be culpable as well. I shuddered and started for the stairs, forcing the image of the blackened teeth and skull out of my mind. "Come on, Sam."

"You won't have to call this in." Sam's boots thudded hard against the stairs.

I glanced over my shoulder to meet his gaze.

"Dad's in attendance."

I stopped. "Why in the world would Eddie show up at an event like this one? He isn't into old home restorations or interior designs. Plus, his case is fresh."

When Eddie had what he referred to as a fresh case, he

spent every waking minute exploring angles and leads. Closing the case consumed him.

"He's not—his, um, new friend is." The way Sam said *friend*, I knew he referred to a woman. "They were behind me on my way over."

"What *new* friend?"

"He's seeing Doc Tatum."

I wondered why I hadn't been informed of this. Not that Eddie had to run his dates by me, but Sam knew. And I spent a good deal of time with Doc Tatum. Considered her a friend even.

Back on the main level of the house, Betsy was refilling the buffet table. Jena Lynn appeared miffed with me as she finished placing warm goat cheese and roasted red pepper crostinis on the platter. Lost in the shock of the unexpected findings, I'd neglected to keep track of time, leaving her alone to deal with the crowds. I nodded for her to accompany me to the kitchen, away from prying eyes and ears. Jena Lynn gave a pleasant smile to the guests and followed me into the kitchen.

One look at Sam and she blurted, "What's wrong?"

"There's a crispy corpse in the cellar," my brother blurted without an ounce of tact.

I scowled at him. He shrugged his shoulders but glanced away. Sam wasn't known for his sensitive side. As in, he didn't seem to have one.

"What?" Jena Lynn's tone rose. "There's another burn victim?"

"Shh," I hushed her. "We don't want to alarm the guests."

"Okay, okay. What do we do?" She began wringing her hands. "I mean, besides the obvious, to report it." The speed at which she spoke exposed her nervousness. "Should we just carry on?" She had been through months of counseling herself a little over a year ago when she, like me, saw our dead mother. Poor Jena Lynn's mind, unable to handle the vision, sent her down the road of a brief mental breaking point. A decision Mama regretted to this day.

"Yes." I hugged her. "I'll find Eddie. This has absolutely nothing to do with the diner or you." *Thank God.* "And we can't make a scene." I gave Sam a pointed stare as he helped himself to blue-cheese–stuffed olives. The crime scene certainly hadn't affected his appetite. When he didn't seem to quite get my meaning, I nodded toward my sister.

"Oh yeah, Jena Lynn, don't worry. Can I help with anything?" Sam glanced around in search of a spare apron.

"That'd be great, Sam. If you could get another batch of mushrooms going in the oven, that'd be a big help." Sam gave a nod and washed his hands. With a task to manage, my sister seemed much more herself. I swiped a tray filled with flutes of champagne as cover. Yvonne had worked way too hard for this evening to go to pot. I'd spare her if I could manage it.

"Sam, watch the door," I whispered, and left the kitchen in search of Eddie.

I moved through the crowd with ease, pausing occasionally when an attendee showed interest.

"The food is just lovely, Marygene." Poppy Davis, owner of the Beauty Spot, and I guess now Sam's new girlfriend, smiled at me as she took a flute from my tray.

"Thanks, Poppy. It was so nice of you to come out and support Yvonne."

She grinned. A little of her pink lipstick was smeared on her front tooth. After telling her, I kept moving. Yvonne preened to her crowd, her brilliant smile, genuine. Several flashes went off as photographers snapped shots of her in the library. It did my heart good to see her gaining the praise she deserved, and that just made me hate this situation all the more.

"Marygene." Mrs. Gentry stepped in front of me, causing me to nearly lose the tray.

"Careful." The edge in my tone had been obvious.

She blanched. "Something wrong, dear?"

I forced my face smooth. "No, of course not. Champagne?"

She shook her head and her eyes narrowed. "You seem jumpy."

All I needed was for the mouth of the South to get wind of the news. "It's the adrenaline of an event. I'm just so thrilled for Yvonne."

"Oh yes. She's done a wonderful job with such a drab old place. I'm surprised by all the attention she's receiving, though."

Don't bite her head off. She's just an old, sad, miserable woman.

"Anyway, I just wanted to thank you for giving my boy a chance. He's been working over at that temp agency for ages. They just never send him out on temps that lead to permanent positions."

"Of course. We'd love to have a hardworking fella like your son." Without being too blatantly obvious, I kept scanning the crowd for Eddie.

"He is a good boy."

I nodded and pasted a smile onto my face as I continued my search and tuned her out when she changed the subject to island gossip. I kept smiling and nodding at what I'd hoped were the appropriate moments. At least until I caught the word *nudity*. I refocused.

Her overly painted face squinched. "Really, Marygene. Your poor mother would roll over in her grave if she knew there were nude pictures circulating of her daughter."

"Circulating?" My stomach lurched.

The old woman's white head bounced around happily. "Well, they could be. Who knows if Debbie Foster gave the digital files over without saving a copy for herself? People can be mighty opportunistic. I'd watch out for that one."

Unable to hold my tongue a second longer, I snipped, "Well, I guess you would know. Since the two of you are such good friends and all. Birds of a feather, right?" Satisfied by the flash of outrage upon her wrinkled face, I decided to leave her to stew.

She gave a little huff in response as I moved on, which I paid no mind to. This was a matter of life and death. Well, just death, I supposed.

Eddie was standing right inside the library. I could see him now that I moved closer. Yes, his *friend* was Doc Tatum, the island family practitioner. She was in her late fifties, tall and slim, and looked ten years younger, with dark amber eyes and a caring smile. She had taken great care of my sister and me after our ordeal last year when an old man dropped dead in front of us in our diner and my sister was falsely accused of murder. We'd both struggled for a while. Eddie appeared relaxed and happy, chatting with his date. Which made what I had to do even more difficult. Not that I had a choice. When he saw me, his smile broadened. I stood and watched him weave through the crowd toward me, Doc Tatum in tow.

"Hey, pumpkin." Eddie gave me a kiss on the cheek. I loved it when Eddie was in a good mood. I hadn't expected to see this side of him until he closed the case. "Everything is wonderful."

"The food is unbelievable. You should be proud." Doc Tatum brushed my arm with her fingertips.

"Thank you. It's nice to see you, Doc Tatum." I wondered how long I should stay and make small talk before taking Eddie aside.

Yvonne spotted me and gave me a little wave. I beamed back in response. My beam must have been dimmer than usual because there was concern etched in her brow.

I refocused on Doc Tatum. "You look beautiful tonight."

She was the picture of Southern elegance in a cream pleated dress, her hair pinned up with a few strands hanging around her face.

"Why, thank you. Call me Lindy." That was telling. Everyone called her Doc Tatum. "It's such a treat to watch you work. You really have a flair for this sort of event."

I forced a smile and shifted my feet before glancing around.

Eddie's eyes narrowed. Damn. Plagued with the inability to hide my nerves from my overly observant father, not that it would take someone with his skills to detect that my day certainly hadn't gone as planned.

A little more abruptly than I had planned, I blurted, "Eddie, could I have a word, *please*." I put emphasis on the word *please*.

He pursed his lips in disapproval.

Over Doc Tatum's shoulder I saw we were drawing attention. "I'm sorry, Doc Tatum, but it's mighty important."

"I can see that." She took a flute from the side of the tray farthest from her. It forced me to readjust my hold to balance it properly, and I let out a huff of disapproval. Why did people do that? Her tone softened. "Is something wrong?"

I let out a horrible fake laugh that sounded like a wheezing donkey. "Of course not. Don't worry about it. Enjoy the party." God, I was rambling. "I just need to have a word with my father. If you don't mind." It came out terse, and Eddie frowned at me.

Thankfully, Doc Tatum hadn't seemed to take offense. In fact, she seemed to always understand me, speaking to me in cool, calm tones that worked wonders in soothing her patients. "Of course not. Don't trouble yourself with any worry on my account, dear. May I take your tray?"

I gave my head a quick jerk forward.

"I've got it." Eddie took the tray from me and placed it

on a small table to the left of the room's entryway. He leaned down and gave me a smile through gritted teeth. "What in tarnation is going on?"

"Not here," I hissed.

With my hand tucked in the crook of my father's arm, I all but hauled him into the kitchen.

"There better be a good explanation for your rude behavior. Lindy has been good to this family. To you especially and—"

"I know, and she's aware of my gratitude. I'll apologize. She'll understand, believe me."

Eddie's postured stiffened when he noticed Sam standing with his back against the cellar door, in a guarding sort of fashion, as he stuffed his face with crostini.

Guilt oozed from my brother's pores. "Hey, Dad." Roasted red peppers hung out of the corners of his mouth. "Doc Tatum having a good time?"

Our father had a way of making you feel guilty, even when you hadn't done a thing to feel guilty for. You'd always wonder, *Have I done something and forgotten about it?* Which, as kids, we usually had. Thankfully, this one had nothing to do with us.

I dropped my arm and stepped aside.

Eddie's gaze shifted from my brother to me. "This isn't just about yesterday, is it?"

I shook my head.

Eddie's face got that sheriff look. "Tell. Me. Now."

"Down there." Sam opened the door.

"What's down there, Sam?" Eddie's tone was low.

Sam and I exchanged a worried glance. Neither one of us knew how to explain what was down there without chancing being overheard.

Sam spoke up. "Trust me. You don't want us talking about it up here."

Eddie's face went to stone. He had this way of wiping

his expression free of all emotion when he worked on a case. I really needed to learn how to do that. He pulled his cell phone out of his pocket, turned on the flashlight, and started down the steps, with Sam and me on his heels. I closed the door as discreetly as possible. I feared we'd been way too conspicuous already.

"Who found the body?" Eddie asked after he turned on the light and squatted down next to the corpse.

"We did." My brother and I stood shoulder to shoulder—well, my shoulder to his bicep. "We were moving the champagne down here."

"When?"

"Just now," Sam told him. "Marygene came right up to fetch you."

Eddie's face was grim. "Gasoline."

Strangely, it had been hard to pick up on when we were down here before. Now, I detected the distinct odor. The burned flesh smell had overwhelmed me before. Eddie took out a pen from his pocket and moved something with it. I leaned in to see what it was. A wadded-up candy wrapper.

"Neither one of you touched anything down here, right?" Our father had gone into full-blown sheriff mode.

"Only the little rope for the light and maybe the wall," I said softly.

Eddie began punching buttons on his phone.

"It's definitely a murder case now, isn't it?" I asked.

"It stands to reason," was all Eddie said before he stepped away to speak to his deputy. "Myers," he barked. "You and Reyes get down here to the Palmer house. Call the Gaskin boy. We're going to need him on this." Silence. "Yeah, we've got another one."

CHAPTER 5

After Teddy arrived, and all the guests in the house had been asked to leave after providing contact information, the diner staff working the event and Yvonne were the only ones remaining. Teddy had an unusual look upon his face and, since my nerves had calmed down, my curiosity was piqued. If I had one guess regarding his puzzlement, it would be the position the body had been in. That had stood out to me as well.

Yvonne sobbed, and I focused on my friend. "I can't believe this is happening."

"It's going to be okay." I wrapped my arm around her shoulders, leaning my head close to hers. "The evening was lovely and everyone had a marvelous time. No one even knows for certain why they were asked to leave a little early."

Yvonne gave me a cool glare. "Don't try to downplay this. They were asked to give detailed contact information and whether they saw anything suspicious. They know something's up. Did you see Mrs. Gentry's face? She salivated at the potential scoop." She tucked a curl behind her ear and glanced away. "Lord help me. There's a dead woman in the basement of the house *I* showcased. Do you have any idea what that's going to do to my selling potential or my appeal?"

Sadly, I did. Despite that awful fact, she'd recover. Eventually. I knew from experience.

"I guess ain't nobody gonna want to have a house designed by the crispy-corpse designer," Betsy said from across the room, where she sat in a Queen Anne chair.

We'd all been asked to wait in the library, where we'd be out of the way.

"I bet this will be a story to scare the kids for years to come. Better watch out. If you go near the crispy-corpse house, you'll end up fried."

I shot Betsy a *not the time* glare.

Her lips twitched and the giggle she was obviously trying to withhold escaped. "Oops, too soon?"

"Oh, jeez Louise, she's right," Yvonne whimpered and covered her face with her hands and slumped down on the cream pouf in front of the fireplace. "How could this have happened? I mind my own business. I pay my taxes early. I'm kind to my fellow man. Will people remember that about me? No. I'll be known as the crispy-corpse designer."

Sam and Betsy snickered.

"This isn't funny, y'all!" My sister's face resembled the epitome of outrage.

The forensic team wheeled the body past the room, zipped up in a black bag. No one was laughing anymore.

Sam broke the moment of silence. "I guess when folks are unsure how to behave, we have inappropriate reactions."

"Sam's right." I rubbed Yvonne's back. "It's hard to wrap your mind around something like this. They didn't mean any harm."

Yvonne nodded but still didn't raise her face from her hands. We all gave her a moment. Betsy kept glancing away, her lips tightly pursed as she still fought to regain her composure. She'd been so proud of her crispy-corpse designer comment. Her shoulders shook in silent laughter. Sam avoided looking at Betsy. Jena Lynn gave both of them that scolding look a mother gave a child when they were in need of discipline.

My father marched back into the room, flanked by Alex and Deputy Reyes. Betsy sat up straight the second she noticed the new deputy. She snatched a magazine off the rack and began fanning herself. She'd switched from comedian to woman on the prowl in two seconds flat.

"Deputy Reyes," Eddie began, "is going to take your statements."

Betsy raised her hand. "I'll go first. I'm always willing to do my civic duty, Deputy Reyes." She puckered her lips, looking absolutely ridiculous.

He ignored her completely. "I'll start with you, Ms. Brooks."

Yvonne lifted her head, weariness evident in her posture.

"If you'd follow me into the kitchen."

Yvonne rose slowly. There was trepidation in her tone when she said, "Of course."

Sam spoke up. "Dad, is it okay if I take Jena Lynn outside to get some air?" Sam was worried about my sister. So was I.

"That'll be okay. Just don't go too far."

"You all right?" Alex asked me after the five of them left. Eddie had accompanied the deputy and Yvonne into the kitchen. Sam and Jena Lynn had gone out onto the front porch. I heard the door softly close behind them.

"Yes." I sighed. It was a lie. I couldn't describe the emotions swirling within me. I needed to speak with Mama. There were questions that only she could answer. "The two cases are obviously connected."

Alex glanced around. "There's always suspicion when two dead bodies are found so close together and the causes of death are similar. We'll know more when we get the reports back from Teddy."

"Poor Teddy," Betsy said. "Was it me or did he look a little green around the gills when he came up from the basement?"

"I noticed it too." This certainly had to be a lot of excitement for a funeral director on a tiny island.

Alex moved tentatively toward me. When I didn't protest, he wrapped an arm around my shoulders and hugged me. "We okay?"

"Not the time to delve into that one." I sagged against him.

"Yeah, you're right. I just needed to check on you. I have to go. Eddie has me canvassing the neighborhood. It'll be an all-nighter."

"Okay."

He lifted my chin with his index finger. "Things aren't good between us right now, but if you need me, you call. I'll move heaven and earth to get to you." His dark, piercing gaze impressed upon me that he meant it.

Alex had owned my heart 100 percent at one time. Now, as much as I truly wanted to believe we'd make it through anything, my faith faltered. He left and I moved over to the pouf Yvonne had vacated and sat next to Betsy.

"Y'all will work it out. You always do."

Maybe.

"Alex can be an ass, but he loves you."

I shrugged, not having the energy to focus on that at this moment. There were two victims seeking my aid in solving how they died. Now that fact was undeniable. The weight of my predicament made my body ache.

"That Deputy Reyes is the sexiest thing I've ever laid my eyes on." Betsy had a little grin going on.

"God, don't tell me you're interested in him?"

"Why? What's wrong with him?"

"He's so rude. You should have heard the way he spoke to me when I gave my statement after finding the first body."

"Well, he was doing his job. He's new in town and probably wants to be all professional." She licked her finger and smudged the stain on her shirt.

"Maybe. Although, in my opinion, he has the personality of an old shoe. He hardly interacts with anyone when he eats at the diner."

She put her hands on her hips. "Old shoes are comfortable. Ain't nothing wrong with them. I think he's that strong silent type. Probably hurt and just needs a little lovin' from a voluptuous gal like yours truly to bring him out of his shell. You'll see. In a few weeks, he'll be a different man." She sounded completely convinced.

I laughed. "If anyone can, it'll be you, Bets."

When the deputy came back into the library, Sam and Jena Lynn had returned. Betsy lit up like a lightning bug. He asked for Sam next. Yvonne's eyes were red rimmed. She'd been crying.

"I'll talk to you later. I'm going to run by Sunset Hills and see Mama. After that, I need to pick up Izzy from Candi's and then I'm going home, draw a bath, and have a bottle of wine." She had one of the bottles from the kitchen in her hand.

We embraced. "I know this feels catastrophic, and it is, but this incident won't define you or your career."

"Thanks for that." She released me. "I fear you're wrong,

though." She ran her index finger between her eyebrows. "Now I have to go and deal with Mama. I've got three voice mails from the nursing staff. She's been unruly."

"That doesn't sound like your mama."

"I just don't know anymore." She slung her purse over her shoulder. "I tried calling Candi, but it went straight to voice mail. She has a bad habit of forgetting to charge her cell. If she comes back by here, let her know I'll be by to pick up Izzy. It'll probably be late. And if you see her before me, tell her she'll need to give a statement as well. If not, I'll handle it when I pick up Izzy."

"Of course."

She sighed. "I'm so out of it. I couldn't even remember the name of the handyman service. I had to find it in my phone."

"Eddie understands the nerves that are associated with trauma. Don't worry about it and call me when you can, okay?"

She gave me a half nod. She gazed off as if she were a million miles away. Shock, I thought. Even though she hadn't seen the body firsthand, this sort of ordeal took its toll.

Everyone else had gone home when it finally got around to my turn. Odd since Sam and I were the ones to discover the body. In the little nook off the kitchen, which originally had been designed for the maids, I sat across the breakfast table from the deputy.

His face held an unusually calm expression, like two burned corpses didn't faze him in the least. I'd bet he thrived in the interrogation department. "I find it unusual that I'm sitting across from the sheriff's daughter for the second time to discuss how she came to discover another dead body."

Eddie chose to not accompany me again. Either he wasn't a bit concerned about me being implicated or the conflict of interest was too great. I'd bet on the first.

"Can't argue with you there." I forced myself to remain steady. "And I must admit, I'm surprised you waited to speak to me until last. Especially since, as you mentioned, the sheriff's daughter finding two dead bodies in the same week is rather odd business."

"I have my reasons." Slight bags hung under his eyes. It had been a late night for all of us. "Can you tell me how you came to discover *this* particular burned corpse?"

Part of me wanted to tell him the truth. That my mama, the island spirit, had caused all this to befall me. Would I have found either of the bodies without her presence around me? Who could say for sure, but I highly doubted it. Instead, I carefully recounted everything in detail and watched his expressions.

"The smell is one I won't soon forget."

"I would imagine not. And twice in one week." He scribbled onto his pad. "Someone with your history of domestic issues, this has to stir up unwanted emotions."

A low blow. "Are you attempting to upset me? Because, I can assure you, I don't need any assistance in that department." I started to ask for Eddie, then decided against it. Like Mama said, he couldn't break me. However, I did find it rather mean—no, downright cruel—for this stranger to use my traumatic past as a weapon.

"Just recounting the facts." He scratched his square-goateed chin with the back of his pen.

"As you see them." I crossed my legs.

"Yes. As I see them. That is my job."

"Please, carry on with your job, Deputy. The quicker we can get through your insipid questions, the quicker I can go home." My tone came out annoyed, and I didn't care.

"Am I keeping you from your beauty rest? How insensitive of me."

"Well, get to it, why don't you? Riling me up about my past isn't going to get you any additional details, because

I'm not hiding anything." My blood pressure rose with my heart rate.

"How did Ms. Brooks seem to you when you arrived here today?"

I sat there, dumbfounded for a moment, that he'd changed tactics. "Normal. As one would expect, she was nervous about the showing. This was a big night for her career."

"How would you describe her demeanor when the body was discovered?"

"Oh, for heaven's sake! She did *not* do this." There was no way on God's green earth I was going to have another person I cared for charged with an obscene crime. "I mean, really, who's going to torch a corpse and hide them out in the basement and then host a career-making event?" I snorted. "It's absurd."

"I didn't say she did, Marygene. And it's Javier." His eyes regarded me oddly as he leaned back and folded his arms across his chest.

I mirrored his movement. "Surely you have better sense than to chase that ridiculous theory down, Javier. And it's Miss Brown to you."

He smirked.

"Besides, the cases haven't even been ruled homicides yet."

He raised an eyebrow and leaned forward. I couldn't raise a single eyebrow, so I took notice. "How many people do you know who pour gasoline all over their body and light a match?"

"None. You?" Obviously, I believed it to be a homicide. But I wouldn't give him the satisfaction of agreeing.

He leaned back. "Then we have the other body to contend with. Cause of death is perceivably to be the same."

"Perceivably. I guess we have to wait for Teddy to clue us in." I resituated my chef's jacket. The dry cleaner must have gone a little nuts with the starch.

He stared at me. I stared back.

After a couple of very long minutes, I'd had enough. "What's your problem with me? You certainly haven't been around long enough to formulate an opinion as to my character. You work for my father and with my, well, Alex. You've eaten at our family diner on numerous occasions and, during those visits, I've been kind to you, welcoming even. So, tell me, what's your deal?"

"There something about you I can't quite put my finger on. Something . . . off."

My heart rate sped up. Again. Of all the things he could have said, that was the absolute worst. "Funny, I have the same feeling about you." I stood. "Listen, I don't know who that person in the cellar is or how they came to be there. I've never set foot inside that cellar until this evening. I have no idea who would pour gasoline on a person and light a match, and I certainly wouldn't care to make their acquaintance." My declaration didn't seem to faze him. "This line of questioning is absurd. You don't like me, fine. I don't much care for you, either. Eddie does, so I'll be civil because you don't mean a hill of beans to me. But, I refuse to remain here and be treated in such a rude manner."

"Surely you wouldn't expect special treatment as the sheriff's daughter, would you?"

Betsy could do way better than this bozo. "Of course not." I placed both hands on the table as I leaned closer to him. "As you so thoughtfully brought back to my attention, not that I needed a reminder, I've had experience with insecure men who need to demean women to make themselves feel powerful." I smiled sweetly at him.

"What are you insinuating, Miss Brown?"

I'd hit a nerve. *Good.* "You're a smart fella, you'll figure it out. My point is, nothing you can throw at me will stick. You know where to find me if you have further questions."

He slid his card across the table. "My personal cell number is on the back. If you think of anything else. Don't hesitate to give me a call."

I snatched the card off the table and slid it into my bag. It might have gotten crumpled in my fist in the process. "Good night."

CHAPTER 6

As I finished piping the cream cheese frosting on the last of the lemon, cranberry, and white chocolate cupcakes, my sister came into the kitchen.

"Are they ready?"

I was trying to get last night out of my mind. Baking always did the trick. I baked when I was stressed. I'd gotten up after a measly three hours of sleep and came in early for the comfort of butter, flour, and sugar. As always, the Peach Diner became a welcome distraction. Part of my late night had to do with my online snooping. I found some interesting tidbits about our audacious Deputy Reyes. He was indeed divorced and his ex-wife's Facebook page held a wealth of information. I might have even texted him with the website she'd created just for him, Javierreyesisadouche.com. I bet he had second thoughts about giving me his card now.

"Yes." I began boxing up the little beauties. "I wonder what made these the pick of the week?"

Jena Lynn shook her head. "I have no idea."

I moved the first peach-colored box in her direction and she began tying it up with our new logo-printed ribbon.

"You okay? I can tell you didn't get much sleep either. I had to take a sleeping pill to finally drift off." My sister looked concerned.

I thought about sharing with her what I'd found about the new deputy but decided to withhold it for now. I'd also found some positive things about the man too. He'd received several commendations and had a reputation for closing cases. He seemed to be a good cop. Certainly a respected one.

Mama's absence propelled me to get ahead of this myself. I needed information so I could prepare for what was to come. Without information, I'd be even more lost.

I smiled at my sister. "I'm surviving."

She leaned against the worktable. "The whole ordeal is simply lunacy. Who would do something so awful?"

"Try not to think about it."

"Yeah, you're right. We have to move on. Poor Yvonne. This has to be crushing her." No truer words had ever been uttered. "Maybe we should take some food by or something."

"I'll call her and check in." I took a box of turtle brownies from the walk-in. When I reemerged, Jena Lynn had moved on. Good timing since I didn't want her to know what I planned to do after my shift ended in ten minutes.

"Marygene." Betsy peeked around the corner into the kitchen. "You leaving?"

"About to, why?"

A grin played around her lips. "I thought we'd run by and see how the investigation is going. Maybe take your daddy and Alex some pastries. With them working so hard and all, it's the least we can do."

"You mean, take Deputy Javier Reyes some pastries."

"Well, he's part of the sheriff's department now and new to the island. It wouldn't be polite not to make him feel welcome." Betsy's face was flushed and she fanned herself with her hand. "He could be the one, Marygene. You never know."

"I wish you would find someone else to set your sights on." I began untying my apron.

"Why do you dislike him so much?" Betsy had that little crinkle between her eyebrows and her hands on her hips.

"Because he's an ass."

She grabbed a box from the cabinet and began assembling it. "Jeez, tell me how you really feel. Maybe he's just different. You can't expect him to act like folks from around here. You aren't giving him a chance. Don't be a snob, Marygene. We can't all be born Southerners."

I snorted. "I'm not a snob." I went to retrieve my purse from the lockers in the office.

Betsy followed me inside. "I think he's just misunderstood."

"You think he's hot." I closed the locker after I grabbed both of our bags.

She took her hobo bag from me with her free hand. "That's an undeniable fact. The man is smokin' hot!"

I pulled my phone from my pocket. "Hot notwithstanding, his ex-wife's story should be a cautionary tale for you. She dedicated a website to him." I pulled up the website and handed my phone over to Betsy.

Her mouth dropped open. "You can't go by disgruntled exes." She used her index finger and thumb to enlarge a photo. "Oh Lord, she's drawn devil horns on him."

I laughed as she handed my phone back.

"Nope, I'm not going to look at this anymore. But forward it to me in case it doesn't work out between us."

"You got it. Just be careful."

She waved off my concern.

"All right then. We have a whole tray of crumb bars that didn't get picked up. Take those." If he hurt Betsy's feelings, I'd add him to the island's crispy corpse count.

"Great! You going to come with me?"

I gave my head a shake as I tossed my bag over my shoulder. "You have to see the douche all by yourself. I've got somewhere to be."

"Okay. Can I swing by your place tonight and pick up that quilt for Meemaw?"

Her meemaw adored quilts, especially homemade quilts. After the remodel of my house, I'd boxed up Nanny's collection. I kept two for a keepsake but offered the others to Jena Lynn and Betsy.

"Sure thing." I swiped the box of brownies from the counter and left.

The parking lot at the Gaskin Funeral Home held a good many cars when I arrived. Not wanting to be in the way of the funeral procession lining up, I parked beside the curb at the end of the lot.

The two-story redbrick funeral parlor, with large white columns to match the trim, had belonged to the Gaskin family since the first Georgia red-clay brick had been laid. Theodore Gaskin, "Teddy" to all those who grew up with him, had mostly taken over the business after his father had been diagnosed with Stage 1 lung cancer. He'd beaten it, his heath had returned, and he was working again, just not at full capacity. Teddy was standing on the stately porch passing out remembrance cards.

"Hey, Ferret, how's it hangin'?" I grinned, using the old high school nickname, and took a card from his outstretched hand.

He laughed and handed out another card to the couple behind me. I stepped aside to allow them to enter the building.

"You're obviously not here for the funeral." He glanced down his nose and took in my state of dress.

"No. I hoped you'd have a minute to chat. I brought turtle brownies." I cracked the lid so he could catch a whiff of his favorite indulgence.

He checked his watch. "The doors to the chapel should be closing in ten minutes. I usually don't like to stray far from the chapel in case a family member needs me during the service."

"It won't take long, promise." I gave him my most angelic smile. "Come on. We never hang out anymore."

"Hang out." He half laughed. Teddy had a good head on his shoulders. He was a real bright guy. My intentions wouldn't elude him. He reached around me and pulled open one of the large wooden double doors. "Go wait in my office. The same one that used to be Dad's, down the hall to the right."

I scooted through the doors before he could change his mind.

"There better be a full baker's dozen in that box," he called after me.

The sickly sweet smell of flowers and air freshener accosted my senses as I traveled down the narrow hallway on the threadbare burgundy runner. The dark cherrywood-paneled walls of the old funeral home were in need of a good polish. I paused by the first viewing room on my right. It wasn't my curiosity as to who lay in the open cream-colored casket but who stood in front of it that caught my attention.

"What are you doing here?" I whispered into the open doorway.

Mama stood in front of the casket, snickering to herself.

After a quick perimeter check, I rushed to her side. "Why in heaven's name are you laughing?"

She pointed at the body of an elderly woman dressed in a denim dress with a red patent leather belt around her middle. "You know how she died?" Mama guffawed. "She choked on a jelly bean."

"That's hardly anything to be laughing at." I kept my tone low and admonishing.

"Carolyn Peterson made the rudest remarks to her daughter at my funeral. She said I deserved to go out the way I did." She leaned in close to Mrs. Peterson's face. "Well, look at you now, Carolyn!" she yelled. "Dead as a doornail! And I'm standing here over your body telling my daughter you deserved what you got! Ha! Choking on a jelly bean." This wasn't the mama I had grown up with. The Clara Brown that raised me would never disrespect the dead.

"What has gotten into you?"

Mama ignored me and reached into the casket and patted the woman's face, still crooning.

I feared she'd mess up her makeup and terrify the woman's family when they came to pay their respects. I wagged my finger in Mama's face. "Stop that!"

Mama straightened and surprise lit her eyes.

"This childish behavior is beneath you. Just because you're dead doesn't give you the right to allow your manners to wane! I'm ashamed of—"

"Marygene?" Mr. Gaskin's voice jolted me out of my rant. I stood there bewildered. "Who were you talking to?" Mr. Gaskin peered around the empty room.

"No one. I, um, was just paying my respects to Mrs. Peterson." I scooted out of there lickety-split, pausing briefly beside him. My God, if I wasn't more careful, my future home would be the loony bin. "I'm supposed to be meeting Teddy in your old office. It's that way, right?" I pointed past him.

He scratched his white beard and mumbled something unintelligible.

"Have a nice day!" I rushed down the hallway.

After I'd placed the brownies on the large mahogany

desk, I slunk down in the leather chair opposite it, mortified. *The island cuckoo* would be the next nickname I'd acquire. I could hear the gossip now. *Watch out for that cuckoo Marygene. She's the weird streaker that talks to herself.* Sweet Lord. They might even dedicate a website to me, marygenebrownisaloon.com. I had some self-analyzing ahead of me.

"Sorry to keep you waiting so long." Teddy closed the door to the office. He sat down in the oversize chair, took his glasses off, and rubbed his eyes. "What a week."

"For me too."

"I bet." He put his glasses back on and dove into the box of brownies. "What'd you say to Dad? He warned me to watch out for you."

I laughed off the comment as if it had been a joke. "I have no idea. Just said hi and asked where your office was."

"Oh, he still calls this his office."

Relief washed over me.

He opened the box and smiled approvingly. "I haven't had time for lunch. And before you ask, I can't tell you much." He shoved a whole brownie into this mouth.

"I'm not asking you to break any laws or confidences here. I'm just curious about a few facts. Accidental death or homicide? Obviously, by appearances, homicide, right?"

He took another brownie from the box, leaned forward, and took a regular bite of that one.

I continued, "You don't have to say anything. Just nod your head if I'm on the right track. See, the first body, I could have bought as an accident. Except for the fact there weren't any boats missing passengers and no accidents reported. But with the second body . . ." I shook my head. "No way. Not that I'm buying the burned-alive theory. I mean, the second body had to have been restrained. The position was as if the person had been sleeping on their side. Who would lie there and be burned alive? I know I sure wouldn't." I patted the desk, resting my case. "Well?"

"Why don't you ask your dad? You could get me in a lot of trouble here."

"Eddie's worried about me and wants to protect me. And I understand his motivations, but these two are keeping me up at night. It'll be just between us, I swear." I crossed my heart.

"I get the keeping-you-up-nights. In all my time working with the deceased, I've never had to deal with anything like this." He dropped the brownie back into the box and wiped his hands.

"Identical crimes are rare, right?"

His gaze locked on me. He *had* found something.

"Have the identities been confirmed?"

"Not yet."

"Come on, you've got to give me something." I leaned forward and placed my hands on the desk.

He checked his watch and stood. "You said it, not me."

"You mean it was identical homicides?"

"*Identical* being the key word there. I really have to go."

Not that I'd quite figured it out yet, but Teddy had given me a clue. And if I played my cards right, he might come forth with further information as he discovered it. I grabbed my bag and stood. "I owe you a lunch. Come by the diner and it'll be on me."

"Lunch and dinner, plus dessert." Where he put all the food he consumed was beyond me. He had the metabolism of my dreams.

I smiled. "You got it."

CHAPTER 7

The Spanish moss–covered stately iron fence that encompassed Peach Cove Cemetery had tarnished, thanks to the salty air. The location directly behind the funeral home made the procession mighty convenient. Folks would drive around the corner or just walk. The mystique surrounding the only cemetery on the island had frightened brave youths, deterring those who'd dared consider pranking or partying here.

Okay, I supposed it just kept me and a few close friends away. If I recalled correctly, Alex and his buddies had been kicked out of here several times after being caught smoking and having make-out parties. Since I was here, I might as well pay my respects to Nanny and Paw Paw's graves. After the heavy showers last night, the ground was a bit soggy. My Crocs would need a good hosing off since they kept sinking into the earth. Just walking under the large ornate gate gave me the creeps. The islanders' morbid fascination with sculptures of sad-looking children on the headstones was highly distasteful. The large crosses and angels dressed in robes were also overdone, in my humble opinion. All the older ornaments were now covered in moss and had gray water stains, and some were missing limbs. It certainly added to the creepy vibe.

Then we had hundreds-of-years-old oak trees covered in draping Spanish moss that created a canopy effect over the small burial sites. The uniqueness of our island struck me in moments like this. We were the Deep South, part of the Bible Belt, yet we still had our island lore to contend with. Now I could add island spirits to the list.

I paused next to my mama's ostentatious graveside display. Leave it to my mama to have the largest monument in the whole place. A massive six-foot-tall archangel perched against an oval headstone. *Loving wife, mother, and pillar of the community. Gone but never forgotten.* "Gone, yeah right."

Next to her grave was the combo stone for Nanny and Paw Paw. I knelt down. "Hey, y'all. Sorry it's been a while."

When I got home, I gaped at my front lawn, where reporters and several news vans were camped. Before I could turn around and flee the scene, camera flashes and a giant light shone in my face through the windshield and driver's side window.

A chorus of "Marygene, can you describe the scene of the crime? How do you feel about finding the bodies? Did you see any suspicious activity?"

One brazen reporter even opened my door once I had the car in park, forcing me to step out.

"This is private property! I want all of you to clear out or I'm calling the sheriff's office!" I shouted once I'd regained my voice.

"What were you doing on the beach so early in the morning? Isn't it odd you found another body at an event you catered?"

"No comment." I slammed the door and elbowed my way

through the mass. Sweat broke out on my forehead. My heart hammered within my chest.

"Why won't you make a statement? Doesn't the public have a right to know?"

I'd almost made it to the back porch. A few more steps and I'd be home free.

"Is your father protecting you from further questioning?" a woman with long dirty-blond hair asked. "What are you hiding, Marygene?"

Something within me woke and I spun around. "For reporters, you all are mighty stupid. Clearly none of you are clever enough to actually gain any accurate information."

"You sound confident. Does your father share information regarding his investigations with you?"

"No. He certainly does not!" The little red lights on the cameras were on and all the microphones were in my face. God, I'd allowed them to actually get something out of me.

"Get off my property! Now!" I pulled out my cell and tapped the contacts icon and hit Eddie's name as I stomped up the back steps, shoved my key in the back door, and slammed it shut on the vultures.

He hadn't answered so I called again. This time he answered on the fifth ring when I was just preparing to leave him a voice mail. "You okay?" More of a bark than a concerned question.

"I've got a situation. My house is swarming with reporters." I attempted to slow my breathing.

"Don't worry. I'll take care of it."

I'd showered and changed into my favorite comfortable yoga pants and a tank top. Settling in my sleek new chaise lounge in my newly remodeled home, thanks to Yvonne, I opened the takeout container from the diner containing my surf and turf burger and fried pickles. I'd kept it in the insulated delivery bag since leaving this afternoon and was pleased to find it still warm. The crab stuffing squirted into my mouth when I took a giant bite. Yum. I needed comfort food. Even with all the blinds closed and curtains drawn, I could still hear the rustling of activity on my front lawn. What did they expect to happen? That'd I'd suddenly have a change of heart and come out for a chat? Idiots. Sure, they wanted to know who could have committed such a horrific crime, I got that. But barging onto property where you aren't welcome wasn't any way to gain favors, friends, or information from someone like me.

Under the assumption that the victims were restrained, I tried to consider what motive someone could have for burning bodies that were allegedly already dead. Covering evidence was the most evident reason. However, with forensics today, surely not much could be hidden that way. It would make identifying the victims more difficult. Fingerprints were no longer a viable option. That left dental records and medical records. Although, that would only be effective if either victim had fractures on record or kept up with dental checkups.

Finally sirens blared. Eddie sure had taken his sweet time getting here. Not that I'd hold that against him. He had a lot on his plate at the moment. Car doors slammed, and shells pinged against undercarriages from spinning tires. I marginally relaxed.

With the burger now resting in the container, I wiped the juices from my hands and started into the kitchen. When I opened the back door, it wasn't Eddie but Alex standing on the other side of the screen door.

"Where's Eddie?"

"He sent me. The reporters are gone now, and I gave them all a warning that if I get a call again, I'll run them in."

I hoped that would keep the wolves at bay. "Well, thanks." I tucked a few strands of hair behind my ears. "I guess I'll see you around." I started to close the door, not feeling prepared to be alone with him and have the overdue uncomfortable conversation about where'd we'd stand after we hashed out all our issues.

He pointed to the latch keeping him from entering. "Going to let me in?"

The door stood half open. "Not sure yet."

"Come on, Marygene. Let's not let this fester. I said I was sorry." He gave me a crooked smile. God, he could charm me even when I wanted to throttle him. "Life is short. It's your decision how you deal with this. Let's forgive, forget, and move on."

That comment doused the charm. "Why is it that when a man screws up, they always pull out the forgive and forget card? And you're right, it is my decision how I deal with this. But it was your decision that got us here in the first place! Yes, life is short. Too short to deal with BS like this."

"Nothing is going on." He threw his hands in the air. "I don't even remember that woman's name. I was sitting at the bar and she sat next to me. We shot the breeze for a few minutes. She had foam on her lip and I wiped it off. That's it."

"Well, maybe I want to wipe some foam off of some hot tourist's lip and shoot the breeze."

"You better not!" His jaw clenched.

Typical double standard.

"Besides, you have some nerve being mad at me. You're the one who's flashing the world."

"Don't be melodramatic. Old Mrs. Foster is hardly the world."

"Me, melodramatic?" His tone rose. "Pot meet kettle, sweetheart." He gave the screen door a rattling tug.

We squared off. "Alex Myers! Don't you break my door!"

"Then let me in!"

"No!"

He gave the door another jerk. It wouldn't hold much

longer. I went to slam the back door on him, but Betsy joined Alex on the back porch. With all the commotion, I'd totally forgotten she said she'd be by for the quilt.

"Hey, y'all," Betsy said cautiously. "Everything okay?"

"Fine. Alex is just leaving. Betsy and I have to get ready to go out. I have to find a tourist to shoot the breeze with."

"Don't push me, Marygene!" He slammed his hand on the doorframe.

"Since it won't mean anything, why would you care? You didn't want an exclusive relationship anyway."

"You agreed! Said you needed some space." He practically had steam emitting from his ears.

"And you knew why. I was working through baggage, Alex."

"Maybe I'll just come back later." Betsy sounded worried and had that expression she got when she was uncomfortable.

An expression I knew well. A furrowed brow while she bit the inside of her left cheek. Now, I felt like a heel. It was beyond rude to have this blowout in front of her.

"No, I'm sorry, Bets." I opened the door. "Please, come in."

Alex stayed out on the porch, and I joined him out there.

"Listen, let's just put a pin in this discussion: Go home. We both need to cool off, and I need to think. Thank you for coming out here and getting rid of the vermin."

"You're welcome, and I'm sorry." He ran his hand on the back of his neck. "It wasn't my intention to start anything or upset you."

"I know."

"I love you. I swear I do, and I am sorry." He started down the porch steps.

I lifted my hand but couldn't scrounge up a smile for him. Our relationship had always had issues. The problem was, I couldn't envision a life without Alex in it. As to what role he would play, that proved more difficult.

I went to the refrigerator and pulled out a bottle of wine. I held up the bottle. "Want some?"

"Like you even have to ask."

I nodded and pulled two glasses from the cabinet.

We heard the sound of shells pelting against metal and the spin of tires.

Betsy's eyes went wide. "If he hurts my baby, I'm going to kill him! He's drives like a maniac when he's mad." She raced out the back door.

I filled both glasses to the brim and sat down on a stool at my granite island. I sipped from my glass and took in my gorgeous kitchen. Yvonne had done a spectacular job with the décor. The white subway tiles laid at an angle behind the stove and down the wall balanced the color in my light gray cabinets. It had a cool, calming feel with the grayish-blue painted walls in the adjoining dining room.

Betsy came back in with a look of relief.

"Car's okay?" I took a sip from the glass.

She sat next to me and nodded as I slid her glass in front of her.

"He's lucky that it is too." She gulped from her glass. "With the day I've had, I'm in no mood to deal with his tantrums."

I heard that.

"My water heater broke and I've got to buy a new one." She blew out a breath.

"That sucks." I propped my elbow on the island and my head in my palm.

"Want to talk about you and my dumb cousin. Alex can be a colossal jerk. Or are you not ready yet?"

"Not ready yet."

"Okay then."

That was what I loved about Betsy. She never pushed. And when I finally reached the point of needing a listening ear, she'd be there. I did fill her in on the reporters.

"I wished I'd gotten here while they were here." She patted her bag. "I keep my trusty revolver with me at all times."

I was so glad she hadn't shown up while they were here.

"How were things at the sheriff's office?" I grinned over my glass. Even if I wasn't a fan of the new deputy, seeing Betsy enthralled could be a fun distraction.

"Did you know Deputy Douche doesn't eat sugar?" Betsy sounded aghast. "Or refined sugar, as he calls it. I mean, really, how can I have a love affair with a man that doesn't eat real food?"

"So it's a deal breaker then." More sips.

"If he wasn't so hot, yes. I guess I could go on a diet and eat clean." She didn't sound happy about it. "He runs too. Like miles." She got up and refilled her glass.

"That doesn't surprise me. He's in great shape. You never noticed what he orders when you wait on him at the diner?"

She made a face. "I just thought he was ordering all those salads to impress me."

I snickered. "I don't think that's a guy thing."

"Huh. Where'd you go after you left work?"

I filled her in on all the details.

She burst out laughing when I got to the part about Mr. Gaskin. I joined in. We sobered when I told her about my discussion with Teddy.

"So we have no idea who those two are?"

I shook my head. "Teddy did indicate the crimes were identical." A thought struck me like a bolt of lightning. "Actually, his exact words were *identical being the key word there*. What if the bodies were so similar that he suspected they were twins?"

"Shut the front door!" Betsy's mouth dropped open.

"It's possible. We do have an abundance of twin births on the island."

"You could be right. According to a file on the non-food-eaters desk, no one has been reported missing, and the only thing they have to go on is the deceased were both women. So they might not be island twins."

I smacked her on the arm playfully. "Betsy Myers! You snooped through his files?"

"He had it lying out there in the open. All I had to do was flip it open when he was speaking with Eddie about Yvonne's assistant, Candi. She'd just left when I got there. Alex was too busy gobbling up pastries to notice." She grinned mischievously.

"What were they saying about her?"

"All I could hear was that she didn't have anything of substance to add to the case."

"Figures. Well, if no one on the island has been reported missing, then it's probably—"

"Tourists." She finished my sentence. "So, now, because of your mama, you have to figure out how they died and who killed them. At least that's how Meemaw said it works."

"Well, Teddy will find out how they died."

"So, it's probably two murders. And the psycho is loose on the island."

I nodded and swallowed. "Or if they were tourists, then the killer could be all the way to Mexico by now. How am I supposed to solve that? I mean, don't you think the victims would understand that?"

"Well, they should. How are we supposed to find some killer hiding out in Mexico? Although, we could get some great tacos while we're there."

I gave her a pointed glare. "We're not going to Mexico."

"But what about tacos?"

"We can definitely get tacos. My burger is cold now anyway."

Betsy hopped up and rummaged through the takeout menu drawer. "So, as long as your spook mama is around, this could keep happening. The dead bodies, I mean."

I blew out a breath. "Yep."

"What god-awful news."

"I'll drink to that."

Betsy held up the menu she'd been looking for. "I'll dial dinner. You open another bottle of wine."

Sounded like a deal to me.

CHAPTER 8

The diner had closed every Sunday since its inception. When Mama and Nanny were alive, we always had a big lunch on Sunday afternoons. The tradition had passed with Mama many years ago. Until six months ago. Jena Lynn had revived it but on a biweekly basis, and we took turns hosting it. We also extended an invitation to our Peach Diner family. Nanny had always referred to the staff that way and the family they had become. Those who didn't have a place to go for Sunday lunch were welcome at our houses. Mostly it consisted of Jena Lynn and Zach, Eddie and Sam, Betsy and her meemaw, and Alex and me. Yvonne and her mama had come a few times. It concerned me how she'd kept to herself lately. I'd left her several voice mails, and she had yet to return my calls. If I didn't hear from her soon, I'd run by and check on her.

Today was my turn to host. Before the remodel, I would have had to pull out the old folding table Mama used to host the gathering. The space in my kitchen-dining room combo had always been large enough to accommodate a crowd and now, with the new furnishings and décor, I had a table that would seat twelve with the leaf installed. Yvonne had found the table at an estate sale in Savannah. We bought gray tuft chairs separately. It worked perfectly in the space. Still had the country feel with a touch of coastal elegance.

Usually this would be a happy time, but with all the drama surrounding the dead women, plus the weird place Alex and I were in, the usual cheer within me had gone. In fact, if he were not in attendance this afternoon, it would also force me to explain his absence. The chicken and dumplings were simmering away on the stove, and I had two large trays of garlic cheese-and-herb biscuits in the top oven and roasted root vegetables in the lower oven. Jena Lynn would be bringing the dessert. Whatever we had left over at the diner always worked well with whatever we served. Plus it made life a little easier.

"Everything smells wonderful." Mama stood over the pot of chicken and dumplings and wafted with her hand toward her nose and inhaled. "That's one of the many downsides to my current predicament. I miss sharing a meal with my loved ones."

I reached over, with an attempt to wrap an arm around her shoulders, and, to my surprise, succeeded. Her form was now corporal to me.

She read the question within my eyes. "We're connecting." A smile spread across her face. Mama had always been a beautiful woman, with high, defined cheekbones that held a natural rosy glow, her nose and lips perfectly proportional on her oval-shaped face, and when she smiled, she could light up the room. "The closer we become, the more real I'll become to you." Interesting. For the first time in years, my mama and I embraced. It may have taken unusual and tragic events to get us here, but we were here.

The alarm went off on the top oven. "Hey, Mama." I pulled the two piping-hot pans from the oven and placed them on the island. "These two victims. What would happen if I stayed out of it?" I placed the oven mitts beside the pans and turned toward her.

Her face paled. "Oh, honey, that isn't possible. And I wished to all that is holy you could leave this one alone. Spirits that have been wronged in life have a sort of vengefulness about them."

"Vengefulness toward the one who harmed them, I get. But you're saying if I don't help them, they'll turn their wrath toward me instead of the one responsible for their deaths in the first place?"

"Sadly, yes." Mama glanced at her hands.

"That hardly seems fair. Eddie could solve this without me."

"If law enforcement could handle the case, then they wouldn't be reaching out to you, hon."

"They've hardly given him a chance. Who are these women, anyway?"

Mama didn't respond.

"You can't tell me who they are. One of those rules." I used my finger to make quotes when uttering the word *rules*. "What could they do to me?"

Again she didn't respond.

"What if their killer isn't on the island any longer? Am I supposed to search the earth to locate and bring him to justice? I'm in food service, not a superhero."

She began to fade and waved. Her lips formed the inaudible word, *sorry*.

"Knock, knock," Betsy's meemaw said as the two of them entered through the screen door.

Everyone used the back door.

"Hi, Meemaw." I untied my apron and went to hug her.

Both were dressed in their Sunday best. Betsy favored her Meemaw greatly. Both had the same emerald-green eyes and fiery red hair. Meemaw's color, of course, came from a bottle now she was well into her eighties. She kept her hair in a tight curly perm that suited her. She smelled of Caesars Woman perfume and baby powder.

"Don't you look pretty today." I released her.

She laughed and waved a hand in my direction. "You're telling tales. I haven't looked pretty in forty years."

"Sit here, Meemaw." Betsy pulled out a chair at the table for her.

"Don't mind if I do. Something sure smells good."

As if on cue, the oven dinged and I went to retrieve the veggies while Betsy went to the refrigerator to pull out a gallon of tea. I'd made four.

"You doing okay? You weren't at church this morning." Betsy put the tea pitcher on the island next to the baskets I'd lined with linens.

"I wasn't in the mood." I began filling the baskets with the hot biscuits. I lowered my tone. "Mama came by."

"Your mama still pestering you?" Meemaw reminded me that there wasn't a thing wrong with her hearing.

I placed the biscuits on the table next to the butter dish and glanced back at Betsy. She gave me a sheepish smile.

"Don't get mad at Betsy. She tells me everything." Meemaw reached into the basket and took a nicely browned biscuit.

"Not everything," Betsy mouthed.

"I've had my experience with island spirits, so don't you worry none. I ain't going to go around flapping my gums." She slathered on a healthy pad of butter and took a bite. "So good. You know, I have a hankering for a cup of coffee."

"I'll get it." Betsy busied herself with the task.

"Suppose you're a bit overwhelmed with those bodies." I took a seat next to her.

She patted my hand. "Best advice I can give you"—she paused to chew the bite she'd taken, her orange-painted lips moving slowly—"is to not draw too much attention to yourself. If one of the dead orchestrates a meeting with their earthly remains, and no one else bears witness to it, walk away. 'Cause if you keep happening upon bodies, they'll either lock you up or try to."

I stared at her, unblinking at her contrary advice.

"I was under the impression I didn't have a choice in the matter. That the spirits would be angry with me."

"Your mama tell you that?"

I nodded.

"Hogwash."

Betsy put a steaming hot cup of coffee next to Meemaw.

"These sure are good. You have a gift, my dear." Meemaw slathered up another biscuit. "I'll never forget that heap of bodies I found—"

My breath caught in my throat. Betsy appeared dazed.

"Sorry we're late." Jena Lynn interrupted our discussion. "Everything okay?" She paused at the table.

Zach was behind her with two giant boxes of desserts from the Peach.

I pasted a smile on my face. "Fine. Just having a chat with Meemaw."

"Y'all come in. Marygene's outdone herself with these cheese biscuits." Meemaw waved a hand.

I rose from the table, hugged Jena Lynn and Zach, and went to finish dishing the food into suitable serving dishes. We always ate family style. I was on autopilot, filling the soup tureen and platters, casually greeting guests with a smile as they arrived. I wasn't even all that fazed when Alex decided to show up. He gave me a swift kiss on the cheek, and I patted his chest absentmindedly before he took his usual place at the table. Meemaw's words kept ringing in my ears: heap of bodies. *Heap of bodies!*

When Eddie had texted this morning that he'd arrive with a plus-one today, I'd assumed he'd meant the lovely

Doc Tatum. Much to my chagrin, he'd brought the new deputy with him instead. Eddie should have asked.

"Hope you don't mind I invited Javier. We could all use a little normalcy."

"Can't argue with you there."

Under the circumstances, Eddie looked to be doing okay. He'd shaved and the circles under his eyes weren't as dark as they could get. Seeing him in such good health made me feel better. Not that I'd forgive him for bringing an imbecile to lunch.

Javier handed me a bouquet of flowers and my favorite bottle of wine. Obviously he'd done research, or maybe Mr. Mason, the grocer, told him what I usually bought.

Eddie clapped Sam on the shoulder when he passed by.

Sam sat mighty close to Poppy. The two made a sweet couple.

"Thank you for having me." Javier discreetly leaned in and whispered, "I appreciated the text you sent me. I didn't even know that site existed. Riveting reading."

"Wasn't it, though? You really can get a sense about people when you hear from those closest to them."

"I couldn't agree more. In my experience, you can get a better sense by viewing them in their natural habitat." He glanced around the kitchen and dining room in my habitat.

Game on. I lowered my tone. "For a real education, you should have showed up early, Deputy Douche."

He gave a bark of laughter, drawing the attention of the whole room. "Javy, please. No need to be so formal."

"Javy," I cooed. "Best be careful." I put my hand to cover my lips away from the others, all secret-agent like. "When becoming too comfortable with your prey, you can get a false sense of security and become devoured in seconds, never to be seen again."

To my surprise, he let out another belt of laughter, filling the entire space. When I turned back around, Alex's attention zoomed in on us with laser focus. With only so much mental bandwidth to work with, I ignored him. It wasn't as if I was doing anything wrong. I didn't even like the new deputy. I rushed to put the wine in to chill and the flowers in a vase.

Once we were all seated, Eddie said grace and everyone dug in. Eddie had placed Javier in between Betsy and me.

Alex, seated to my right, passed the soup tureen. "Moving on already?"

I gave him a scowl and decided not to dignify his question with a response.

I passed the tureen to Javy. "I'm not sure we'll have much to your liking, other than the roasted vegetables. We Southerners are all about refined sugar and flours."

"You don't eat sugar or flour?" Sam's eyebrows reached his hairline. "God, what else is there? I mean, don't get me wrong, I'm a carnivore through and through, but I couldn't live without breads and desserts."

"Sam!" Poppy gave him a disapproving look. Maybe she could polish my brother, although I doubted it.

Javier ladled several scoops of chicken and dumplings onto his plate. "I try to eat clean. But it's not as if I don't ever splurge. I love a grain-free veggie pizza with no cheese."

The table gasped.

"Veggie pizza with no cheese!" Meemaw looked appalled. "That's not pizza. What's the point without the cheese?"

Javy passed the tureen to Betsy, who scowled at her grandmother. "It's still pizza, Meemaw. I might try that sometime."

Alex choked on a sip of tea. I elbowed him as Betsy leaned around Javy to glare at her cousin.

"I agree that on occasion, you gotta splurge."

Alex laughed under his breath. "Cheese is your favorite

food group, Bets." The idea of Betsy eating clean really seemed to tickle his funny bone. He was lucky she wasn't sitting closer to him. He'd pay later.

Her knuckles were white as she gripped her knife. "And yours is beer foam."

The table went silent.

"What's that? Beer foam." Meemaw glared down the table toward Alex. "What have you done, boy?"

Eddie glanced around as if he'd missed something. Javy's focus went from me to Alex. Wow, was he getting a lesson in the life of Marygene Brown today. Damn. My face heated and Alex seethed next to me. When I glanced up, Sam looked excited. *Oh dear God, please let's not have a brawl in my new kitchen.*

Betsy whispered something to Meemaw and she shrugged, focusing on her meal.

"Eating clean must take lots of discipline. I certainly don't possess such a quality," Zach chimed in, saving me from what could be a seriously horrific conversation. I let out the breath I'd been holding.

"And it shows." Jena Lynn patted her husband's middle, which had expanded since the wedding.

Betsy and Poppy forced laughs.

"Hey, more to love." He leaned down and nuzzled her cheek. Zach dwarfed Jena Lynn with his large stature, which was a stark contrast to his mellow personality. His laid-back demeanor was the perfect balance for my sister's somewhat high-strung personality.

"Get a room!" Sam pretended to be sick.

Poppy genuinely giggled. Her eyes sparkled in the lovey-dovey sort of way that new couples experienced. It was sweet.

"I guess some folks are meant to be and some aren't." Sam took another jab in our direction.

"Guess so," Meemaw agreed around a forkful of food.

Javy was all smiles.

"Enjoying yourself?" I asked barely above a whisper through gritted teeth.

"Immensely." He stabbed a brussels sprout.

"Eddie." Meemaw scooted closer to Betsy and focused her attention on my father seated across from me.

"Ma'am?"

"Y'all found out who those gals were that were killed?" Meemaw scooped a heaping spoonful of dumplings into her mouth. She was a straight shooter, no-nonsense kind of person. An attribute that I usually appreciated.

Eddie wiped his mouth with his napkin. "No, ma'am, not yet. But don't you worry, we're on it."

"Seems to me someone would come lookin' for their loved ones. Wonder why ain't nobody come forward yet." Her ringed fingers wrapped the handle of her coffee mug. "And why wouldn't they dump them both in the ocean? Odd that one would end up in the cellar of Thelma Brooks's daughter's place. What's the connection there?"

Javy glanced across the table toward Eddie and appeared to be waiting to see how his sheriff would respond.

"Those are mighty good questions. We're looking into it." Eddie sounded kind and confident.

Pride welled up within me.

"They're probably tourists." Betsy put in her two cents.

"Could be." Sam nodded. "But why would anyone want to kill a couple of tourists?"

"Maybe whoever they were vacationing with decided they were more trouble than they were worth and offed them before leaving." Betsy smiled, apparently pleased with her theory.

"That's good, Betsy. They might be what you call, working girls." Meemaw's eyes lit up with her addition to her granddaughter's theory. "Y'all know, hookers."

"Y'all leave the theories to the sheriff's department."

Alex tried to sound authoritative, glaring at Betsy. Was he trying to take a leadership role over the new deputy?

"You can't blame a body for being interested in the case, Alex. Folks have got questions. We deserve answers." Meemaw took up for her favorite granddaughter, and Betsy gave Alex a *ha!* grin. "Could be that—"

Alex stood, walked around the table, and spoke gently to his grandmother. "Meemaw, can I get you a piece of pie or pastry? I see some boxes from the diner over there." This was the side of Alex I'd always adored. He never disrespected his elders.

She nodded. "I could always go for a slice of pie. Warmed with ice cream, if Marygene has some."

I smiled in her direction. "I have whipped cream I made last night and vanilla bean ice cream."

"Oh good. Alex, I'll have a scoop of ice cream and a dollop of Marygene's whipped cream."

"Yes, ma'am."

Javier leaned over in my direction as I sipped from the glass of tea. "Would you pass me the roasted vegetables, please?"

I reached across around Alex's plate and retrieved the platter. Javy's fingers brushed mine when he took the platter. To my surprise, they lingered there for a few seconds too long. When I glanced up, he stared directly through me. Brazen. I couldn't for the life of me figure this guy out. One minute he was rude and the next he actually seemed to like me.

"Marygene," Alex called. "Can you help me with Meemaw's dessert?" He must have noticed the exchange.

Eddie certainly had. He cleared his throat and I returned my attention toward the kitchen behind us.

Meemaw said, "Boy, you can't heat up a piece of pie by yourself?" She struggled to her feet. "I'll help ya. Lawsy mercy, Marygene's been cooking all morning. She deserves to sit a spell. You Myers men are helpless in the kitchen."

"Meemaw, you sit." Betsy was on her feet. "I'll make it."

"Thank you, honey. Alex, run out to Betsy's car and fetch me my purse. I've got to take my blood pressure pills."

He did as he was told, but he glared in my direction as he went by. I'd be lying if I didn't admit I enjoyed his jealousy. And boy, did he deserve it.

"How are you settling in here on our little island, Javier?" asked Jena Lynn, who was seated adjacent from our guest.

"It's a very different experience than living in New York. Slower paced, but I'm adjusting."

Jena Lynn refilled his glass with tea. My sister was nothing if she wasn't hospitable. He thanked her.

"So that's where you're from, New York?"

He forked some root vegetables. "Originally I'm from Puerto Rico. I lived in Buffalo for ten years and took a job on the force there."

Jena Lynn and Zach nodded.

"What brought you to Peach Cove?" Betsy asked as if she hadn't already known. She'd read enough from the website to know his marriage had tanked in a terrible way.

His father-in-law had actually filed a lawsuit against him regarding his daughter's trust fund.

She placed Meemaw's dessert in front of her and retook her seat next to Javy.

The man shrugged in a nonchalant manner. "Went through a messy divorce and needed a change." He slanted his eyes my direction, and I wondered if he worried I might pull out the website and share it with the table.

I ignored him completely. We Southerners had manners.

"Marygene went through a messy divorce last year," Sam piped up. Well, with the exception of Sam, we all had manners.

I shot him a warning glare.

He ignored it, making it perfectly clear he no longer cared for the idea of Alex and me together and had decided not to wait on word from me. Not that I blamed him. I'd be the same if I'd caught one of his girlfriends as he had Alex. But this pushing for me to go out with another deputy had me irritated.

"You two have a lot in common," he added.

I'm going to kill you. I hoped my eyes were shouting at my brother as I glowered.

"Lots of people have gone through messy relationships that ended badly." Betsy stared longingly at Meemaw's plate. She'd hardly touched her meal, which consisted of barely a spoonful of chicken and dumplings and a large serving of vegetables.

Javier made her feel self-conscious, and that annoyed me, too.

"All I'm saying is that Javier might need a friend." Sam continued meddling.

With a playful pitch to his tone, obviously enjoying my squirming, Javier said, "Always good to have a friend."

"That's true," Betsy agreed, then gave me a narrowed squint. She must've detected my helplessness because she turned on Sam with a heated glower.

Alex returned just as Sam exclaimed jovially, "See! That's all I'm saying. Could be good for Marygene and Javier to get to know each other better."

Alex stood as if planted beside Meemaw.

Sam opened his mouth again but one look down the table at his dad shut him up. Hopefully for good.

Meemaw slapped Alex on the arm. "Give me my pocketbook, boy. What's wrong with you?"

"Eddie, do you know if the mayor is still planning on us holding the Taste of Peach Cove event to kick off tourist season?" Jena Lynn changed the subject, thank God.

With everything going on, I'd completely forgotten about that. She gave me that look that said her feelings were hurt I hadn't confided in her about my situation. These family lunches might not work out for me in the long run.

"I haven't heard different." Eddie placed his napkin on his plate.

"Marygene, maybe you should invite Javier to come along with you." Sam's face was the picture of innocence.

Betsy's face went red. The table went dead silent.

Alex had a murderous expression on his face but wisely kept his lips sealed. Sam, obviously ready for a fight, bared his teeth at Alex before he took a bite of biscuit. He'd baited and waited.

Poppy appeared nervous and focused on her plate.

Eddie just looked agitated. "That's enough, Sam."

Meemaw took a bite of pie, smiling. "This is better than one of my daytime shows."

Zach stifled a laugh after Jena Lynn elbowed him in the midsection.

"I have to work." I attempted to defuse the situation. "Maybe Betsy could show him around."

Betsy brightened. "I'd be delighted."

"That's kind of you. I may take you up on that," Javier said politely.

That did nothing to alter the tension between my brother and Alex. The two still regarded each other like battering rams, and I was afraid Sam was about to ask Alex to step outside. Idiots.

"All right!" I stood and clapped my hands. "I think Meemaw had the right idea. Who wants dessert?"

Sam grinned broadly and raised his hand.

CHAPTER 9

The morning rush of customers had nearly tripled. And by midmorning, the line for seating wrapped around the side of the building. Betsy and Heather were overwhelmed by lunchtime, and I had to go out onto the floor and help wait tables. Even with the three of us hustling, we hardly got a breather until about one o'clock.

Yvonne sat down at the bar in my section.

I held my hands up in exasperation. "I've left you like a thousand messages. I almost came by your house last night. You won't believe what happened at lunch yesterday."

"What?" Her eyes brightened with interest.

"I'm not telling you until you explain why you've been MIA. We're friends. You don't hide from me."

She deflated. "I'm sorry. Just dealing with a lot."

I poured her a cup of coffee and put a peach muffin in front of her. On a bad day, she always ordered coffee and a muffin while waiting on her lunch. She was lucky too. She'd received the last one. I yelled back to Jena Lynn to bake off more.

"I know." I gave her hand a quick squeeze. "I just worry about you, that's all. I care and want to be here for you."

"I love you too. And I'll do better with sharing, promise."

I placed menus in front of the guests who sat next to her.

"Have you read the paper this morning?" Yvonne tapped the tip of the paper that peeked out of her bag.

"Haven't had a chance. You want the lunch special? It's roadkill, potatoes, and gravy."

She nodded and pinched a bite from the top of the muffin. I filled out the ticket and hung it on the wheel for Sam.

Junior smiled as he wiped down the vacated spaces at the counter. Jena Lynn had been right about him. He worked his tail off and proved to be extremely reliable. A good hire indeed.

"My career is over." Yvonne shoved another bite into her mouth.

I hung the ticket for another special from the customer to her left.

"It isn't." I turned back around.

Betsy pointed to the back booth that new customers had just occupied.

"Sorry, I'll be back. Hold that thought." I placed the peach tea in front of the gentleman who'd ordered a lunch special and rushed off to greet the new arrivals.

"Afternoon. Welcome to the Peach Diner." I placed the laminated menus on the table and glanced up, smiling.

My heart went into my throat when I met the gaze of the reporter Roy Calhoun. He still wore the same black square frames. His hair was different. A little longer and no longer gray but the color of charcoal. He'd also grown a beard. No wonder I didn't recognize him at first.

"Calhoun."

"Hello, Marygene. You're looking well."

"Thank you." I smiled, regaining my composure.

He pointed across the table at the younger man. "This is my nephew, Darryl."

"Hello." I nodded in his direction. "What can I get you, gentlemen?"

"What's the special today?" Calhoun glanced at the menu.

"Roadkill with potatoes and gravy."

Darryl's mouth dropped open. "What's roadkill?"

"It's a chopped steak with onions and mushrooms." Calhoun laughed. "It isn't actually roadkill." He gathered up both menus and handed them to me. "We'll have two of those, a peach tea, and—" He glanced over at Darryl, who said, "A Coke, please."

I nodded and got their orders in.

I'd been so busy I'd not had time to inquire as to his presence on the island. Not that I truly needed to ask. We had two dead, burned victims and the media ran with it, like they always did. Yvonne left word with Betsy she'd call me later. She could tell how busy I was. Calhoun had left a more-than-generous tip and held up a hand before leaving.

Things finally slowed down around three, and we were all pooped. Betsy was happy. She'd doubled her usual tips, as had Heather, who'd rushed out the door the second her shift ended. She didn't stay around and chat like she used to. She had a new boyfriend and he and the kids kept her pretty busy.

I'd shoved the paper Yvonne had left behind under the counter after she left. Now that I had time to read it, I completely understood her emotional distress. Huge articles took up the front page with the headlines: *Is the Peach Cove Sheriff's Department up for the Task?* and *Two Jane Does Found Burned to Death within Days of Each Other.* Yvonne's name and her house were mentioned.

My suspicions regarding Calhoun's presence were confirmed.

"Awful, huh?" Sam said from behind me. "Dad's going to hate being second-guessed again. And poor Yvonne. It's not her fault someone got whacked in her basement. It's been good for our business, though." He put his plate filled with a double portion of roadkill on the counter.

I sat next to him. My feet were killing me. "I'm still mad at you, you know."

"Why? Because of Javier? Don't be like that. I'm just looking out for you."

"Alex swears it was nothing."

He slanted his eyes in my direction.

"It looked bad, I get it. Forget it. I'll figure it out. No more pimping me out to any eligible men you come across, got it?"

"Fine." He didn't sound as if he meant it.

I leaned over the counter and picked up freshly wrapped silverware. I stabbed a mushroom off his plate.

"Hey, get your own."

"Stingy." I ate my prize. I loved mushrooms. "Calhoun came in. Did you see?"

He shook his head. "The vultures are circling."

Betsy sat down with her plate. "You okay on your own till I finish eating?"

"Yeah." I pushed the paper over to her. "It's practically dead now anyway. No pun intended." I glanced around the diner floor. Junior was cleaning up the back two booths. "Don't forget to take your lunch, Junior."

"Yeah." Betsy patted the stool next to her. "Come eat with me. I'll go back and dip you up the last of the special."

Junior nodded after wiping down the last table and went to wash up.

Teddy came into the diner and sat at the bar next to Sam.

"Hey, Teddy."

"How ya doing, Sam?" Teddy picked up the paper I'd left on the bar.

"Can't complain." Sam shoveled the last of his potatoes into his mouth.

"What'll you have, Teddy?" I forced myself up from the stool.

"A slice of pie, any kind, and a cup of coffee."

"I'll have to brew a fresh pot."

He nodded as I dumped the sludge from the pot and gave it a rinse. "Want a glass of water while it brews?"

"Sure—no, on second thought I'll take milk, two percent."

I reached into the small refrigerator and pulled out two small cartons of two-percent milk and placed them on the counter, along with a glass. I sliced him a piece of pecan pie and slid it to him.

Sam had already scarfed down his entire plate by the time the coffee brewed, and he was back at the grill. I waited on two more tables before Betsy and Junior finished, and then she took over the floor. Junior went home for the day. He'd paused to ask me if I would like him to stick around and accompany me home. He pointed to the paper when I gaped in surprise.

"That's okay, but thanks for the offer." I'd patted his shoulder and he went on his way.

When I took a load off and sat next to Teddy, we each had a steaming hot brew in front of us and he was on his second piece of pie, apple this time. "Any news?"

He raised his bushy brows.

"Anything you can tell me?"

He filled his mouth full of pie.

"You identified the bodies?"

His facial expression gave it away.

He had! "Anyone I know?" My heart hammered. Could this be it? If I convinced my old friend to confide in me and found out the identities, maybe I could point Eddie in the right direction and this whole nightmare of the deceased seeking my aid would be over.

He shook his head and the wind in my sails stalled.

"Anyone you know?" I chewed on my bottom lip.

Again, he shook his head.

"Can you give me anything verbal?"

He finished his pie and kept looking at the menu. Teddy was a stress eater like me. "I think I want a cheeseburger and some fries."

"Sure." After I hung his order, I went into the back and loaded a box full of his favorite brownies and presented them to Teddy and warmed up his coffee.

He stared at the bribe. "God, you're persistent."

"Fine. If you don't want the brownies." Before I could reach the box, he tucked them close to his chest.

"Hey, I've gotta eat, right?" He grinned. "All I can tell you is Yvonne is safe from being charged or even being re-questioned. You and Sam are too."

Blindsided, I took a minute to organize my thoughts while I searched his face. His nearly black intelligent eyes stared back, unblinking.

"Were they tourists?"

He shook his head.

I blew out an exasperated breath. "If they weren't tourists, then they had to be residents."

"Keep your voice down." It came out as a nervous hiss.

"I'm barely speaking above a whisper. Come on, this is affecting me. I'll keep your confidence. I swear it." I held up scout fingers. Not that I'd ever been a Girl Scout.

"Hey, guys, what's going on?" Betsy interrupted us and Teddy looked relieved.

He stood. "Can I just get that order to go?" He glanced at his watch. "I'm running late anyway."

Betsy relayed the change to Sam and he boxed it up. I

dug out twenty dollars from my apron pocket and handed the ticket and money to Betsy to ring up. "I'll walk you out, Teddy."

"No need. Thanks for the lunch." He snatched the to-go bag from the counter.

I looped my arm with his and walked him out anyway. Betsy stared on with interest.

When we got outside, I gripped his arm tighter. "My shift's just about over. I'll shadow you for the rest of the day if I have to. You have no idea how this ordeal has impacted my life. I'm desperate."

We were attracting attention.

I let my hand drop from his arm.

"Melodramatic, much?"

"Come on, Teddy." I held my hands together and pleaded.

"Wow, there is something odd going on with you, isn't there. Dad keeps telling me to give you a wide berth."

"Well, that's plain rude."

"Dad's not himself these days." His fingers drummed on the box of brownies peeking out of the top of the bag. "I suppose everyone will find out soon anyway. Nevertheless, I mean it, if it gets to your dad I told you, I'll never speak to you again."

"You have my word."

He glanced around and I feared he might change his mind. I waited with bated breath as he leaned in and whispered, "Remember when I said *identical* was the key word?"

"Yeah."

"They were twin sisters."

"I was right!" I nearly fist pumped.

"Shh! That's not the breaking news." He motioned for me to follow him around the side of the diner in the alleyway. "Not a word. Got it!"

I held up my scout's honor sign again.

He all but rolled his eyes at me.

"Okay! Not a single word. I swear."

"After I discovered the similarities in the corpses, I managed to gain access to dental records amazingly still on file. From there identifying them was a breeze. A missing-persons case was filed for Kayla and Pamela Dryer over two decades ago."

I gasped.

"And that's not the most interesting. The bones weren't those of older ladies, but young women in their early twenties."

"Oh. My. God." I felt my eyes widen.

"I have your word." He put his finger to his lips.

I nodded and he darted across the street.

CHAPTER 10

Alex showed up at my house late. With the condition of the current climate, our problems were now in perspective. When he phoned, I'd not hesitated to agree to his request to come over. We were sitting in the living room with coffees and sweet-potato pound cake. With the bomb Teddy had dropped on the department with the victims' identities, they were putting together a special task force. Well, that was how Alex had referred to it. The more he explained, the task force notion seemed like a stretch. Come to find out, I hadn't had to twist Teddy's arm after all. Alex, completely intrigued by the case, had told me everything. He'd enjoyed my mock-shock expressions. And with the new developments, empathy for the victims overwhelmed me.

"So, basically Eddie is going to hire another deputy?" I leaned back and cradled my warm mug in my hands.

"He wanted to, but Mayor Bill shot that down. No budget for it, he says. So Teddy will be in our meetings regarding the case and asked to speak and answer questions regarding the cause of death and conditions of the corpses."

Poor Teddy. He didn't really like being the center of attention. I wondered how he was handling the news.

"And they're bringing in a cold-case consultant from Atlanta."

I didn't know there were cold-case consultants.

Alex put an oversized bite of cake into his mouth. "The sheriff told the reporters and he instructed us, if Javier or I are approached, to say that a special task force will be formed to investigate the case. Where this gets even more dicey is that the twins' missing-persons cases from twenty-five years ago were led by Eddie."

My mouth momentarily dropped open. "He had to have been a rookie then." The identities had to be a major shock for Eddie for different reasons entirely. "The reporters still believe they're Jane Does?"

Alex nodded.

I tapped my mug with the nail of my index finger. The pin wouldn't stay in that grenade for long.

We settled into silence for a few minutes while Alex polished off his second piece of cake. Once he'd satisfied his sweet tooth, he turned his attention back to me. "Now that we're cooled down, can we have a civil conversation about us?"

The word *civil* irritated me instantly. For him to imply I needed a reminder to conduct myself in a civilized manner, when he started this whole thing, was a tough pill to swallow. But swallow it, I did. "I can manage that."

He sighed and ran a hand through his thick, wavy hair. His duty belt made a cracking noise as he sat on the edge of the seat. "We love each other, right?"

"I thought so." I placed my mug on the coffee table.

"I thought so too. I suppose what I need to know is, can we get past this? Or should we simply take a break?" He raised his hands. "Staying close friends, of course."

His words struck me like a punch to the gut. Yeah, I'd had similar trains of thought, but hearing the words from his lips caused me to nearly lose my breath.

He wants to break up.

I stared across the room at his tan face. His big hands clasped together in front of him. He'd been patient while I worked through all my issues. Maybe my issues were part of the problem.

"Your brother obviously hates me now. He's dying for you to get rid of me and go out with Javier. Plus, with this massive case ahead of me, it might be a good time to take a breather. What do you think?"

"My brother doesn't hate you."

His lips pursed into a thin line.

"Okay, he does hate you, but he'll get over it. And the notion that I would date Javier is absurd."

Alex appeared relieved.

"And you might be right. A break could be healthy. All this fighting certainly isn't." I heard myself say this in a monotone, revealing, at least to me, my deep sadness.

He searched my face as I fought for the right words to continue.

"I'm not the same. My marriage changed me. In the beginning, when I first told you about Peter, you were so loving and kind to me, and even after. I'll always love you and be grateful for that." Emotion began to flood me. "What I walked through altered both of us, I think. Neither one of us could have predicted how it would affect our relationship. Loyalty is everything to me. Being able to trust the man I choose to spend the rest of my life with is paramount. Not that I'm even ready to go down that path yet. Or if I ever will be again."

Alex sat there frozen for a few beats. He seemed to be battling his own emotions. "I do love you. And I can't believe we're actually saying these things."

"Yeah, me either."

We both stood. He approached me slowly. I slid my arms around his neck and rested my head on his shoulder. I took in his smell of sandalwood, light sweat from a long day's work, and my cooking.

"This is just a break. Maybe I rushed you when you needed time to heal." Even when he spoke the words, it felt like more than a break to me.

"You didn't rush me. Maybe you weren't ready for the type of commitment being with someone with trust issues would bring. And that's okay. Besides, you're right. This case is going to keep you busy."

He held me tighter. "The case is big and attracting a ton of attention. Not that the job is more important than you."

"You don't have to say that. My dad's your sheriff." I half laughed in an attempt to lighten the mood.

"Right, I forgot." He tried to join in with a small chuckle. "*Friends* means we still see each other regularly, right?"

I nodded against his shoulder.

"I have to know you mean that and this isn't the friends line that we'd give other people when breaking it off." He pulled my arms and separated us to gaze into my face.

"I always want to be friends, Alex. But let's give each other some space first. Just a bit. You need to figure out what it is you want and so do I, without concern that our needs will hurt the other."

He sighed and nodded. "We're not saying we're over for good. A break to evaluate and just deal with the messes in our own lives."

Our gazes locked and, for a few long moments, I got lost in the smooth, silky milk chocolate of his eyes. "Agreed."

When he left, both his cheeks and mine were damp.

I hardly had time to process everything that transpired over the next few days. My schedule kept me from obsessing. Eddie had made the announcement that the identities of the victims had been determined. The press went nuts.

The island was abuzz with speculations. Mama didn't show herself, so I couldn't run anything by her. She knew something of great importance. I could feel it in my bones. It had been the way she'd said she wished I could leave this one alone.

I spent all day at the diner, then ran by Sunset Hills to check in on Ms. Brooks. She loved my peaches-and-cream bars. I took her a full box and she was so pleased. She recognized me the second I came into her room. I guess she'd been having a good day. I was surprised to run into Candi, Yvonne's assistant, when I left. She said Yvonne sent her to check in on her mama. Yvonne must be really busy or really upset and hiding out from reporters after that article. I left her a message about seeing her mom.

My evening was spent in room A at the Baptist church, the room the pastor allowed us to use for group counseling. On autopilot, I'd set up the table with two coffee urns, one decaf, one regular, and trays of baked goods. Dead on my feet, and with the Taste of Peach Cove scheduled for tomorrow, I left without participating.

The buzzing of insects in the warm night greeted me as I walked toward my car, where Roy Calhoun casually lounged. He'd always had a knack for locating me when the opportunity arose. That was what reporters did, I supposed. Find people and information. The easy grin on his face almost made me smile.

"Lovely night, isn't it?" His arms were folded across his chest as he gazed at the stars.

"If you're here to try and get some inside information from me, forget it. All I know is what Eddie told everyone else. I'm tired and need a shower and my bed." I'd made my tone firm. *Don't push me*, I hoped he heard.

Calhoun didn't budge from where he stood at my driver's-side door. His green gaze met mine and we connected. He and I shared one of those moments in life that bound two people on a molecular level. Some experiences had to do with great trials that lead to great triumphs. Other experiences could be the miracle of new life. Ours had been death and the investigation of a murder. We'd parted ways shortly after. In truth, I'd never expected to lay eyes on him again.

Calhoun had once professed his feelings for me. Sadly, like many relationships, we were like ships passing in the night, with two different destinations charted.

"Sorry if that came out harsh. I had a bad experience with some reporters, but I shouldn't take it out on you. You look well." The wind blew and forced me to tuck my hair behind my ears. "How've you been?"

He pushed his frames up on his nose. "Good. I'm back out in the field full-time. My nephew is interested in the business. I'm giving him a taste of what surviving on limited sleep and out of a suitcase is like."

"That's good of you."

"Not really. My sister asked me to scare him straight. She wants him back in pre-law. His father has visions of the family firm."

"Ah."

We sort of settled into a strange silence.

"I really don't know anything else."

"I'm not here for that. I just wanted to see how you were. We parted on such abrupt terms and I regretted that. I heard that you're helping out here." He motioned toward the church.

I nodded. "Giving back."

"That's wonderful. I'm so glad to see you doing so well. You and Alex still seeing each other?"

Uh-oh. I hoped this wasn't going where I feared. "It's complicated." I hiked my bag higher on my shoulder.

"I see. Well, that's too bad." He pushed off the car.

"You seeing anyone?"

"For six months now." His face brightened.

"She makes you happy. I can tell." I gave him a genuine smile this time. Thrilled that he'd found love.

"She does. The funny thing is, we clashed when we first met. Sort of reminded me of you, her stubborn streak and temperament."

I laughed. "My nanny used to say a woman without fire wasn't worth spit."

"Valerie would agree with you." He laughed just as his phone rang. He checked it and took a step away from the car. "Well, I'll let you get going. Have a good night. I'll see you tomorrow at the Taste of Peach Cove." He lifted his hand and stalked over toward his car, the phone to his ear. Then he paused. "Oh, hey, there was a little gal with spiky hair about yay high." He held up his hand to about his shoulder. "She was peeking into your car windows when I got here."

That sounded like Candi. What would she be doing peeking into my car?

"Thanks for the heads-up."

He nodded. "Let me know if I can be of any help." He went back to his call.

CHAPTER 11

Colorful tents lined the square in front of the local businesses and beyond. The event had the potential to become an annual affair that featured restaurants and caterers showcasing their best food and drawing new clientele. Taste price ranges varied from one to five dollars a head, more than reasonable since overall admission cost two dollars a head or five for a family. In addition, local artists and musicians came out to offer live music and personal portraits.

The sheriff and fire departments teamed up to organize and operate a kids' corner with dunking booths, batting cages, inflatable jump houses, and games. The ice cream and food trucks had been strategically parked right beside the kids' corner. Mayor Bill had installed a large stage at the opposite end of the square for the local bluegrass bands.

We couldn't have hoped for a more beautiful day with temps in the low eighties, thanks to a tropical depression that had caused a cool snap. The wonderful smell of wood and pork smoking in the portable smokers down the street made my mouth water. Betsy propped the door open to the diner, where our tent backed directly up against it. Folks could stroll straight through to sample our offerings. My job this morning couldn't be easier—selling tasting cards at the front of the tent and passing out the small pamphlets Jena Lynn had made up telling our diner's history, before directing people into the diner. No-brainer. And perfect for me today, since I'd spent long hours preparing the samples.

"You all right?" Betsy sidled up next to me after I ran a man's card through the reader and handed him the iPad to sign.

"Enjoy." I smiled brightly at the couple, handed the man his card back, and showed them through. "You spoke to Alex?" I asked Betsy after they'd gone inside.

Betsy grabbed a foam cup of tea and took a sip. "I can't imagine the two of you not together."

I did the same from my own cup. "We both needed to take this break. And six months ago I would have agreed with you. Now, I don't know." A few more people strolled up to the tent and I took their cash and let them through. "Hey, have you seen Yvonne around anywhere?"

"Welcome to the Peach." Betsy beamed and handled the next transaction.

"Wow. It sure smells wonderful," the gentleman said.

"And a bargain." His lady seemed pleased by our prices. That's one of the things that I enjoyed so much about food service. We got to make people happy. We comforted them when they were sad. Celebrated with them on their successes. And were there to start their day off right with a good breakfast. We prided ourselves on pleasing our clientele and making them feel at home.

Betsy turned to me when the couple had passed us. "Nope. Haven't seen her. Why?"

I sighed. "Last night her assistant, Candi, was snooping around my car while I served at group."

"Well, that's weird."

"I know. I couldn't reach Yvonne last night, so I was hoping to speak with her at some point today."

Betsy nodded. We smiled and allowed a small group to file through.

"What about you? Don't you have that date with Javier this afternoon?"

She scrunched up her face.

"What?"

"Well, I kind of ran into him at the market the other day and he asked me out for coffee." She paused as we both greeted a few more arrivals. "Actually, I asked him out. But that's not the point." She fanned herself with our sample menu. "Anyway, he's real dull, with no sense of humor. And I'm funny!" She threw her hands in the air.

"Uh-oh, what'd you say?" I smirked. My day just got brighter.

"His ex-wife was right. He's a douche. He hardly said two words on the walk over to the coffee shop. So, to break the ice, I told him I was bilingual like him and started speaking pig latin. I asked him about his family and ordered our coffees in pig latin. The little gal behind the register laughed to tears."

I burst out laughing.

"See! I got nothing out of him but raised eyebrows. Not even a snicker. So I made up an excuse and got the hell out of there."

"Betsy!" Jena Lynn called.

"Oops. We'll catch up after. If Javier comes by looking for me, tell him I'm not here." She darted inside.

The line started to stretch down the block. Thank God we'd printed up so many tasting cards that showed tasting prices and our offerings. I spotted Teddy in the line with his dad and waved. Teddy brightened but his dad avoided making eye contact. I didn't blame him. I focused on the smiling faces of the little girls holding tightly to their mother's hand. "Can they have a sucker?" Once the mother approved, I held the jar out for the girls to choose their favorites.

When my shift ended, I roamed the streets after popping into a few tents, ate some fabulous barbecue, and bought a double scoop of heavenly hash on a waffle cone. The cool chocolate awakened my taste buds. The sun, close to setting, had done nothing to disperse the crowds. The island event was alive with residents, tourists, and the dreaded reporters. I'd been approached twice. As politely as I could manage, I said *no comment* and kept moving. A gust of cooler air caused the aromas of the vendors' food to swirl around me in an intoxicating way. Despite the trials I had, I loved my island.

"I love it too," Mama said, now at my side. "If I have to be stuck somewhere, I'm glad it's here. It's a shame they waited until after I passed to begin this tradition."

Her appearances no longer startled me. The only way I could describe it was like a sort of disturbance in the air around me right before she appeared. "Where have you been hiding?" I used my ice cream cone as cover.

"Now, Marygene, I told you—"

"I know, I know. You only have a certain allotted amount of time and you don't always get to choose when that time begins." She clasped her hands behind her back as we strolled. The breeze blew her dress delightfully around her calves. It astounded me how alive she appeared to me. It could be a hard concept to adjust to, the spirit world.

"I suppose since you've been informed of the identity of the victims, you're hoping to be off the hook?" Mama glanced around and seemed to be enjoying the sights.

"Honestly, Mama, I don't see how I can help. Sure, it bothers me, but it's been over twenty years. I'd never even heard of the sisters, and the storm that's brewing regarding their disappearance needs to be handled delicately. Eddie headed up the missing-persons case, as I'm sure you're aware of." She confirmed my statement with a nod. "Besides, Meemaw described your vengeful spirit notion as hogwash."

Mama snorted in an extremely unladylike manner, completely out of character. "You should speak to Betsy's meemaw again. I assure you, it isn't. And darling—" Mama sighed. When my mama said darling it sounded like *dahlin'*. Truly old Southern and always made me smile. "I will lose the advances I've made toward my crossover if I must protect you from the vengeful spirits." Mama furrowed her brow. "It's complicated."

She spoke truth. I don't know how I knew it, but I did.

The weight of my situation slowed my walk. In all honesty, I believed the dead needed a voice too. The violence that cut their lives short angered me as much if not more than the stories from those I met with in group therapy. They deserved justice. I'd have to tread mighty carefully. The more thought I gave her words, the more compelling helping the sisters became. "All right. I'll do my best."

Mama gave my hand a quick squeeze. Her energy was stronger. It came across as conflicted on so many levels. Uneasiness overwhelmed her.

I glanced in her direction and she turned away. "I wish you'd confide in me."

"I would if I could, honey. You have to believe that."

"I do." I blew out a breath and nearly stumbled off the sidewalk. Thankfully I righted myself just in time.

I spied Calhoun and his nephew throwing large softballs at Mayor Bill dressed as a clown in the bright orange dunking booth. Bill Gentry was always a good sport. He made faces and stuck his tongue out a second before the seat released underneath him and he plummeted into the water. Mama and I laughed.

"Who's that?" Mama pointed over by the dunking booth.

"Who do you mean?" I searched the crowd.

"That girl speaking with Evelyn."

There, off to the side of the booth, stood Evelyn Gentry and Yvonne's assistant, Candi. Evelyn's head bobbed around as her mouth flew. The girl gave her a death glare before saying something that had Mrs. Gentry's head flying back as if struck. Candi whirled around and stomped off. That woman was always making enemies. I wondered what Candi had done to ruffle her feathers, or vice versa.

Startled by the encounter, I didn't notice Yvonne strolling toward us until she shouted my name. Her mama by her side waved, and little Izzy on leash, dressed in a pink tutu, pranced next to her feet.

"Poor Thelma. Someone should really take better care of her."

I cut my eyes in Mama's direction, not caring for her accusation. Yvonne was doing her best for her mama. Sunset Hills had a stellar reputation in their field, providing excellent care to their residents.

"Hello!" I waved to the pair.

Poppy had done a great job on Yvonne's mama's hair. I could tell it'd just been set. A lovely shade of gray, curled close to her head. When they reached us, I hugged each of them, petted little Izzy, and made sure to compliment Ms. Brooks on her hair and Yvonne on her dress, which I must say screamed fabulous. Off the shoulder, blue and white striped that hit mid-thigh with three-quarter-length flounce sleeves.

"Thank you. I got it at my favorite little store on Amelia Island." Yvonne's face had transformed since the last time I saw her. Her eyes sparkled with joy and her cheeks had a bright rosy glow.

"Well, you're looking better than I expected. Did you get my voice mails?" I folded my arms.

She touched my shoulder. "Yes, and I'm so sorry. I went to Savannah for an interview with one of the local papers. And *Modern Day Business Woman* is going to run a piece on me."

Both hands flew to my mouth a second before I squealed in delight. "Wow! That's fantastic news!" Overjoyed for my friend, I nearly choked up. "I saw Candi at Sunset Hills and she didn't mention it."

"She told me she saw you when I picked up Izzy. She's begun dog sitting for me and it's been a godsend." Yvonne's smile nearly spanned her entire face. "Candi wanted me to be able to share the news. But I'd instructed her to get you a message since my cell died on the way home on the ferry. I had just enough juice to tell her I was on my way home. She was supposed to call you. I guess my cell died before your number came through to her phone via text. She said she tried to catch you before group but missed you." Ah. Well, that explained her presence. But not why she would snoop. Perhaps she was checking to see if the car was mine.

"That ice cream looks good. Yvonne, get me one of those." Ms. Brooks licked her lips as her eyes fixed on my cone.

"Sure, Mama." Yvonne squeezed her mother's hand. "I'm bursting! A few days ago I thought my career had ended with that awful article, but instead it stimulated interest. I've had so many calls and people wishing to tour the house. My little business is booming! I've had to put an ad in the local paper and on my Facebook page for additional help. I don't mind training someone. It'll ensure that things are run my way. Especially after the bad experience I had working with a full-fledged partner in Atlanta last year. It was pure relief when he bought me out." That made sense to me and exactly the way we handled kitchen staff in the diner. "At this rate, I'll be booked through next summer."

"That's splendid news! And well deserved."

"And"—her eyes twinkled with an intentional dramatic pause—"*Georgia Coastal* is going to run my article in their next issue!"

We were both beaming.

"We have to celebrate!"

"Y'all can celebrate after I get my ice cream," Ms. Brooks said.

Yvonne laughed. "I'll catch up with you later."

We hugged again.

"I'm so happy for you! Don't forget about us little guys when you're the designer to the stars."

"Never." She laughed.

Mama and I watched them cross the street. "That's wonderful for Yvonne. I always liked her. She reminds me of Thelma back when we were young."

"Ms. Brooks and you were close then?"

Mama nodded. "We had our little group. Thelma, Debbie, Vi, Evelyn, and—" Her face changed and she blurted, "I've got to go. Start singing. And smile."

"What? Who else?"

"Sing!" She began to fade.

"You're crazy." I shook my head and smiled anyway. I couldn't carry a tune to save my life.

"Good afternoon," a deep accented voice said from behind me.

Startled, the corners of my lips turned up as I began singing, "'Crazy for feeling so lonely . . .'" Slowly, I whirled around to find Javier Reyes.

"That looks good on you." He wore khaki cargo shorts that showcased his muscular calves and a blue and white linen button-down shirt.

"Hello. What looks good on me?"

He took a step closer. "That smile looks good on you."

"Thank you. I hope you're enjoying the event and getting to know our island better. See you around." It came out polite, without welcoming further conversation. With a pivot, I continued to the opposite end of the square, where the bluegrass band had just started their second set.

He followed. "You don't like me very much."

"I've said as much. You don't like me either." I kept my gaze straight ahead and continued to eat my melting ice cream.

"I never said that."

He confused me to no end. "You didn't have to. Your actions spelled it out plainly. Now go away."

He didn't walk away. He matched me stride for stride. "I apologize if I offended you at lunch. That was a rude way to behave. I have an unusual sense of humor. Not everyone gets my personality."

"According to Betsy, you don't have a personality."

Again, his face held surprise. Surely he wasn't that dense.

Intrigue took hold. "She told me about your interesting coffee date."

"Interesting is an understatement. That woman is a lunatic." His face contorted in a distasteful way, but his eyes were laughing.

"That's one of the traits I love about her. According to her, you don't possess a sense of humor either. And just an FYI, I'd be careful going around calling her a lunatic. You might have another website dedicated to you."

"God forbid. And obviously, Betsy left out a lot of details." He put his hand on my lower back and guided me out of the way of a group of running boys, but not before what was left of my cone got knocked from my hand.

"No running," he barked and they skidded to a halt.

"Sorry, Miss Marygene," the older of the boys said.

I recognized him as one of Heather's kids. For the life of me, I couldn't remember his name.

"That's okay. Say hello to your mom for me."

He nodded politely, despite several of the boys' snickers. When he glared in their direction in a furious sort of way, they all shut their mouths and the group moved down the street. Clearly, he held the alpha position in their little pack.

When we reached the stage, I took an empty seat in the back. Javier sat next to me.

"So, you didn't enjoy Betsy's pig latin?" I wiped my hands on the spare napkin I had in my left hand.

His head shook in a bemused fashion. "The pig latin struck me as odd, but"—he paused and glanced around— "the grand finale happened when she blurted, quite loudly, the reason she suddenly had to leave."

My turn to be confused.

"She left that part out?"

My expression must have shown how out of the loop I'd been kept.

"How shall I put this?"

"Just say it. I find it takes far too much energy coming up with a tactful way to put most things. I'm a straight-shooting kind of gal." My foot involuntarily tapped the ground to the beat.

"Good to know. Well, when her performance didn't get the response from me she desired, she crossed her legs and waved her hands in the air while she shouted"—his tone raised in mock falsetto—"'Lord help me. Aunt Flo has arrived! Gotta go!' And she bolted out the door."

I hooted in a delayed response. For a few seconds, I couldn't believe Betsy had gone so far as to use such a tactless excuse.

Javier joined in. When he laughed, really laughed, it changed his face completely. The furrowed, stone-chiseled face softened. He had a nice laugh. His head fell back slightly and the corners of his eyes crinkled delightfully.

Once we'd both regained our composure and I'd wiped the tears that had leaked from my eyes, he stunned me with a question. "Do you make it a habit of having conversations with yourself?"

Thankfully, I had an answer on the ready. "I wasn't talking to myself, I was singing."

He studied me closely. Probably observing to learn my tells.

I echoed his eye movement. "But sometimes I do when I'm on edge. It's thinking out loud, really," I added just in case Mr. Gaskin opened his big mouth. "These two bodies have rattled me a bit."

"How so?" He swatted a fly away from his face. "I mean, I get that the sight would be immensely troubling to civilians and all, and I'm sure on this small island where sealed lips is an impossibility, you're aware that with the circumstances surrounding the victims' disappearance, your friends and you would've been in diapers when the victims were murdered. Although, I suppose you may have information you're withholding. In that case, feel free to unburden yourself."

A couple of girls ran up to us selling cookies.

"Aren't y'all adorable." I dug through my purse to locate what spare cash I had on hand. Waiting tables had its benefits. I never had cash on hand until I moved back home. "Give me five boxes. I'll take two home and you girls can each have a box on me."

Grins split the faces of the little dolls in braids.

"Thank you," said Bonnie Butler, owner of Bonnie's Boutique, who stood behind the girls. Her red hair, usually fluffy and shaped in a football helmet, had fallen flat from the humidity. "I've got my granddaughters until the end of the week. Their parents are on a cruise for their anniversary. We've got to get these sold and"—she softly pinched the oldest child's freckled cheeks—"no one told Grammy until this morning that the due date to turn in the money is tomorrow."

"In that case." Javier dug out his wallet. "How many do you have left?"

Bonnie glanced into the red wagon they pulled. "Twenty boxes."

He handed Bonnie the appropriate amount, buying the lot. Relief washed over the poor, weary woman's face.

"You don't eat refined sugar." I grinned.

"Take them to the sheriff's department on Monday morning and leave them with the secretary," he instructed Bonnie Butler.

"Young man, you are my hero." And with that, the girls and Bonnie strolled away.

He might not eat sugar, but I sure did. I tore into a box of thin mints, my favorites.

"Trying to win the island over?" I bit into a crispy cookie.

"Perhaps you misjudged me. My ex's website played a vital role in the judgment, I'm sure. Thankfully, my attorney got the site pulled down. A gag order being in place should have prevented such action. The lawsuit's been dropped. And it was just Maria's way to lash out at me." He sounded a bit bewildered before perking up. "Maybe I'm a kind person with trust issues." *Like you*, his eyes implied. He laid the charm on thick.

"I'm a fairly good judge of character. The website aside, and based upon the first impression I had of you at the sheriff's department, followed by the second impression at Yvonne's, I'd say"—I squinted, taking him in—"pardon the expression, but you're an ass."

He put his hand over his heart and slumped slightly forward as if I'd wounded him.

"And melodramatic." I wiped the slight perspiration

from my brow and lifted my face to the direction of the wind, thankful for the salty breeze.

"Listen, I'm the new guy on the force here and when the sheriff put me in charge of interviewing his kids, well, I sort of saw that as a test." Okay, that sounded like something Eddie would do. He certainly hadn't made a point to be included in our interviews.

"Did you pass?"

He shrugged. "I'm still here. Admittedly, I felt concerned I'd been too hard on you. Interviewing daddy's little girl is a precarious situation to be in. I'd not been very thorough in my research. I knew you had issues with your ex, but when I discovered to what extent, I felt like a heel." There it was, the dreaded *history*. "I must ask you for your forgiveness. I behaved like an imbecile, and you had every right to expose my error to your father."

I shook my head. "No. But be more careful when dealing with those with a traumatic past."

"I swear it." His expression looked serious.

"Okay. I'll give you a pass. Just an FYI, every man worth anything stands when a lady leaves the table or desk. It's the Southern way." I wanted to get off the topic.

"And therefore the correct way?"

"Exactly."

A smile spread across his face. "Duly noted."

I went back to the subject I had a keen interest in. "And why wouldn't finding two terrible bodies bother me? Someone went to great lengths to not only take their lives but to preserve and hide their remains. Their poor family must've grieved for decades, unable to lay their loved ones to rest. I feel as if I owe them in some way. I have this sort of—and I get this may sound weird and if it freaks you out, I'm sorry. There is a connection between us. The deceased and me." Had I actually said that? *Aloud?*

"How's that?"

Too late to back out now. "It could have happened to me. Or anyone in my recovery group. We all suffered from abuse that could have ended us. Those two weren't as lucky." I put the half of the cookie I had between my fingers back in the box, my appetite now lost.

"I see."

I stared off, listening to the band. I'd meant every word, not knowing if the desire to solve their murders came from my link to Mama or from my own life. It no longer mattered. We were connected, the twins and me. Mama was right. If the victims believed the department could solve their crime and apprehend the responsible party, they wouldn't have sought me out. Hopefully, all that would be required of me would be to nudge the department in the right direction.

"Your father was the lead on the missing-persons cases." His words pulled me from my contemplations.

Not sure what he was insinuating, I decided not to respond. If he had a question, he'd have to ask.

"He's going to have to explain the case publicly."

"Eddie is strong and competent. The islanders trust him. You should too."

We settled into silence.

"My *abuelita* believed she had a connection to the dead."

Of all the things I would have guessed to come out of his mouth next, that had never crossed my mind. "Did you believe her?"

"Yes."

I turned to him. "Are you saying you believe I have a connection with the dead?"

He shrugged. "Maybe."

"Are we actually communicating with a purpose of getting to know each other?"

He took a second to ponder before replying. "Yes, I suppose we are."

"Are we becoming friends, douche?"

"Not if you keep referring to me as a douche."

"Fair enough."

CHAPTER 12

Since Betsy and I had taken the first shift, we were in charge of cleaning up the outside. A completely fair trade-off from our perspective. Junior had come by and offered to do the heavy lifting, which we'd appreciated. The drop in temperature made the air crisp and easy to breathe. When Junior left, I began teasing Betsy. We'd just finished disassembling the inside of the tent.

"Seriously, you couldn't come up with anything else?"

Betsy had tears streaming down her cheeks as she guffawed. "I'm usually so good at coming up with excuses on the fly, but when I dug down into the recesses, while staring into his beautiful hazel peepers, I got nothing."

"Other than your tactless comment, you mean." I snickered.

"Yeah, other than that."

We were so caught up in ourselves that we'd not noticed Mr. Gaskin approach.

"Good evening, Mr. Gaskin. Sorry, we don't have anything left in sample form. I could pop into the diner and see what we have in the back, if you'd like." I smiled at Teddy's father. His gray beard was a stark contrast to his mocha skin and usually warm obsidian eyes. Tonight, though, something colder lurked there. His bald head shone in the moonlight.

He sliced his hand through the air. "Nah, don't trouble yourselves."

"It's no trouble at all, Mr. Gaskin. I'll go see what we have." Betsy held out her hand for the key, which I tossed to her.

Mr. Gaskin waited until she'd gone before he spoke further. "Actually, the reason I'm here is to have a word with you."

My curiosity was piqued and wariness loomed. "Want to go inside?" Better to have a witness.

"No. Here's fine." He unfolded a couple of chairs and we took seats. He gave me a pearly white grin. "Theodore is a fine young man. He's hardworking, ambitious, and dedicated to both the funeral home and his new job with the sheriff's department."

I nodded to show how in complete agreement we were.

"This business with you showing up or bargaining with him for information is highly irregular and could jeopardize his job with the department, not to mention tarnish his good reputation."

My cheeks burned. "Mr. Gaskin, my intention—"

"Your intentions, young lady, are irrelevant. Theodore needs to focus on his business and not have his head turned by a troubled young woman seeking attention."

I flinched. "I beg your pardon, Mr. Gaskin." I cleared my throat. "I'll respect the boundaries you desire for your son. He's my friend, and I certainly wouldn't want to, as you put it, jeopardize his career, and for that I take no offense. But I do take umbrage at your insinuation that I'd hurt Teddy because I'm desperate for attention. Sir, you didn't see the condition of those bodies. I did, and not by choice. I want whoever is responsible to be brought to justice." I gave him a pointed glare. "My interest in this case isn't unfounded. However, your opinion of me, sir, is."

He stood and folded up his chair, seemingly unaffected by my words and tone, which had come out as sharp as a two-edged sword. "Now, young lady, I don't mean to be hard on you. I know you've had a hard row to hoe. A lot of us have and, like the rest of us, you learn to deal. If your mama was alive, I'm sure she'd agree with me. And I know your daddy will." His chastising tone had my blood nearly to a boiling point.

Betsy chose that moment to come out with a box in hand. She stood statue-still while Mr. Gaskin continued his scold.

"This case is going to stir up a shit storm, 'scuse my French, but it is. Cook your little food. Run your family's diner. Stick to the kitchen, where you belong, before someone else's life is ruined." He turned and stalked off.

"Who does that guy think he is?" Betsy's tone edged on venomous. "And what century is he living in?" She dropped the box and put her hands on her hips and mocked, "*Stick to the kitchen.* If I didn't like Teddy so much, I'd go stomp his old decrepit bones into the ground."

Slowly, I folded up the chair, too flabbergasted to speak. Irritation continued to creep up my spine. My mind swarmed with thoughts. How had I become the target of such venomous allegations? And by someone notorious for his kindness and mild demeanor. Sure, I got it. The peace had been disturbed. *Did he just threaten me?*

Oh God! This man had the facility to preserve the bodies for all this time. After tonight, he certainly was a suspect. More questions flooded me. Why not incinerate them? Unless he planned to use them as a message to someone. No, that didn't make sense. What message could he possibly be sending Yvonne by dumping a body at her place? Confused, and feeling scatterbrained, I muttered under my breath, "What in sweet baby Moses is going on here?"

My thoughts again drifted back, as they sometimes had, to the infamous detective Thornton, who had been called in to aid Eddie with a murder case last year, and his reference to the secrets harbored on this island.

"You know, Bets," I said when I could finally regain my ability to speak. "His intent to discourage me from involving myself has had the exact opposite effect. I'm even more convinced that those women need me and, by all that's holy, I'm going to help them."

"Damn straight they need us!" Betsy did a fist pump. "I know you see this as a curse and, don't get me wrong, if I had my dead mama popping in on me, I'd probably fart out a chicken. Especially since she died when I was too young to remember her." That Betsy, such a way with words. "That being said, you and I are an awesome team. I mean, if it wasn't for us, the sheriff's department would still be looking for the Ledbetter killer."

Not to toot my own horn, but I fully believed that as well. A gust of wind swirled around me and a deep desire to find the truth gripped me. By whatever means necessary, these women would get justice. Unearthing this island's secrets would be top priority. I imagined the two young women standing a few feet from me. They stood arm in arm, one a mirror image of the other. Chestnut hair against milky-white skin and whisky-colored eyes. As if synchronized, their mouths opened and the words *thank you* echoed around me.

"Hello!" Betsy waved her hand in front of my face, pulling me from my reverie.

"Sorry. I got lost in thought."

A truck rumbled up, laden with tables and chairs. A couple of guys hopped out and began loading up the rented items propped in front of the diner. On autopilot, I signed the digital screen presented in front of me.

Once they pulled away, I turned to Betsy. "We need to pull out that whiteboard. The first suspect on my list is Mr. Daniel Gaskin."

Betsy's eyes twinkled with excitement. She loved this stuff. She opened her mouth to say something, then her eyes went wide as she stared over my shoulder. "Tonya, what's wrong?"

Tonya Wrigley rushed toward us, pushing a blue stroller, her face drawn in what I deduced as utter panic. "Oh, Betsy, Marygene. I'm so thankful y'all are still around. I'm in the depths of despair." The stroller came to a stop in front of me.

A quick glance inside revealed a black-and-white cat with one completely grayed eye. Mr. Wrigley, I presumed. I reached in to pet him, only to receive a feral response. I managed to get my hand out before he clawed the devil out of me.

"Mr. Wrigley, stop that!" Tonya scolded. "He can sense when something is wrong."

His eyes narrowed into slits, daring me to invade his space again.

Betsy hugged Tonya. "What's happened?"

"My sister called from over in Savannah. My granny is ill. I have to go and help care for her for an indefinite amount of time, and I have no one to look after Mr. Wrigley." She reached in and stroked his large black furry head.

He purred happily.

"Why don't you take him with you?" I suggested. He obviously loved her.

"I can't. My sister and granny are allergic."

"Well, I'd take him," Betsy said, "but you know I have

Killer, and he doesn't get along with any other cats. You remember when I tried to adopt that kitten two years ago?"

Tonya nodded.

"It was awful, Marygene," Betsy informed me, since I'd
been living in Atlanta with my horrible ex at the time. "I
had to keep the two separated at all times. Killer is mighty
protective when it comes to sharing my affection."

I'd never actually met Killer. Every time I went by
Betsy's house, he'd made himself scarce.

"Marygene could do it, couldn't you?" Betsy volun-
teered me without a second thought.

Both round faces turned toward me.

"Well, I would, but I have a lot going on at the moment,
and Mr. Wrigley doesn't seem to like me all that much. Besides, I'm more of a dog person myself. There's no one else
that could possibly look after him?"

She gave her head a shake.

"I hate to be this way, but I'm not sure I have the time to
dedicate to properly caring for an animal." I shifted from
foot to foot.

"That's the beautiful thing about a cat. Unlike a dog,
they pretty much look after themselves. You won't have to
worry about bathing him or taking him out to go potty. Just
make sure he has food and water. He'll be no trouble at
all." Tonya made it sound so easy.

Unfortunately for her, I recalled our previous conversation regarding Mr. Wrigley. "You said he had a sinus condition!"

"I have nasal spray for that."

I took a step backward. "No way on God's green earth
am I ever shoving a nozzle up that cat's nose."

"You don't have to use it while I'm gone. It's from the
herb shop. It isn't prescribed."

"Come on, Marygene. Look at that face." Betsy lifted
the little sunshade.

The furry feline began licking his snow-white paw. The act I supposed could be perceived as slightly endearing.

"He'll warm up to you, I swear. He's a real sweetie once you get to know him. He loves to go out for strolls. You only have to tether his harness to this little hook here."

I groaned.

"I have nowhere else to turn." Tonya sniffed and I softened. "I have to leave in the morning. Finding a home for a rescue animal is daunting in itself and the foster homes that are available aren't suitable for Mr. Wrigley. He had a hard time in the home before mine. I've done my best to show him the love he deserves. That's why I spoil him so."

"Come on, Marygene. Just pet the little bitty guy." Betsy said *little bitty guy* in a baby voice.

I dared another reach into the carriage. This time he didn't hiss or launch an attack. Not that my strokes on his head brought the same purring enjoyment that Tonya's had, however; as if he sensed the desperation of his situation, he allowed it.

"All right. We'll give it a try. But I will not use the nasal spray and I'm not pushing him around town in that thing." I made my tone firm on the spray and stroller statement.

"No problem." Tonya beamed, and I received a rewarding round of smiles.

"Bring him by in the morning. Use the back door, the front door sticks a little."

Tonya flung her arms around my neck and wept.

"I'm proud of you." Betsy patted my shoulder.

CHAPTER 13

Tonya dropped Mr. Wrigley off an hour before I had to leave. She set up his food and water bowls in the kitchen and litterbox in the laundry room off of the kitchen. Luckily she'd purchased one of those fancy types that cleaned itself. When full, I had to simply remove the tray from the bottom. I hoped she'd be back before that time came. I'd dog sat for Yvonne before, but Izzy and I were old pals. I worried I might not be a very good cat sitter. Tonya assured me we'd be fine. She mumbled something about the cat and me being kindred spirits. Whatever that meant. She handed me typed, detailed instructions for his care, which, to my surprise, actually appeared quite simple. His food and water were self-dispensers. Again, super simple.

"Mr. Wrigley." Tonya opened the door to his pet carrier.

The cat darted out in a flash and dashed through the living room and up the stairs.

"Oh dear." I had no idea what to do next.

"Don't worry. He just needs some time to adjust to his surroundings. He did the same thing when I brought him home."

I nodded. He needed space, I got that. As long as he didn't come clawing me in the middle of the night, we'd probably be okay.

Tonya hugged me again. "Thanks again for doing this. And if you have any questions, just call me." She asked for my number and texted me so I'd have hers.

"Okay. Thanks." I gave her a nervous smile. "I'm sure we'll be fine."

She glanced at her watch. "I've gotta run." She paused. "Did you know that your front door is spray-painted yellow?"

"What?"

"Yeah. I couldn't read it from my car but definitely could make out the yellow."

I followed her outside. She went to her car, stressing about being late for the ferry. I waved bye as she pulled down the driveway, wiping the tears from her cheeks. Poor thing.

The yellow stood out. When I made it up onto the front porch, my front door read in yellow spray paint, *Leave it alone. Hussy.*

What? Who would do this? Mr. Gaskin could have, but he came to me directly and surely he wouldn't stoop to name-calling. It didn't seem likely. I racked my brain to come up with another option and drew a blank. I took a picture of the door. I'd decide what to do about it later. A little spray paint seemed more like a coward's scare tactic than an actual threat. Time for more coffee.

With the whiteboard rehung in my new office, which had once been my old bedroom, and a fresh mug of coffee, I got to work. At the top of the board, I put the words Cold Case, with Kayla and Pamela Dryer's names underneath. I planned on stopping by the sheriff's department to see if I could get a look at that cold-case file. I had a tentative time line drawn out but needed dates to fill in the gaps. I wondered how Eddie would play into all of this since he handled the missing-persons case way back when. Obviously, no one would suspect the local sheriff of foolishly freezing the remains and discarding them in a perfunctory fashion. Being in law enforcement, he would be able to dispose of the remains and evade suspicion. Not that Eddie had the maliciousness within him to begin with. Still, I needed to have a gander at that file.

Daniel Gaskin went onto the board simply because he'd drawn attention to himself, had the facility to preserve the bodies, spewed hateful remarks, and possibly spray-painted my door. Although, he seemed too refined for a stupid, childish stunt. It could have been random kids. Graffiti had been a problem with the younger teens in the past. Eddie put them to work cleaning the side of the road, and that seemed to fix the problem. Maybe we had a lone wolf.

I checked my watch. Time to take the rollers out of my hair. I gave it a fluff and a good dousing of hairspray and slid into my red pumps that matched the red blossoms on my cream dress. If you wanted to know everything there was to know about the island—gossip- or history-wise, you went to the one place where you could have all the senior women together in one location: church. And it just so happened that today Peach Cove Baptist Church hosted their annual homecoming with what they referred to as dinner on the ground, which basically meant the members brought a dish from home to share with their church family in the fellowship hall.

Last night I raided the freezer to see what I had on hand. With a few steamable bags of broccoli and the two large containers of my homemade chicken stock, I'd had just enough to make a huge pot of broccoli and cheese soup, and I'd used two frozen loaves of sourdough bread to make crouton toppers. With my coffee travel mug in hand, I was good to go.

I found my way to the fellowship hall to drop off my contribution with the ladies tasked with setup and food warming. It had been a while since I'd attended a service, but the music minister's wife and her daughters, and what looked like granddaughters, were still the ones handling the prep work. For a minute, I hung around the doorway to the large commercial kitchen and watched them talk, laugh, and work.

"Hello." The music minister's wife noticed me lurking and gave me a lovely smile. She stood tall and lean, with her dress reaching her ankles. Pretty pink toenails peeked from just underneath. "Why, Marygene Brown, how wonderful it is to see you."

One of her granddaughters, a bright-eyed girl, took the thermal travel bag from me and smiled as her grandmother hugged me.

"I've been praying for you, dear."

"Thank you. I do appreciate it. I can use all of the prayers I can get."

She released me. "You poor thing, you've been through so much since your mother passed. It's awful about the sisters." She tsked. "All we can do is pray."

"True."

"You look just beautiful, though."

"Thank you, ma'am. Did you know the twins?" I started helping her unwrap paper plates.

"Knew of them." She scratched her forearm. "They were the only missing-persons case I can recall the island ever having." She glanced at the ceiling as if attempting to recall a fact. "I bet I was only twenty-seven or twenty-eight at the time. Everyone feared for the safety of their loved ones then. It took a while for folks to resume normal activity. I mean, land sakes alive, one minute the twins were shopping in the market and the next, poof. The abandoned car they found belonged to Kayla."

I reached under the counter to retrieve another package of cups and followed her out of the kitchen to set up the large serving table.

"It sure was a shock for me to find them." I wanted to encourage the dialogue.

"I bet. After all these years too." She placed the stack of cups neatly on the table. "There were some crazy things happening on the island at that time, too."

"What crazy things, Nanny?" the youngest of the girls asked.

I ventured she was about nine. Pretty little thing with long brown hair and big blue eyes.

"Never you mind." She patted the girl on the shoulder. "You run along to your class now." Then she turned to me. "Listen to me going on and on about ancient history. You'll be missing the service if you don't hurry." She hugged me again. "I do hope to see you in attendance more often."

"Thank you, ma'am. I'll do my best." Reluctantly, I left and moved quietly through the vestibule as the music had already started. I heard hymns being sung. I slipped into the back of the sanctuary and onto the pew next to none other than the bird watcher, Mrs. Foster. Just my luck. The glance she shot my way as I took a hymnal from the back of the pew in front of me proved she still harbored negative feelings about me and my lapse in judgment. She received a smile from me anyway as I sang out, "'What a friend we have in Jesus.'"

When the service ended, I found Betsy and Meemaw sitting with Ms. Brooks and Yvonne at a table in the middle of the fellowship hall.

With my plate piled high with fried chicken, mashed potatoes, collard greens, macaroni and cheese, and a giant hunk of cornbread, my insides did a little happy dance. These church women sure knew how to put on a spread, and I was starving. The tables were so close together, I

weaved around toward my saved seat, pausing here and
there to exchange pleasantries with those who were glad to
see me. Everyone wanted to ask about the condition of the
bodies. Not suitable conversation for lunch, I kindly re-
marked. I received nods of acknowledgment.

I squeezed in between Betsy and Yvonne. We sat elbow
to elbow, my idea of family style. Meemaw carried on with
her conversation about the birthday party Betsy had promised to throw her next week. She had it all planned out—
Meemaw that is, not Betsy. Betsy kept cutting her gaze my
way until I finally laughed and agreed to cater the party.
Thrilling Meemaw and relieving Betsy.

"I want one of those tiered-up cakes with a zebra pattern
on it. Oh, and one of those glittery gold toppers. You only
turn eighty-five once." She took a bite of potato salad. "My
party is going to be a doozy! Viola is coming to town for it
and everything."

"Then a zebra cake you shall have. It'll be nice to see
Aunt Vi. She's been missed around here." I dug into my
plate. Everyone called Betsy's aunt, Aunt Vi. Never having
had children of her own, she insisted on it. Even as a child,
I'd recognized her eccentric personality. She'd always
been so much fun.

"How's Mr. Wrigley?" Betsy asked.

I explained to everyone at the table how I came to be sitting with the little fella. "Don't know. He's in hiding."

"That's normal. He'll come out and socialize when he's
ready." Betsy grinned.

Yvonne leaned closer in to the table. "The news about
those twins has circulated even farther off island. I had a
call from a reporter in the Carolinas just the other day."

"It makes sense it would attract such attention. I mean,
with the bodies being preserved the way they were, then,
um, burned," I whispered.

Yvonne shook her head. "It's awful and a little frightening, but it sure has brought a lot of attention to the island and, for me, that's been a real positive."

"Good for the diner too." Betsy cracked the shell of her chicken potpie.

Sadly, it seemed that bizarre activity drew lots of tourists. And with tourists came revenue.

Mrs. Gentry caught my eye, and I recalled seeing her with Candi the other day. I decided to ask Yvonne about it before it slipped my mind again. Something about it seemed off to me. Perhaps that was just my suspicious nature, but still, it needed to be fleshed out. After I explained what I witnessed, Yvonne didn't appear surprised in the slightest.

She rolled her eyes. "Mrs. Gentry had me come by and discuss completely redesigning her home. Since the publicity, I suppose she believes my plebian status revoked, and now I'm worthy to enter the grand Gentry family home. Not that I'd turn the business away, but all the designs I presented she immediately squelched. She probably decided to take it out on Candi since I stopped returning every single call."

The entire table showed their disapproval for Mrs. Gentry's antics.

"That Evelyn needs to be put in her place. I don't know what's happened to her over the years. She's turned into a right witch," Yvonne's mama said.

Meemaw and Betsy snickered.

Yvonne whispered, "Mama, we're in church."

Alex moved past our table, and we all settled into silence. He leaned in and kissed Meemaw on the cheek.

"Lawdy mercy, I'm surprised the church didn't cave in when you crossed the threshold."

Alex chuckled at his meemaw's teasing. "Come on, I'm not that awful." He chanced a glance my way and I smiled.

We were supposed to still be friends after all.

"You're here to snoop. I know your game, boy." Meemaw waved her hand playfully. "Go do your job. We can't have a maniac on the loose." Perhaps Meemaw had my number as well. Her party would be the perfect opportunity to inquire about that *heap of bodies* reference she'd made.

Yvonne leaned her head close to mine. "I still can't believe you two broke up. Remind me to tell you something later. I don't want to bring it up here."

What else has Alex done now?

"They're calling it a break," Betsy interjected.

"That's the stupidest thing I ever heard. In my day, we didn't take breaks. We fought it out and then moved on. When you're married as long as I was, fifty-three years, you don't even like each other half the time. But you stick it out." Meemaw never kept her opinions to herself.

Time to change the subject. "The minister's wife said the twins vanished without a trace. They'd been shopping in the market and then vanished, their car left in the parking lot."

"That's true." Meemaw forked a piece of fried okra.

It looked so good, I wished I'd gotten some.

"Poor Kayla and Pam. They were such sweet girls." Ms. Brooks stunned us all. "They had such a hard life, living with their stepdaddy. Their mama up and died when they were only thirteen. They should have gone to live with their kin in Savannah. They'd have been safe then."

"You knew them?" I leaned forward.

Ms. Brooks bobbed her curly head. "They were part of our group."

"That's right, Thelma," Meemaw added. "I remember them now. It was you, Debbie Foster, my Viola, Clara, Evelyn Gentry, and the twins. Thick as thieves they were."

Betsy, Yvonne, and I sat in utter silence for a few moments, exchanging glances. It didn't surprise me that each of us had a family member who grew up with the twins, but it seemed to shock all of us that they'd been so close.

"Sad how they disappeared." The elderly lady I didn't recognize from the table next to us leaned over and joined in.

Meemaw and Ms. Brooks weren't low talkers.

"My Rita knew them too."

I glanced over to the woman seated to her right. I recognized her but, until her mother said her name, I couldn't have placed her. Now I recalled that she was the sister of Nita Collins, a regular at the Peach. She had curly black hair and a pleasant round face that glowed with kindness around the purple glasses perched at the end of her nose.

"We knew of them but my sister, Nita, and I weren't part of their seaside sisters."

I turned farther in my chair. "Seaside sisters?"

She took a sip from her red cup. "That's how their group referred to themselves, the seaside sisters. And from what I recall, after high school, they kinda got into some wild stuff."

My mama? Wild? We all turned to stare at Ms. Brooks, the only member of the seaside sisters at our table. She spooned potatoes into her mouth, completely unfazed.

Before I could inquire further, we were interrupted when the pastor took to the microphone and introduced the Peach Cove Pickers and they began to play. I had to bite my tongue to squelch the urge to probe for more answers. Ms. Brooks wasn't always lucid, and I wanted to take advantage of the opportunity. Maybe later. However, Mama had her wits about her all the time, and she would have a lot to answer for when she made her next appearance.

As the group sang, I surveyed he crowd. There sat that hoity-toity Evelyn Gentry, the picture of an upstanding woman of the community. What I wouldn't give for a few minutes alone with her in the interview room, with her strapped to a polygraph. This island and their secrets! *Seaside sisters, indeed.*

CHAPTER 14

Sam and I finished loading the van with all the breakfast items Eddie had ordered for his meeting with his "special task force." To my surprise, a few reporters had received an invite. I had no idea what Eddie had been thinking when he invited the bottom-feeding cretins. Well, other than Calhoun. He clearly would be included in the exception clause of my previous statement. He'd been nothing but kind and helpful. And, I supposed, the article Calhoun wrote had also helped Yvonne's career. Okay, perhaps I needed to reconsider my opinions.

"Let's get this over there before the breakfast rush begins." Sam started up the engine.

We hauled the food to the department. The conference room had been thrown together, utilizing cubicle walls around the sides and back of the partitioned room. The front, since they'd obviously run out of partition sections, was left open. I assembled the breakfast while Sam set up the coffee urns. I arranged one platter beautifully, with peach rolls, apple cider doughnuts, mixed fruit turnovers, and healthy slices of cinnamon streusel coffee cake. On the other, breakfast burritos—Eddie's favorite—mini spinach and crab quiches, and bagels with smoked salmon, cream cheese, and chives. I'd just finished scooping the last of the banana-nut oatmeal in the chafing dish when Sam leaned in, seething. "That's her."

"Her? Her who?" I put the serving spoon in the dish and glanced across the span of the long rectangular table.

"The one Alex flirted with at the bar." A tall, wavy-haired blonde had legs up to her neck, which she didn't mind showing off. Her skirt, if you could call it that, showed her flawless skin. Not a lump or bump anywhere. I loathed her. She flashed her movie-star smile as she giggled at something Javy said before she sauntered around the corner, swaying her hips elaborately.

"Are you sure?" I thought I might be sick.

Sam gave his head a jerk of confirmation.

"You've got to be flipping kidding me. That"—I pointed to where she'd walked—"is the chick he wiped foam off of? What's she doing here? She's a tourist, right?"

Sam shrugged. "Sorry, Sis."

Alex walked past the conference room and flinched when our gazes locked. He made an about-face and slipped into the room. "Let me explain."

My fists clenched at my side.

Sam put his hand on my shoulder. "Not here. Think of Dad and what a scene would do with all these reporters. He ain't worth it." Sam was on the balls of his feet.

Alex kept his distance. "Come on, Sam. You know me."

"I do. And I stand by my previous statement. Not. Worth. It." He was a good brother.

Alex ran a hand on the back of his neck, his eyes weary and his face pained. I still didn't feel sorry for him. "It isn't what you think. Lucy needed a job. She applied at Yvonne's design company, but she turned her down."

So, that was what she wanted to tell me.

"She needed income, and we needed a receptionist. Eddie

said she had references and everything. She's rented one of the cottages on West Beach." His hands were raised in a defensive posture as he rambled.

"Oh well, then it's all okay. *Lucy* needed a job," I said in mock falsetto. "It makes complete sense now."

"She had nothing to do with the break, I swear."

Break, my ass! God, would I never learn?

Javy entered the room. "Everything okay here?" He glanced around the room, clearly uneasy.

My brother briefly squeezed my hand hard. It redirected my focus long enough to make the decision I'd be fine. Eventually. I let out the breath I'd been holding. My tone came out calm and together. "Just finished setting up. We'll get out of your way."

"Good to see you, Javier." Sam clapped his hand on Javy's shoulder. "Marygene and I were just saying we should have you out to her house for a cookout. I'll bring Poppy along and we'll make a night of it."

Alex seethed.

Javy glanced in my direction as if to assess if the invitation had indeed come from me.

In my current mood, I nodded. *Why not?*

"Sounds good. I'll get back to Marygene on my schedule."

"Perfect." Sam beamed.

Eddie chose that exact moment to join us. "Smells great in here." He appeared to be in a decent mood. He had a distaste for theatrics. It served him well in his position of authority. Eddie had once told me *Never give anything away and always keep a level head, pumpkin.* It worked for him, most of the time. The fact that he hadn't sensed the tension in the room and that he'd hired that pouty-lipped Barbie doll were clear indicators of his stress levels. He usually didn't miss much. I chastised myself for labeling the woman. And despising her. The fault didn't lie with her. She probably had a terrific personality and could carry on an intelligent conversation. Just because my pride had taken a hit, it shouldn't give me the freedom to assassinate another's character, and I wouldn't engage in such behaviors. Or I'd try really hard not to.

"Good luck today." I gave Eddie a kiss on the cheek before my brother and I strolled out of the conference room. Neither of us spared Alex another glance. Just like Sam said. He definitely didn't deserve my anger or pain. *One foot in front of the other. I can so do this.* My life's mantra. *Positive mind, positive life.*

And it worked up until I passed the reception desk and *Lucy* spoke to me.

"You must be Marygene." She sashayed around the desk to thrust her hand in my face, her pink nails wiggling at chin level. She had a couple of inches on me, she was about ten pounds thinner than me, and her hair had a life of its own. Not in a bad way either. It flowed and bounced in an attractive eye-catching way.

Now that Alex no longer had his attention, Sam couldn't help the appraising glance he gave her.

"I've heard so much about you. As I'm sure you have me."

I furrowed my brow as if I were completely confused. "I'm sorry, but I'm afraid I haven't. You are?"

My retort contorted her face in an unattractive manner. Maybe she wasn't so nice after all.

"Lucy Carmichael."

With a cordial smile, I took her hand and shook it, firmly. "How are you enjoying our island, Lucy Carmichael?"

She shrugged. "This place is sort of like the land that time forgot in some places, and in others it reeks of old money and high-end taste. Where I'm staying is a cross between the two."

I nodded and took a step back, ready to be back at the diner.

"We should hang out sometime." She flipped her hair over her shoulders. "Especially now I'm working with your dad. Alex said you two were good friends. It'd be fun."

"Maybe, but work keeps me real busy." *No chance in hell.*

She crinkled her nose and then blurted, "Oh right, you're a waitress."

"Sometimes. But I own the Peach Diner, along with my sister. We're extremely proud of our family business."

She laughed and looked down her nose at me. "Honestly, I was trying to be nice. Someone like you could use a friend like me to elevate your circumstances."

My nails dug into my palms.

"And with me working as the new secretary, you needn't worry about those hilarious photos leaking."

My palms stung.

"The last secretary just left the flash drive lying around. Anyone could have gotten ahold of them." She tsked.

That didn't sound like Tonya.

She would not get the best of me. I forced my face to relax. "I'm a free spirit," I said in a flippant tone, by way of explanation. "Better watch your p's and q's. Eddie runs a tight ship. He doesn't care for loose lips within the ranks."

"Good to know. I'm just so grateful to Alex for speaking up on my behalf."

I grinned so hard my jaw ached. "Yes, he's so thoughtful like that." *He'd better not be the one who showed you the pictures.*

"He's a real sweetie." She actually batted her long fake lashes. "He offered to take me out on his boat."

What?

He just said two seconds ago that his only goal was to help her out with a job. Now this deranged woman baited me with a date he'd asked her on. My nails dug deeper into my palms.

Sam cleared his throat. "That's nice. Come on, Mary-gene."

A couple of reporters came through the doorway. Cal-houn and his nephew were among them. Lucy's expression altered from catty to welcoming.

Phony bitch.

"Good morning, gentlemen. If you'll just go right on in to the conference room there." She pointed around the corner. "There are refreshments we've catered in. Just help yourself. The sheriff will begin in approximately twenty minutes."

"I hoped breakfast would be catered in from the Peach. I'm looking forward to this. Fellas, this woman is a genius in the kitchen. You're in for a treat."

"Thank you, Calhoun." I gave the reporters a smile. "I hope you gentlemen enjoy it."

One of them took an interest in me and stepped over. He had a wide build with a pudgy midsection. His face was round and ruddy. "You're the sheriff's daughter. I wondered if I might have a word with you later. I'm extremely curious about your discovery of both bodies."

"She's given her statement to the department and that's where this ends." Sam wrapped an arm around my shoulders.

"Ah, the brother. You were with her when the second body was found."

"I was. I have nothing further to add either. The sheriff will answer all your questions."

Calhoun cast an apologetic smile my way and herded them into the conference room. Not that it stopped them hurling questions and insinuations over their shoulders. This just wasn't my day.

Sam and I had just turned for the front doors when Lucy opened her stupid mouth again. "Oh, wait, Marygene. I wonder if you know of any good shops nearby. I'm in dire

need of a few light sundresses. This heat down here is brutal." She gave me the up-down. "You know what, never
mind. I'll just order online."

My body froze and I began mentally counting to ten.
Don't mar, maim, or murder Eddie's receptionist.

"Maybe you could make us a picnic lunch for my date
with Alex. You know, I'd like to surprise him. The Peach
does that sort of thing, don't they?"

Dead woman talking!

If there was one woman on that jury, I'd never be convicted. I pulled out of Sam's hold and took a step forward,
ready to claw her sterling-gray eyes out. Contacts, obviously. Lucy instantly retreated for the safety of the desk.
Like that would save her.

Sam grabbed my arm and jerked me toward the front
door. "We'll be glad to take your to-go order. Just call
ahead." Sam kept his voice cheery. "Have a nice day!"

"You are way stronger than you look," Sam said as I
stomped to the van. "I told you he wasn't worth it, and
going after that girl isn't going to help."

I sat down hard and slammed the van's door.

"Don't take it out on the van either. Plus, I got you a date
to get your mind off of the loser." Sam grinned, a smug expression upon his face.

"I told you, I don't need you pimping me out." When I
thought about how Alex reacted though, I grinned. "You
get a pass on this one. The timing was perfect."

Sam nodded. "I'm smooth like that." He started the engine.

"I've got to get that stupid flash drive."

"The one with your nudies on it?" Sam cringed.

"Yes, Sam. God, they could end up on the internet and
some of them aren't so flattering. And I hate Lucy. She's
lucky you were there to save her. She better watch out.
Something awful might happen to her."

"Don't let her get to you. She just wanted to rile you up and you took the bait. Now you're wanting something bad to happen to her because she's after your loser ex-boyfriend."

I folded my arms and glanced out the window. "I'm not saying I want something horrific to befall her, but if it does, it wouldn't hurt my feelings."

Sam burst out laughing.

CHAPTER 15

Behind the counter, I placed the pre-sliced pumpkin cheesecake with caramel pecan topping into the refrigerated glass display case. My cheesecakes were a thing of beauty. The delicate, spicy ginger-cookie crust gave the bottom a nice firm bite at the end of the airy whipped cream-cheese filling. It boggled my mind as to why people only indulged in delicious pumpkin once a year. Not at our diner. You could get a cup of pumpkin-and-black-bean soup with lump crabmeat or shrimp, or a spiced pumpkin muffin, on certain days of the week throughout the year. We attempted to rotate our daily offerings to keep them fresh and desirable.

After the horrendous morning I'd had, I feared I'd burst into tears at any moment. So I'd avoided Betsy and Jena Lynn by throwing myself into the day's tasks. Went above and beyond to keep busy. And when Heather came into the diner full of cheer, it was a welcome distraction. Her dark hair had been styled with beach waves and she'd put on a few pounds, a good thing for her. She had a healthy appearance now.

She wiggled a ringed finger in front of us. "I'm getting married, y'all! And this time I've finally found a good one." Squeals of delight went round until she announced the news that she'd be moving away. Her fiancé's family lived in South Carolina, and she needed a fresh start. It made sense. We all told her how sad we were to see her go, but understood. Jena Lynn got her new mailing address so we could all pitch in and send them a wedding gift, before excusing herself to the office for a moment. I would be filling in out front some, until we hired a new waitress. Sometimes it could be challenging to find an employee who actually stuck with it.

"I'm so happy for you!" I gave her a giant hug.

We both shed a few tears.

"Sometimes a change can be liberating. Though, rest assured you'll be missed."

"After last year, I didn't think I'd ever love again, then I met Larry." Her face creased in a grin. "He's wonderful and the kids love him. I just hate leaving y'all without help. I would've given more notice, except the house sold faster than I expected and we close on our new house early next week."

"Don't worry about it. We have several fill-in waitresses looking for full-time work." I hoped that still remained the case. With the influx in tourists came the need for jobs. A good thing.

Betsy flashed her pearly whites as she passed with her tray full of food.

Jena Lynn came back into the dining room and hugged her next. Then she slid an envelope into her hand. "I do wish you could have the wedding here, though. Maybe this will help since we can't cater your wedding."

Heather teared up when she glanced inside. "Y'all are too good to me."

After one last group hug, she went off to begin her new life. She deserved happiness. I wished her many wonderful years of it.

After my shift, I baked Meemaw's birthday cake, rolled out black fondant while the cake cooled, and cut out the zebra patterns. I placed the dowel rods in the center of the first layer, to hold the second tier in place, when Jena Lynn came in with a face on her like thunder. "I can't believe you didn't claw that woman's eyes out! The nerve!"

"Sam told you, huh?"

"Yes. That girl has to be the instigator. Alex would never be vile." She folded her arms. She'd always loved Alex and I got that, but it still bothered me. It was as if she took his side over mine.

With the cake fully assembled, I began the crumb coating. A good crumb coat was essential for a clean-looking design. The soothing motions of spreading the buttercream while spinning the turntable helped me relax while I chose my next words wisely. "Why does everyone believe it couldn't be Alex? Apparently, he asked her out. Sam heard it same as I did."

"From her, not Alex." Her opinion certainly didn't match my brother's.

I sighed.

Jena Lynn leaned against the counter opposite the work table. "I'm in your corner, Marygene. We're sisters. I'll admit my feelings were hurt you didn't confide in me about the troubles you two were having."

"What's to say? He's a flirt. We're supposed to remain friends while we both work through our own junk. But now, I think we're really done."

"I get it. I guess I'd hoped that, you know, you and Alex

would settle down and be happy together. Maybe even have a couple of kids."

Without pause, I began placing the fondant pieces on the cake. "If there's one thing I've learned in this life, it doesn't always turn out as we plan. That's not necessarily a bad thing. Besides, my happiness doesn't have to correlate with marriage and kids. I can be happy all by myself."

"Wow. You don't sound all torn up like I thought you would."

"I suppose I've got other things on my mind too. Plus, you can't force a relationship. It's an entity of its own and it either works or it doesn't. Alex and I tried. Will we ever try again?" I shrugged and filled a piping bag with frosting. "God only knows. One truth I've come to realize over the last few years is whether I'm in a relationship or not isn't going to make or break my happiness."

"No, I know. I get that. Um, you said *other things*. You mean all the island drama?"

"Something like that. Hey, did you know Mama belonged to a group called the seaside sisters when she was younger?"

Jena Lynn shook her head. "Doesn't ring any bells."

"For me either, but a lot of the senior women on the island knew all about them and their shenanigans. And want to hear the most interesting part?" I paused over the cake, piping bag poised, to meet her eyes.

Her brown eyes were as wide as saucers. "Tell me."

"Kayla and Pamela Dryer were part of the seaside sisters, along with Ms. Brooks, Aunt Vi, Debbie Foster, and Evelyn Gentry."

"No way!"

"Way. And I plan to get to the bottom of it." I piped large round white dots at the joining of each tier.

"Oh God, not the whiteboard again. Why don't you just

quit the diner and join the sheriff's department?" she joked, and I knew we were back on better terms. "You could apply to join the new task force and work alongside *Lucy*." Lucy's name came out all nasally.

We both had a laugh.

"All right, I've got to run. I've got to make up the guest room. Zach's oldest sister, Hannah, and her husband are coming to stay with us awhile."

"Why's that?"

She rolled her neck around, stretching. "A pipe burst in their house while they were on a cruise. The floors are completely ruined, along with most of the appliances."

"Yikes." I changed piping bags to one with a number-three round tip to write *happy birthday* in bright pink around the base of the cake. The color would be a nice contrast to the gold foil board and topper.

"Yeah. I told Zach they better get right on that. I don't care if they have major jobs in the works. I love his family and all, but I don't want them living with me indefinitely." She glanced at her watch.

I could completely understand that.

"You good here?"

"Fine. I'll close up as soon as I finish this cake. Betsy's wiping down tables and refilling sugar packets now." I was dead on my feet. These double shifts were murder. "Hey, didn't you say Hannah was interested in working here?"

"Yeah. Since both her kids are now school age, she has time. She's a real good baker. If you want, I could see if she wants to do a sort of apprenticeship. I know we talked about expanding and having extra help; someone we could train to make things our way would be good."

"I think that'd be great!"

"Okay. I'll bring her in for a half day and we'll see how it goes. The cake looks beautiful. Meemaw will be pleased."

I waved bye and continued my task.

With the cake now in the walk-in, I untied my apron and tossed it over my shoulder. My shorts were a mess and my shirt might not make it, even with stain remover. I shut off the lights and rounded the corner. To my surprise, Eddie sat at the bar with a cup of coffee. Must have been the last of the pot because Betsy had already gone and she always cleaned the pots before she left.

"Hey." I leaned against the counter.

His brows were drawn together as he stared down into the mug between his hands. All the enthusiasm from this morning had vanished.

He lifted his face and offered me a smile. I couldn't help myself. I closed the distance and took the seat next to him, wrapped my arm across the expanse of his back, and rested my head on his shoulder. I found another reason to involve myself in this case. To ease the stress it caused my father.

He patted my hand. "I'm all right. I just needed to see my daughter's pretty face for a few minutes." When I lifted my head and rewarded him with one of my one-hundred-watt smiles, he grinned and it went all the way up to his eyes.

"This case is getting to you." I retreated to my own space.

He nodded. And when he began to speak, I went quiet as a mouse. Eddie didn't come forth with information often, and I planned on hanging on every single word. He ran his hand through his hair. "When those little gals went missing, I'd only been a deputy a few years. We searched high and low for them. Made a plea on television to the residents. Even sent out several search parties into the protected land. No one ever came forward and no one recalled seeing them after that afternoon."

"How can not one but two people simply disappear like that?"

"I don't know, but they did. We didn't have CCTV cameras like they had in Atlanta or Savannah. All we had to go on was eyewitness accounts, and that didn't amount to much. Their stepdaddy had died several years prior and their aunt had come to live on the island while they finished school. I sort of got the impression she wasn't around half the time anyway. The girls practically raised themselves." He shook his head. "He was a real sumbitch, their stepdaddy. Little did we know that their extended biological family had their own issues with the law. When I reached out to the family they had off island, they refused to even come in and sit down with us. I had to go to them." He pushed the mug away. "That's when I found out why they insisted on keeping silent. A lot of the family had rap sheets as long as my arm." He motioned to his elbow. "Petty crimes mostly. B and E's, theft by taking, and one, I think"—he sat up straight—"did time for armed robbery."

"Wow."

He swiveled in his chair and faced me now. "I've got to talk to you about something."

His piercing blue stare made me instantly nervous. Would he be asking me about the bodies? Had he recalled what Betsy said about Mama? Maybe he was worried about my sanity.

"This business with you and Alex and that girl I hired as a receptionist."

I had to force myself not to let out a sigh of relief.

"I picked up on a little trouble at lunch the other day, but I didn't know you'd decided to split up."

"Honestly, Eddie, don't worry about it. It was a mutual decision. And if he ends up with that Lucy, fine. I don't like her, but that's his business, not mine. I'll get over it. There are far more important matters than who Alex dates. His relationship status with me shouldn't have any bearing on his job. We aren't married."

He slid a flash drive across the bar. I gripped the small plastic device in my hand.

"It's been locked up in my drawer. So, no worries about anyone else seeing them."

That relieved me. Lucy had just been yanking my chain.

"And if I'd known about the issue with Alex, I'd never have hired the girl. We don't need that kind of drama inside the department."

"Thanks for this." I held up the drive. "Still, don't fire her on account of me. Truly. It's no big deal."

"She's just a temp anyway. I won't keep her around. Hopefully when Tonya's grandmother gets well she'll be back."

I hoped so too.

"And as for the drive, there's nothing on it we can use for the investigation."

I started to tell him about my spray-painted door, but when he placed both big hands on the counter and stood, I decided it could wait.

"Come on, I'll walk you out to your car."

When we reached my car, I finally got up the nerve to ask Eddie what had been on my mind for some time. "Are you worried about secrets that could come to light during the investigation? I heard things at church about Mama and her friends."

He opened my door for me. "Pumpkin, there are always secrets we wish could remain buried. This island is no exception. I'm just glad your mama isn't around to be put through all the in-depth questioning and interviews that will need to be conducted." He urged me into the driver's seat. "Drive safe." The car door shut.

CHAPTER 16

Tonight I drove home on autopilot. The disturbance in the car began the second I turned down my long driveway lined on both sides with gnarled, moss-draped oaks that formed a canopy. "Hey, Mama. You've got some explaining to do."

"Don't take that tone with me, young lady. I'm your mother. You're not mine. You best remember that." Mama's arms folded across her chest as I put the car in park.

"Never been confused on that point." I slung my purse over my shoulder and exited the vehicle. "What I am confused about is why, after all these years, these two are just now surfacing. Poor Eddie is worn slap out." I went up the back steps of my farmhouse, aware she still followed behind me. "You should've seen him tonight." I shook my head. "This case can't drag on. He won't be able to handle it." I didn't stop after I entered the kitchen. I marched straight up the stairs, stripped, and jumped into the shower.

"I detest that this is putting pressure on Edward." Mama sounded weary yet annoyed.

I began removing my makeup.

"But he's the sheriff. He coveted that position for years.

Lord knows I tried to convince him to pursue other fields. Cases like these go with the territory."

"No, cases like these don't." I rinsed the shampoo from my hair. "Cases like these are in the movies or documentaries. Preserved bodies resurfacing after twenty-five years isn't the norm. Why now?"

"I don't know, Marygene."

"But you do know about the seaside sisters. Kayla and Pamela were in your little group." I stepped from the shower, thankful to feel clean, and wrapped a towel around myself. "People are talking about shady things that took place on this island. Things that I believe you have knowledge of and perhaps even took part in."

Mama handed me my night cream. "I put all that out of my head once I married and had Jena Lynn. We were all young and dumb. Playing with fire, your nanny used to say, and she was right. All of that nonsense went on in our late teens and ended in our early twenties. For me at least. I can't necessarily speak for the others in the group."

I stared over my shoulder at her as I smeared on the cream.

"I'm ashamed of some of the choices I made, and people were hurt by some of them."

"Just tell me this: Do you know who killed those twins?"

Ever so slowly, she nodded. The act appeared to take effort.

"Well, for heaven's sake, tell me! I can steer Eddie in the right direction and we can put this all behind us for good." I put the cream down and pointed at her. "You always said take responsibility for your actions. And now, it's time you practice what you've preached because your actions are affecting Eddie, Sam, your precious Jena Lynn, and me. Lord knows Jena Lynn needs peace, and I need peace! Come on, Mama, help me." I put my hands together in a praying fashion, pleading with her. It was a low blow to attempt to manipulate her by throwing up her past favoritism toward my sister. She'd apologized for allowing my presence to be a constant reminder of her infidelity. I'd forgiven her and had mostly come to terms with it all. Sometimes my bitterness reared its ugly head.

Before I could ask for her forgiveness, she opened her mouth but nothing came out. She appeared shocked. She opened it again and again—nothing came out. Her hands went to her throat, her brown eyes wide with what could only be described as terror. She glanced straight up a single second before she disappeared. The force shoved me to my knees. I sat there completely stunned and prayed she'd be okay.

Sunday rolled around and no Mama sightings. Today Meemaw celebrated her eightieth birthday. I finished helping Betsy put up the pink, black, and white decorations, and the cake sat beautifully on the round table, covered in a pink tablecloth, positioned in the middle of the fellowship hall of the church. Betsy had booked the hall for seven, perfect timing for when Sunday-night service let out. All Meemaw's friends could simply walk down the stairs and be at the party.

"So, she just vanished?" Betsy asked as we began putting food in chafing dishes to keep it warm.

"Yep." I popped a crisp bacon-wrapped asparagus into my mouth. "And the weird thing is, I think she got in trouble for breaking the rules or something."

"Really?"

I nodded. "I got the distinct impression someone forced her to leave and shut off all forms of communication. She knows who the killer is and, for some stupid reason, whoever is pulling her strings won't let her divulge anything that might be remotely useful."

Betsy put out the zebra plates and napkins and black forks on the cake table, glancing around warily. "Maybe it's God. And here you are calling him stupid. Get away from me. I don't want to be struck dead."

"I didn't say it was God. And things like that don't happen."

A loud clanging sound nearly shot me out of my own skin. Betsy and I both shrieked. Napkins went flying. It took us both a second to realize the noise had come from the double steel doors at the back of the room and it hadn't been the Almighty. Alex stood there, gaping at the two of us huddled together.

"Alex!" Betsy hissed, composing herself. "Service is still going on upstairs."

"Sorry. You said to get here early to help set up, so here I am."

I turned my back and busied myself with arranging the rolls, croissants, and mini baguettes around the crab dip, leaving Betsy to clean up the napkins. My heart still pounded.

"The chairs are over there against the wall on the chair dollies. Situate six to a table," Betsy instructed her cousin.

"Where are Jena Lynn and Zach? Zach said he would be here to help with the heavy lifting."

"They both have the stomach flu that's been going around." I poured mock champagne that consisted of ginger ale and grape juice into the champagne fountain. Then I went to retrieve the cups from the kitchen. The doors closed again. That was when I heard Betsy really get riled. She never had mastered the art of whispering.

"How dare you bring her here? Do you have any idea how that will affect Marygene?" My heart nearly stopped beating.

"Marygene made it perfectly clear we are through. Do you know who she hung out with at the Taste of Peach Cove? Javier! Lucy saw them all cozied up, listening to blue-grass music."

One, two, three, four, five . . . I clenched the plastic champagne flutes in my hands. *Six, seven* . . .

"Why, Marygene Brown, I do declare you look prettier than you ever have!" The voice echoed around the kitchen, and I opened my eyes to see Betsy's aunt Vi dressed in a pirate-wench costume, complete with a stuffed parrot sewed to her shoulder. Her red frizzy hair stuck out from underneath the green trifold hat, and her lips were painted a scarlet red. She charged me and squeezed me so tightly I feared for my ribs.

"Good to see you too, Aunt Vi."

"Aunt Vi!" Betsy squealed and the two plus-size women dashed across the kitchen to embrace. Aunt Vi had been the one who stepped in when Betsy lost her mama at the tender age of four. She'd told me she had no memories of her mother. Meemaw raised her, of course, but Aunt Vi had been the one she'd leaned on during the rough patches. It warmed my heart to see the two so happily reunited.

Betsy howled. "What in tarnation are you wearing?"

"Mama said she was having a costume party. Isn't this a hoot! I love it so much I've worn it grocery shopping twice. It's a real dude magnet at the senior center."

That coaxed a chuckle from me.

Betsy wiped the tears from her eyes. "She changed her mind last month when we booked the church. I can't believe she didn't tell you."

Aunt Vi smirked. "She did."

The two burst out laughing all over again.

"I should have worn my cat costume. I've got this spandex number I wore last year for Halloween and . . ."

I left them to carry on their conversation while I put the flutes out on the table near the champagne fountain. Then I went to work on the chocolate fountain. Everyone loved warm glossy chocolate over fruit and cubes of pound cake. The real crowd pleaser only required a microwave to heat the chocolate with a little corn syrup, then the mixture would be poured into the base of the stainless steel fountain.

Alex and his date gave me a wide berth, which I was completely happy with until his mama arrived, giving me the evil eye. Judging from his mother's reaction, I'd bet money Alex played the wounded and misunderstood card during his description of our breakup, leaving me to be perceived as the bad guy. Now I wanted to track his lying tail down and rip him a new one. Obviously, he'd left out the part about Lucy when he told her we'd broken up. Yet, there she stood in all her skanky glory, wearing a stripper dress to a birthday party at church, no less.

No, it wasn't any of my business anymore. Whatever and whoever Alex did had nothing to do with me. I paused. What if it had been Lucy who spray-painted my door? She glared in my direction. It certainly seemed plausible. Well, I wouldn't even acknowledge it. I'd call our handyman to come paint it, and act as if it never happened. I focused on Meemaw, feeling quite proud of myself. She had her pink birthday-girl banner on, was wearing a feathered boa, and had a crown upon her head. And she appeared to be having the time of her life.

"You all right?" Aunt Vi sidled up next to me as I stood in the corner of the room next to the kitchen pretending to be available to refill whatever ran low. She didn't wait for me to answer. "Don't let him get to you. Myers men are stubborn as mules. He's only with that little trollop to make you jealous." She took a bite of roasted shrimp cocktail.

"All's fair in love and war, sweetie. You're a beautiful girl. I say have fun with it while you have it. Believe me, one day you'll look down and the girls will be at your knees."

I giggled and wrapped my arm around her shoulders. "Thanks for the advice. Can I ask you something completely off the subject?"

"Sure. You know me, I'm an open book. Just make sure you want the answer before you ask. Look at Evelyn sitting over there all high-and-mighty." Aunt Vi put on a fake smile and waved a pinky in Mrs. Gentry's direction. Who, in turn, acted as if she didn't notice her. How could you not notice the only person in a pirate-wench's costume? "And there's Debbie next to her. Thick as thieves, those two."

Huh, Mrs. Gentry had warned me about Mrs. Foster, and here they were, like Aunt Vi had stated, thick as thieves.

That Evelyn Gentry, the notorious busybody, annoyed me to no end. Junior sat next to her with a solemn expression. I smiled and waved at him. He instantly perked up. He probably hadn't wanted to spend his Sunday afternoon this way. Poor guy.

"Hey, there's Thelma and her little Yvonne. I'll be right back." She scooted across the floor.

Alex and Lucy walked up to the table together. She had her hand tucked in the bend of his arm. Alex's gaze locked on mine as he opened his mouth to speak when Lucy whispered something to him. My heart ached and I felt utterly ridiculous all at the same time. Thankfully, Betsy signaled the chocolate fountain was running low.

I had the giant-handled mixing bowl in the microwave when I heard Alex say, "What are we doing?"

I swallowed the lump in my throat. "I'm melting more chocolate. You're here with your date who just the other day, according to you, meant absolutely nothing to you, yet you brought her to your grandmother's birthday party."

"I feel like I'm losing my mind here."

I turned around to see him pulling at the roots of his hair with both fists.

"You're losing your mind?" I kept my tone low. "You did this." I pointed my finger at him. "You!"

"I know! If I could only go back and fix it."

I snorted. "You're here with her. Let that sink in."

The microwave dinged and I pulled the chocolate out with my mitted hand and left him standing there.

By the time I'd completed my task and retaken my place in the corner, Aunt Vi came back. "I heard Alex and that girl arguing before they walked out the back door. She's not a keeper."

"Whatever Alex does has nothing to do with me anymore."

"Good for you!" She gave me a quick hug. "He's my nephew and I love him, but he needs to grow up. You're a prize." She speared a meatball from the hors d'oeuvres plate she held.

"Anyway, if you don't mind me asking . . ." I had to get this in before she got distracted again. "What can you tell me about the seaside sisters?"

She hooted. "Those were the days. It was all about free love and herbal remedies. Nothing was bad for you then. We even had our own little Woodstock-like commune here on the island. Did your mama ever tell you about that?"

I shook my head and my mouth dropped open. I instantly closed it.

"Of course not. When Clara got married, not only did she gain a husband but also a stick up her hind end."

"What're we talking about?" Betsy joined us.

"The seaside sisters." I scooted aside to allow Betsy to squeeze in between us. "Aunt Vi said they had their own Woodstock here on the island."

"Get out!" Betsy said a little too loudly.

"It's true! We even did the nudie stuff. People came

from all over to spend a long weekend to have new experiences."

Betsy and I gaped.

"Maybe that's why your mama is stuck. She was certainly no angel." Betsy snickered.

"Viola!" Meemaw called. "Come on over. We're about to sing 'Happy Birthday'!"

Aunt Vi handed Betsy her plate. "Go and fetch a lighter, Marygene. Not to worry. I know all about island spirits and the pains they can be."

I was dying to ask what information she possessed.

Aunt Vi could clearly see the eagerness on my face. "I'll be in town for a while." She leaned in and wagged her eyebrows. "Girls, do I have some stories to share with you."

CHAPTER 17

Doc Tatum came into the diner the next morning, early. Sam, who always came in to help unload on delivery day, had let her in. The open sign had yet to be flipped, and I had a large sheet of puff pastry rolled out to the perfect dimensions. With Jena Lynn out sick, I needed to get a jump on all the pastry that needed baking. I'd had to call down the list of subs to see who I could get to fill in out front. I'd also posted the position for a full-time waitress on our new Facebook page and one in the local paper. With business booming, combined with the prospect of expanding, we would need to hire a few more employees soon anyway. Jena Lynn had hired a temp girl before she became ill. She'd be reporting for work today, I hoped.

"What a nice surprise." I wiped my forehead with the back of my flour-covered hand. "I have warm cinnamon rolls cooling and a pot of coffee going. If you'd like, you can help yourself."

Doc Tatum gave me one of her caring smiles and held up her travel mug. "I brought coffee from home, but thanks." Something about the tone she used when speaking to me made me feel as if everything would somehow turn out all right. I imagined it as the way a doting mother would speak to a child. Mama certainly hadn't been that when we were growing up, which was most likely the reason my sister and I leaned toward the high-strung side.

"Okay, what can I do for you then? Not that I'm not always happy to see you." I cut the puff pastry into squares. I paused and wiped my hands on the hand towel over my shoulder.

"Please, continue. I can talk while you work." Doc Tatum sipped from her mug.

"Okay then." I began spooning the apple mixture in the center of the squares. The scent of spiced cinnamon apples, with hints of orange zest, delighted my senses.

"I've been told your participation in therapy has become less frequent lately, and I wanted to be sure you're managing all right. You've been through a lot. And sometimes when we experience additional trauma, even unrelated, it can be a trigger and stir up anxiety."

"I'm okay. I've been utilizing my coping techniques and trying to separate the false alarms from reality." I sealed the small pastry pouches and began putting them on the sheet pan. "Some days it isn't easy. I won't lie."

"Of course you wouldn't. You aren't a liar, Marygene." Doc Tatum made a point to make direct eye contact with me when she spoke. She'd explained that she needed me to see for myself that she believed what she told me. I was lucky to have her.

"Thanks for that. You have my word. If I need help, I'll ask. No more hiding or pretending everything is fine. I want to do the work and take control of my life." After a quick brush of egg wash, I slid the sheets into the preheated oven.

"That's good to hear."

"So, now that we've established I'm okay, tell me about you and Eddie."

She blushed ever so slightly. If I hadn't been watching her closely, I'd have missed it.

"Well, well." I pulled the biscuits from the second oven and brushed them with melted butter.

"He's the first man I've dated since my husband passed. This case has kept him so busy we haven't had that much time together lately."

"It's a rough one. He's got a lot on him at the moment." I took a minute to pour myself a cup of coffee. "Did you know the twins?"

She gave her head a shake. "I was still in Savannah at the time. Your father is taking this case extremely personally, and that worries me a little. Not the fact that he cares so much. I believe that's what makes him such a great sheriff." She fidgeted with her cup. "He's a good man."

I slid the biscuits into the warmer drawer. "Don't worry. This case will close soon enough and he'll be back to his old self. A cold case like this isn't run-of-the-mill. Combine that with reporters peppering questions about the case belonging to him when he was a rookie and that his daughter and son found the bodies. That's a lot. Not to worry. Eddie's tough, and I assure you he can handle it. And you're right, he is a good man, the best."

"Who's the best?" Sam carried a large box of shrimp into the walk-in, pausing momentarily for me to check the freshness. Not that Sam hadn't already checked, but it was always good to get a second opinion. Smelled fresh to me. "Dad?" Sam's face split into a grin.

I nodded. Both of us were grinning like loonies now.

"All right. I've got to get to the office and open up." Doc Tatum turned to leave. "On second thought, I will take one of those biscuits." I wrapped her one up in a parchment.

"Thank you. You kids be good." She took a bite and left the kitchen.

We waited until we heard the door chime before Sam and I exchanged a pleased expression. "I can totally see them together for the long haul."

"Me too. I like her or I would have used my *Are you going to be my new mama?* line."

"You're awful!" I laughed and threw my dish towel at him. It came back at me with way too much velocity.

"Ouch." It had been a tad damp.

He ran before I could retaliate.

At three, I finally managed to get a break and eat a meal. Betsy grinned from ear to ear. The pockets of her apron were filled to capacity with tips.

"How's Rebecca doing?" Rebecca had applied via our Facebook post. She'd waited tables for a few summer jobs and now that she was taking a break from college, she'd been looking for full-time work. We always hired on a temp-to-perm basis. Our employees not only needed to be hard workers but friendly to our customers and mesh well with our current staff. There wasn't anything worse than dreading coming to work every day because you couldn't stand the people you worked with.

"She's a slip of a girl but a hard worker. Good attitude and the customers seem to like her. She'll do fine."

We both watched the girl, her long, dark hair fashioned up into a messy bun, whisk away the menus from a back table. She had a bounce in her step, even after the breakfast and lunch rush. That was the difference between nineteen and practically thirty. Rebecca cast a wary glance toward Betsy as she scooped ice into glasses.

"What's that about?"

Betsy smirked. "She got a little scare is all. You had an applicant for the night-shift waitress come in, and I had to run her off."

My mouth fell open. I put down my fork. "What'd you do that for? We need help!"

"Trust me, you wouldn't have hired her anyway." Betsy went on counting her tips.

"How do you know? And now, what if Rebecca quits because she's scared of you? There is no way you can manage out here alone with the new influx of patrons. Seriously, Betsy, I have no idea where your head is." My appetite left and I put my napkin on my Cobb salad.

She huffed. "Look, don't get all snippy with me. I'm always on your side. And here I was trying to spare your feelings, but will you let me? No." Betsy's face was flushed.

"What are you talking about?"

She threw her hands in the air. "It was Lucy, okay? She thought she could get me to put in a good word for her. Crazy, right?"

I nodded numbly.

"But you need help, so, if you want me to run out and find her, I'm sure she'd love to come on back in with her newly injected lips. She'd probably be a main attraction and bring in even more patrons."

"You made your point." It took me a second to recompose myself. "She had the audacity to come into my establishment and apply for a job? Guess she isn't getting paid all that much at the department. Eddie said she was only temping for now."

The more I thought about it, the more my anger grew. "I thought Rainey Lane was bad, but this chick is in a league of her own." Rainey Lane Ledbetter had been a pain in my backside all during school. She'd moved away after graduation but still came back for visits up till her father-in-law passed.

Betsy plopped down on the stool, nodding smugly. "Yep, Rainey Lane ain't got nothing on Lucy." Betsy put her money away. "I told her I'd yank her hair out by the roots if she didn't get out of our diner."

I choked on a sip of coffee. "No, you didn't."

"Did so. And I'll tell you this right now. If she dares show up at any of my family functions, she's leaving bald."

I burst out laughing. Betsy was the best. "Go make nice with Rebecca. We're going to need her."

CHAPTER 18

The diner was locked up tight for the night and I took my weary self to my car. I spotted Teddy walking out of the market with a small bag and I lifted my hand.

He came trotting over. "You look awful!"

I ran my hand through my ponytail. "Gee, thanks. You sure know how to make a gal feel good. I had to work open till close. Jena Lynn is sick."

"Sorry. I didn't mean that the way it came out."

"It's fine. How ya doing?"

He shoved his free hand into his pocket. "This case is getting hairy."

"You mean with all the re-interviews?"

Relief washed over his face. Obviously, he needed to talk to someone but didn't want to divulge secret information. "Yeah. And I found out something that I have to tell Eddie about."

"What?"

"My dad and Kayla were, you know." He glanced around. "Lovers."

"So?" I shrugged.

"He was married to my mom at the time."

"Oh." I pursed my lips.

"I know."

"How'd you find out?"

He smacked his forehead with the heel of his hand. "Stupid me decided it was time to clean out the storage room. I found all sorts of love letters. Kayla wrote something about a pregnancy."

"Kayla was pregnant? Did you find evidence of that during the autopsy?"

"The internal organs were too damaged to tell. And I'm not sure if Kayla was pregnant. The letter had some water damage. I have to turn them over, right? I mean, I hate to. Dad would've never done anything like this. But with us owning the funeral home, it'll lead to suspicions."

"Because your dad had the facility to store the bodies." It looked bad for Mr. Gaskin.

"See! That's what I'm afraid of. His health hasn't been good, and I don't want to put him through duress."

He'd seemed pretty spry to me the other night when he'd threatened me. "It's a tough spot, for sure. Um, why are you telling me? You want to protect your dad. Why tell anyone?"

He appeared confused. "I honestly don't know why I told you. I saw you and just needed to tell you."

Creepy. Could this perhaps be Mama's intervention? Or the twins'?

"Probably because we're friends and you know that you can trust me." I smiled reassuringly.

He scratched his head. "Yeah, probably. I'm going to talk to the sheriff."

I patted his shoulder. "Get some rest. Things will seem clearer in the morning. Eddie isn't going to put your dad through the ringer unless he finds probable cause. They've known each other for a coon's age." I opened my car door.

"You're right. Drive safely."

The second I started my engine, my phone rang. I hit the button on the steering wheel.

Yvonne's frantic tone came across the speakers. "I'm at your house! Where are you?"

"I had to close. Jena Lynn's sick. What's wrong?" I pulled out of the space and noticed Teddy standing beside his car staring oddly toward me. I'd ponder that later.

"It's Mama. She told one of her care workers that she was responsible for the twins' deaths."

"What?"

"Yeah, and they called the sheriff's office. Ever since Eddie went on the news asking for people to come forward with information, Mama's been going on and on about the victims. She had details that the staff at Sunset Hills couldn't ignore."

"You told Eddie that she'd been watching the news when he got there and about her condition, right?" It seemed cut-and-dried to me. "Of course she has details. They were friends."

"Well, that would have been one way to go."

I turned onto Cloverdale. "You left Sunset Hills with your mama before anyone from the department could get there." That's why she was at my house. "There's a key in that rock in the front bed. I'll be there in five."

"Okay. You'll talk to your daddy for me?"

"I'm calling him as soon as I hang up here." Fatigue and I were becoming old friends.

Eddie's phone went to voice mail, so I called the answering service for after hours. They forwarded me to the available deputy, who happened to be Javy. "Hey. Thought y'all would appreciate a heads-up. Yvonne brought her mama to my house. If anyone had plans on chatting with her, they better go there."

"Good to know. I'm at Sunset Hills now."

"She's an older woman and isn't always in her right

mind." I drove under the canopy of Spanish moss–covered trees that lined my driveway. All I wanted to do was take a shower and go to bed. I'd been so busy, I'd hadn't even had time to reach out and check in on my sister. Selfishly, I prayed she would be well enough to work tomorrow.

"We still have to question her," Javy said.

"Sure. That's why I called."

"You wouldn't happen to have a pot of coffee going at your house, would you?"

"Don't you worry. I have a Keurig. I'm parking now."

"Thank God." He sounded as exhausted as I felt.

"Okay, bye."

Yvonne paced the floor of my kitchen, wringing her hands. A glance into the living room answered my unasked question as to where her mama was. She sat happily in the recliner with a cup of coffee, eating a pastry, watching *Andy Griffith Show* reruns on the television with Mr. Wrigley on her lap. Her hand stroked him from the top of his head to his tail. I slogged to the coffeemaker.

"I'm sorry. I didn't know what to do."

I waved her apology away and looked around for my bag. I really needed a Tylenol and I'd thrown them in my purse before I left this morning. Ugh. I left it in the car. I made a mental note to get it later. "We're friends. My door is always open to you. Javy is on his way over. This is absolutely nothing to worry about." I turned on the Keurig and slid my favorite K-Cup blend into the machine. "I can't believe Mr. Wrigley is sitting with your mama. Do you know since he's been with me, he's avoided me like the plague."

"That is odd. Izzy loves you."

"I know. I don't know what's up with that cat. Listen, I'm going to chug this cup and then take a quick shower." I glanced at my dirty clothes. "My hair probably smells and I feel grimy."

I squeezed Yvonne's hand as I took the now piping-hot brew from the machine. "I promise your mama is going to be fine. Just give me five minutes and I'll be back."

My usually together friend appeared disheveled. Her hair was flat and her face barren of makeup. Usually meticulous about her clothing, tonight she wore gray yoga pants and an oversized pink T-shirt.

I put the mug down and hugged her. "Trust me."

She nodded into my shoulder a second before I felt her shuddering.

"Oh, honey, it's going to be okay."

"She keeps saying she did it. That she's responsible for their deaths." More sobs.

"Let's not get ahead of ourselves here." I released her but kept my arms around her shoulders and walked her to the opening between the rooms. "Does that look like a woman who's guilty of murder?"

Ms. Brooks laughed at something Barney said.

"No, you're right. I'm sorry." She wiped her nose with a paper napkin she'd been twisting in her hands. "Take your shower. I'll be fine. I promise."

"You're sure?" I searched her watery blue eyes.

She managed a quick nod.

"Okay. I'll be fast."

Ms. Brooks waved at me as I entered the living room. I took a chance and reached out to pet Mr. Wrigley, thinking he'd finally come out of his shell. He rewarded my kindness with a hiss before leaping from her lap and darting up the stairs. Ms. Brooks cackled as I followed him, moving much slower. It shouldn't bother me that Mr. Wrigley wanted nothing to do with me; nevertheless, it did. Oh well.

When I emerged a few minutes later, I was clean, but exhaustion had settled into my bones. I'd stood under the spray for a few minutes longer than I'd intended, enjoying the quiet and having to do absolutely nothing. My friend needed me and I'd be darned if I wouldn't come through in her hour of need. I'd called to Mama a few times, hoping she'd return. When she didn't show, I debated telling Javy about Mr. Gaskin.

I slid my legs into my favorite pair of cotton pants and pulled on a pink tank top. I worked a comb through my tangled mess of hair as I made my way down the stairs.

Javy sat on my coffee table, speaking softly to Ms. Brooks, who had moved to the sofa. Yvonne sat next to her, holding her hand. My heart ached when I saw the helpless look on both their faces. Ms. Brooks had sorrow and regret written all over her face. Now she did look like a woman who had something to hide. That expression would give any deputy pause. Or at least contemplate the truth in her words. Ms. Brooks broke down in tears and Yvonne quickly followed.

Javy turned and our gazes locked when I reached the last step.

I said evenly, "Ms. Brooks seems to need a break, don't you think?"

He turned his attention back to my friends and, for a second, I feared he might ignore my suggestion. When he said, "I'm going to give you ladies a little break," the tension in my muscles eased.

Yvonne nodded and I gave her a sad smile and moved the box of Puffs toward her. "Y'all okay?"

"Yeah. We will be." They clearly needed some space.

Javy followed me into the kitchen, where my now lukewarm mug waited. I drank it anyway and put another pod in the machine. I grabbed another coffee cup from the cabinet for Javy. When I glanced up, he was staring at me with such intensity that my heart skipped a beat. Dark circles encompassed his eyes, and his uniform was a bit wrinkled. He visibly swallowed.

"Your cheeks are all flushed." His finger brushed my cheek.

I stepped away. "Well, I just got out of a hot shower. You want strong or regular brew?" I placed the mug on the Keurig.

"Sorry about that. Strong, please."

Silence stretched out between us.

"It's okay." I focused on the stream pouring from the machine.

When I handed him his mug, his fingers brushed against mine and, despite my wariness, my stomach did a flip-flop. *Get a grip, Marygene.* My life was complicated enough.

This clearly could be nothing but rebound attraction. Plus, my friends were in the other room, sobbing. I cleared my throat as my shoulders slumped. "You might want to wait on Eddie before going back in. Yvonne's mama isn't well and, although she slips some, she knows him and would probably open up more."

Before he could answer, the back door opened and in walked my father. "What a day."

"You said it." I held up a mug in offering.

He nodded eagerly in response. "How've you handled the situation?" he asked his deputy.

I made his coffee while Javy caught him up on what had transpired. He greedily took it from me and thanked me before he instructed the two of us to remain in the kitchen. He didn't want to further upset the old woman and thought he'd get more information from her without Javy. I grinned. I liked being right.

I wanted more information myself. Betsy and I needed to spend some time with Aunt Vi. She never held anything back and I was sure Eddie would be speaking to her, being a member of the seaside sisters and all.

"You've been good friends with the Brooks family for a long time?"

I swallowed a sip from my mug, trying not to focus on how close Javy stood next to me. Every second he seemed to be inching his way closer.

"Yes. All my life. They're a good, honorable, and respectable family. The poor woman is in a retirement community and has a difficult time getting around. There's no way she could heft either of those bodies to either location. But, she may be hiding some things. I've recently found out a lot of secrets were buried and folks never thought anyone would ever start digging them up."

"You plan to? Dig them up, I mean."

Aware he kept staring straight through me, I focused on everything in the kitchen except him. "I do. People talk to me. And like I told you, I feel obligated to help. Don't go all macho like Eddie and order me to stay out of it. I won't interfere with the investigation."

My favorite creamer still sat on the island. I scooped it up and poured a little into my mug, not offering him any, as he took his black. Then another pod went into the machine. I stood tapping my nails on the counter.

"Is there a reason you're avoiding making eye contact with me?"

"Yes."

He chuckled. "You going to tell me?"

I glanced up then. "You're too pretty. And that's dangerous in my current state."

His eyes crinkled around the edges, and he covered a bark of laughter with a cough. Not the time to be, as they said, ROFL with the sheriff's daughter.

"Shut up." I reached for his mug, which he held playfully and wouldn't relinquish.

The screen door closed loudly and there stood Alex Myers with a face like thunder. Javy released the mug.

I hitched my thumb toward the living room. "Eddie's in there with Ms. Brooks. I didn't know you were coming by."

"Obviously." His lip curled in disgust.

"Don't start with me. You want a cup of coffee?" I spoke smoothly and politely. When he didn't respond but shot daggers Javy's way, I made him a cup anyway. Javy, to my surprise, seemed unperturbed by Alex. I liked that.

"Eddie instructed us to stay in here." I put a mug of coffee on the island for Alex. Even went as far as adding his cream and raw sugar. "You want some pastry? I have your favorites." I slid the platter over to him.

"Thank you." His tone softened slightly and he seemed to simmer down some after that. Still, he made a point to move around my kitchen, showing his familiarity with everything. When he moved closer to me, I worried he'd try and prove something in front of Javier. I gave him my *Don't push me* face. He spoke softly. "Meemaw loved her cake. I wanted to thank you for making it for her. Especially after, well, everything."

I took a step backward. "I love Meemaw. Just because you and I aren't together anymore doesn't mean I stop loving your family. Betsy and Meemaw are my family in my heart. You know that."

The Keurig warmed up again. I cast a glance over my shoulder to see that Javy had helped himself. He looked oddly right at home.

Eddie came back in with Ms. Brooks. She had her hand in the crook of his arm and was all smiles. Eddie covered her hand with his. "I'm going to take Ms. Brooks back to Sunset Hills."

I glanced back at Yvonne trailing behind them, and she shrugged. She'd driven her mother here, which begged the question as to why Eddie would drive her home.

"Yvonne, you coming to say good night now, aren't you?" Ms. Brooks glanced back at her daughter.

"Yes, ma'am. I'll be right behind you."

"I'll need to have a word with the two of you after I see the lovely lady home," Eddie instructed his deputies.

"Here or—" Alex began.

"Heavens no, not here. I've got a business to run and I've been on my feet for sixteen hours now." I'd cut him off intentionally. They could have a powwow somewhere else.

"At the station." Eddie smiled at Ms. Brooks. He made me so proud.

"Thank you for the coffee." Javy rinsed his mug off in the sink and put it in the dishwasher, stunning me.

Alex had never put a single dish in the dishwasher.

"You're welcome." I stared at his back as he followed Eddie out the back door. He paused to keep it open. "Alex, you coming?"

Alex's brown eyes shut to slits. Again Javy simply smiled, as if being kind. I fought a grin.

"Night, Alex." I turned and left the kitchen, grabbing Yvonne by the arm.

When the back door closed, I sat on the sofa. "I know you have to go, but what in the world happened? I couldn't hear much from the kitchen."

Her face had relaxed after their conversation with Eddie. "I simply don't know. Mama was all over the place, talking about a commune on the island, where she and your mama plus their friends used to practice nude living on the weekends. She said things got crazy for a while and they were eating wild mushrooms and talking to spirits. How if she'd encouraged the twins to never return to the island, they'd still be alive. But she'd been weak and not said a word and the wolf in sheep's clothing swallowed them up. Crazy stuff."

"Did Eddie ask who the wolf was?"

She nodded. "She laughed and told Eddie he knew exactly who the wolf was and if he wasn't careful, the wolf would huff and puff and blow his house down. If that wasn't bad enough, she changed the subject to Junior. How he looked a lot like his daddy and that Evelyn must be pleased. Then how much you favored your daddy and what a sweet girl you were. She said, sounding incredibly disappointed, that I came out not favoring her in the slightest."

"Wow." I stood.

"It's been a long night."

We embraced.

"Thanks for your help." She released me. "Get some sleep. You look terrible."

"Yeah, that's what I hear." I watched her leave, locked up, and heaved my weary bones up the stairs. So many stairs.

My thoughts were consumed with so many things, I feared I'd never fall asleep. Where did Mr. Wrigley hide all day long and could I fit? Then my thoughts drifted to who Ms. Brooks's wolf really was. She knew something, even if she didn't realize it. I wondered if Eddie would question her further. The idea that my conservative, never-a-hair-out-of-place mama had been a hippie caused a bubble of laughter to escaped my lips. A few minutes later I couldn't catch my breath, guffawing, and I felt immensely better. Laughter truly was one of the best medicines.

"Mama, you nudist, if you can hear me, I don't ever want to hear another word about my skinny-dipping." I drifted off to sleep with a smirk.

CHAPTER 19

Pressure on my chest startled me out of a deep slumber. When I cracked my lids, I saw Mama's face for a split second followed by a giant furry flat face. There on my chest sat the giant cat. I shrieked and sat straight up and the cat shuffled to the left side of the bed, meowing loudly.

"Now you decide to socialize?" I gaped at the cat, who aggressively paced the left side of my bed. "What is it?"

That was when the smoke detector went off! Mr. Wrigley leaped into my arms and I flung the covers from the bed. My feet hit the floor with a thud. Smoke filled my nostrils. With the cat tucked under my right arm, I sprang for the door, testing it with the back of my hand. It was warm, and I knew that meant I shouldn't open it. I had no choice in the matter, being on the second floor. The drop to the ground from the window could be damaging.

Gasping for air, I glanced at Mr. Wrigley's highly flammable fur. I made a split second decision. Racing to the bathroom, I flipped on the shower and threw the towel from the hamper into the spray. He wouldn't like being covered with the cold wet towel, but it would save him from harm.

"You're simply going to have to deal." I covered as

much of us as I could manage. My roommate hardly protested. He must've understood this was for his own good.

The next thing I knew the bedroom door burst open. "Come this way!" Junior shouted as he rushed in and scooped me up with his right arm. Junior hoisted me so high off the ground that my feet barely touched the steps as we charged to the first floor.

Flames were visible from the staircase coming in from the kitchen and lapped the edge of the rug in my living room. A howl of protest, along with claws to my forearm, came from Mr. Wrigley. I kept him close anyway. Both our hearts raced beyond the healthy range.

"Cover your face!" I shouted over the roar of the flames. Junior lifted his shirt over his nose. Billows of smoke threatened to suffocate us. He and I choked and sputtered. My eyes stung so badly I could hardly see.

Junior managed to get the front door open and dragged us out into the torrential downpour. Rain pelted down in hard, fat drops as we sloshed as far from the house as we could manage. The three of us collapsed on the lawn. Sirens were getting closer, and the flashing lights came down the long driveway.

"I kept you safe!" Drops of rain ran down Junior's face. "That bad man lit a fire in your old burn barrel out back. I hit him on the head with my fists." He showed me how, lifting both fists and bringing them down hard. The man had to have been shorter than Junior, based on the motion he mimicked. "He fell but scrambled away before I could catch him. His jacket was too slick. I tried to put out the fire, but the barrel was too hot. I flung it away and it went through the kitchen window. Then I dialed nine-one-one." Junior was out of breath when he finished his account.

I glanced at his burned forearms. "Oh, Junior, you're hurt!" I wrapped the wet towel that had covered us over his arms. He thanked me softly.

Mr. Wrigley sought a dry spot. I tucked him against my skin. It was the best I could do.

My brain fought to decipher what had transpired.

The next thing I knew, the firemen were already unhooking their hoses and moving toward the scene. Mr. Wrigley, Junior, and I were hustled onto the back of the paramedics van. Thankfully, the downpour had turned into a light shower, but the ground had been saturated and my bare feet sunk with each step, dirt creeping between my toes.

Shudders crept up my spine as we were wrapped in thermal blankets and I held my new furry friend close. Despite the warm temps, the chill had settled in my bones. Shock. I recognized the symptoms well now.

While the two of us were being checked out, I sunk my hands deep into Mr. Wrigley's fur and watched as my family home went up in flames. My beautiful kitchen. The years of memories, both good and bad, incinerated before me. Unshed tears burned my eyes but nothing fell.

The paramedics bandaged up Junior's arms and he grimaced. The adrenaline must be wearing off and he was feeling the pain now. I vaguely recalled one of them telling me I did the right thing by wrapping his arms in the wet towel.

When Mr. Wrigley began to purr, I settled down some. Everything happened lightning fast. If it hadn't been for Junior, I might not have made it out alive. And if Junior hadn't flung the burn barrel through the kitchen window, there wouldn't have been a fire.

Slowly, I regained my faculties and questions mounted.

I turned to Junior. "What on earth were you doing here this time of night?"

The rain had lightened up to nothing but a drizzle now.

He leaned closer. "Must keep Marygene safe. I saved you."

I spoke calmly. "Thank you. I appreciate you keeping me safe, but why are you here?"

"It's a secret. I'm not supposed to tell." He glanced around warily.

"I'm good at keeping secrets. And since I'm the one you're supposed to keep safe, I'm sure it'll be okay if you tell me."

He rocked back and forth, cradling his injured arms.

"Please, Junior. I need you to talk to me."

Then barely above a whisper, he uttered the words, "The ghost. She told me to keep Marygene safe and she would make the scary dreams go away."

Mama! How dare she manipulate this sweet man.

"Are you mad?" He actually looked like he might cry.

My heart literally ached. He didn't deserve this. "Not with you. I am with the ghost. She shouldn't have done that. Listen. People are going to think you started the fire."

His eyes went wide and he vehemently shook his head. "I didn't!" He sounded agitated. "I saw the bad man leaving your house with a box when I got here."

"I believe you. But some people might not. You ask for your mama and daddy. Tell Eddie about the ghost and I promise you the ghost won't get upset with you."

"No way Jose! The ghost said don't tell nobody." He rocked more.

"Okay, how about I tell Eddie about the ghost and then you can give a little nod. Then you won't actually be telling him anything. How about that?" On one hand I was furious with Mama, and on the other, if she hadn't intervened, I might not be here to be angry.

After a brief moment, he nodded. "Yeah, that'd be okay."

"You just say you told Marygene and she'll tell them." He nodded again.

I gave the man a hug. He had saved me. At first, he bristled but a microsecond later, he hugged me back with all his might, being careful of his forearms. I grunted under his viselike grip around my ribcage.

"Oh, sorry, sorry." He released me from his modified bear hug. "I'll tell them about the bad man. She didn't say nothing about that. And I got a piece of his jacket too." He pulled a torn raincoat hood from his pocket the second Eddie came over.

Fear and concern etched my father's brow. "Are you all right?"

Numbly, I nodded. "My house." My voice came out distant sounding.

"I know, sweetheart." Eddie wrapped an arm around me. "It's just wood and nails. All replaceable. You, however, are not."

"Junior got me out." I stifled a sob. "He said he almost had the man who did this."

Proudly Junior held up the hood.

"That's real good, Junior." Eddie moved in front of Junior and put the hood in a bag. "And I'm real grateful for you for keeping my daughter safe." He softened his tone. "Can you tell me why you were here?"

Junior shut his lips tight and pointed to me.

"He said a ghost promised to keep his bad dreams away if he kept me safe."

Eddie kept a cool expression and understanding registered.

"I'm sort of cold." Junior shivered. "And I want to call my mom and dad."

Eddie called the EMT over. They were taking Junior to the hospital. The EMT said standard procedure would be to keep him overnight for observation. I'd received oxygen as he had and my lungs were clear. I refused to be taken in.

"I'll call your parents and make sure they meet us at the hospital." Eddie placed a hand on Junior's shoulder.

When the ambulance left, I stood watching my house burn. Suddenly, a loud crack caused me to jump. Right before my eyes, the top floor crumbled. Even at this great distance from the house, you could feel the radiating intensity of the blazing inferno. The firemen kept dousing the flames, but it was no use. My house, the only thing I could call all my own, crumbled into ashes bit by bit. I feared someone wanted me consumed within the flames. Exactly like the twins. Burned to nothing but bits of bone and tissue. The tears began to flow.

CHAPTER 20

Eddie turned and glanced inside his truck, where I now sat. He let out a string of curse words. "Stay put. I've got this." He stomped away. Reporters and the media were back on the scene. From my vantage point, in the dark I couldn't make out most of the faces but one, Roy Calhoun. He moved to the front of the line. He and Eddie exchanged a few words.

I hugged Mr. Wrigley closer. He shook in my arms. There was too much commotion going on. I didn't know much about animals except for the fact that they were good at sensing emotion from their owners. I focused on my breathing techniques. Hoping that if I calmed, he would as well. Because if he bolted from my arms, I might never find him.

I slid from the truck, feeling antsy. My house still smoked, but the fire had been mostly doused. Clueless as to what I needed to do next, I stood. My limbs were heavy as I watched the flurry of movement from the firemen, law enforcement officers, and local news crews. When Betsy put an umbrella over my head and stood inches from my face, wearing a hot pink satin robe and slippers, I sort of came to. She had those old-fashioned sponge curlers in her hair and her mouth moved in such a hurried fashion, it sounded as if she spoke in a foreign language. I caught, "Ohmygodmarygene." And, "Whatonearthhappened."

"I'm homeless." I burst into tears.

"Oh, honey." Betsy wrapped her arms around me. "It's going to be okay."

I blubbered about everything. I told her about Mama coercing Junior and how he'd saved me. How Mr. Wrigley had woken me. How upset I was at her for doing that to such a fragile man.

"Wow. Well, I know it's awful and all to use someone like that. But, Marygene, if you'd died in that house, I'd have died along with you." Betsy's eyes welled up with tears.

We were the best of friends. Shared just about everything. Emotional like this, we weren't. We usually dealt with tragedy with humor. It worked for us. Now we were both blubbering uncontrollably. And Eddie was right. It was only a house. I counted my lucky stars and felt beyond grateful for Junior. Mr. Wrigley and I were alive and that was something.

I wiped my face with the blanket. "Like the hair." I tapped her curlers.

She used the bottom of my blanket to wipe her nose. I handed it over to her. She laughed. "I stayed with Aunt Vi tonight. She insisted on putting my hair in these ridiculous things." She began taking them out and tossing them in her giant shoulder bag.

When Javy came tromping through the side yard, crushing my azalea bushes, he held a case in his hands. Recognition hit. It'd been Nanny's. She kept all our family albums in it. She always said if there was a fire, grab the kids and get them to safety and then get the case. I passed Mr. Wrigley off to Betsy and sloshed through the yard.

"Where'd you find that?"

Javy's round hazel orbs were wide. He set the case on the ground and took off his jacket and put it across my shoulders. That was when I realized I was standing in the middle of my front yard in nothing but a soaked nightie and there were people snapping pictures everywhere.

"Thank you," I whispered softly.

"Welcome." He picked the case back up. "I found this out in the woods while canvassing the area. Junior appears to be telling the truth. There were two sets of footprints leading off your property." I reached for the case. He pulled it back, his latex-covered hands reminding me this would have to be dusted for prints. "Sorry."

"Prints. I know. Please be very careful with it. It's all I have left." I wrapped my arms around myself. Why would whoever did this take Nanny's case? And how would they know about the case, and where to find it?

Mist covered his lovely, olive-toned face. Those expressive eyes locked onto mine. For a few short seconds we just stood there in the rain. "I want to scoop you up in my arms and make it all better." His accent thickened with emotion.

Stunned into silence, I watched his well-groomed-goateed jaw go slack. I believed he'd surprised us both with his outburst. And in that moment, I wanted to be scooped up, for someone to make this all better. I'm also ashamed to admit that if we'd been the only two people there, I would have let him comfort me.

Eddie cleared his throat as he joined us. "Thanks for loaning her your jacket. She's in shock."

"It's Nanny's case," I choked out.

"I recognize it." He wrapped his arm around me, and I leaned into him. "You don't need to be standing out here in the middle of the yard." The three of us walked back to the truck.

"Of all the things to take from the house, why that? It's all our family albums." I leaned up and searched Eddie's face.

He scratched the stubble on his chin. "Maybe Junior took it." He shrugged. "If it wasn't him, I bet we come up with nothing. We'll dust it anyway." He tossed a glance over his shoulder to Javy. "Go lock it up in your cruiser."

"Listen, pumpkin. I know you're feeling vulnerable right now, and I don't want to butt in and tell you how to run your life." He paused. The expression on his face was indicative of the discomfort he felt speaking to me this way. "Promise me you'll use caution regarding who you let close to you."

He cared and I appreciated it. "I promise." With the events of the day, it felt good to have Eddie looking out for me. My life was a mess. Again.

Alex strode over and propped his arms on the truck. "I gave a statement to the reporters, but I think they're going to camp out anywhere you are."

I closed my eyes. "Fine. I'll give one statement to Calhoun and be done with it."

"I'm sorry, Marygene. I know how much this house means to you with all the renovations you made." Alex gave me a lopsided smile. "Good memories." His eyes roamed over me and he seemed to notice I wore Javier's jacket and little else.

I turned to Eddie. "I'd rather get this statement over with, if you can get Calhoun away from the fray. I don't want any pictures. I look a fright. Besides, they've gotten a lot of footage and shots of the house, or what's left of it, I'm sure."

Eddie sent Alex to fetch Calhoun.

My thoughts shifted. "I can't open the diner today and I think Jena Lynn is still sick." I know it sounded petty to be concerned about the diner, but it was the livelihood of my family and our employees. "I'll have to call Sam and see if he can manage for a few hours until I can get there. We'll have to run on a limited menu." My shoulders felt heavy and my chest constricted.

Jena Lynn and I were really going to have to discuss hiring more kitchen help. Now more than ever I wished we had gotten Hannah in and trained. Although, she could possibly be ill as well. Those viruses could run through an entire house.

"I don't even have any clothes."

"Pumpkin, one thing at a time. Alex spoke to Betsy. She's on the phone now. He knew you'd be worried about the diner." Well, that was kind of him. "The good news is you're okay. Clothes we can buy. I'll speak to Zach's dad in the morning and have him get over here to quote out how much to rebuild. I'll call Wally over at Sterling Insurance and find out about filing an insurance claim."

I let out a ragged sigh. "No, I can do it. You have enough on your plate right now."

Eddie walked us away from prying eyes. "I'm your father. I can manage my job and my children. I want to help you. Let me."

I swallowed the lump in my throat. "Okay. Thanks." I leaned my head on his chest.

He squeezed me tight.

As we stared at my family home, now a pile of burnt wood and ash, I recalled my conversation with Teddy. "Hey, you need to speak with Teddy. He stopped me on my way home tonight, telling me something about letters he found between one of the dead girls and his dad."

"Okay. You think he had something to do with this?" He motioned to the house.

"Oh no, not Teddy." My mind went back to Mr. Gaskin. He had threatened me. Perhaps he thought I would convince Teddy to take his findings to Eddie. That would mean he had to have knowledge as to what his son had found. "And someone spray painted an ugly warning to me on my front door the other day."

He took me by the shoulders. "Why am I just hearing about this now?"

"It said something like, mind your own business, hussy. I thought it was Lucy or kids." I chewed on my bottom lip. "Now I'm not so sure. And . . ."

"Tell me."

"Mr. Gaskin sort of warned me to stay away from Teddy at the Taste of Peach Cove. He said his boy didn't need a troubled young woman like me interfering in his life and that I should keep myself in the kitchen or I might get hurt."

A muscle worked overtime in Eddie's jaw.

"I didn't want to upset Teddy, so I left it alone. Now I have no idea what to think."

His fingers gripped my shoulders and his voice came out raspy. "You can't keep shit like this from me."

Shocked by his tone, tears began to flow again.

"I'm sorry." He crushed me to his chest. "I could have lost you tonight and that isn't something I'd come back from. I'll speak to Teddy. Don't worry. I've got this."

I sniffed and tried to get ahold of myself. "I should've told you. I'm sorry." I shivered, the shock of everything overwhelming me.

"You're cold." Eddie pulled Javy's jacket tighter around me and zipped it up. "I need to put the pieces together. The spray paint aside, this may not have even been about you."

"What do you mean?" He had my full undivided attention.

"It might've been a message for me."

"What?"

He shook his head. "I have to work it all out first." His eyes told me he was definitely hiding something.

Fear gripped me.

"I know you like your space, honey, but staying with me is an option. The other is your brother's apartment, but I can assure you, Sam's bachelor pad only has the one bedroom and well, you know what kind of shape it's in."

Sam's apartment looked like a hurricane hit it. I couldn't go to Jena Lynn's either, her in-laws were there. I loved Eddie. I just needed my own space, a place where I could cry, scream, or do whatever necessary to get my berries back in the basket. My cousins ran an inn. It crossed my mind to get a room there. But then there would be the problem of Mr. Wrigley. I doubted they allowed pets and I couldn't ask them to make an exception for me. That would open them up to a host of problems with guests with pet allergies.

Betsy sidled up and must have caught the end of our conversation. "You could stay with me except for the conflict with Mr. Wrigley and Killer." Betsy chewed on her bottom lip. "Hey! Why don't you stay with Aunt Vi? She's rented Pelican Cottage on the far end of Laguna Beach. She didn't want to be where the tourists were on West and Santa Rosa beaches. I'll call her for you if you'd like. She'd love to have you!"

My spirits lifted marginally. Not only would I have access to the one with the knowledge of island history but I'd also be living with a free spirit who wouldn't bat an eye at any of my crazy therapeutic antics. Still, I might be putting someone I cared about in danger.

"Does the cottage have a security system?" Eddie asked Betsy.

Betsy shrugged. "I'll ask when I call."

"I don't know, Bets. Some crazy tried to burn down my house. I don't want to bring my drama to her doorstep." I wrapped my arms around myself.

"Nonsense. She loves drama. I'm going to call her now. She won't mind the late hour."

"Will you ask Sam to come get Rustbucket?" I glanced over to where my Paw Paw's old 1960 brown truck sat. We had a love-hate relationship, the truck and me. He'd gotten me around when I needed him most. Sam loved him. "Tell him he's all his." I couldn't bear to leave Paw Paw's truck next to his burned-down home.

Betsy gave me a thumbs-up before she and Mr. Wrigley scooted off to make the calls.

Alex trotted over. "The reporter is waiting over by his car. The rest cleared out when they heard he got the exclusive. I don't think that's the end of it, though." He moved closer to me. "But perhaps it will keep them at bay for a bit." He rocked back on his heels. His soaked, tangled mess of hair hung down around his ears.

"Okay, well, on second thought, ask Calhoun if he'll meet me at Aunt Vi's if I get the okay. First I want a shower and to change into anything she has that will fit."

"Not a problem. He's lucky he's getting an interview at all." Alex and Calhoun didn't have the greatest of relationships.

"You can stay with Aunt Vi if she agrees." Eddie's face took on a stern appearance. "I'd feel better if you had some sort of security, though."

Mama's old revolver went down with the house and honestly, I didn't do so well with guns anyway. I hadn't had near enough practice, and only kept one near if I deemed it absolutely necessary.

"I can't say I'd be thrilled about staying at Aunt Vi's, but I could sleep on the sofa for a few days. That could be the easiest solution," Alex said.

Great idea. Then he could bring Lucy over and the four of us could play cards.

My chest tightened. "No. I'll be fine."

Alex and I weren't in the best of places. And with my anxiety already through the roof, I couldn't add him into the mix.

Eddie seemed to intuit my meaning. "I need you with me at the hospital. We'll have both Evelyn and Bill there at the same time. It'll be good to separate them and question them individually and informally." Eddie raked his fingers through his hair. "And before I have to call either of them in on an official capacity."

"I can go over afterward," Alex said.

"I believe the Pelican is the cottage next door to me." Javy's accented voice drifted over from behind me, and Alex grimaced. "I've rented Sand Dollar. Is Betsy's aunt a flamboyant redhead in her fifties?"

Eddie confirmed it with a head nod.

A ragged sigh left my lips. In my current predicament, I'd prefer having Javy next door to Alex staying over. "That'd work then. If Aunt Vi agrees to allow me to say."

"Marygene." Alex moved closer to me. "Let me do this for you."

I scrounged up the courage to make eye contact. He must have seen the raw sentiment on my face. We knew each other too well. I could no longer feed my delusion that we were meant to be, and that aside, I couldn't deal with the emotions he brought out in me. Not yet.

I gave my head a shake. His jaw clenched. Bitterness filled his gaze. Disappointment overtook me. Even now, at my lowest, he took my denying his protection as more of an insult than the emotional weight it'd be adding to my already heavy load. And Javy's offer as an encroachment on *his* territory. He stalked away.

That was when I closed the lid on Alex and me. I had to. So, all those feelings went into a little box and I sealed it up until the time came to unlatch and deal with it. In therapy,

I'd learned many things. One, that the issues I had that resulted from the abuse I'd incurred in my horrendous marriage would never truly go away. But I could box them all up and put them away in the closet—via my coping mechanisms—and one day when they returned, and they most assuredly would return when something triggered a response, I would repeat the procedure of boxing and putting them away all over again. Then I could manage another day, then another and then another. One day at a time. And each step I moved farther from the episode or flashback, the stronger I'd become. I was learning to accept the things I couldn't change.

Betsy gave us a big thumbs-up from her car. I guess I was moving in with Aunt Vi.

"So, it's settled." Eddie agreed. He turned toward his deputy, his eyes hard, his face stern. "If anything remotely out of the ordinary happens, I expect a call. And needless to say, if anything happens to her, I'll have your ass."

Wow. I hadn't expected that.

"Understood, sir."

CHAPTER 21

"Thanks for the nightie." The long gown that Aunt Vi had loaned me hit me at my ankles. It surprised me that her choice in nighttime wear was as conservative as something Mama would have worn. She had such a boisterous personality and her usual attire was so utterly different than what I now wore. It had two large pockets in the front and snaps down the center, securing the pillowcase-shaped gown. I supposed I'd have to do some shopping tomorrow, or I guess actually today, since the clock had struck two a.m. I plunged my fingers through Mr. Wrigley's fur. He hadn't left my side since arriving. Betsy had provided some food and a spare litter box, for which I expressed my great gratitude. It was all those little things that could make one feel so utterly overwhelmed.

"Not a problem, sweetie." Aunt Vi handed me a cup of hot chocolate and took a seat next to me on the cozy white wicker love seat. The sound of the waves served as a comfort. I focused on the linen curtains on the open French doors, moving languidly against the Spanish tile flooring.

A phone rang, causing me to nearly leap out of my skin. I laughed, putting a hand over my heart.

"It's okay. It's only my cell phone." She handed me a cookie and went to answer it.

I could hear her speaking from the other room while I nibbled on the chocolate chip cookie.

"She seems okay. Just really shaken up, understandably so. Uh-huh, of course." Silence.

I put the cup on the glass-topped coffee table in front of me. My hands visibly shook. The weight of my ordeal threatened to suffocate me. The tendrils of panic swirled within my midsection, taking hold. Sure, everything could be replaced and I had kept up on the insurance payments, but it truly wasn't about the stuff. Losing your home, the place you sought for comfort and security, rendered you to this childlike state of instability. Or at least that was how it affected me.

Breathe. In for seven seconds. Hold. Out for ten. I'd done this three times before I heard Aunt Vi speak again.

"I'll tell her. She'll be safe. That strapping young deputy is right next door. He'll be over when the reporter arrives. Yes. We're on the quiet end of the beach. Mostly fixer-uppers. Right, that's the place. You couldn't pay me to rent one of those the tourists frequent. Way too many people for my taste." Silence again. "Bye."

Perched on the edge of the seat, I waited for her to tell me who had called and what was said.

She sat back down and sipped her hot cocoa. "You get the next couple days off from the diner. Jena Lynn had planned on returning to work tomorrow anyway, and she insists that you get some rest. She said to tell you she loves you and that everything will be all right." She wrapped a chubby arm across my shoulders and hugged me tight. Then she proceeded to give me the wettest kiss on the cheek I'd ever had. When she released me, I fought not to wipe the moisture away but failed.

"I should go in and help her."

"Whatcha gonna wear? You need clothes and shoes. I mean, hon, you're not even wearing a bra, and none of mine will fit you." She laughed. "My bloomers would swallow your bony little ass whole. Besides, I don't have clean ones left. I need to do wash. If you insist, I'll dig you out the cleanest pair."

The thought of wearing her dirty bloomers had me nearly gagging. When she started laughing so hard she snorted, I figured out her game. The old softy had effectively pulled me from the depths of despair via her nasty underwear. God, no wonder I loved her. She reminded me of an older version of Betsy.

This time I didn't jump nearly as far when a rap came from the front door. I pulled the thin throw off the back of the love seat and covered myself. Mr. Wrigley bolted for the bedroom we'd be sharing. I supposed he'd had enough excitement for one day. We both had.

Javy came in, escorting Calhoun. I started to get up and greet them when Calhoun raised his hand. "No, Marygene, please stay where you are."

I reached for the cup on the table and took a sip. Javy stood while Calhoun perched on the wicker chair adjacent to me. I focused on the pink hibiscus that bloomed across the cushions. A small circular coffee stain stood out. I rubbed at it with my thumb.

"Thanks for coming all the way out here," I forced myself to say.

"If you want to reschedule, we can absolutely do that."

I lifted my gaze to meet Calhoun's observant green gaze. At least he appeared concerned.

With a shake of my head, I let out a sigh. "No, let's get this over with."

He placed his phone on the table in front of me.

Later, when I crawled between the sheets, I hardly recalled any of the questions he'd asked or my responses. Mr.

Wrigley curled up next to me and the two of us drifted off into a restless slumber.

When the sun came peeking through the slits in the blinds later that day, it took me a few moments to orient myself. First, the light shining brighter than I normally experienced had thrown me. As I glanced at the pink and green tropical comforter, everything came violently crashing back. I wondered if the house still smoldered. If anything I owned survived. Who could have done this to me? And why?

"I'm so glad you're okay," came Mama's voice a second before she sat on the bed.

Bolting upright, I glared at her. So lost in my own head, I'd not felt her as I usually had. "You manipulated Junior?"

She toyed with her hands in her lap. A flush to her face that I attributed to shame came next. "It was the only way I knew I could keep you safe. He's a sweet boy and didn't deserve any of this." She lifted her palms in time with her head, tears spilling over her cheeks. "I saw the blip in the future, the fire that would consume you along with the house. So, I broke the rules. Again."

I took her hands in mine. "You got into trouble? For me? What did they do to you?"

She shook her head. "Nothing for you to worry about. It'll take me longer to be able to cross is all. And I regret that more for you than for myself."

The door slowly creaked open and in walked Aunt Vi, with two mugs of coffee. "Thought I heard you up. You talking to your mama?" She placed the mug on the bedside table and then leaned against the doorframe.

"Hey, Clara!" Aunt Vi waved toward the bed.

I glanced from Mama to Aunt Vi.

"She can't see or hear me." Mama smiled. "She can feel

a disturbance. Vi is sensitive to the other side, like Mee-maw."

"Oh, Marygene, your sister dropped by earlier and left a sundress and flip-flops for you." How thoughtful of her. I would need something to wear while I did some shopping. I dropped Mama's hands and retrieved my mug from the bedside table and took a long, deep sip.

"It's a good thing Jena Lynn has better taste in clothing than Vi. Tell her I said hello and she really needs to do something about her ridiculous fashion sense."

Aunt Vi wore skintight parrot yoga pants and a hot pink tank top. Her ears were adorned with parrot earrings. Strangely, I thought it worked for her.

"Mama says hi and it's good to see you." More sips from the mug.

"She said no such thing. She made a smart remark about my pants, didn't she?"

I laughed, nearly spitting coffee. "Are you sure she can't hear you?"

"I can't. But I know Clara. She never got my style." She snorted. "And, Clara, no need to thank me. I'm going to straighten this mess out. Your girl here needs to know the truth if she's ever going to solve the murder. Don't you worry. I'm not going to hold anything back." Aunt Vi gave Mama's general direction a saucy wink.

Mama moved to her feet.

"Oh my. I'm going to get all the gossip on your nudist days." I grinned at Mama.

"She's upset, isn't she?" Aunt Vi snickered.

Unbeknownst to Aunt Vi, Mama now stood inches from her. I informed her.

"Right here in front of me?" Aunt Vi giggled and put her mug next to mine.

I nodded, snickering.

Mama was ranting warnings at Aunt Vi to watch herself. Aunt Vi went into some sort of modified karate stance and began slicing through Mama with her hands.

"Hi-ya!" Another slice down Mama's face. "Judo chop!" Mama didn't seem amused.

I nearly snorted coffee out of my nose when Aunt Vi lifted her hands high and tried to balance on one leg. "Get ready for the crane kick, Clara! I'm gonna take you out, karate kid style." Her leg went wild, and she landed on the bed next to me. "Dammit, Clara! I think you hurt my hip."

I patted her back as she floundered, and stifled my giggles. Her wailing wasn't a true sound of pain, so my concern was minimal.

Mama gave her eyes a dramatic roll. "She's fine. Ever the flair for dramatics. I hate to admit it, Vi is right. There are things you need to know that I'm unable to tell you. Although, some of it I'd hoped you would never learn." She glanced upward, then back to me. "Be careful, my sweet girl. The more you peel an onion, the more tears it'll bring." She faded from sight.

Having Aunt Vi believe in Mama's spirit should've, by all intents and purposes, solidified my question in regards to my sanity, i.e., seeing my dead mother, but as hilarious as Aunt Vi's display had been, that she engaged in it at all gave me pause. No, I reconsidered. Aunt Vi, the ever eccentric, certainly showed no signs of lunacy.

"Oh look! My favorite." Aunt Vi, now fully recovered from her quote-unquote hip injury, peered over the edge of the bed, crawled to the floor, and picked up what I hoped was an M&M before popping it into her mouth. My hopes regarding validation were dashed.

CHAPTER 22

After snipping the tags from the bra and panties Jena Lynn had obviously bought for Zach's benefit, I slid the skimpy items on. Tight, but it'd have to do. Jena Lynn took more after Mama, with a petite frame. Thankfully, the aqua dress, a nice forgiving A-line cut, hung nicely. I went into the dinette, where Aunt Vi sat, undoubtedly enjoying her turnover, her moans the evidence.

"Your dad dropped off your car this morning. Your purse is on the love seat." She took another large bite, her jaws stretching wide. "Want one?" From what I could tell from the contents in her mouth, she'd offered an apple turnover. Guess that M&M didn't fill her up.

I gave my head a shake and pulled at the top of the dress. "I'm afraid that if I do, I'll split the bra I'm spilling out of."

"I've got an appointment with Poppy this afternoon. I'm in need of a new do. If you want, I can reschedule and go shopping with you. I can help you find your new style."

Uh-oh. Aunt Vi looked as though she'd love to make me over.

"No need." I went to the coffeepot and refilled my empty

mug. "Thank God, I was so exhausted that I left my purse in my car last night."

She lifted a nonchalant shoulder. "Okay then. There's a spare key on the counter there." She pointed to the key next to the toaster oven.

It didn't escape me that she'd sacrificed her space for me. She'd lived most of her life as a loner, never marrying or even engaging in a relationship longer than a year. She enjoyed her solitude.

"Thanks for letting me crash here."

"Think nothing of it, sugah. I'm looking forward to having a roommate for a bit." She glanced off into the distance, her eyes darkening. "Plus, I owe Kayla. I'll do whatever I can to help bring the girls peace." She gave me a sad smile.

I had to fight the urge to question her. No, she would tell me when she felt ready.

"Knowing this island and its lore as I do, you're the best chance they have." Her bright emerald gaze regained its usual playful mischievous glint, and she lifted a fist. "I'm team Marygene!"

Surprisingly, my day had been okay. No one stalked or attacked me. Everyone I came in contact with had been pleasant and accommodating. No judgment whatsoever. So, for me, that meant success. I sat in the food court eating a large gyro and fries with all my purchases surrounding me. My credit card was now nearly maxed out on essentials alone. Well, okay, essentials and a few splurges. A gal had to lift her spirits when necessary. And, boy, was it necessary. Once I got the insurance check, I planned to pay the balance off anyway.

I'd decided to go off island and take the Cove ferry into Savannah to visit the mall. Running into inquisitive neighbors was the deterrent to spending money locally. Explaining what had happened and how I was doing were topics I'd rather not get into. My cell rang and, after a slurp from my straw, I answered it.

"Hey, Jena Lynn. I saw you called a couple of times. I'm at the mall, shopping, and you know how loud it can be in here. How are things at the diner? You feeling better?" I dipped a fry in ketchup before shoving it into my mouth.

"I'm recovered and I've got Hannah here with me today. You'll be so pleased with how fast she's picking things up." That sounded promising. Hannah, already being an accomplished baker, should only need to adjust her quantities to fully grasp the position, that and the exorbitant amount of preparation it took to bake off massive quantities of baked goods. "More importantly, how are you? You aren't alone, are you?"

"In shock and yes, I'm alone but fine. I can't believe our family home is gone." I sighed and pushed my meal away.

"Eddie came in. He said he had everything in motion on the insurance payout. There'll have to be an investigation first, though." Legalities, I got that. "You could have come and stayed with me, you know."

"I'm good at Aunt Vi's. She's got a nice size place."

"Really? Aunt Vi is so . . ." Polite Jena Lynn, not knowing how to nicely put that Betsy's aunt had the reputation of being a complete nutcase, was completely adorable.

"Lovable, generous, and kind but a fry short of a Happy Meal. I know. That's what I love about her." Nothing in my life surprised or upset her. I kept that last part to myself.

"Right. And I bet she's glad to have the company. Um"—I heard shuffling and supposed she'd stepped into the office—"they're holding Junior."

"In the hospital, right? I should have called to check. I feel awful. He saved my life." Well, he and Mama.

"No. He's in county lockup."

"What?" My voice rose louder than I'd intended.

A few unhappy tables around me cast unpleasant glances my way.

I turned to the side. "Seriously, Junior didn't do this. Eddie knows that."

"How can you be so sure? And I feel horrible for insisting we hire him. The man obviously has an obsession with you. I'm not supposed to know this, but Alex came to me because you aren't returning his calls either. Junior has made a shrine wall of you. In his bedroom." She was silent a moment while that sunk in. "He's a proper stalker."

"Okay, that's a bit weird. Still, I don't think he's guilty. He got me out, for heaven's sake. He had a torn hood from the coat of the guy he ran off. Plus, there were two sets of footprints at the scene."

"Maybe he brought it with him and doubled back to use as a cover story. Then had second thoughts and got you out. I don't know."

Listening objectively, as any other citizen would do, her argument held plausibility if we'd been talking about anyone other than Junior. What would Junior gain from burning my house down? Nothing. That wouldn't matter to a jury. Nutjobs did crazy things all the time without cause.

Jena Lynn brought me back from my contemplations. "Mayor Bill and Mrs. Gentry are furious. The old woman stormed in here demanding to speak with you this morning. And when she found out you weren't here, she threatened to sue you for slander."

"Slander? That's absurd. If anything, I've been on Junior's side." With my appetite now lost, I gathered up my bags and the tray, dumped what was left of my dinner into the bin, and placed the tray atop it.

"I'm sorry. You were probably trying to escape all of

this for a while and I've ruined your day." The regret in her tone traveled across the line with the weight of a freight train.

"You haven't. There's no escaping any of this. Love you, and thanks for calling. I'll come in tomorrow."

"You sure?"

"I need to work. You know I bake when I'm stressed, and I don't even have a kitchen anymore." I made my way out to the parking lot. The night felt warm and reassuring against my skin.

"Okay. But only a half day. This is a lot, Marygene. Don't push yourself."

"I won't." With my bags now in the trunk, I fired up the engine.

CHAPTER 23

As I sat on the ferry, I tried to reason logically why they'd be holding Junior. One, Eddie must have good reason to keep him. Sure, the evidence to hold him was there. Still, he'd given me no indication he believed in Junior's guilt. The key to the pattern of destruction was arson. Both bodies had been burned beyond recognition, then my house torched. No chance on God's green earth did Junior kill the twins. He'd only been a baby then. Whoever did, fire had been their weapon of choice. They were cold, calloused, and brutal. Could he be using Junior's hold to give the killer a false sense of security? That sounded like a brilliant move. And knowing Eddie as I did, he wouldn't put Junior in county. He might allow the press to believe he had, though, and even Junior's parents.

With the decision to leave Eddie to his business, when I got back to Aunt Vi's, I considered the possibilities. I'd bought two new mini whiteboards from the office supply store on the second floor of the mall. The sooner I solved this, the sooner I could get my life back.

The boards hung side by side over the dresser, where the mirror had been a few minutes before. I wrote the Dryer

Cold Case at the top of the board. The seaside sisters took their place on the corner: Mama, Mrs. Gentry, Ms. Brooks, Debbie Foster, Aunt Vi, and the twins. Mr. Gaskin went up as the prime suspect. One, he had motive, he dated Kayla. Two, he had the facility to house the bodies. Three, he'd threatened me. Four, he might have caught wind of me talking to Teddy the night my house caught fire. It would make sense he knew about Junior following me around. His timing was perfect. Maybe he was who Eddie attempted to trap by holding Junior. It made complete sense.

Betsy came barging into the bedroom. "Hey! I brought pizza." She stopped short, taking in my board. "Mr. Gaskin is the killer?"

"Hmm?" Aunt Vi followed her, chomping on a slice of supreme and I did a double take. Her hair was the craziest shade of red I'd ever seen. I mean, fire-engine red, with burnt sugar lowlights. She'd had it cut short into a wild pixie cut. Pieces of hair stuck out all over her head. She reminded me of a porcupine.

"Aunt Vi wanted something different." Betsy made eyes toward her aunt's hair.

"Well, she succeeded." I smirked.

"Thanks, girlies. You know"—Aunt Vi walked closer to my board—"Daniel and Kayla had a terrible breakup. She came to me so upset before she and her sister left. Kay said Daniel wasn't what he seemed. I'd been out of it at the time. A little too much herbal remedy back then, and blew her off. I have to admit, Daniel was there for us when . . ."

Betsy and I were keenly interested.

"Let's go eat some pizza." Aunt Vi whirled around and left the room.

Betsy and I were on her heels.

"Aunt Vi?" Betsy sounded concerned.

Aunt Vi's cheeks were wet and a ghostly pale expression had taken over her face. "Those are memories I've tried to forget. They're the reason I fled the island in the first place. I'm not as strong as the others."

Others? "You mean the seaside sisters?"

She nodded. "I will tell you. I just can't right now. I promise we'll talk about it, girls, but right now, I'm sorry, I . . . can't."

Betsy hugged her aunt, patting her back. "It's okay. We'll put a pin in it, right, Marygene?"

"Yes, of course."

Aunt Vi never showed emotion like this. Whatever had her so upset had to be serious and related to the case.

"I'm going to take a shower." Aunt Vi patted Betsy's cheek and then strode down the hall toward her room.

My hand went to my mouth. "Could Mr. Gaskin be the killer? I mean, he's Teddy's dad. Always the first one at all the high school football games. He donates his time to helping the vets at the senior center. Until recently, he's never uttered an ugly word to me."

"Anything is possible." Betsy got another slice from the box.

"But why wouldn't he incinerate the bodies? Keeping them all these years is beyond the realm of sick." I scratched my head.

Betsy scrunched up her face. "Some guys are, you know, freaks."

We shivered in disgust. Surely not.

"Though, my bet is he didn't have the bodies cremated because there would have been a record of it. They don't have a crematory at Gaskin Funeral Home. Folks' loved ones who need cremation, and they are few and far between here, get sent over to Savannah."

Oh. Well, that made sense. Still. To keep them all these years.

"I hate to say this, to even think it." I glanced down the hallway to make sure Aunt Vi wasn't in earshot. "Do we have to look at the seaside sisters? Obviously something horrific happened. Could they have been involved?" I pointed to the hallway where Aunt Vi went.

Betsy chewed on her bottom lip. "That would be accusing yours and Yvonne's mama and my aunt Vi." Along with the others. I assumed that point would be understood. "Ms. Brooks did go on about being guilty. Maybe she killed them and someone tried to cover it up by getting rid of the bodies. It could have been Yvonne. She did try to hide her mama out at your house."

"Oh, come on! There's no way Yvonne torched the corpses."

Betsy shrugged. "She's been acting weird lately. The job to destroy the bodies was majorly botched. Maybe she planned to dump both bodies in the ocean but one at a time. She's not that strong. And when the first dump didn't go so well, she thought she'd plant one in her own basement to throw the sheriff's department off the scent."

I put my hands on my hips. "Seriously?"

"You never really know anyone."

"Well, if that's true, what if you did it to save Aunt Vi? Perhaps her coming back to the island was timed with the bodies. You could have planted one in Yvonne's house to throw the sheriff's office off your scent."

Betsy's mouth hung slack. "I'm not that dumb. I would have hacked up the bodies into pieces. Then put them in several trash bags, those big black heavy-duty kind. Ducttaped them to bricks or rocks or something, then dumped them way out in different sections of the ocean. By the time the bags deteriorated, the body parts would be nothing but fish food. And I certainly wouldn't dump them on the side where the tourists swim and cruise ships frequent."

"Geez, Bets, remind me to call you if I ever kill someone."

Betsy smiled, pleased with herself. "When are you ever

going to learn. I'm not only a pretty face. And I was totally kidding, playing devil's advocate. Yvonne doesn't have the stomach for burning corpses. She'd have to call us for that. Now let's eat."

Corpses and pizza weren't a great combination for me.

"I'm going to take a walk on the beach. Clear my head and think this through."

"Okay. I'll save you some."

"Thanks." I closed the door softly behind me.

The waves crashed against the shore as I strolled down the beach, guided by nothing but the bright moonlight. The sand between my toes felt glorious. I needed to become reacquainted with my first love, despite the horrific memories of the human remains. Inching closer to the water's edge, I felt the caress of the warm water across my foot. Bliss. This far down the beach was all but deserted. There were a few cottages and houses. Something about property value and proximity to stores and nightlife made them undesirable. Funny, it was what made them the most desirable to me.

On the way back, I mulled over what I'd learned and felt I had insufficient evidence to actually bring anything of substance to Eddie. I'd done what I could by informing him of Teddy's intention to have a word with him and what he'd found. Ms. Brooks sure felt a similar weight of guilt, which reminded me of Aunt Vi and her determination to make up for not being there for Kayla when she was younger. Could Mama and her friend have had something to do with Kayla and Pamela's deaths? Perhaps Mr. Gaskin had been part of whatever had taken place. An accident, surely. I hoped.

When I got back to Pelican Cottage, I sat down on the beach, not ready to go back in. Wondering if my mother and her friends were capable of manslaughter had discombobulated me. If Betsy called me in the middle of the night, with an accident, would I go running and try to help her cover it up? Was there a fine line between right and wrong? Not that Betsy would need me. After tonight, I understood that my best friend could make half the island disappear without a trace, all by her little lonesome.

"Nice night."

I jumped and a squeak left my lips.

"Sorry." Javier strolled surreptitiously over beside me. "May I?" He motioned to the ground.

With a hand still on my rapidly beating heart, I motioned for him to sit. "Geez. You sure move stealth-like."

He sat, leaving a foot or so between us. "Habit. I should have made more noise to announce myself."

"Ya think? You're lucky I didn't have a heart attack. News flash. Nervous folks startle incredibly easily." I shook my head and took in his muscular tan legs stretched out on the sand. Seeing him in casual wear felt sort of wicked. Clearly, I had issues.

"Got it. How are you doing?" He placed his palms on the sand behind him and leaned back. Casual posture, nice touch.

"I'm fine. Well, not fine but okay." I stared out toward the ocean. The crashing of the waves soothed my soul. "You know, I always thought I'd buy one of these fixer-uppers and make it my own. My dream has always been to live this close to the water."

"Why didn't you?" His tone sounded as smooth as a good whisky.

I shrugged. "I moved away from home and then when I returned, I had to rebuild my life. Mama had left the old place to me. It's paid for."

He hitched a chin over his right shoulder. "I might buy my rental."

"If you do, Yvonne could help you with interior design. She redid my whole house. Gave me the kitchen of my dreams . . ." I tucked the edges of my dress underneath me. It had stretched out some and now I really liked it. Jena Lynn wouldn't be getting it back.

"I'll keep that in mind. I certainly don't have an eye for that sort of thing. I can do a little construction, though, so that'd save me a few dollars doing some of the renovations myself."

"We going to keep this small talk up much longer?" I sat up straighter.

He raised a brow.

"Oh, please." I straightened and sat cross-legged, tucking my dress underneath me. "I'm relaxed now. You've done your best to make me feel like we're two new friends having a chat about commonalities. You don't need to socialize to keep an eye on me. What do you want to know? Ask." Upon further deliberation of his declaration about scooping me up, I wondered if that had been a brilliant tactic to gain my trust. There was an attraction between us, sure, but that could also be used as a tool.

"I thought we were friends."

"We hardly know each other."

"Well, what would you like to know?" He kept his tone smooth, edging on seductive.

I gaped. "You're not seriously coming on to me right now."

"What?" He chuckled. "I've seen you raw. I thought you'd like to level the field."

I squinted at him. "Fine. Tell me about your marriage. I know her side. From the website, you worked as head of her father's security firm. Crossed some lines by taking bribes or something. Add that to the cheating, and she dumped you."

He shook his head, his face completely somber now. He gazed out over toward the ocean. "The truth is, while working as head of security, I uncovered her father's plot to rob some of the businesses he worked for. He has a gambling problem and planned to use what he stole to pay off depts. So, daddy's little girl took his side and operation submarine happened from there. I managed to salvage most of my reputation. Even got my position back on the force and agreed to divorce Maria. She hasn't proof of cheating because I didn't cheat. Money is that woman's true love. I gave her everything, but that wasn't enough. They wanted to destroy me by going after my family. The agreement was if I left, they'd leave them alone. My sister has kids and has her sights on a few good schools. She could get a letter of recommendation from my ex-father-in-law if I left. It made sense at the time. Now, I sort of wished I'd stood my ground." He rubbed his chin.

We sat in silence while I processed. "Okay, you were open. Now be honest with me."

He turned toward me, looking surprised.

"You don't quite trust my dad or me, do you? Your past dictates that you would naturally develop suspicions about the character of those closest to you. I get it. Ask your questions and I will be as honest with my answers as I can be without breaking certain confidences. And even then, I won't lie. I don't lie, Javier."

He sat up, intrigue filling his eyes. "Did you pay Junior to burn your house down on purpose?"

Of all the things I'd mentally prepared for him to ask, this wasn't one of them. "What? No. Hell to the no!"

"It makes sense. Your dad is mixed up in some old case that came back to bite him. Someone has something on him. He finds out about Junior's adoration for you. You help Junior concoct some elaborate story about a ghost. Instruct him to have everyone ask you about it, because you're afraid he might screw the story up and implicate you and your dad."

I sat there, blinking. "You're nuts. Why would I want to burn my own house down and nearly myself with it?"

"The fire got out of hand. Your dad was infatuated with your mama. Perhaps she and her friends were close to the victims. Maybe he helped cover up the crimes. Perhaps whoever has something on the sheriff, could be Gaskin, orchestrated the discovery of the victims to blackmail him." His accent got thicker when he spoke quickly.

"Um, sure, I can see the plausibility in your theories. Although, there's no way Eddie would risk my life to save himself. That's just nuts." I made the universal sign for crazy. "My master plan executed to perfection nearly cost me my life? Yeah, right."

"It's possible."

"Okay, how about this? You're paranoid because you were screwed over by your trusted employer/father-in-law, so your judgment is skewed."

"Possible. And I really don't believe you're responsible for any of this, I wanted to gauge your reaction to see if you're hiding anything. I knew when I saw you standing in the yard looking so wounded."

I had to admit, Javy's tactic had been brilliant. I'd file it away for future use. If I had been protecting the guilty party, it could have shown.

I turned my body back around to face the ocean.

"You're right, I am jaded by my past."

"That's okay. I'm jaded too." I didn't want to talk about me anymore. "Did Eddie speak to Mr. Gaskin?"

"He's scheduled to come in tomorrow. We know he had a relationship with Kayla Dryer, but that doesn't make him a murderer." No, it didn't. "Viola Myers is supposed to be questioned tomorrow as well."

I wondered what Aunt Vi would tell them. I shifted on the sand.

"Ah, that got a reaction."

I nodded. "She said something tonight about Kayla telling her that Mr. Gaskin wasn't what he seemed. She feels bad she wasn't more of a friend to her." I turned toward him now. "Y'all better be gentle with her. She's a good person with a big heart."

"This is a murder case," he said firmly but gently.

Of course it was. And I had firsthand knowledge of how he went after a potential witness or suspect.

"The sheriff is even going to be deposed."

I opened my mouth to question his statement, then closed it when I thought it through. Naturally, he would be. "Eddie's an honorable man."

"I will say he's willing to lay the case out and be questioned. Most sheriffs would push back."

"Eddie's tough."

"Not as tough as his daughter, I think. You're a survivor." Javy's gaze fixed on me so intensely, unease ran up my spine.

Eddie's words about being careful who I allowed close to me came back. Slowly, I rose and dusted the sand from my dress. "Good night."

He visibly swallowed. "Night."

CHAPTER 24

The next morning went surprisingly fairly normal. Other than being dead on my feet, that was. After reassuring my sister for the umpteenth time, I made loads of pastries and decorated more than a dozen cakes. I ignored the article that had been printed in the paper with my exclusive interview and the local news. Other than polite responses to customers, I'd not really engaged in conversation.

Still, the twins were consuming my every thought. Aunt Vi hadn't emerged from her bedroom before I went to bed. Betsy worked the late shift today, so we'd only seen each other in passing. I worried about Aunt Vi and her interview today. She'd seemed so fragile last night.

My thoughts drifted back to my conversation with Javy here and there. Although I'd defended Eddie and our island, I did fear Eddie hid something serious. His comment that someone might be targeting him never left my thoughts.

It was funny. When I served seniors in the diner, they appeared such sweet, cordial people. One would never suspect that they had a sordid past or hid appalling secrets. How my view had changed.

My brother stopped me on my way out. I had to be over at the sheriff's office in fifteen minutes to make a formal statement. "I'm sorry about the house."

I stood there by the grill line, watching him flip burgers and scatter hash browns.

"Yeah, it sucks. At least I'm alive." I gave him a half smile.

"That's the important part. Hey." He came a bit closer. "I've got a shotgun in the toolbox on the back of my truck. You take it over to Aunt Vi's with you." He gave me a stern look that read he'd not take no for an answer. "I don't know what's going on around here lately. Seems like folks have gone batshit or something. You take it for protection, you hear?"

"Sam, It's been forever since I fired a shotgun."

"It's either take the gun or come stay with me. I'll take the sofa." He plated up the meals and put them in the window.

"Thanks for the offer, but I'm not moving into your pigsty, Sam."

"I'll walk you out." He hollered to his helper to watch the grill line and he walked me outside.

"I appreciate you caring, I really do, but—"

"I'm not going to hear it, Marygene. There's nothing to it. Put it against your shoulder like Dad showed us, aim for the midsection, and squeeze the trigger. It'll kick."

I recalled the kick. It knocked me on my rear when I was sixteen. I hesitated when Sam extracted it from the toolbox on the back of his truck and held his hand out for my keys. Seeing he wouldn't be moved on this, and feeling uncomfortable standing in the middle of the street with my brother while he held a gun and shotgun shells, I hit the key fob to unlock the trunk.

"Dad said Javier is next door. I know I talked a lot of

smack about you going out with him." With the gun now secured in my trunk, he put a hand on my shoulder and lowered his head next to mine. "Listen, we don't know him. He seems like an okay guy. That doesn't mean he'll lay his life down for yours. We have to look out for each other and Dad." Sam made a lot of sense.

"Okay." I wrapped my arms around his waist and squeezed. "You're a good brother."

He patted my back awkwardly.

I laughed.

"See ya."

I watched him trot across the parking lot before I drove around the square and parked in front of the old brick building adjacent to the town hall, which housed the sheriff's office. I noticed Meemaw sitting on a bench outside, between the two buildings under a large oak tree.

"Hey, what are you doing here?" I slid onto the bench next to her.

She smiled at me, despite the fact she looked worried. Her brows were knitted together and her lips pursed. "Waiting on Vi. I insisted on coming along for moral support. She asked me to stay out here." She shook her head. "Poor girl is carrying so much guilt. And part of it's my fault. I should've done something all those years ago. I wanted to tell them in there. Vi was adamant I stay out of it." She hmphed. "All those bodies."

"What bodies? The twins?"

She gave her head a shake. "No, all those others. When my Vi was young, she and your mama were two peas in a pod. Went everywhere together. They had their little group." She smiled in a reminiscing sort of way. "They were young and the Peach Cove hippy movement took hold of 'em. They used to go out to the conservation land. Stay there for days. Living in tents and smoking and drinking. They made big bonfires on the beach. Stark naked sometimes." She shook her head. "Didn't like that none. Your nanny and I went out there, threatening to tan some hides when we found out. I had an island spirit then, my sister, Ruthie." She grimaced. "She was a real brat. That's probably why she didn't instantly cross. Always complained about having a headache when we were kids and it was time to work in the fields. Took my car without asking when we were teens. Forever trying to one-up me as an adult. She drove me crazy, even in death."

"Meemaw." I gently touched her arm to get her back on track. "You found the bodies."

"They drew me to them because of Ruthie. They were all naked and lying in a circle on the far end of the beach. They'd eaten mushrooms or some sort of fungus. They were all dead." Tears sprang into her eyes.

I dug through my purse and handed her a Kleenex. Then I squeezed her hand.

She blotted her cheeks. "I didn't know how to help the kids who accidentally killed themselves. If I'd gone to the authorities, our girls would've been questioned and maybe arrested. Lord help me, I just turned and walked away. Paid for it, too. The nightmares got so bad, I went to see a psychiatrist and got something to help me sleep. My Henry thought I'd gone crazy and right nearly did. Finally, one day I got better." Now I believed Mama had been dead-on with the vengeful spirit warning.

Vi came out of the double doors and hurried over to us. "Mama, are you okay?"

"Fine. Just an old softie remembering the olden days," Meemaw lied through her teeth. "Maybe we should mosey on over to the diner and have a slice of pie."

"Sure, Mama." She helped Meemaw to her feet. "Marygene, you going to be okay on your own?"

"Perfectly fine." I kissed Meemaw's wrinkled cheek.

She'd earned each and every one of them and wore them proudly.

God, I loved her. "Meemaw, you tell whoever waits on you that Marygene said whatever you and Aunt Vi have is on me."

She perked right up. That was the admirable trait all the Myerses possessed. They rebounded quickly.

"Well, that's right nice of you, sweetheart. Thank you."

I learned something about Meemaw in that moment as I watched the two of them walk to their car. Meemaw had her own little box where she kept her pain and troubles. Respect overwhelmed me. That woman was the epitome of a survivor.

Evelyn Gentry came storming over. "Marygene Brown! How dare you accuse my Junior! He wouldn't hurt a fly and you know it. Just because he's a large man doesn't make him a brute."

If she thought to intimidate me like she had Candi, she had another think coming. "Mrs. Gentry, I'd appreciate it if you would lower your tone. This display is quite unbecoming. How do you think this looks? You, the wife of the mayor, verbally assaulting the victim." I tsked, as she had me at Yvonne's function. I'll admit I took a little too much pleasure in it.

Her huffy red face made it all worth it.

"I assure you I don't believe Junior is guilty. I never accused him of anything and would testify to the fact he is the most gentle soul I've ever met."

Her face contorted to a full pucker and she poked me in the arm with her bony finger. "Oh, well, you can tell your daddy that then. My Bill's had a time keeping those reporters at bay. That's all my Junior needs right now. Bill's going to hold a press conference and you're going to get my boy released before he takes the podium."

She matched me stride for stride up the steps, her eyes slanted toward me continuously. Once inside, she slammed her hand down on the receptionist's desk. It made a loud smacking sound. Lucy jumped.

"Get me the sheriff this instant."

"He . . . he's in a meeting. Can I take a message?" Lucy fumbled with the pens in the holder. The sight was mighty amusing.

"Girl, if you don't want me to come around this desk, you better get the sheriff out here this second."

Lucy appeared petrified of the old woman. Not their first meeting, I guessed. Someone must not have informed her that you didn't mess with or get between a Southern woman and her child. For a half second, I considered intervening. Almost instantly, I decided against it.

"Forget it. You're useless. And take heed, girl. If you see me around town, walk the other way." Mrs. Gentry wagged her finger at the young woman.

"Y . . . yes, ma'am." Well, that almost made this whole ordeal worth it.

"Edward Carter!" Mrs. Gentry bellowed. "I've got your daughter here and we're going to straighten this out once and for all!"

I gave Lucy a finger wave as I passed her desk.

Mrs. Gentry and I were stunned into silence at the sight in front of us. Mr. Gaskin stood at the end of the hall in handcuffs and Junior kept pointing to him, nodding. I knew Eddie didn't have him in lockup. Did this mean Mr. Gaskin was *actually* guilty?

Eddie spotted us and waved us back. Junior grinned and waved vigorously; both his forearms were still bandaged. Javier hauled Mr. Gaskin into the interview room.

"Junior!" Mrs. Gentry sounded so relieved to see her son.

It was sort of sweet. Even if I didn't appreciate all of his mother's qualities, she did love her son and would do anything for him. They embraced.

"Your son is free to go, Evelyn." Eddie clapped Junior on his back. "He's been a big help."

Mrs. Gentry checked her son over as if she expected to find further injuries.

"I scratched him," Junior said proudly. "They got skin to test from under my fingernails with this toothpick thingy. It's him, though. I didn't know it was him until he came in and then I remembered."

"You used my boy?"

"Now, Evelyn, Bill knew about the whole thing. We drove him to lockup for the press to get word, but he wasn't booked. We brought him back here. He had a nurse with him in the back room, the one with a cot, the entire time. We ordered him pizza and got candy from the vending machine."

"Bill knew about this?" the old woman seethed. Whoa. She reminded me of a viper, ready to strike without mercy.

"Mr. Gaskin burned down my house?" I changed the subject to the most important matter here.

Junior stared at me with a sad expression. "I'm sorry I didn't stop him before he did that. I tried to watch over you."

"You're sweet, but you don't need to watch over me anymore."

Junior began chewing on his nails; worry etched his brow.

"That's right, honey. Marygene has her daddy to watch out for her. You come along home and I'll make you a grilled cheese and tomato soup. Mama's going to have a long chat with Daddy." Poor Mayor Bill was going to get it.

"He's around the corner there." Eddie motioned.

Junior winked at me as they started down the hall. Not

quite sure how to take that, I watched Eddie walk with the pair.

Javier came out of the room and went into the viewing side, leaving the door marginally ajar. Curiosity took hold. Was that an invitation? A second later, I decided yes. With a quick peek around to ensure I wouldn't be seen, I power walked across the hall and slipped inside, closing the door behind me.

CHAPTER 25

Mr. Gaskin had been handcuffed to the little metal doohickey on the old scarred metal table. He didn't exactly seem upset, and that bothered me. His eyes stared straight through the glass and then me. At least it felt that way. He couldn't literally see us on the other side of the glass, and I knew that. The haunting, knowing expression on his face read that his fate was sealed. Why would he do such an awful thing? To pull off such an act of desperation would give anyone cause to consider him a suspect in the murders as well.

I glanced at Javy, standing with his arms folded across his chest. The emotion he showed me last night had vanished. Other than the invitation to join him, he stood before me the consummate professional.

"He has scratch marks on his neck and arms. Defensive wounds. We've taken samples from underneath Junior's nails to run a DNA match. He isn't talking."

"Poor Teddy." I couldn't imagine what he must be going through.

"His son is in Eddie's office. He's hired an attorney. We're waiting on the attorney to arrive before we begin questioning Mr. Gaskin. I thought you deserved the right to face him, even though this is the only way."

"Thank you." I swallowed hard. "Do you think he's guilty of killing the twins?"

"It fits." It did.

"And your opinion of Eddie?"

He stood silent. No comment. Okay then.

After what Meemaw had told me outside, there was far more to the story than everyone let on, or perhaps even knew. What about all those bodies? Their deaths were presumably an accident. Although, why would the deceased enlist Meemaw's help if it had been? I rubbed my forehead. There were so many pieces, my brain had difficulty keeping up with them.

"Were there any other missing-persons cases filed within a few years before or after the twins went missing?" It could have happened before Eddie joined the department. My timeline on all of this information was more than a bit fuzzy. I wondered, if cadaver dogs were dispatched on that part of the island, what they would find.

"Not that I'm aware of. Why?"

"Just wondered." I kept my gaze trained forward.

Mr. Gaskin sat stoically. Was I staring into the face of a killer? He certainly had attempted to kill me. Or had he? Junior said he tried to put the fire out. In his efforts, the barrel went through the kitchen window. Perhaps Mr. Gaskin had simply been attempting to scare me. I had to get in there.

"Javy, I need a few minutes with Mr. Gaskin before his attorney gets here. I'm not in law enforcement, so if I get out of there before anyone finds out, it shouldn't be a problem."

Javy blinked a couple of times before giving me the "you're insane" glare. I was getting so sick of seeing those. "You can't go in there."

"I bet Teddy would have no objections." He might until I told him I had doubts regarding his dad's guilt regarding the attempted murder of me.

"It isn't Teddy's call."

I grabbed the handle of the door. "It isn't yours, either. If you want to rat me out to Eddie, fine. Or you could stand here and see if I can get any of those secrets that have been needling you revealed." I didn't wait for a response and, a few seconds later, I sat across from the man who potentially hated me so much he might have made an attempt on my life. I really wished Mama would make an appearance. She could give me something to crack this nut open with.

He swallowed. A simple gesture, but a telling one. The man didn't have nerves of steel. He faked it well, though.

"Mr. Gaskin." I kept my tone low. "I'm going to be honest with you and I would appreciate it if you returned the favor, please, sir. This isn't being recorded. Your rights are being respected. Javier is on the other side of that glass." I pointed behind me and glanced where I guessed he still stood. "He's giving us a few minutes to chat before your attorney arrives. None of what you say to me will hold up in court. You know that. This is for me." I hoped Javy would run a little interference until I got what I needed.

His gaze darted around the room before settling back on me. I allowed my pain to climb to the surface. He needed to see how his actions had affected me. Betrayal from a neighbor that I'd known my entire life made me question everything I'd been raised on. "I don't understand. Teddy and I have been friends since kindergarten. When you were undergoing your chemo treatment, my sister and I brought food to your house."

Regret flickered across his face for a brief moment, then it was gone.

"You were worried I'd hurt Teddy. But look what you did! This will definitely rip him apart." I lifted my palms.

"Help me out here. Why would you do such a thing? Why do you hate me so much?"

His shoulders slumped. "I don't hate you, child. And I never meant for that night to go the way it did. I started with the spray paint, hoping that would be enough. I left the barrel on the back porch, right next to the smoke detector on the other side of the wall in the laundry room. I broke into your house and I took the box your mama used to talk about. The one with the family albums. I figured that if the detectors were slow, the albums might be harmed. That boy showed up and hit me. He tried to pick the can up and then threw it. Stupid kid. It slipped my mind that I'd dumped the spray paint can in the barrel out back until after I saw the house go up in flames. Then I ran like a coward after I saw the boy pull you from the house."

I felt both shock and relief that he'd decided to come clean to me.

"It was a scare tactic, nothing more. You kept pestering folks. Making them recall the past. You wouldn't let this thing with the twins go. Why?"

"A scare tactic that could have killed me!"

Shame filled his expression.

I promised to be honest and I would be. Completely. "Have you ever heard of an island spirit?"

His brows shot up to his hairline.

"Never mind. When I found both the bodies, they gripped me to my core and wouldn't let go. That someone could murder two young women and their killer never be brought to justice is an outrage. They were stuck, frozen in their youth as time marched on. I couldn't bear it."

He appeared appalled. "I didn't kill Kayla or Pamela. Kayla and I were in love." He shook his head. "I know it was wrong to still see her after I got married. Before, though, I wanted to marry her. We were going to, but she couldn't leave her sister. I don't know why. Whenever she visited and I saw her again, I simply couldn't help myself. I would have never hurt her."

"Then why go to all *this* trouble? To scare me off of something you aren't even guilty of."

The door burst open and Eddie, along with an outraged attorney, barged in. "What is the meaning of this? None of what my client has said is admissible. I'll file a motion to have all of this thrown out. The case too."

It was a risk I had been willing to take. If the case got thrown out, so be it. I stood and avoided Eddie's furious glare.

To all of our surprise, Mr. Gaskin spoke directly to me. "Marygene, I feared your digging would bring to light what I've been hiding from for years."

"Mr. Gaskin, I must advise you to keep silent." His attorney's long, thin face reddened. He slammed his case on the table.

"It doesn't matter now. They have my DNA." Pain and remorse filled the room, along with sweat.

"I request the room. Now," his attorney demanded.

"I'm sorry, child."

I paused at the door and spared him a second glance over my shoulder.

"I'm glad your mama has passed on, for your sake. Leave this alone. What you seek will only bring more pain to so many, and you still may not find the answers you seek."

His lawyer closed the door on us.

Eddie took me by the arm and hauled me into his office. I glanced around for Teddy. He wasn't there. "What were you thinking? You may have blown the entire case!" Eddie raked his fingers through his hair.

"I'm sorry. I needed to find out why."

"That isn't your job! And I had him, dead to rights." Eddie's fury made the air thick and hard to breathe.

"I honestly don't believe he'll even fight it. He kept talking even when you and his lawyer were in the room. Even after his lawyer cautioned him. You heard him apologize to me. This is far bigger than my house, Eddie."

He cupped my face in his hands, and suddenly I was a child again. "Nothing is bigger than your life."

I closed my eyes to stop the tears from flowing. It stung, but I managed to hold them at bay.

He dropped his hands. "What's going on with you? How is it that you keep stumbling upon bodies?"

He'd obviously given this a lot of thought.

How could I possibly tell Eddie what only the insane or those who experienced island spirits would believe? No. It was out of the question.

"Marygene, I'm running out of excuses to explain this to myself. These types of crimes are hard to explain and have only been occurring since you've returned home. I'm not saying it's your fault, but you've got to admit, it looks odd. And now your interference with my suspect might well tank the entire case!" He threw his hands in the air. "What are you doing, girl? What are you after?"

Emotion churned within me. I wanted to scream, cry, and fight all at the same time. "What happened during the hippie movement on the island?" My fists were balled at my sides. My nails stung my palms.

"For the love of God! Stop listening to Viola. That's ancient history and, quite frankly, none of your business."

"Fine. But the murder of the twins happened while I was in diapers. That had nothing to do with me." I threw my hands in the air. "I certainly didn't enjoy finding those women."

"I know that!" His cheeks were bright red and mine heated up as well.

"They've stuck with me." I sniffed. "If I could get them out of my head, believe me, I would."

"I'm working the case and everywhere I step, there you are, poking your nose in. Again."

Mama stood there, glaring at Eddie. She apparently didn't approve of his tone, either. To her credit, she kept silent and allowed me to make my own decisions, and I appreciated that.

He jabbed a finger in my direction. We were a couple feet apart. Two bullheaded members of the Carter bloodline squaring off.

"If I catch you where you aren't supposed to be another time or find you interfering in my cases again, I'll lock you up."

Before I could think it through, I lashed out. "Just because you dropped the ball on the missing-persons case doesn't mean you get to take it out on me. If you'd done your job all those years ago, we wouldn't be having this discussion and my house never would have burned down. And my life wouldn't have been in jeopardy!"

He flinched as if I'd slapped him with his own guilt. Thoughts he must've railed at himself for days.

Whirling on my heels I darted out of the room. I made it outside before the hot tears flowed and regret weighed on my shoulders. I should have kept my mouth shut. Said *Yes, sir*, and left. Mr. Gaskin was right. Already the people I loved suffered. Meemaw and Aunt Vi, even Mama, dealt with regretful emotions. Now Eddie. If I could leave it alone, I would. Sadly, the decision wasn't mine to make.

CHAPTER 26

Over the course of the next couple of days, the island was in turmoil. All the living seaside-sisters clan were called into the sheriff's office to be questioned about Daniel Gaskin. If they saw anything suspicious and if they had information they might not be aware of. Debbie Foster and Evelyn Gentry had similar stories regarding threats Mr. Gaskin hurled at Kayla. Neither one of them was quiet about what they'd told Eddie. It dominated the chatter at the diner. Aunt Vi couldn't say for sure but she did come clean about Kayla telling her that her old boyfriend wasn't what he seemed. What confused me most was that there wasn't a single mention of the bodies Meemaw had referred to.

Another thing that had me scratching my head: Ms. Brooks was the only one of the group who didn't agree with the testimonies of her old friends.

Or so Yvonne told me while we lounged on the beach in the late afternoon after my shift. "She said it was the person they all least suspected." Yvonne sprayed on some tanning oil while we sipped Coronas with lime. "The wolf in sheep's clothing thing again. I barely held it together when she burst into tears and claimed to be guilty. Again. She told Eddie that Pamela experienced the worst of it. No one should have to give up a piece of themselves."

"A piece of themselves. What did she mean by that?" I flipped onto my stomach to sun my back.

Yvonne did the same. "Heaven only knows. Jeez Louise. I'm so sick of all of this. Even though Eddie said he wouldn't need to question Mama anymore, she hears about it and it's in the paper and on the news. It's really got her in a tizzy. Last night she called Evelyn and Debbie liars." She finished her drink. "She said they'd split hell wide open. Started rambling about mass graves and bodies. They had to sedate her."

"Do you think there's any truth to what she's saying?" I knew there was regarding the bodies but didn't want to break Meemaw's confidence. And she'd not mentioned that Ms. Brooks had known about them. That concerned me regarding the seaside sisters and their involvement.

She adjusted her sunhat. "No. I don't know. One minute she's laughing about something she and one of her friends did years ago and then next she's claiming one of them stole precious jewels. Which one, changes all the time. She didn't even know me yesterday morning. She thought I was a nurse."

I squeezed her arm. "I'm sorry. That's got to be tough on you too."

She wiped the tear that leaked from her eye. "She's all I have left."

"You've got me," was all I could think to say.

We locked hands. "I know. But you've got your plate full too."

"I'll always make time for you. You're my sister from another mister." That got me a genuine smile. "You should call Doc Tatum. Maybe her meds need to be adjusted."

"I'll do that. How are things going with the insurance payout on your house?"

"Now that Mr. Gaskin has been arrested, I'm getting it soon." I sprayed a little more oil onto my arms and laid them out above my head.

"Are you rebuilding, or buying something beachfront?"

I sat up. I'd never considered not rebuilding. At least not seriously.

Yvonne lifted her sunglasses. "You love the beach. It's always been your dream to own property out here. You planned on putting your mama's house on the market when you first moved back. Now's your chance."

"Could I do that?"

"Sure you could! It's paid for, so you can get a cash settlement. If you had a mortgage, the check would be issued into the lender's name and you'd have no choice other than rebuild. I had a client a few years ago who rebuilt her house after an electrical fire. That's how I know." She twisted open another bottle. "What time is it?" When I shrugged, she picked up her phone from out of her beach bag. "Shoot! I'm so late." She bolted upright and put on her cover-up.

"Think about what I said. There are several properties I've had my eye on that I'd love to remodel. If you let me showcase it, I'll cut you an amazing deal on my services." She winked as she slid her feet into her sandals.

Aunt Vi came sauntering out the French doors, wearing her giant pink sunglasses and matching hot-pink string bikini. Yvonne and I shared an amused smirk. She exposed so much flesh the strings weren't visible in some spots.

She bent to retrieve a lounge chair when Yvonne waved at her.

"Take mine. I've got a meeting to get to. See y'all."

Aunt Vi plopped down onto the chair next to me and slathered herself up with baby sunscreen SPF 50+. "How's Thelma?"

"Yvonne said she's having a hard time." I handed Aunt Vi a beer from the cooler beside my chair. "She keeps touting that the killer is a wolf in sheep's clothing."

"Interesting." Aunt Vi put the bottle to her lips. "The question is has she lost her marbles or does she know something she's afraid of telling?"

"You mean like she's been threatened?"

Aunt Vi nodded. "A body was placed in her daughter's house. Possibly to keep her silent. Eddie not keeping you in the loop?"

I swigged from the bottle. "We had a huge fight. I crossed a line. I left him a message apologizing, but he hasn't called me back. Alex and Javier are working round the clock, so I haven't even seen them either." I shrugged.

"I wish we could let this drop." Aunt Vi finished her bottle in one long, loud gulping session.

"Mr. Gaskin said something to that effect, for me to drop it. I don't want to hurt anyone, Aunt Vi." I flipped in the lounge and lifted the back so I could sit up. I stared out over the ocean. "I can't do what Meemaw did and walk away. I don't have the mental strength to deal with nightmares and vengeful spirits. Sometimes I'm furious with Mama for putting me in this position and sometimes I feel like it's a calling I was destined for."

Aunt Vi sighed. "Mama told you about the bodies."

I nodded slowly.

"She thinks we never found out about them." That explained a lot. "It was crazy times then. Our little group thought we were changing the world with love and acceptance. Once word spread about our little private piece of the island, we had all sorts of nomads take part. We didn't even know the real names of most of them. People called themselves flower, kitten, or even something like lemon, anything that they chose and we went with it. Our lifestyle hadn't been all about partying and getting high. We organized protests against any and all potential wars and environmental pollution. We truly believed we were doing good. Then someone brought some bad mushrooms and all hell broke loose. When Mama and your nanny came out to rein us in, they threatened to bring the sheriff. That old coot wasn't a good man like your daddy. He would have locked us away for whatever charges he thought he could make stick. It was sort of a tough love approach. We were getting out of hand. The sheriff found out anyway, and he put a stop to our shenanigans. Tore down all of our tents and had all our stuff hauled off. Most of the visitors went back home, some to college and some had jobs. Still, our little clique snuck out there some nights. The shock we all had when we found the deceased. Those poor kids must have snuck off farther down the beach with their mushrooms." Tears streamed down Aunt Vi's cheeks.

"Your mama, Thelma, and me, along with Kayla and Pamela, went farther down the beach one weekend to avoid detection. That's when we discovered the decomposing bodies." That explained Ms. Brooks's statement. She swallowed hard and I waited for her to compose herself. "We freaked out. They'd been dead awhile. Kayla held it together fairly well. She called Daniel and told him that she found the bodies, on her own. He worked for his uncle then. He took care of the situation for her. After that, we decided that our flower power days were over. We all went our separate ways for a while and swore an oath of silence. Time marched on and no one came looking for them. Not one single inquiry and after that, I could almost convince myself it hadn't happened." No wonder she'd left the island.

I reached out and took her hand. We sat in silence, staring out at the crashing waves. I wouldn't add to her suffering by asking any more questions. She'd endured enough and those poor people took their own lives, inadvertently, of course. It hadn't been her fault.

"Years went by and we all went about our lives. Your mama got married and so did the others in our group. Babies were born and peace restored. Kayla had come to me after they moved to Savannah. Daniel had married. Kayla had a new boyfriend then. Still, they were addicted to each other, couldn't help themselves. His wife found out. Bad business." She sighed. "And with Pamela losing Bill to Evelyn, neither of them had much left on the island."

"Wait, what? Pamela dated Mayor Bill?"

"Didn't you know that Pam and Bill dated before he and Evelyn got together?"

I shook my head.

She shrugged. "Ancient history now. Back then the riff between Pamela and Evelyn got ugly. I believe it was part of the reason the twins left."

That made sense. "Um, if the twins lived in Savannah, how did a missing-persons case get filed here?"

"Their family never reported them missing. I did. I saw Pam's car parked on the square. It stayed there unmoving for three days." I nodded, recalling Eddie's take on the family.

"You know the rest. One minute they were shopping in the market and the next, they simply vanished. There's a dark place in hell for whoever robbed them of their lives. I hate to think it was Daniel. He got to carry on with his life after they lost theirs." She struggled to her feet. "I'm going to take a dip."

CHAPTER 27

The next morning I met Wally, my insurance adjuster, over at the house. He had to double check a couple of things with the investigator. Wally had a great reputation on the island for being fair. He didn't like to try and get out of paying claims. The man nearing sixty had adapted the Quiverfull way of life. To say he had a large family would be an understatement. Those in that Christian movement usually did. He and his wife had thirteen children, and I lost count of how many grandchildren they now had. I didn't know how they did it, but they managed to make it look easy. The man's integrity stood for itself. And for that I was grateful.

I'd decided I needed to see the property. Face it, really. I'd yet to go back since the fire. The ache in my heart to see the place in ruins had me close to tears.

"You okay?" Wally Sterling asked.

I nodded and accepted the folder the heavyset man extended to me.

"I'm sorry this happened to you. You've been in our prayers."

"Thanks." I glanced at the folder.

"Everything seems to be in order now. If you decide to take a payout, let me know and I can have a check direct deposited into your account after you sign the pertinent paperwork."

"Thank you, Wally."

The man had a ruddy round face, and when he smiled, it expanded.

"I'll make my decision on rebuilding soon."

He nodded and we shook hands.

I stayed behind after he left and walked around the property for a few minutes. It almost felt like a death. The wind kicked up and a flicker of gold wrappers caught my attention a few yards from where my back porch used to be. I reached down and picked all three of them up. They'd gotten trapped under some debris. My heart fluttered as I recalled Eddie had found the same candy wrapper in Yvonne's cellar.

I stuffed them into my pocket and strode to my car. After my shift at the diner, I'd take them by the sheriff's department. It seemed like too much of a coincidence not to. There could still be some DNA on them. I hoped touching them hadn't destroyed any evidence that might remain.

The square had exploded with camera crews, reporters, business owners, and curiosity seekers trying to get close to the municipal building where Mayor Bill stood in front of several microphones. Eddie stood on his right side and Alex and Javier on his left.

Forced to double park, I elbowed my way through the crowd and sidled up next to Betsy. "What's going on?"

"There's an outstanding warrant for Mr. Gaskin in Atlanta. He's being extradited to the city."

My jaw went slack.

Betsy nodded. "Apparently he's been hiding out on the

island all these years to get out of facing the charge. His DNA got a hit. Mayor Bill said he's also being charged for the murders of the twins and the attempt on your life, which the mayor's son thwarted."

I guessed they would make the charges against him stick on my case after all.

"Did he confess? To killing the twins?"

Betsy shrugged. I spotted Teddy standing over by the green space. His clothes were rumpled and his appearance gaunt as he stared at Mayor Bill, who took questions from the reporters.

I meandered my way over to Teddy, stopping only to hear a few "poor thing" comments and answer questions on how I was doing. When I reached him, I placed a hand lightly on his shoulder.

When he turned, his slack expression concerned me further. "What's happening?" He searched my face for answers.

I took Teddy's hand. He followed me like a lost pup across the street and into the empty diner. I flipped the sign to closed and locked the door, just in case someone lost interest outside and wanted to come in.

"Teddy, I want you to listen to me." I moved him by his shoulders to sit down on a stool. Then I poured him a glass of water and sat in front of him. He stared down at it as if he had no clue what it was or what to do with it.

"I spoke to your daddy yesterday."

His posture went rigid and his head whipped up. "How? He won't see me."

"Long story. What your daddy needs is for you to get him the best attorney you can afford. Unless he confessed to the murders, I have no idea how they're going to prove such a case." If he turned out to be guilty, they had to have more evidence and he'd be convicted anyway. Right now, my friend needed hope.

"Why are you helping me? He burned down your house."
He slouched forward and his wounded-puppy expression
tugged so tightly at my heartstrings that I hugged him. He
laid his head on my shoulder.

"I don't believe he intended to burn it down or harm me.
He attempted to protect himself and probably you from the
discovery of his outstanding warrant. I have no idea what
that's about." I rubbed his back like you would a small
child. "You should go and try to see him. Find out."

"He couldn't have had those bodies housed in the funeral home all these years. I would have found them."

I released him but held on to his shoulders. "We don't
always know our parents as well as we think we do. Ask
him about the time he helped Kayla out with a problem."

Teddy abruptly stood and stumbled. "What problem?
Are you trying to pin more charges on him?" Poor Teddy
acted as if he couldn't decide if he was angry with me, or
grateful. The emotional roller coaster he rode would last
for a while, I supposed.

I used Doc Tatum's technique of a soothing, calm tone.
"A lot of crazy things happened on the island when our parents were young. If your dad is innocent, he may know
who's actually guilty. And that could help his case."

A knock on the door pulled our attention. Jena Lynn
stood there with her hands in the air.

I went and let her in, along with a rush of customers.
While my back was turned, Teddy rushed around me, bump-
ing me into the front door. He didn't look back as he charged
across the street.

Folks were riled up while I helped Betsy serve up meals.
She and I hustled while trying to calm the masses. Everyone wanted to ask me questions.

I avoided most with simple responses. "I'm grateful to

be here working today. And it's only a house. Thank you for your prayers."

"I honestly can't believe it." Debbie Foster sat at the end of the counter. "All these years we lived on the same island as a monster. I mean, I had my suspicions about him all along, but, without proof, what could I do?"

Several nods went around from her seniors group. The encouragement appeared to fuel her need for attention. I re-filled their mugs with coffee.

"You're a hero, Debbie. If you and Evelyn hadn't gone forward, he might not be locked up where he belongs."

I fought the urge to roll my eyes

"I know Marygene is grateful." One of the old women, whose name I couldn't recall, placed a hand on my arm.

"Yes, ma'am. I do feel awful sorry for Teddy, though."

Sympathy nods went around from everyone except Debbie. She didn't seem to like for the attention to be shifted from her.

"We better keep an eye on him too. Like father like son, I say."

Nods again.

"Teddy is distraught. I don't think it's Christian to blame a son for his father's sins. Judge not lest ye be judged." And with that, I spun on my heels and went into the kitchen, thankful my shift was over.

As I waited for Betsy's last few tables to leave so she could end her shift, I sat in the office chatting with Jena Lynn. We'd been discussing Mr. Gaskin as well. "Not to change the subject so abruptly, but I wanted to get your take on me not rebuilding Mama's house."

Her fingers stilled on the keyboard, where she was plac-ing our weekly order. "What?"

"Well, you know I never intended to live there perma-nently anyway, and now that I have the opportunity to cash out and buy something else, I'm considering a beachfront fixer-upper."

Tears began to spill down her cheeks. I had no idea this would upset her so much. She wiped the mascara that had smudged under her eyes.

"Jena Lynn, what is it?"

She smiled through her tears. "Nothing and everything. I'm an emotional mess. I always saw one of us raising a family in that house, and if you aren't going to rebuild, that'll never happen."

Emotional mess? Family? "Jena Lynn, are you pregnant?"

Her face glowed through her tears, and I rushed to crush her in a bear hug. "That's wonderful news. If you want the property, rebuild the house, it's yours."

"You mean that?"

I released her. "Of course. I would have given it to you in the beginning if I'd known you wanted it."

"Well, Mama left it to you."

"So. We'll work something out. I only need enough cash to purchase something and a little to fix it up."

"Oh no. The cash settlement is all yours. I'm married to a contractor, remember. I'll even buy the land from you."

"Don't be stupid. You aren't buying it. I'll sign it over to you." I locked hands with my sister and did a little dance. "We're going to have a baby!"

Despite the forthcoming topic of discussion, there was a bounce in my step as Betsy and I left the diner to meet Yvonne. With unfolding events, this conversation was paramount.

Jena Lynn had sworn me to silence on the pregnancy news. She explained that it was still early and she didn't want to tell anyone until the second trimester, which was still a couple of weeks away. Originally, I'd planned on including her in our powwow, but with the revelation regarding her condition, I decided to spare her.

I rode with Betsy over to Yvonne's place of business. She pouted, clearly annoyed that I wouldn't give her a hint as to what we needed to discuss. I didn't want to go through it more than once.

She'd even gone so far as to stick out her bottom lip. "We're a team! Whatever you know, I should know."

"You will. Look, we're here already. It hasn't killed you to wait fifteen minutes. Jeez." I shut the car door and went up the stairs of the lovely Palmer house.

"It is killing me. You know I don't have any patience and like to be the first to know everything. It's my thing." She huffed a few steps behind me.

"Being nosy is your thing?" I smirked at her over my shoulder.

"Yeah!" She swung her arms as she marched. "Today's been a big day for news. Does it have anything to do with Mr. Gaskin?"

"Yes." I held the door open for her. "Along with Mama, Ms. Brooks, and Aunt Vi."

Betsy tilted toward me and her lips slightly parted. "Oh . . . juicy."

We hustled inside.

Twenty minutes later, we all sat in the library and I had laid it all out for my friends. Betsy and Yvonne sat holding their cups of coffee, staring blankly at me.

"I can see your mama doing this, but not mine. No offense." Yvonne took a sip from her mug.

"None taken." I understood her position. Her mama had been a doting and loving mother, supporting Yvonne at every stage.

"What do we do with this information?" Betsy wrapped her arms around herself.

"Nothing." I placed my mug on the coaster on the end table. "We have no evidence and, with Mr. Gaskin working for a funeral home, he'd know how to get rid of bodies and have access to the chemicals to destroy evidence." That fact was the reason I questioned his guilt in the twins' murder case. "No one ever filed a police report. They were nomads."

"They were human beings. People with lives." Yvonne briskly shook her head.

"Yes. And your mama is a person. And Aunt Vi is a person. Neither one should face charges for illegally disposing of a body." I'd had my own inner struggles. There wasn't any evidence. Even if we came forward, we had nothing of substance to report. "Let's be realistic here. What's there to report? Who would back up the claim? Mr. Gaskin isn't going to say anything. It would only hurt him. Plus, he claimed he loved Kayla and did it for her."

"So you think he's innocent?" Yvonne crossed her legs, swinging her foot while fiddling with her hands in her lap.

I shrugged. "He's guilty of a lot. As to those murders, I just don't buy it. But, I could be wrong."

"Well, I'm not going to worry about that." Yvonne uncrossed her legs. "And Marygene's right. There really isn't any way to substantiate the claim. It's absurd. If Kayla called Mr. Gaskin to"—she swallowed—"dispose of remains, the two of them would be at fault. All the others are simply guilty of foolishly keeping silent. They were practically kids anyway."

"So we're agreed, then. We won't speak of this again?" Betsy gave us a solid nod.

"I certainly won't. I have enough on my plate. I have to find a new assistant." Yvonne rubbed her forehead.

"I thought Candi was working out." I finished off the rest of my coffee.

"She turned in her notice. I've got two weeks to replace her."

"Well, at least she gave you notice. At the diner some employees are no-call no-shows." Betsy ran her fingers through her ponytail. Some waitstaff were notoriously unreliable. That's why when we had a good one, we tried to hang on to them.

"I guess. Izzy loves her, and, well, I assumed she hadn't any complaints about the job or at least she never voiced any. I hoped she'd be around for a while. Not that I don't understand. She said she'd come into some money and planned on moving to a more lively area. She's a city girl at heart." There was something about that girl that didn't seem quite right. I'd put a pin in it for now. Yvonne didn't need anything else to worry about. Besides, I hadn't anything solid to present, other than her odd behavior. And there was no law against that.

Betsy and I wished Yvonne luck, then Betsy dropped me by my car and I drove home to Aunt Vi's.

CHAPTER 28

When I pulled into the drive, I noticed the darkness in the house and the absence of Aunt Vi's car. I hoped she felt better. Reliving painful memories could rattle you for days. I had a box of peach rolls that I set on the table before opening the French doors to let the breeze in. The ocean sounds gave me a sense of calm. The uncontrollable power of the sea reminded me that something bigger than me, stronger than me, and infinitely more powerful existed.

I let out a long breath. Breathing here came easier. I held the salty air in my lungs and smiled. My phone rang and I stooped to scoop it from my bag on the love seat and hit the answer icon. "Hi, Doc Tatum."

"Hello, hon. How are you doing?"

"Fine." Confused why she'd be calling, I checked my calendar. "Oh shoot! I forgot to set up the snack table. Doc Tatum, I'm so sorry." Consumed with what'd been going on, it had completely slipped my mind.

"No, it's fine. No one expected you to keep that up after the fire."

Oh.

"I'm calling because I saw your father last night."

I cringed.

"I really think the two of you should talk."

"I appreciate your caring, I do, but this is between my father and me. Besides, I left him a voice mail days ago. He hasn't returned it."

Silence. "I didn't know that."

"Probably because he didn't tell you. When it suits him, Eddie has a way of keeping important facts to himself." I walked out onto the patio.

"He seemed so upset about the fight you two had. I mean, I understand this case has taken its toll and all, but his part is done now. I must admit, I'm confused as to why he didn't mention the call." The strong notion that this case was far from over reminded me about the shotgun my brother had insisted I take, which I'd placed in the coat closet next to the front door. Now I felt grateful to have it. Javy wouldn't be watching out for me like he had before.

"Well, thanks for understanding about the snacks. And for caring."

"If you need to talk, I'm here." She sounded confused but sincere.

"Thank you. We're lucky to have you in our lives."

"Why, thank you." I could hear she meant it. "I'll let you go now."

"Okay. I hope I didn't cause a rift between you two. I shouldn't have said that about him keeping secrets. I'm just upset. Ignore me. We'll work it out. We always do."

"I'm sure you will. Bye, dear." She ended the call.

The lights came on in the living room of the Sand Dollar. I needed a reason to pop over. I couldn't take the peach rolls, given Javy's aversion to anything that tasted good. I went through Aunt Vi's fridge. Beer, cheese, old pizza, Chinese takeout container, and oh look! Perfect.

Moving silently onto his patio, I tapped on the sliding glass door. When I got no response, I tapped harder. Then pounded. The door slid open with force. Javy still wore his uniform and didn't appear happy about my visit.

With my plastic smile in place, I waved. "Hi, you're home. I almost left."

"Is that why you beat on my door for a full two minutes? I was on a call."

"Sorry about that. I only wanted to drop by and bring you a welcome-to-the-island gift. I recalled that I hadn't done that yet and, with you being so far down on this end of the beach, I didn't think many of your neighbors would venture down to do so." I presented my offering with both hands.

He glanced and smirked. "Carrots."

"Organic carrots. It's the good stuff."

He picked up the bag and examined it precariously. He must have gotten a whiff because his nose crinkled. "I think they're past their prime."

"No, that's the organic you're smelling. I think they were grown in manure, organic manure, that is."

"There's mold on them."

"Oh well." I shrugged. "It's the thought that counts."

"Not much thought went into these." He lifted the lid on his outside trash bin and dropped them inside. They hit with a thud.

"It's all Aunt Vi had in her refrigerator that you would eat." I clasped my hands in front of me. "Aren't you going to invite me in?"

"Hadn't planned on it." He propped himself against the doorframe.

"Oh, come on!" I smacked his bicep playfully. "We're friends now. We were great in that interview."

"Being your friend almost got me fired." Gone was the man who had shown a little interest in me, and an ornery, suspicious man remained. I didn't blame him. He'd been sabotaged once. He wouldn't allow it to happen again.

I grimaced. "Sorry about that. I'll fall on my sword again if you'd like. I'll take the entire blame. Eddie will believe me too. He's not such a fan at the moment."

He studied me for a few long heartbeats. His stern expression softened, slightly. "No. Come in."

I ducked under his arm and took in his abode. There were no prints on the walls. A folding chair sat in the corner of the room and a small sofa against the wall. The kitchen right off the living room was dated but clean. This cottage had a similar floor plan to the Pelican. It sort of felt sterile, unlived in.

"Sit down."

I perched on the edge of the white leather sofa. He didn't strike me as a white leather kind of guy.

"The furniture was here when I moved in."

I guess my face showed my surprise. I nodded. "Ah. I hope they aren't charging you extra for it."

He plopped in the seat in the corner. It creaked under his weight. He wasn't amused.

"Did Eddie really nearly fire you?"

"Yes. And he forbade me or Alex to give you any information about the case." Not a surprise there. "Not that it matters. The case on the Dryer twins is closed. We have our guy."

"Is the department sure of that?"

He sat stoically, staring.

"Wow, taking Eddie's command literally." I clasped my hands in my lap. "Well, to me, it doesn't make sense. Mr. Gaskin has access to all sorts of chemicals. He runs a funeral parlor, for heaven's sake. If he were guilty, he could have found a way to get rid of their remains or would've sent them under another name to be cremated in Savannah. He couldn't have kept them in the funeral home all these years; his son would have found them."

"Maybe his son did but didn't realize what he saw. Killers rarely if ever make sense. I once had a case where a guy kept the tongues and eyeballs of his victims in a fish tank beside his bed."

My lips curled in disgust.

"And don't even get me started on gang members. One guy got caught because he made a necklace out of human ears. He wore it around his neck with pride." He shook his head.

He made a good point. Killers didn't always make the best judgment calls. If Mr. Gaskin killed them, then why did I feel so uneasy about it? Wouldn't the twins' spirits have moved on, since the killer had been brought to justice? God, where was Mama when I needed her? She'd know.

"You obviously knew that your dad cut you off. Why come to me? Why not go to Alex? You have a history with him."

"It's because of our history I didn't go to him. We both need a clean slate." I didn't exactly feel comfortable talking about Alex with him. Not that any of our issues were much of a secret any longer. Neither Alex nor I was known for our quiet demeanors.

"He still talks about you all the time."

Unsure of how to respond, I kept silent.

"I think he worries I might be interested in you."

My stomach flip-flopped.

"He said you two had been together since high school."

The fact that they talked about me had my palms sweating. "On again and off again."

"Off for good this time?" His question sent chills down my spine.

I shrugged. "We're in two completely different places in life. He's never been married or dealt with a divorce. Granted, my issues run a little deeper than that. He supported me through rough times." I gave him a sad smile. "Trust is a big issue with me." I glanced away.

"Divorce is something that alters you. Makes you wary of moving forward. Especially if your ex *es muy loca*."

When I glanced up, he cracked a smile.

All the air seemed to be sucked from the room. He scrutinized me in a way no one else ever had. As if he wanted to peel my skin away and see what made me, well, me. My heart began to race in an uncomfortable way.

Abruptly, I stood. "I better go. I don't want to get you fired."

He stood as well but made no move toward me and said nothing to stop me.

"Marygene."

I paused with my hand on the door.

"Thanks for the carrots."

"You're welcome. Maybe next time I'll bring you some edible ones."

CHAPTER 29

Teddy came into the diner the next day. The hush that came over the folks eating shouldn't have surprised me. It had. Poor Teddy looked terrible. He'd lost weight and his face was gaunt, with giant bags under his eyes. I poured him a cup of coffee and slid it in front of him.

"Thanks."

Whispers were just loud enough to make their way over to us. "How can he even show his face around here anymore? If it were me, I'd move away. I'm not going to use that funeral home anymore. I don't care if it's the only one on the island."

Teddy started to rise.

I grabbed his hand and smacked a serving tray down on the counter. The sound popped loudly and the diner went silent. "What is wrong with you people? Can't y'all see this man is in pain?"

Several gazes swung toward me. Others didn't have the guts. Good. I was beyond fed up.

I pointed to the table at the back corner. "Mr. Davis! Weren't you saying the other day how Teddy let you make payments on your late wife's funeral expenses? Even cut you a deal because you'd let the life insurance policy lapse."

He ducked his head in shame.

"Miss Sally, didn't Teddy bury yours and Miss Glenda's Yorkies in the cemetery?"

"He sure did," Miss Sally said proudly.

Her sister nodded in unison. "He even created a pet cemetery and now provides services for those of us with fur babies." She glanced lovingly in Teddy's direction. "He was so kind to us. Let us pay whatever we could afford."

Our new waitress Rebecca chimed in. Her usual quiet demeanor fell away. "This man was a godsend when my sister, Lizzy, lost her baby prematurely." Her voice cracked. "Our family doesn't have much money, and Teddy allowed my daddy to trade in lieu of payment. He never treated us any differently neither, and allowed us the privacy we needed in order to grieve."

A few tears were shed then. I smiled down at my friend.

Teddy became visibly uncomfortable, shifting in his seat and taking quick sips from his mug.

Sam, who'd apparently overheard the commotion, came out with two tall stacks of pecan pancakes. I took them and set them in front of Rita, who was dining with her sister, Nita.

Sam glared over the heads of the diners. "Teddy was born and raised on this island, like most of you." His metal spatula roamed over the dining room. "This island has seen its fair share of troubles and tragedies since the first settlers arrived. And one thing that has held us together as a community was that we stuck together. In good times and bad."

A chorus of agreements went up.

Poppy, who'd been eating down at the end of the counter, gazed at my brother, starry-eyed. He was pretty great.

"Now I believe I speak for my sister and Jena Lynn here

when I say we have the right to refuse service to those who attack others when they're down-and-out."

I nodded firmly in agreement. Jena Lynn, who'd just come out of the kitchen a moment ago, wiped her hands on a towel and jutted out her chin, signaling to the crowd that we were all on the same page.

"I'd be careful making those kinds of threats, boy." An old man in the back stood. "Folks round here don't care for ultimatums. I'll be eating my breakfasts at home from now on."

"That's your prerogative," I said calmly.

He dropped a few bucks on the table and strode out the front door. We waited to see how Sam's statement impacted the remaining diners. When no one else made a move for the door, we considered the situation handled.

Smoke came billowing from the service window. "Shoot!" Sam rushed back around the corner to put out the small grease fire.

Teddy rose and walked out the door. Confused, I whispered to Rebecca to check my tables for coffee. She rounded the counter, coffeepot in hand, while I chased after Teddy. The tingling of the bell above the door sounded a little rougher than usual.

"Teddy, wait!"

He didn't even slow his charge across the street toward his car.

I gave chase before checking oncoming traffic. A large pickup truck honked and I froze.

The driver shouted, "Watch it!"

"Sorry!" I held up a hand before continuing after my friend.

When I caught up to him, he had already slid into his car and started the engine. "Wait! I don't understand."

His face held a flurry of emotions as I tapped on the window.

"I'm sorry if we embarrassed you. We were only trying to help. Those people in there needed to be reminded of who you are."

His knuckles were white on the steering wheel. I readied myself to jump back if he decided to peel out of the space. Relief overtook me when he finally rolled down the window.

"I'm a quiet, private person. I don't like attention, and I don't want yours or anyone else's pity." His teeth were clenched as he stared straight ahead.

"I get that. This is your home. You should be allowed to go wherever you please without hearing gossip."

"I just want to be left alone. I'm up to my eyeballs in attorney's fees. My dad won't say anything. He still won't see me. I have no idea what is going on except for what I can get from his attorney."

"He didn't confess to the murders, did he?"

Teddy shook his head. "He has to ride the rap for the theft in Atlanta. It was a dumb crime a kid would commit. He stole copper out of some old buildings, with friends. Somebody got hurt during the robbery." He turned and faced me then. His eyes were softer now, pleading. "It would do him some good if you could speak up on his behalf on the arson charge."

I stepped back and bit the inside of my cheek.

"I know it's a lot to ask. Consider it, will ya? You said you spoke to him. Encouraged me to hire a better attorney."

"Teddy, I—"

"Please, consider it." The poor man was on the verge of tears.

I nodded. "I will. I'll consider it."

A sort of peace seemed to rush over him. Maybe he felt like he'd done something for his dad.

"Please don't be a stranger. I'm still your friend."

As he pulled away, I held up a hand, stepped up on the grassy curb, and stared across the street toward my diner and its glossy peach sign. The diner had seen all sorts of crazy island catastrophes. Still, it stood and beckoned folks to come in for some comfort food and a nice friendly chat.

"I want you to leave that boy alone." Eddie's stern voice from behind me caused me to jump.

"What?"

"I mean it, Marygene. He's been through a lot and you pestering him about details regarding the cold case isn't good for him. We need our coroner clearheaded and ready to work."

I blinked and looked into my father's face. His glare held the stern command. Anger boiled my blood.

"What's going on with you?"

He appeared conflicted.

"You have no idea what we were talking about. He's my friend. I have every right to check on him." I waited for an explanation. An apology would have been nice too. When neither came, I turned my back and stalked across the street and got back to work.

My nerves raged like a hurricane. Something was off about Eddie.

Yvonne called later that evening. She'd made the mistake of asking her mama, while lucid, about the hippie movement, referencing the bodies in a tactful way. Her mama became increasingly agitated, and Doc Tatum had to be called to the retirement community.

"I'm so sorry." I languidly enjoyed a glass of wine out on the patio.

Aunt Vi, now recovered, had her newly organized book club inside, and I didn't want to intrude. I had a sneaking

suspicion the club might have more to do with the signa-
ture cocktails she created for each title they planned to read
than the books themselves.

"It's my own fault. I should have let it lie." The call
went silent, and I guessed she needed a sip from her own
glass of wine. We had these wine chats often. "I had a hard
time picturing my straitlaced mama participating in any
sort of hippie movement. She described it as a variation of
the movement. That it wasn't like Woodstock. She and her
group had modified their chapter to something more suitable. Suitable, Marygene! Dancing naked around a fire
while smoking isn't my mama."

I laughed. "Sorry. That visual you painted tickled me."

We both snickered a little then.

"She's doing better now, though. Doc Tatum said she'd
call in new meds. She believes this new drug they've been
testing holds great promise."

"That's great."

"So, tell me about Eddie."

I'd briefly mentioned him before I heard that she needed
to spill first.

I blew out a frustrated breath. "He's all bitter and angry
with me. He's forbidden Alex and Javy from talking to me
about the case, and he made it perfectly clear he wants me
to give his coroner a wide berth. Teddy and I were friends
before he became one of Eddie's minions. I'm trying to
help Teddy."

"Well, it sounds like y'all did a good job setting expec-
tations at the diner."

"Yeah. Sam made me proud."

"*You* made me proud."

I heard the smile across the line.

"Thanks." Then I told her about the decision to look for
properties and that Jena Lynn wanted to rebuild and move
into the house. I left out the part about the family. That was

Jena Lynn's big news, not mine. I'd not been around a lot of babies in my life, and the idea of having one close thrilled me. I wasn't sure I was the mothering type. Especially with the island spirit nonsense I had to deal with. But an aunt, that I could totally do.

"That's wonderful news! Please let me help you. I have a listing agent I work with. She's great too. You'll love her. She knows the market and gets amazing deals for her clients. Want me to have her call you?"

"That'd be great!" Excitement at the prospect of a new beginning began to fill me. Well, that and the wine.

"Have you thought about the style you want to decorate in?"

"Nope. I'll leave that to you."

She squealed. "As much as you love the outdoors, we should definitely consider bringing the outdoors inside. Sliding pocket doors would be perfect. They're all glass and allow you to extend the outdoor living space into the main part of the house. All that light, Marygene. Imagine cooking in your open Southern-chic kitchen decked out with the most gorgeous Viking range while having a spectacular view of the ocean."

The constant sound of the crashing waves and the salty air swirling around me while I tested recipes in a beautiful kitchen sounded like heaven. I told her so.

"So, we'll be looking for a kitchen with a house attached to it."

"You know me so well." I brought the glass to my lips.

A strong disturbance in the air forced me to drop my glass. It shattered against the stone patio. I shrieked.

Mama appeared, her face full of terror.

"Send Yvonne over to Thelma! Now!"

"What?"

"Do it!" Mama's mouth continued to move, but no other words were audible.

What was going on? That's when it hit me. She'd broken more rules.

"Marygene, are you there! What's wrong?"

I stood, avoiding the glass on the ground. "Yvonne, I want you to listen to me and not freak out."

"You're scaring me."

"How much wine have you had?"

"Not even a glass. What's going on?"

I walked off the patio and grounded myself with my bare toes in the sand. "You need to get over to Sunset Hills now. Call on your way over and have a nurse go and check on your mama."

"I don't understand."

"And you don't have to. Do you trust me?"

"Y . . . yes. You know I do."

"Then hang up now and call. Once you've taken care of your mama, call me back. Okay?"

Dead silence on the other end.

"Yvonne! This is serious! Okay?"

"I'm going now!" The line went dead, and I started to pray.

CHAPTER 30

Time moved at the pace of pouring molasses. For the past several hours, I'd walked up and down the beach to not upset Aunt Vi. She'd had enough to deal with. The way I saw it, unless I knew something for certain, there wasn't any need in alarming anyone else.

When I finally did receive word, it didn't come from Yvonne. "Okay. I'm a believer," came Javy's accented voice across the line.

Uh-oh. That meant Yvonne had told the authorities I alerted her to the danger.

Not willing to admit to anything, I asked, "How's Ms. Brooks?"

"She's in a coma. You saved her life."

No, Mama saved her life.

"Yvonne is with her. Sadly, this isn't only about her. Two other residents were sent to the hospital. One DOA and the other they're not sure if she'll make it. She has a heart condition."

I gripped the phone tightly as I fought to regain control of my vocal cords. "What happened?"

"Her medication was changed and she had some sort of bad reaction with something she took with it. The other residents apparently had the same cocktail."

"Oh my God."

"Doc Tatum has been called. Apparently she made a mistake or the pharmacy did."

That didn't sound like Doc Tatum.

"Your dad is signaling me. I just thought you should know."

"Thank you."

A few minutes later, Yvonne's picture showed up on my iPhone. I slowed my breathing before answering. "Hey. How's your mom?"

"I nearly lost her. The doctor said that if I had called a couple minutes later, it would have been too late." I could hear the thickness in her tone.

"I'm getting dressed right now. You're not sitting with her alone."

"Thank you. Just you though, okay. We're in the ICU. I'll inform the nurses that you're family and they'll buzz you in."

"I'll be there as fast as I can."

The spaces in the parking lot of Bay Memorial were mostly unoccupied at midnight. I'd talked to Mama the entire forty-five-minute drive over. Unsure if she could hear me or not, I decided I'd chance it anyway. The pertinent people were notified regarding Ms. Brooks's condition before I left the house. The responsibility shouldn't fall on Yvonne's shoulders. I left telling Aunt Vi to Betsy.

Jena Lynn switched my off days. A Saturday at the diner without me could be rough on her. I'd stressed my concerns regarding her condition, but she'd assured me all was well.

My eyes were closed as I sought comforting words to offer my friend during her time of crisis. When the elevator doors opened on the appropriate floor, I was careful not to crush the paper cups in my hands containing coffee from the vending machine. As I turned the corner down the long corridor, I spied Alex discussing something with Javier. Neither one of them had seen me yet. If they were here, then perhaps this wasn't ruled as an accident. And if that were true, then surely they had ruled Doc Tatum out. If it had been her mistake, a deputy wouldn't be stationed outside the ICU.

Both men's heads lifted at the same time. I'd been seen.

Javy said something to Alex, then strode toward me, pausing briefly. "You okay?"

I swallowed and forced a nod. "Eddie has y'all standing guard?"

"Upon requests of the families, yeah. We're rotating out, hoping that our presence will give the grieving and ill a sense of security. We've coordinated with the onsite security, which isn't any better than mall cops anyway. We're making sure no one gets through without a badge or okay from a family member."

That made sense.

Javy touched my shoulder when my attention wandered toward the double doors ahead. "I've got to go and meet the sheriff. We've got to get this guy."

I swallowed. My insides churned with the mere idea of the type of person it would take to commit this sort of crime.

"I meant what I said on the phone. You have a gift."

The gift comment threw me. I'd always considered it more as an affliction. Yet, today, it saved my friend's mother.

He gave me a small smile before he glanced over his shoulder at Alex, who watched us like a hawk. "I'll see ya."

"Yeah, okay." I shuffled forward.

"I'm glad you're here." Alex greeted me. "Yvonne is beside herself."

"Understandably. How did this happen?" I studied his face.

Alex put both his hands on his duty belt. "We're trying to sort it out. If Yvonne hadn't called to check in on her mom before bed, she wouldn't even be here right now."

"I'm so glad she did."

We both glanced toward the closed doors to the ICU wing, where Ms. Brooks and another Sunset Hill resident lay, fighting for their lives.

"Are they in danger?"

"I can't go into it all, but the lethal combination given to Ms. Brooks and, um, another resident doesn't appear to have been an accident. And Doc Tatum didn't authorize the prescriptions they took."

My mouth went slack.

"We could be looking at one of those angel-of-mercy killers." Alex put his hand on my shoulder.

"Oh my God."

His phone chirped. "That'll be the sheriff."

"Okay. I need to be with Yvonne anyway." I started for the door and paused. "Alex."

He turned. His handsome face still made my heart rate speed up a little and I supposed always would. "I'm glad you're here too."

He rewarded me with one of his lopsided smiles. "I'll tell you a secret." He lowered his tone, closing the distance between us. "I took the first shift because I knew you'd be here." His lips brushed my forehead. The simplest of gestures, yet we both shivered.

My life was a mess.

A kind nurse dressed in pink scrubs noticed my hands were full and opened the door to Ms. Brooks's room for me. Yvonne sat next to her mama, holding her hand. A lump developed in my throat. "She looks so peaceful, doesn't she?" Yvonne's voice was thick with emotion.

I placed the paper cups on the small table next to her sleeping mama and pulled a chair over next to the bed. They had tubes sticking out of her. Her skin was pale and devoid of natural human color. Monitors beeped and pumps hissed.

"Yes, she does," I lied.

Yvonne needed to believe that and she was allowed.

"You saved her life. How did you know?" Yvonne's tearstained face filled with questions.

"You ever have one of those weird feelings about something? Like, you left an appliance on or a person you met has something dreadfully wrong with them?" I struggled to explain. All those thing were true about me.

She thought for a moment, still stroking her mama's blue-veined hand. "You mean like when Mama says she's got a chill because someone walked over her grave or an angel is whispering in her ear?"

"More like when we used to laugh at my nanny when she said she knew when something bad brewed. Or they better watch out for this or that fella."

Nanny had been right about things on more occasions than we could count. Then though, I'd rationalized it away.

"I sort of remember. Well, whatever gave you the feeling that I needed to check in was a blessing."

Mama stood over her old friend, stroking her hair. This time, however, she didn't appear fully corporeal.

I only managed to make out her outline. "Yes. A blessing indeed."

Mama smiled at me. "Trust your instincts, sweetheart. They'll guide you to the truth."

I raised my eyebrows in question, but Mama had turned her attention back to Ms. Brooks.

"The nurse who works nights, who took a liking to

Mama, told me she'd been a little agitated after her bath. The other ladies who were brought in to the hospital with her are her friends. The ones she confided in about Kayla and Pamela." She wiped the tears from her cheeks. "I never should have put her in there."

I squeezed her arm. "Stop. She knows you love her. You didn't do this to her."

"I know." Yvonne sniffed.

"Has the doctor given you any news?"

"Which ones? Three came in at different times once she'd been stabilized and moved into the ICU."

"Any, all."

"The next twenty-four hours will be crucial. She'll either wake up or she won't. She has brain waves, so that's a good sign."

"She'll make it." Mama's voice whooshed around me like the whispers of angels.

"She's going to be okay." I wrapped my arm around my friend. "We're going to pray and have everyone we know pray. Your mama is a fighter. She won't leave you yet."

Yvonne sobbed on my shoulder. I did something that I hadn't done in a very long time. I prayed aloud for my friend and her mama and gave thanks to the heavenly Father for protecting her, and silently for Mama.

The nurse shooed me out of the room at three a.m. I paused by the doors when I caught the profile of someone familiar in pink scrubs. She looked familiar, but I couldn't place her. After another double take at the girl's long black hair, I gave up on figuring it out. She saw me, ducked her head, and rushed into the room beside Ms. Brooks. Her reaction struck me as odd.

"Miss," the heavyset nurse who had made me leave a few moments ago said. "You really do have to leave now."

"Yes, of course. I thought I saw someone I knew is all."
She hit the square silver pad on the wall and the double
doors that secured the ICU wing opened. As I walked
through them, I chalked up the whole ordeal to fatigue.

Alex was slumped in the chair against the wall. He
looked so sweet and peaceful when he slept. I walked over
and brushed a curl from his head. He jumped. His eyes
went wide. "Oh God! I fell asleep."

"It's okay. I'm heading down to the cafeteria to get
some coffee. You want some?"

He stretched and nodded.

A loud whirling sound came from the other side of the
doors. "Code blue!" was being shouted. My heart went into
my throat. Could Mama have been wrong?

Alex leapt to his feet and hit the call button on the door
and shouted his creds to the woman on the other end. Petrified, I held on to his arm. When the doors swung open, I
rushed in behind him. A flurry of movement went on. Several carts were being wheeled into the room next to Ms.
Brooks. Nurses and doctors swarmed. It all happened as if
in slow motion.

Yvonne stumbled from her mother's room to see what
was going on. I rushed to her side.

"That's Ms. Frances Harris's room."

I intuited that to mean Ms. Brooks's friend. The two of
us huddled together, waiting to see if the poor woman
could be saved.

When the room went silent, wails of agony took the
place of the machines. Tears streamed down cheeks. My
heart broke for the family. A man came bursting from the
room yelling for Deputy Myers.

Yvonne had been allowed to go back in her mother's
room. I was sent out again. I waited in the chair Alex vacated during the commotion and still sat there when Javy
arrived. I'd spent that time pondering the events. I started

to put pieces together. If the son or grandson called for Alex, they must suspect foul play. The girl I saw kept sticking out in my mind. I couldn't swear one hundred percent, but she favored Candi. But how could that be?

Before I could speak to Javy, Eddie arrived. Too numb to care if he yelled at me for being here or not, I sat staring at the sterile white tile flooring. Alex came out then with the man who had called for him.

"Y'all were supposed to be keeping her safe!" The short, stocky man's voice sounded ragged. "Some nurse no one seems to know came into her room and switched out her IV bag. A few minutes later, she flatlined!"

"Calm down, Mr. Harris. We're going to get to the bottom of this." Eddie's tone came out low, yet firm. This was bad. "What did she look like, this nurse?"

Javy had his pad out, ready to take notes.

"She was small and thin with long black hair. Her name tag read Cindy. The staff says there isn't a nurse named Cindy in the ICU. Now, she's . . . she's gone." The man broke down crying.

Alex put his hand on the man's shoulder, but he shoved it off.

"Are you sure about the description?" Eddie asked calmly.

"Yes, I'm sure. Damn sure," he choked out angrily.

"I saw her." It came out in a gasp. When no one seemed to hear me, I managed to say it a bit louder. "I saw her."

All gazes whirled around to me.

"When I left Yvonne's room, I saw the girl he's describing. And I think I know who she is."

CHAPTER 31

The hospital went on shutdown. No one in and no one out. I sat in a little room in the hospital security office, watching footage on three monitors with Javy and Eddie. Next to me sat Mr. Harris. Eddie got a phone call and stepped from the room. A minute later, he called Javy out and when Eddie came back in, Javy wasn't with him.

My eyes were tired, but I stayed glued to that screen. I wanted this girl caught and Ms. Brooks safe. A flash of the profile I saw caught my eye. "That's her!" I pointed to the screen.

"She's right! That's the woman."

She exited the elevator on the ICU floor. She walked right past Alex, who slept propped against the wall, and had been easily admitted by a hospital staff member. *Scary.*

"Your deputy fell asleep!" Mr. Harris roared. "My mother is dead because your stupid deputy fell asleep! I'm going to sue your whole department."

"I understand your anger. If I could get you to refocus on the screen for a minute to give us an identification of the woman you saw, we want to apprehend her and get justice for your mother."

The rolling chair went flying as Mr. Harris stood. "I told you she's the nurse."

The technician had frozen the angle of the partial profile on the screen once the subject entered the ICU unit.

He pointed to the screen one last time. "That's. Her." He stormed from the room.

Eddie rubbed the back of his neck. He hadn't said a word to me yet, other than asking what I'd seen.

I turned back to the screen. "Can you zoom in closer? Or maybe find a better angle?" I asked the young tech whose facial expression showed pure shock.

"I can try." He went through the footage and we managed to get a decent angle of her exiting the ICU. She went right past me. With all the commotion, I'd not even seen her. She'd done a decent job of hiding her face from the cameras until she made the mistake of glancing back at Yvonne.

"There! Stop!"

The image froze.

"I think that's Yvonne's assistant Candi."

"Are you sure?" Eddie asked.

"Fairly positive. She's wearing a wig. Obviously, I can't be one hundred percent, but if you search the rest of the footage, I bet you'll find her other places in the hospital. There might be an even better angle to get a clearer image." I sat back in the chair.

"Did Yvonne say they were at odds? Perhaps she was a disgruntled employee?" Eddie put his hand on the doorknob.

I shook my head. "Candi turned in her notice. Said something about coming into some money. I don't see any reason why she would do this to Ms. Brooks or the other women." It didn't add up. "I don't know. All I can say is that girl"—I pointed to the screen—"looks an awful lot like

Candi. I don't even know her last name." I slumped in my chair, put my elbows on the desk, and shoved my fingers through my hair.

"Print that image for me and send a JPEG to my cell. Then send the entire footage over to the Peach Cove Sheriff's Department." He handed the tech his card.

He nodded and began completing his task. This had been an exciting night for the security tech. His eyes were wide as saucers.

Eddie touched me on the arm before he opened the door. I forced myself upright and willed my legs to move. Why would Candi do this? Then a thought occurred to me. What if the money she came into was for performing a task? The task of getting rid of the last remaining islanders with information on the twins' death. A shot of adrenaline pumped through my veins as we entered the elevator. I glanced over at Eddie. He stared straight at the doors. We still weren't sharing. Got it. I was sure Eddie had figured out that the shutdown happened too late. The murderer had fled.

Helplessness overwhelmed me. I wanted to help. Eddie wasn't having it.

"What are you hiding?" I whispered low.

He heard me, I could tell by the rigidity of his posture. Stubbornly, he said nothing.

It took two hours for the hospital to resume some semblance of normal activity. I'd been sitting in the closed cafeteria. I didn't feel right leaving Yvonne alone, even though they would no longer allow anyone other than her into her mother's room. The best option for us both was for me to be a few floors below. Betsy called at five a.m. I'd been dozing with my head on my arm.

I jerked upright and wiped the drool from my cheek. Yuck. "Hello." I cleared my throat.

"I'm on my way into the diner to help Jena Lynn open

and you won't believe what I just saw!" When Betsy got
excited, her voice sped up so fast, I had a hard time understanding her.

"Slow down!"

"Sorry. Three cups of coffee talking. I saw Mrs. Gentry
getting out of the back seat of Javier's cruiser. Mayor Bill
followed behind in his car. And from what I could see, he
was fuming mad. He stomped up those steps with a purpose."

"Was she in cuffs?"

"Not that I could tell. But why else would she be at the
sheriff's department this early in the morning if they didn't
suspect her of trying to off Ms. Brooks?"

My hand went to my mouth. "Why would she do something like that? They're friends. Or were."

"I have no idea. How's Ms. Brooks doing?"

"She's still in a coma, but I think she'll pull through.
Mama says so anyway. Bets, all hell broke loose a few
hours ago."

"Tell me."

I gave her the short version of what had transpired.

"Sweet baby Moses. Marygene. Be careful."

"Promise. Call you after your shift."

How did this all fit? *Think.* Were they separate crimes or
could they possibly be linked? How did Candi fit into all of
this? If she did. As tired as I was, how could I be sure about
anything?

My thoughts drifted back to Mr. Gaskin. He claimed innocence for the murders but admitted his guilt for his other
crimes, including setting fire to my house. My phone
chirped. It was a number I recognized. Roy Calhoun.

**Are you okay? I'm outside the hospital with the rest of
the vermin lol. I'm getting strange information from a
nurse on the inside.**

I replied. **I'm okay. I'm in the cafeteria.**

The little dots that showed he was typing kept beginning then disappearing. It wasn't like Calhoun to be indecisive. Finally his text came through.

See you in five.

Calhoun took a seat at the table opposite me. "After I got the call from my nephew, I drove nonstop to get here."

"You left your nephew behind to snoop?" That sounded like Calhoun. The young man didn't look old enough to be a reporter and could slip in and out of places asking questions without attracting much attention. "Smart."

"When does this cafeteria officially open?"

I'd been sitting here in the dark. "Supposedly at six a.m." I'd come in and taken up residence at a table in the back anyway. My coffee, or sludge, came from a vending machine. Along with my breakfast. I passed the half-eaten bag of M&M's across the table.

He took a few from the bag and popped them into his mouth.

"What do you know?" I asked.

"If I share, will you tell me if you were there or not? When it went down." He was all business.

"I can tell you I was there and that I am an eyewitness."

His face held sympathy, but he couldn't hide the glint in his eyes. A good story always excited Calhoun. He leaned in closer. "From my inside source, the old woman was intravenously given embalming fluid."

I blinked several times and then shook my head. "What?"

"The IV bag that contained saline was switched with a bag containing a mixture of formaldehyde, glutaraldehyde, and methanol. With her bad heart, it killed her in minutes."

The sheer horror of his statement made me physically ill. I thought I might be sick. "Who told you that?" I gasped.

He leaned back and gave me his *I can't reveal a source*

look. If what he was saying was true, the only person I knew with access to embalming fluid was Teddy. Could he have snapped? The gossip floating around the diner about *watching out for that one* and the *like father like son* comments came rushing back. Surely not!

Could Teddy have known all along about his father? Maybe even helped him with the bodies? But why would he do something like this?

I needed more information. I pulled out my phone.

"What is it?"

I held up my finger, signaling he should wait, and typed the twins' names into Google and sought out any old news articles relating to the case. I found none. Then I typed Dryer into Facebook and searched with the criteria location of Savannah. Several popped up. I copied and pasted several names into Google and searched. I got a hit.

Amelia Dryer had made a statement to the press regarding the discovery of her distant relatives' bodies. She basically enjoyed her moment in the spotlight, not having any relevant information. What did stand out in the article, though, was the mention of her mother and how she dealt with the news that her cousins' remains had been located. According to the article, the twins had lived with her parents a short while. I needed to have a word with this woman.

I showed him the article I found with the name of the twins' cousin who lived in Savannah. "Could you find her?"

"Of course." He slid my phone back to me. "What can you give me? The identity of the fake nurse?"

I weighed out the pros and cons. "No. I can't give you that. The image I viewed wasn't clear enough for a positive identification. And divulging who it may be could jeopardize the investigation. But I can give you something."

He folded his hands on the table and waited.

"Mrs. Gentry is being questioned at the station."

He laced his fingers behind his head and stretched. "She's the office manager at Doc·Tatum's general practice, correct?"

I nodded.

"The mother of the man who was at your house when it burned down. The mayor's wife?"

I nodded again.

"I might be able to do something with that."

"Leave Junior out of it, though. I mean, don't say anything nasty about him."

"Okay. I'll get you the address. I'm going to hang around and see if I can get my source to give up more information. This island has become a good source of revenue for my paper." He stood. "I'll text you when I have the information. I don't want anyone who knows you to see us together, and that Hispanic deputy just arrived to change shifts with your ex; a little bird told me he had a major foul-up in this case."

Too tired to keep my face blank, I frowned. "You know everything, don't you?" My tone came out flat.

He made a fist and tapped my chin with it. It felt like a friendly gesture. "Like I told you before, I'm good at my job. Plus, that one was an easy one. The family is talking to anyone who will listen. I appreciate your being straight with me."

CHAPTER 32

The media frenzy outside the hospital made it nearly impossible for me to make it to my car. After I checked in on Yvonne, who, I'd been told, had fallen asleep beside her mom, I left word with the front desk of the ICU to have Yvonne call with any news and that I'd be back soon. She'd be aware they wouldn't allow me in, but she could come out if need be.

Aunt Vi was out when I got to Pelican Cottage. I checked Mr. Wrigley's food and water, gave him a scratch behind the ears, took a long, hot shower, then crashed for several hours. Aunt Vi came home while I slept, leaving a note on the fridge that instructed me to eat. It read, *Don't worry. I didn't cook.* Aunt Vi couldn't boil eggs, much less cook anything. A large wrapped sub sat on the top shelf of the refrigerator, along with a tub of potato salad and a container of banana pudding. Thank you, Aunt Vi! I turned and shrieked when I saw Alex asleep on the love seat. His disheveled appearance was an indication of our night.

He startled awake.

"What are you doing here?" I set my food on the table.

He sat up and scrubbed his face with his hands. "I couldn't go home, with the media and all. Eddie's putting me on desk duty, and I needed to crash someplace."

"Well, you can't stay here. Go stay with Betsy."

"Why?"

"Why?" I sounded incredulous to my own ears. "Alex, you know why. We're on a break, edging the fine line of permanent."

He glanced away. "What if I don't want it to be permanent?"

"What if pigs fly? I don't know. Life is beyond crazy right now for both of us. We need to deal with our current situations before we even begin to delve into our mess of a relationship."

He threw his legs off the sofa; his bare feet landed on the floor with a thud. He rested his elbows on his knees as his fingers plunged into his mess of hair. "I'm in deep trouble and needed to be close to you." He glanced up. "I thought it was, you know, our usual kind of fight. That this tragic situation would make us see that our problems weren't . . . problems."

"That's childish thinking, and I'm not a child anymore. Sure, in the grand scheme of things, what's happening now is on a different level entirely. But, honey, we can't fall back on each other because it's convenient and then live as if we're teenagers without commitment when life settles down."

"You want something serious now? To what, settle down and start a family?" His face became a picture of panic.

I smiled. "I'm not saying I'm ready to marry again or if I'll ever be. I'm taking life one day at a time. What I do want is something more stable. I need that."

"I can do stable."

"You're rushing to say that because you need me now. What happens when you don't? You like playing the field and having fun, and that's okay."

He stood. "That's not true."

I held up my hand, traffic-director style. "Let's put a pin in this, please. There's a murderer out there, and our friend's mother is fighting for her life. There's a man we've known our entire lives being indicted for a murder I'm not sure he committed, and now his son might be being framed."

"You think Mr. Gaskin is innocent? That's preposterous. Teddy has been behaving erratically since his dad's extradition. Not that I blame the poor guy, but it does appear suspicious." Sure, Teddy was having a hard time, but still the idea that he could be involved in a murder didn't feel right. Maybe I simply didn't want to believe it.

"What about Candi? Have they found her?"

"We don't know if that woman is Candi, and not since I last heard." He checked his watch and shoved his feet into his boots. "You're right. I shouldn't have showed up and dumped more on you. I've got to get to the office anyway."

"Is Mrs. Gentry being questioned?"

He blew out a breath. "Who told you?"

"Betsy saw Javier bringing her in."

"Eddie will be pissed off if he finds out I'm telling you anything." He buttoned up his shirt. "What the hell. You seem to find things out anyway. Yeah. Evelyn Gentry overstepped her position as receptionist. She admits to using Lindy's log-in to send updated prescriptions to their patients at Sunset Hills. Mrs. Gentry claims she was only trying to help. They were closing up and Lindy had a patient emergency. She sent in the wrong prescriptions that seemed to be too perfectly lethal when matched with the Valium someone gave the victims at the hospital."

Oh my God. Poor Doc Tatum.

His phone rang. "Sheriff." He grabbed his belt and flung

it on. Holstered his weapons and said, "Okay. I'll be there in fifteen," and disconnected the call.

I waited.

"Ms. Brooks is stable. A private security firm has been hired to watch over her at the mayor's expense." Alex put his hands on his hips and appeared lost in thought.

Everyone would know the mayor did that because of Alex's mistake and the heat the mayor feared he'd receive. It'd be the mayor's only way to exercise damage control. That and offer compensation, which I wouldn't be surprised if he had or would do soon.

"We're okay, right? I mean as much as we can be? I couldn't bear it if you hated me. Eddie let Lucy go anyway. She got a job at the credit union."

I opened my mouth to stop him, to tell him that his caring about her employment status said something.

"Please, let me get this out. I was in the wrong. I admit that to you. I need us to be okay, on some level."

That had been tough for him, and I decided that what went on between him and Lucy no longer mattered. And he had a lot to deal with moving forward. I wouldn't add to his load. With a sigh, I wrapped my arms around him. He crushed me tightly against him. We stood there in silence for a long moment.

"We're okay. Now go. Eddie needs you."

After I ate I called Yvonne, but it went straight to voice mail. I left a message and decided to go into town. I felt confident the new security detail wouldn't let me on the ICU floor anyway. Still, I needed to do something for my friend, to find the one responsible. If Mrs. Gentry still remained a guest, courtesy of the Peach Cove Sheriff's Department, the island would be abuzz with information. Secrets were hard to keep on a small island, which was why I'd been so surprised to find out about the twins and the activities of the senior generation. Something inside me told me all of this was linked somehow. And Mama had instructed me to trust my instincts. She'd been right about everything thus far.

When I pulled into the only empty space I could find, way down at the end of the square near the municipal building, I spotted who I thought could be Eddie. His head bobbed around as if he was really telling someone off. Curiosity spiked.

Slowly, I made my way around the giant hedges that separated the municipal park and the public green space. It *was* Eddie! And Mayor Bill!

I crouched down way out of sight and listened.

"I won't be strong-armed, Bill!"

My heart thudded against my chest.

"This has to play out legally. Evelyn isn't going to be charged. And there'll be no record, so be grateful for that."

"Grateful!" Mayor Bill bellowed. "You know this island, the rumors. It took us nearly ten years to stop the swirling vicious gossip surrounding the disappearance of those Dryer twins."

I froze and my legs felt weak.

Eddie barked, "You assured me the case would never come back to bite us. Now look! I've got to deal with the bodies and a case that's practically been spitballed together."

I covered my mouth to prevent the bile from rising from my stomach.

"Now someone is going after Thelma Brooks, not to mention the two deceased seniors. Thelma knows something, Bill! Her mind is able to put the pieces together yet."

"It's the DA's problem now, not ours. I want a public press release with an apology to Evelyn, or life will get mighty uncomfortable for you, Eddie. And whoever is making my life a living hell and costing me an arm and a leg in security detail better be found and charged. Keep that idiot deputy on desk duty too or he's gone. We can't afford another foul-up."

"You better watch yourself, Bill. Don't tell me how to run my department or my deputies."

"I'll do whatever I damn well please. And another thing, you keep that girl of yours away from my boy. He's got some cockeyed notion he's supposed to protect her. Thinks he's in love with her. I have enough to deal with without having my wife on my back about that."

"You leave Marygene out of this. Your son is your problem. He was at her house, not the other way around. She hired him at your wife's request."

My stomach churned.

"I'm warning you, fix this, Eddie, or I'll tear your life apart bit by bit."

Doors slammed and Eddie let out a string of curses that blistered my ears. What did Mayor Bill have on Eddie? Eddie was one of the good guys. He had to be. Another door slammed. There had to be another explanation. Oh God, not Eddie.

Keep it together. I can do this. I wiped the sweat from my face and crept back around to the street. Now I really worried about Eddie. What had he gotten himself into all those years ago? Before I made it to my car, I spied Alex heading up the steps to the sheriff's department. He had a couple of takeout containers from the Peach.

"Hey," I called, and he halted.

"What are you doing here?"

A few reporters snapped pictures as they stood outside the yellow barricades that had been placed in front of the sheriff's office steps. The rest must still be at the hospital.

He glanced around before we both continued up the steps. "You shouldn't come inside. Eddie's in rare form."

"Eddie's always in rare form." I was absolutely going in there. For one, I needed to see for myself that my father was okay. To lay eyes on his face and read him. A stupid thought crossed my mind. Where would Eddie fit on my whiteboard?

Alex turned and blocked the entrance. "I mean it. He's on the war path after Doc Tatum had to be brought in. Even though the prescriptions were traced back to Mrs. Gentry, it makes her office look bad, and that infuriated Eddie."

That made me sort of happy. He had finally found someone who cared for his stupid, stubborn self. And Doc Tatum was a real treasure.

"He's on no sleep, completely pissed at me, and the mayor has made it clear he wants this case closed in forty-eight hours. I think this is Eddie's first meal of the day."

Eddie was the last living parent I had. There was no way I would stand by and allow him to tank his reputation or his life for the likes of Mayor Bill. "As an eyewitness, I can help."

"He already took your statement and he made it crystal clear you should stay home. He's really worried about you."

"Why?" I moved past him and opened the door. "What's the worst that can happen? He'll yell at me."

Cuffs were slapped onto my wrists the second I walked into the building. And I looked up to see my father seething that I'd crossed him. "No, he'll arrest you."

My choice to show up and check in on Eddie might be perceived as rebellion. The cell smelled of vomit and bleach. Whoever cleaned it needed to be fired. I stared over at the stainless toilet in the corner of the room. I had to pee like crazy but would hold it as long as humanly possible. My shorts stuck to the bench when I shifted to try and get comfortable. Surely this couldn't be legal. If I got sick from being in here, Eddie would be sorry. It was a childish thought, one I was slightly embarrassed for having.

"You doing all right?" Alex asked from the other side of the bars.

"I'm about to start making tally marks on the walls to mark time. I've lost count." I tried to keep my spirits up. If I focused on Eddie too much, or Ms. Brooks, I'd start bawling.

He smirked. "It's been twenty minutes."

"Is that all? Feels like forever." I squirmed. "And I've really got to pee."

"So, go."

I pointed to the disgusting toilet. "In that? No way! It smells and there isn't any privacy."

"Well, it isn't the Ritz."

"No kidding. I don't have any idea why I'm even sitting here. What's the freaking charge?"

Alex shrugged. "I told you he was in rare form."

I blew out a breath. "How long is he going to keep me here? Yvonne might need me."

"You know he isn't talking to me at the moment. Except to bark an order. Not that I don't deserve it."

I leaned my face between the bars. "What's going on with him and the mayor?"

"Mrs. Gentry made a mistake when she sent the prescription change in. She got Ms. Brooks and another patient confused. Both had prescriptions to be called in to the same pharmacy on the same day. The other two victims were overdosed on Valium. Completely unrelated to Mrs. Gentry's mistake. She feels awful about Ms. Brooks. I've never seen an old woman cry with so much snot in my life."

"So the drug mix-up *was* an accident?" I raised an eyebrow.

"Looks like. At least on her part. Did you know that Yvonne's assistant used to be a nurse?"

I shook my head.

"Yeah, she got fired after being caught stealing drugs. We found a wig and scrubs in the trash bin on the first floor. She changed before strolling out of the hospital right under our noses. Theory is, she had a grudge against Yvonne and took it out on her mama. The other deaths were probably to throw us off the trail. Honestly, Ms. Brooks shouldn't be alive with the additional drugs she received because of Mrs. Gentry's screwup. They pumped her stomach just in the nick of time."

What a mess. "So no one is looking at Teddy then? This is all on Candi?" I was kicking myself for not speaking up earlier about my suspicions of the girl. If I'd only said something, maybe this whole horrific situation could have been avoided. Still, I couldn't imagine what she'd have against Yvonne. She'd been an excellent employer.

"Teddy's in Atlanta. He has more than a dozen witnesses. And while he's accounted for his staff at the funeral home, he reported a break-in last night. That's where we think Candi got the drugs."

"Alex!" Eddie's voice boomed.

"Hi, Eddie. Don't worry. He isn't trying to bust me out of the joint. We're discussing my conjugal visit."

Caught completely off guard, Alex covered a chuckle with a cough. Eddie, however, didn't even crack a smile. The glare he gave Alex spoke volumes. I mouthed my apologies to Alex before he tucked tail and ran.

My father breathed in and out laboriously as he took in the sight of me.

"It's rough seeing your only daughter in the slammer, huh?" Still not a grin, smirk, or lip twitch. I wanted to connect with him on some level. To get to the man I'd known my whole life. "I only wanted to make you smile. This person"—I waved my hands in his direction—"I don't know who he is." I studied his face. I caught a flicker of regret. The tiniest of flickers. Had I been completely wrong about why Mama wished I could let this case go? Had it nothing to do with her past and everything to do with Eddie?

That thought chilled me to the bone, and I took a step back from the bars.

His expression altered to one of pain. "You're scared."

I swallowed. "You locked me up." What in God's name was going on here? Not Eddie. Never Eddie. I didn't believe he killed the twins. As much as I hated to think it, in the back of my mind was the niggling thought that he had some involvement, as had Mayor Bill. Mayor Bill had dated Pam before Mrs. Gentry. All the pieces of this twisted puzzle began to take form in my mind.

He raked his hand through his hair, which I swore held more gray than it had a week ago.

"Are you charging me with something, or can I go? I feel helpless. I'm not allowed in to see Yvonne. If the theory y'all are working is correct, she's going to be torn out of the frame with guilt. She isn't answering her cell. Alex is riding a desk because of a stupid mistake. Reporters keep pestering me about my involvement. You obviously aren't eating or sleeping. You're right. I am scared."

He closed his eyes and pulled the keys to the cell from his pocket and released me from captivity. "I shouldn't have put you in here. Everything in my life is unraveling, and you're always in places I'd rather you not be. At least in there, I knew where you were and that you were safe."

We settled in silence and stood awkwardly in the holding area. I'd never felt this disconnected from him.

I'd had enough of the distance. I stood on tiptoes and wrapped my arms around his neck. "I love you, Eddie."

My words seemed to shake him from his trance. "I love you too. You're my baby girl."

We parted and I let out a shuddering breath. "I know you made some mistakes in the cold case. And no matter what, I forgive you for them. Don't forget who you are and what you mean to Sam and me."

He blinked a couple of times but said nothing.

"Be careful."
He managed a nod.
Turning, I left him there.

When I reached the hospital, Yvonne hadn't left her mother's side. It took a lot to coax her down to the cafeteria via phone when she finally answered. The security team vetoed my request to come up. I'd run by the diner and gotten her favorite. A warm goat cheese and fruit salad and a Sam's Surf-and-Turf Black-and-Blue. I'd decided a couple lemon-cranberry-and-white-chocolate cupcakes were in order as well. Ms. Brooks had woken up. Only for a few minutes but long enough for the nurses to give Yvonne a good report. It'd take time, but she'd recover. I didn't bring up anything to do with Mrs. Gentry or Candi. Yvonne didn't need that right now. She looked worn-out and fully aware of how she needed time to process things. I respected her boundaries.

"Thank you for the food. This cafeteria is the worst." Yvonne wiped her hands on a napkin. "Don't feel obligated to stay. I mean, they won't let you up on the floor. Mama's recovering. She spoke to me a few hours ago."

I scooted closer. "Was your mama able to formulate thoughts? Perhaps tell you anything?"

Yvonne shook her head. "I've been told to expect memory lapses. She probably won't recall a thing. She did recognize me." Yvonne smiled.

I hugged my friend. "That's wonderful, sweetie. She'll make a full recovery, you wait and see." I settled back into my chair. "Do you need me to do anything? Want me to keep Izzy? Bring you a change of clothes or a toothbrush?"

Yvonne shook her head again, since her mouth was full. She covered it with her hand. "My cousin brought some clothes by and she took Izzy home with her. She has kids and Izzy will be happy there. Besides, you've got Mr. Wrigley and the two wouldn't get along." For a moment, I'd forgotten about the little guy and yes, that was the understatement of the century.

"Mr. Wrigley barely gets along with himself."

He tolerated me now, and that said something.

"Aww, you've bonded." Yvonne took a sip of Diet Coke.

"Yeah. He's grown on me."

Yvonne took my hand and squeezed. Her eyes went dead serious now. "You know that thing your nanny had, that you inherited?"

I nodded slowly.

"Can it help you find Candi?"

When I searched her gaze, I expected to see pain, anguish, and even guilt. What I hadn't expected to find was sheer rage.

I gripped her hand in return. "It doesn't exactly work that way, but I won't stop until I find out what happened here and why. I'll scorch the earth to bring the responsible parties to justice."

My response seemed to satisfy her. We said our goodbyes, and I drove to the Pelican. My mind filled with turmoil. Calhoun had sent a text with the address of the twins' cousin, and I thanked him. I felt like I needed to bake. Unfortunately, Aunt Vi's little kitchen wasn't quite conducive. I went with my second choice. I walked the beach.

CHAPTER 33

The next morning I checked my messages and saw two texts from Yvonne and a voice mail from a number I didn't recognize. Alarm shot through me. Clicking on the icon, I read.

Mama's awake and eating.

Immediately my fingers moved on the buttons. I told her how thrilled I was and that I'd continue to pray for her.

Tara Reynolds from Sunshine Realty had left me a voice mail this morning. Her tone was chipper and encouraging. She spoke quickly and concisely regarding properties that might interest me. She said a friend told her I was searching for a new home and eagerly invited me to join her one day next week on a tour of several properties, if I was free. It was one of those calls that reminded me that life marched on. No matter what, people worked, ate, slept, and found some way to carry on.

Aunt Vi came into the kitchen wearing a—wait for it—yellow polka-dot string bikini, dragging a cooler. "Morning, sweet pea. I've got friends coming over for a day on the beach." She dumped the contents from the ice maker into the cooler. "We need a break from all the crap that's going on. The vibe on the island isn't good for anyone at the moment. You doing okay?" Her face wrinkled with concern.

I didn't want her to worry about me. "I'm fine." I smiled.

She let out a breath. "Good. What happened to Thelma was a wake-up call to me. Life is short. No more living conservatively."

My brows shot upward. *Conservative* and *Aunt Vi* didn't belong in the same sentence, in my opinion.

"I'm taking life by the cojones and making the most of my remaining days." She stood up after she filled the cooler with drinks. "And I'm moving back. For good." She gave me an emphasizing nod after the word *good*. "I'm hoping my good vibes will improve folks' lives."

"Well, that's great! I know Meemaw and Betsy will be thrilled with the news of having you home. I know I am."

The doorbell rang. "Oh, and hon, I love having you here, but when do you think you'll be moving out?"

I couldn't be more stunned if she'd slapped me. "Um, I'll start looking for a place as soon as possible."

"Sweetie pie, please don't be upset. It's just"—she stared at the metal pelican piece that hung next to the front door—"I'm not kicking you out or anything. I gave that Tara woman your number. She assured me she could find you something wonderful. And, in the meantime, maybe we could set some ground rules."

In a million years, I hadn't suspected Aunt Vi as the friend Tara referenced. "Is it Mr. Wrigley?" My brows drew together, and I tried to figure out what I'd done.

"No, I love the little guy." She let out a huge sigh and flung her arms up in front of me. "I can't compete with that."

My eyes followed her movement. "What?"

"You, Marygene, you! Sure, thirty years ago maybe, but lying in the sun next to you has made me realize I'm not as firm as I used to be. You have your friends over to sunbathe and it's like an episode of *Baywatch*. When I start bringing dates home, they'll see y'all." She huffed.

Aunt Vi wanted to play the field in a real way. Good for her!

"Listen, how about when you have a date over, I make myself scarce until I find a place. I promise not to have friends over to sunbathe without checking with you first. And I'm going to call the Realtor back the second things calm down. So, I shouldn't cramp your style too much longer. I get that once you get accustomed to living alone, it's hard to get used to sharing space with someone."

"And your feelings aren't hurt?"

"Not a bit."

Her facial features relaxed. The doorbell rang in complete succession with no break between dings. "I'm coming! Keep your pants on!" Aunt Vi stared at me.

"Oh. We're starting this now?"

The consummate bachelorette's head bobbed up and down and, in turn, so did her exposed flesh. I gave her a thumbs-up and darted to my room to dress for the day.

"Aunt Vi is on the prowl!" Betsy hooted after I relayed the events of the morning while we sat on the ferry. "I wonder who she has in her sights. I bet she visited the senior center and made a hit list." More guffaws.

On the drive over to the address Calhoun had provided me, I let Betsy in on what I'd witnessed, and about Eddie locking me up. Her jovial mood now soured, she stared out the window, her elbow propped on the door while she nibbled her nails. Neither of us seemed to know what else to say. Candi puzzled me the most. Especially her motivations for hurting those people. Money was the only reason I could fathom. Mayor Bill wanted her found, and Eddie did too.

Savannah had a different vibe than Peach Cove. Southern to its core, with a friendly atmosphere, it still moved at a slightly faster pace than our little island. Each year the coastal city saw hundreds of thousands of visitors attracted to its Spanish moss emerald-green canopies, the historic district with cobblestone streets, and the array of coastal-cuisine-infused restaurants and eclectic artists and vendors. The city, unlike Peach Cove, thrived with the hustle and bustle of tourism.

Some of the city's yearly tourists had spilled over onto our island via the Cove ferry. Our island attracted those seeking a little solitude, endless beaches, and an old-fashioned flair. For a while we'd felt invaded. Slowly we'd become accustomed to new faces filled with joy to be visiting our home. For me, it afforded a new appreciation for what we sometimes took for granted.

The GPS took us to a small street with a gray detached duplex with a cement porch and wood siding. The place, clearly dated, hadn't received a paint job in quite a while. Betsy and I parked on the street. Cats meowed by the garbage cans streetside. They were scrawny and skittish. We found that out the hard way when Betsy stooped to pet one. She'd been rewarded with a long scratch on her right forearm.

"Do you think I'll get cat-scratch fever?" Betsy panicked as she cradled her arm to her chest.

"You'll be fine. If it worries you that much, have Doc Tatum take a look at it when we get home."

We mounted the small set of five steps that led to the front porch, littered with old newspapers and Lego Duplo pieces that had seen better days, and a few smelly garbage bags. Sad that people actually lived like this. I hoped the inside was better kept as I rapped on the front door.

A crackly smoker's voice bellowed, "I ain't buying

nothing! I don't want Jesus! I have nothing to donate. We like weeds. My lawn is fine. Go away!"

Jeez. "Miss Dryer," I made my voice sound cheery. "My name is Martha Avery. I'm from Peach Cove," I lied smoothly. "I wondered if I might have a word with you about your deceased cousins that were recently found."

We heard the cock of a gun, and Betsy hit the deck. She literally dove onto the nasty bags of trash with flies swarming around them. I, however, had sidestepped to the left of the door, where buckshot hopefully couldn't reach.

"Oh my sweet Lord!" Betsy squealed and squeaked. "Something moved in one of these bags!" She rolled around like a beached whale, trying to get up, but kept sliding on whatever oozed from those bags. She would need to be hosed off.

I, on the other hand, decided to take a page from Roy Calhoun's book. He'd once told me how he got entry into reluctant witnesses' homes.

"Sorry to have bothered you. I thought you might be interested in the reward for information. I tried to call first." I listened as Betsy slipped and slid as she tried to get up.

"Phone's been dead a year." Well, that was a relief because I'd totally lied about calling. The door cracked open, the chain still secured, and an old woman's nose peeked out. She appeared to be a little older than Aunt Vi but younger than Meemaw. "You ain't cops, are ya?"

"No, ma'am. We certainly are not cops."

"Reward, you say?"

"Yes, ma'am. Ten thousand dollars if I'm not mistaken." The chain latch came undone in a hurry and a woman about four foot eleven stood before us in an old house dress with a cigarette sticking out of her wrinkled lips. Nonplussed, she spared a glance toward Betsy, who had finally gotten to her feet.

I jutted my hand forward to draw her attention. "Martha Avery." I beamed.

She shook my hand with her bony one then put her cigarette between her fingers and flicked ashes onto her porch. "Who's that?" She cocked her head toward Betsy.

"Oh, I'm . . . um." Betsy's eyes darted rapidly around as she searched for an alias. God, she could blow this. Suddenly she blurted, "I'm Gingersnap Harder."

The old woman gave a bark of laughter. "You a stripper?"

Betsy flushed, dusting off her green tank top that matched her eyes. "Thank you. I get that all the time. But no." That was so not a compliment.

"I'm Marta's partner."

"You mean Martha?" The old woman's eyes narrowed in suspicion.

"Oh, I call her Marta. It's a pet name." The stripper winked at me, and I fought the eye roll threatening to emerge.

"Whatever floats your boat. Come in and tell me about this ten-thousand-dollar reward." She moved to the side and let us into her dark, dingy home that needed an air-out.

Betsy and I perched on the plaid sofa, and I desperately tried not to focus on how oily it felt. Bird cages were everywhere, and the constant squawking and chirping, combined with the smell in here, had a headache on the rise.

"Yes, well"—I focused on Mrs. Dryer, who sat opposite us in an old glider rocker that had seen better days—"we're searching for any information that might clue us in to your cousins' lives. Why they left the island. Who might have visited them here. What their state of mind was. Why they returned. That sort of thing." I got out my phone. "Do you mind if I record this?"

She poured herself two fingers of Wild Turkey from the bottle on the folding end table to her left. Then she held the bottle out to Betsy and me.

"No, thank you," Betsy said politely.

I put a little space between Betsy and me. She really stank. I could smell her over whatever had this place reeking.

The old woman shrugged and downed her drink. "Go ahead."

Smiling, I hit record and placed the phone on the table, hoping the birds wouldn't interfere with the recording. "First, I wanted to ask if you've seen this woman? Did she drop by or ask about the twins?" I motioned to Betsy and she showed the woman Candi's Facebook profile picture.

"Nope. Never seen her before." The woman waved the phone away.

"She might have had long black hair when she came by."

"Ain't nobody come by. What's this got to do with Kayla and Pam?"

"Probably nothing. Can you tell me about your cousins?"

"Those two were attached at the hip since birth. When they were little, they even had their own made-up language that only the two of them could understand. I was older than them, so I got stuck watching them whenever their mom came over. You know those kind of people who are just plain weirdos?"

Betsy and I nodded vigorously.

"Well, that's how they were. But I'm a kindhearted soul, and when they needed a place to stay, I let them stay over the garage out back in the mother-in-law suite." She leaned forward. "Were they grateful? Hell nah! Complained that there wasn't any air-conditioning. And the tap water turned brown. Meh." She slapped her hand through the air. "If you ask me, someone probably whacked them because they were giant ingrates." She poured herself another drink.

"Did they seem okay when they first moved here?"

"From what I recall, Kay and Pam seemed normal. Normal for them, anyhow."

I folded my hands in my lap. "How long did they live over the garage?"

She shrugged. "A few months, maybe a year. It's a little fuzzy." She tapped her head. "I'm on disability and have to take a lot of pain meds. Some man kept coming by, though, to see Pam. Last name Gerald, no, Jenkins." She gazed upward. "Maybe Jerkins."

"Gentry?" I offered.

"That's it!" She pointed her finger at me like a gun. "Pow."

Okay.

"Pamela commenced wailing after he left. Went on for months. Then one day he stopped coming by." She had another drink.

"Did you ever find out why he stopped coming around?"

"Nope. Honestly, I never asked." Such a caring relative she'd been.

"How long after he stopped coming by to when they went missing?" I tried to keep my tone neutral, despite the fact my disdain for this horrible woman was growing.

She shrugged. "All those two ever talked about after that was moving to California or Colorado. I don't know, someplace. So, when they left, I figured that's where they went."

"They just packed up one day and left?" Betsy edged closer to the end of the sofa cushion.

She scowled. "They didn't pack jack. They left all their shit for me to deal with. I had two little ones underfoot too."

"What happened to their stuff?" Hope sparked within me.

"The clothes I sold along with their television."

I deflated.

"Well, Kayla's clothes. Pamela started eating too much and ballooned up."

Probably depressed about her life.

"Some of their junk is still up there. Never could rent the place, so no point in cleaning it out. The state said it was uninhabitable. Something about lead paint." She waved a hand through the air. "Idiots."

"Could we take a look?" Betsy asked eagerly. "There might be something we can use to get you that ten-thousand-dollar reward."

"Go ahead." She leaned closer to my phone. "But I ain't responsible for any damage you incur from venturing up there. Snoop at your own risk." Satisfied, she leaned back and smiled a partially toothless grin. I supposed it never occurred to her that I could simply erase the recording.

CHAPTER 34

Betsy and I slowly weaved our way through the jungle the old woman called a backyard. I wished I'd worn pants. There were probably chiggers imbedding in my exposed skin. I pushed the thought from my mind as we made it to the derelict building she referred to as a garage. The door had swollen to its cracked position and forced us to squeeze inside.

"You sure that staircase is safe?" Betsy asked as we precariously eyed the ten termite-eaten wooden slats that had once been a functional staircase.

"How could I be sure? Stay down here if you like. I came all this way to get to the bottom of this. I survived the old woman and the snake-infested jungle. I'm not leaving without exhausting all my options. I promised Yvonne I'd do everything I could, and I plan to. Once this case is closed, I'm taking a week off and doing nothing but lie on the beach. Hopefully, with no more dead bodies floating in the ocean. After I buy a house, of course."

"That sounds nice."

Idyllic was how it sounded. Now all I had to do was survive long enough to bring my vision to fruition.

The wood creaked under my weight so, with each step, I kept my weight suspended on my tiptoes. Having no idea if it made any difference or not, I rushed the last two steps. A huge sigh left my lips as I made it to the top.

Betsy threw herself against the wall, panting. "We made it! Praise Jesus, we made it!"

"Lead paint." I pointed to the flaking olive walls.

"Ick!" She began dusting herself off.

The room was mostly vacant, except for a stack of old plastic crates. Betsy pulled dishwashing gloves from her purse and handed me a pair. "It's all I could find on short notice and I thought we might need some gloves if we were going to do some real snoopin'."

"Good thinking." I squatted down next to the first crate, pulled the gloves on, and dug in. Latex gloves would have been a better choice. Old moth-eaten towels and sheets were all that was left in the first crate. The next one held old faded photos of the twins, and bank statements. One photo of the seaside sisters caught my eye. There Mama stood with her arm draped over Aunt Vi's shoulder. Her fingers showed the universal sign for peace. They wore long dresses and flower bandanas.

"Look how young they were." Evelyn Gentry had her arm around Kayla's shoulders. Both young women were smiling and had long braids.

I slid that photo into my purse.

Bank statements were fairly boring. They had a few thousand dollars in their joint account, nothing out of the ordinary.

"Look at this!" Betsy handed me a statement she'd been reading.

A deposit for fifteen thousand dollars and the cleared check, from Bill Gentry to Pamela Dryer, had been stapled to the back of the statement. And in the envelope was another Polaroid.

"Bets! You might have something here."

Betsy wiped the sweat from her face and beamed. The heat was brutal up here.

I slapped a mosquito off my arm. "It had to be taken there." I walked the photo over to the opposite side of the room where a giant peace sign had been painted. Faded now, but it clearly had been there. A twin bed had been against this wall and one of the girls, not sure which, lay on the bed with a swollen abdomen.

"One of the twins was pregnant. This must be Pam. She and the mayor were an item before he married Mrs. Gentry. Maybe they had a fling after he got married. Could Mayor Bill have been involved in their death? This picture proved they were involved. That would explain his need for Eddie to drop the case. It fit. I felt sure Eddie hadn't known that Mayor Bill killed them. But someone did. And my bet was on Mr. Gaskin. Mayor Bill must've known about the warrant and the two kept each other's confidences."

"Then, when you started snooping, Mr. Gaskin flipped," Betsy added. "God, we are so good at this! We busted this case wide open!"

"We still don't have an explanation for Candi's involvement." I hesitated to engage in her celebration. "Or know where she is."

"The mayor could have hired her, then killed her too."

"After hearing the way he spoke to Eddie, it's a possibility. He could have hired security and cracked down on the sheriff's department to find Candi, and all along knew she was dead. And if he had Mr. Gaskin store the bodies, that would explain why he'd had a way to pin the murder on him. Still, though, why not destroy the evidence and be done with the whole ordeal?"

Betsy shrugged. "Maybe Mr. Gaskin told the mayor he had."

I sighed. "I don't know. Well, hopefully the check will

be enough to have him questioned. Except, with what might be going on between him and Eddie, I don't know. Maybe we should—"

"Run over and try to get him to slip up."

I nodded. "Come on, Gingersnap. You stink and need a shower."

After we gathered the evidence, Betsy and I started down the stairs. Slowly. When Betsy put her full weight on the last stair, after I'd made it safely, it gave way. She screamed and covered her face with her hands.

"Betsy!" I shook her shoulders. "You're fine."

She slowly took a peek between her fingers. Her feet had landed on the concrete slab inches below the last step. "My life flashed before my eyes. And if I hadn't made it, I wouldn't have crossed right over, either. I'm not as good a Christian as I ought to be." She panted, patting her chest.

"Good to know."

We took turns squeezing through the opening.

The cocking of a gun had Betsy and me frozen, with our hands raised. We were facing the old woman holding the gun and two chunky men about my and Betsy's age on either side of her. "This here's my nephews, Coover and Jim Bo."

"Pleased to meet you, Mr. Coover and Mr. Jim Bo. They look like fine young m-men," Betsy stammered.

"Can it, Gingersnap!" the old woman yipped. "You two thought I was a dumb old broad you could take advantage of. I want that ten thousand dollars, and I want it now."

"Money," said Coover.

"Now," finished Jim Bo.

"Shut up, you morons. I'm the brains here." The old woman scowled.

"Well, the thing is, Mrs. Dryer, we're only the messengers." I chanced a smile. "I can give you the name and number of the man that's offering the reward."

"My main squeeze is right," Betsy added. "His name is Alex Myers, and he's a wealthy business owner. I have his card here somewhere." Betsy dug through her bag. "I'll get him on the phone and you can arrange to pick up your money."

The next thing I knew, Betsy pulled out an old revolver and started shooting. Bullets went everywhere. Coover and Jim Bo hit the ground with a loud thud. The old woman fired back, but the shot went wild as she went flying on her butt. I grabbed Betsy's arm and we hauled ass out of there. We made it to the car before the goons could catch us. They were on us the second I fired up the engine. Betsy fired at them out the window, but the *click click* sound told us she was out of bullets. Betsy rolled up the window, screaming. One goon stood in front of the car and goon number two took up at the rear.

"Floor it!" Betsy pounded on the dashboard.

And floor it I did. Coover, or maybe it was Jim Bo, rolled off the hood. Relief washed over me when I saw him rise from the ground, seemingly uninjured. They didn't seem bright enough to take down my license plate, so for that I felt grateful.

Neither of us relaxed until we were safely on the ferry. We'd decided to stay in the car for the ride back. Despite being stuck in the car with a stinking Gingersnap, I felt safer with the doors locked.

Betsy turned in her seat toward me. "Well, are we hard-core gangsta or what?" She celebrated with a happy dance.

That was when I noticed her left shoulder had a stream of blood rolling down it. My eyes went wide.

Betsy followed my line of sight and screamed. Again. "I'm hit! The pain. Oh, the excruciating pain."

I grabbed her arm to inspect the damage. I blew out a breath and grabbed some napkins from inside the glove compartment and pressed them to the tiny nick on her arm.

"It's a graze, you big baby!" I said to calm her as my stomach revolted. I wasn't good with the sight of blood.

She got up the nerve to remove the mock bandage I'd pressed to her arm. "Oh yeah. It's nothing. Phew."

Then I started laughing. I couldn't help myself. All this pent-up emotion had to come out somehow. Betsy laughed along with me, and when my laughter turned to tears, so did hers. We were such a mess.

CHAPTER 35

Betsy showered and changed and the two of us were on our way to the Gentrys'. Neither one of us had ever set foot in the mayor's abode. The old plantation-style house had large white columns and a double front porch, one on each level. Our plan was to hopefully have a word with Mr. Gentry and get him talking. Betsy would have her phone set to record while I came bearing gifts. I had a gift basket we threw together with whatever crap Betsy had around the house. Luckily for us, she kept old Christmas and birthday gifts she didn't like in the guest bedroom and regifted them. The problem was, if Betsy didn't like the items, it was probable the Gentrys wouldn't either. Oh well, I still hadn't figured out why Candi had been recruited and how the mayor knew she'd been a nurse.

We parked on the street, worried that if Mr. Gentry got riled, he might try to take us out, like he had the twins, and perhaps Candi. We wanted to be able to run if necessary. And now that night had fallen, we didn't want to worry about backing down the long driveway.

"Okay. Deep breaths."

Betsy and I inhaled and exhaled.

"Let's do this."

We marched up the brick steps onto the front porch. I carried the gift basket.

Betsy used the large door knocker to pound on the front door. "This here's a proper door. A giant could live here."

To our surprise, Junior opened the door. His face lit up. "Marygene! Betsy! Nice to see y'all."

"Hi, Junior. We brought your family a gift basket."

Betsy tapped on the basket. "There are M&M's in there."

I'd made Betsy include her family-size bag in the basket. We'd argued over it, but eventually she'd given in.

His eyes brightened and he took the basket from me. "Come in. Mama's having cocktails in the kitchen."

"We like cocktails." I smiled, and we followed Junior down the long hallway that led to the kitchen.

The place had obviously been professionally decorated with old Southern charm. The hallway was adorned with wall-to-wall paintings, each lit for maximum viewing. Her kitchen square footage had to be as much as the Pelican's living room and kitchen combo in totality. I gaped at the marbled beauty: a country-style sink and brick oven in an archway, not to mention the enormous Viking range.

"Mama! Marygene and Betsy brought us a present."

Mrs. Gentry stood, a tad off-kilter, at her massive island, blending up a batch of margaritas. "Isn't that nice, honey. You go ahead and take whatever you want out of it."

He kept hold of the basket. "Marygene, you want to watch TV with me?"

"Maybe in a bit."

He grinned and went into the room off the kitchen.

"Mrs. Gentry, we wanted to stop by and see how you and Junior are doing. This ordeal with Mr. Gaskin has been awful, not to mention the accident with Ms. Brooks and that crazy girl on the loose."

She poured herself a drink and slurped it down in one

long gulp. Betsy reached into her purse slowly, pulled out her phone, and placed it in her front pocket. She received an approving nod from me.

"Awful is an understatement. Thelma and I were friends since grade school. It's all been a horrible accident." The remorse she exuded seemed real.

"Is Mayor Bill at home?" I leaned against the counter as she poured herself another drink.

Then Betsy and I watched as she opened a bottle of orange-colored pills and popped one in her mouth.

"I have awful muscle spasms." She washed down her pill.

I was no doctor, but I felt quite sure that mixing alcohol with a muscle relaxer wasn't advisable.

"You girls sure you don't want a drink?"

"Okay. A drink would be nice."

She stumbled to the cabinet and stumbled back with two more glasses. Filled them both to the brim and sloshed them to us.

"Thank you." I took a tiny sip and my lips puckered. Strong.

Betsy downed hers and readily accepted another. I gaped at her.

She mouthed in response, "What?"

I set my drink on the island and wiped the spill on my hand onto the tea towel hanging on the stainless dishwasher that sparkled more than a diamond. Her housekeeper was worth every penny. When I put the towel back, I spied the small decorative bowls filled with candy in shiny golden wrappers.

Mrs. Gentry gulped more margarita. "Bill's never home anymore. I have no idea what he's up to. Ever since this stupid case, he's been so stressed out that he can't sit still. I don't know what to do." She saw me staring at the candy. "Help yourself, Marygene. My boys love those toffees."

I swallowed hard. Those were the exact wrappers I found at my house and Eddie found next to the body in Yvonne's cellar. "Thanks." I took one from the bowl and slid it into the pocket of my jeans. My heart hammered.

"That's awful of him." Betsy patted Mrs. Gentry on the back. "He should be here supporting you. You're the one who had to go through the ordeal of getting questioned."

Mrs. Gentry nodded. "That's what I told him. Dealing with that, and Junior believing that he's seeing ghosts, I'm at my wits' end. He's so selfish. I don't know what I ever saw in him."

Betsy nodded sympathetically.

"I want to take Junior to a doctor in Savannah or Atlanta. My pregnancy with him was high risk, so I saw a doctor in Savannah. They have excellent medical care there."

It was probably during those trips that her husband visited Pamela. The jerk. His wife was having his baby while his mistress, also having his baby, lay in that oven waiting on him to leave his wife. I started to feel sorry for Mrs. Gentry, but we had to get out of there. Something felt very wrong.

"We were just in Savannah today," Betsy offered and I realized she also seemed a bit tipsy.

"Were you?" Mrs. Gentry sounded keenly interested.

Alarms were going off within me and I gave Betsy a discreet warning shake of my head to subliminally signal, *Abort mission!*

Betsy gave me a cockeyed questioning glance before turning back to Mrs. Gentry. "Yes. We spoke with an old woman who was related to the Dryer twins." Betsy helped herself to another refill. My message had vanished over her head and into the oblivion of intoxication.

I had one hope, that our hostess had snockered herself into the same state and the words wouldn't register.

The old woman froze mid-sip and, with laser focus, turned all her attention to my rambling partner in crime.

"Let me tell you, that lady was nasty! And she shot me! Can you believe that?" Betsy stuck out her arm that had a tiny Band-Aid covering her war wound.

"You don't say?"

We have to get out of here! "We probably should get going."

In Betsy's condition, she'd didn't possess a filter. Not that she normally did, but, with a few drinks, it was no holds barred. We needed to catch Mayor Bill unawares if we were going to be able to extract any information. Plus, after the toffee discovery, I feared Junior, unbeknownst to him, had been roped in by his dad as an accomplice.

"Nonsense. You just got here."

"Yeah, we just got here, Marygene. Don't be rude." Betsy made a disapproving face at me while Mrs. Gentry topped up her glass.

"What did this old lady tell you?" Mrs. Gentry sidled closer to Betsy. She appeared relaxed, casual, and completely uninterested in my presence. However, she stood on the balls of her feet, ready to pounce. Impressive after all the alcohol.

"Nothing worth listening to. She prattled on about how they were ingrates and that they wanted to move to California."

I wanted to slap that glass from Betsy's hand.

"She let us snoop in their old apartment. That's where we found that canceled check from your selfish husband to Pamela." Betsy wrapped an arm around Mrs. Gentry's shoulders. "How did you ever put up with him for all these years? You gave the man the best years of your life. Now you're all dried up and wrinkly."

"Betsy!" I jerked her arm. "We really need to get going."

Mrs. Gentry cackled. "Was it a check for fifteen thousand dollars?"

Betsy's eyes went wide and she dropped her arm. "You knew?"

"Of course I knew. Pamela worked for Bill as a receptionist after we were married. She and I were dear friends. When she got pregnant with Daniel's baby, we decided to give her a little something to get started. Daniel certainly wouldn't man up."

Betsy put her hand over her heart. "You're a saint."

This woman seething beneath that fake smile was no saint.

I could almost see the wheels begin turning in Betsy's addled brain.

Her eyes moved rapidly side to side. "But"—she put her hand on her jutted-out hip—"Kayla and Daniel were an item. Not Pamela. I think your jerk husband lied to you. I think that baby was his and he killed them both to cover up."

Rage poured from Mrs. Gentry. Betsy wisely took a step back. Any second her head could spin around and green stuff could come spewing out. She looked that possessed. A shriek left her lips, and Betsy and I stumbled into each other.

"You listen to me, you stupid little bitches. I don't care what you think you know. You're both going to hand over whatever you have and keep your fat mouths shut or you'll both be sorry," she snarled toward Betsy. "You're as screwed up mentally as your psychotic meemaw and deranged aunt."

Betsy's face turned crimson. She bowed up, ready for a fight, and lunged forward. I grabbed the back of her shirt and tugged with all my might, her swipe at the old woman barely missing.

"You listen to me, you wrinkled-up bag of bones. I don't care if you're possessed by Satan himself. If you talk about my family again, I'm going to stake your ugly gray ass!"

Junior, who we'd not seen enter the room, started screaming and holding his head. "Make it stop!" he screamed over and over and went to the floor.

"It's okay, baby. Mama's here." Mrs. Gentry rushed to his side. Betsy and I took advantage and fled out the front door.

CHAPTER 36

Betsy and I had flown out of the neighborhood on two wheels. The only intelligible words I could make out as Betsy shouted were, "Ohmygod, ohmygod, ohmygod." Betsy turned the air up and placed her face at the vent.

My hands shook and my brain struggled to process what to do next. By the time we rounded the corner toward Cove Square, I'd decided to go straight to Eddie. There wasn't another option, and I hoped we had enough for him to make a case. "We're making a bad habit of pissing bad guys off. This isn't a good trend, Bets."

I started to pull into the space next to the truck with Peach Cove Sheriff's Department painted down the side when I spied the black Cadillac that belonged to the mayor.

"The sheriff's department is out! That demon-possessed freak might follow the scent of her husband." Betsy began fanning herself. "Be careful, Eddie. He might be infected."

"What were you thinking, drinking all those margaritas?"

Betsy held her stomach.

"There was way too much tequila in them. Couldn't you taste it?"

She moaned in response and slid lower in the seat.

"Okay, plan B." I circled the square and hit the call button on the steering wheel and instructed the automated voice to call my father. Voice mail. Again. "Eddie, it's me. I saw your truck outside the department. I need to speak with you ASAP. It's a long story, but I'd rather not run into the mayor. We have evidence that the mayor paid off Pamela Dryer. She must have been extorting money from him because she carried his child. And yes, I have proof of that too. I visited their cousin in Savannah. She talked to us, since we weren't cops. I have bank statements and everything. Betsy and I are on our way to the diner. It's closed, so it'll be a neutral place to meet. We have evidence recorded. Hurry!" I disconnected the call.

The parking lot was empty in front of the diner, except for Sam's truck. The dining room was illuminated. I didn't know why he was inside and didn't care. Relief washed over me. Having a male presence while we waited on Eddie would be wonderful.

Betsy held her head and groaned. "Uh-oh."

I didn't like the sound of that.

"I left my phone on the island in that possessed woman's kitchen."

I gaped. "We need that recording!"

She opened the door and puked. After she pulled herself together, I had to help her inside the building.

"I'm sorry. Seeing a possessed woman scared me to death, and then when she threatened Meemaw, I forgot all about the phone."

I helped her onto a barstool and paced. "I need to think."

Sam's face held surprise when he came into the dining room. "What are y'all doing here?"

I pinched the bridge of my nose. "Long story. What are you doing here?"

"I left my wallet in the locker. I thought I lost it while

out on the water, and I tore my boat apart searching for it, then I remembered I never had it with me in the first place." He took in Betsy's appearance and poured her a glass of water. "Looks like y'all been partying."

"Hardly." My legs trembled. This was bad. So very bad.

"She doesn't look so good." Sam smirked.

"Mrs. Gentry tried to poison me." Betsy drank her water.

Sam finally noticed my demeanor. He turned serious. "Tell me."

Once I had, he leaned against the counter with a dumbfounded expression. I could tell he was having a hard time comprehending that Betsy and I had done all of that on our own.

"Am I being punked?"

"Nope. We're badasses." Betsy slumped against the counter.

I pointed to my green friend. "What she said."

"So, you had a type of confession but Betsy left it behind."

I nodded. Betsy looked abashed.

"How does Candi fit in?"

I started to tell him that I hadn't quite figured that out when the bell above the front door jangled loudly, and in stormed a furious Junior. When I spied the shiny butcher knife in his right hand, I shuffled to my feet. Betsy did the same. I could have kicked myself for not locking the door.

Sam held his hands out in a placating way. "Junior, whatcha doing, buddy?"

Junior had tears streaming down his cheeks and his face had red splotches on them. "She hurt Mama!"

I couldn't tell if he pointed at Betsy or me.

"Mama started crying after they left. She said something had to be done. It's all Betsy's fault!"

He wiped his eyes with the back of his hand, the one that held the knife.

"Me! I brought you the M&M's. Your mama is a meanie."

I glowered at her.

He stomped and yelled, the sound terrifying.

"Betsy's sorry, Junior." My voice wavered. "Aren't you, Betsy?"

Slowly, we inched away.

Betsy's head bobbed up and down.

"I love you, Marygene. I'm supposed to protect you."

Sam started to edge closer to the counter and, in turn, Junior.

"Stay back, Sam!" Junior pointed the knife toward my brother, and he took a step back. Junior got dangerously close to Betsy and me. Within arm's reach.

Betsy gripped my shoulder.

"Junior, please don't hurt my brother." My legs felt like jelly. "I thought we were all friends."

Sam slid his phone from his back pocket and hit a few buttons. I sent a silent prayer that someone would answer.

In stumbled Mrs. Gentry. She took in the sight of her son holding the knife. Fear flashed across her face. To her credit, she kept her distance, standing by the front door. With the amount of alcohol and drugs in her system, it surprised me she could stand. "Junior, honey, what are you doing?"

"Fixing it." His free arm struck out like a rattlesnake, shoving me down. He had Betsy trapped in front of him with the knife at her throat.

"Junior, please!" I said from the floor.

He put his back to the counter. He had a full view of the dining room where he stood, leaving no room for anyone to sneak up behind him.

"Go over there, Marygene. I don't want to hurt you."

In fear he would hurt my friend, I did as he said. Tears slid down my cheeks as I saw Betsy's face pale. Her green eyes were wide as saucers.

"Junior, honey, let the girl go."

He glared at his mama. Anger radiated off him.

Mrs. Gentry should shut up. She's wasn't helping the situation one bit.

"Betsy won't leave this alone. She's making Marygene bad."

Betsy made a noise that sounded like a frightened mouse. A trickle of blood slid down her neck.

I tried reasoning with him. "Betsy will leave it alone now. She's awful sorry for upsetting you and your mama."

He shook his head.

The door flung open and a panting Alex came in with his gun drawn. He'd obviously sprinted over. Oh God, it hadn't been Eddie's truck. I'd forgotten about Alex being stuck on desk duty. Sam must have called the department line directly and left the line open. *Where is Eddie?*

Alex and I locked gazes a second before he attempted to engage Junior. His chest heaved. It was the first time in my life I'd ever seen him petrified. "Junior, hey man, look at me."

"Go away, Alex! Marygene ain't your girlfriend no more." He tightened his hold on Betsy.

She wrapped both hands around his forearm.

"You've got my cousin, Junior. You let her go, okay? I don't want to hurt you."

"Alex Myers! Don't you dare hurt my baby." Mrs. Gentry took a step toward Junior.

He screamed, "I'm not a baby!"

"No, you're right. I'm sorry, Son." Mrs. Gentry wiped the perspiration from her forehead with her free hand. The other kept her bag clutched to her side.

Flashing lights reflected off the diner windows. Eddie exited the vehicle, along with the mayor. Alex motioned for them to stay out.

The mayor ignored him and came bursting through the door. His face paled at the sight of Junior with a knife to Betsy's neck. "Son, what in God's name are you doing? Let that poor girl go." His tone came out broken.

"She's a problem! I have to fix it!"

"No, Son, you don't." The mayor's voice sounded stronger this time and with more authority. "Put that knife down."

Eddie slipped in from the kitchen, his weapon drawn as well. Sam must have come in the back way and left the door unlocked.

"Eddie, don't," Mrs. Gentry warned as she caught sight of him. I gasped when my gaze swung toward the old woman holding a Glock as she stood behind her husband, pointing it directly at his temple, as he slumped in the booth. Her purse was now discarded on the floor.

Mayor Bill's eyelids slid shut. "For God's sake. What's wrong with you, Evelyn?"

"See! It's Betsy's fault Mama and Daddy are arguing. All Betsy's fault. She poisoned Marygene against me and all I wanted to do was protect her, like the ghost told me to. The ghost in the yellow dress."

"Look at our boy!" The mayor sounded exasperated. "He needs help and here you are with a damned gun pointed at my head!"

"Shut up, Bill."

The situation quickly escalated to catastrophic proportions. "Put the guns down, Eddie and Alex, and kick them over to me."

Surely they wouldn't do that. It was suicide.

"Hey, Junior." I waved at him, drawing his attention. "This is getting scary, don't you think? Betsy hasn't turned me against you. And all the people we love are in this room. We don't want anything bad to happen to them, do we?"

"Marygene is right. Junior, let's put the knife down, okay?" Eddie spoke calmly as he put his gun on the floor. "See, I'm putting my weapon down."

What the hell is going on here?

"I have to fix it," Junior insisted and stomped his foot, jarring Betsy. "Mama said dump the bags in the ocean. Way out in the deep, but I . . . I thought it didn't matter and stayed closer to shore than I should have. It was rotten meat. Just rotten meat!" He wailed. "That stupid ghost turned the meat into dead bodies. I shot one body with the flare gun. It caught fire, and I dumped it into the ocean. The ghost said to take the other one home and put it back into the broken freezer."

"Junior, honey, quit talking." His mother sounded shaken now. "He isn't in his right mind. He's seeing ghosts, for God's sake. He has no idea what he's saying."

Junior ground out, "Yes. I. Do. You said burn the other body the ghost made and put it in the pretty girl's house, I thought I was going to have to break in, but the back door was unlocked, like someone left it open for me. You said if I did that, all this would go away. It didn't. So, when the ghost said I should watch over Marygene, I did."

"You did protect me, Junior. And I'm so grateful." I smiled at him.

"But you're protecting the bad one! She has to die!" Junior's face tensed.

My pulse raced. Something had to be done. Out of the corner of my eye, I saw Mama run through Mrs. Gentry toward Junior. He paled and the knife went slack in his hand. Sam noticed at the exact moment I had. I'd read it all over his face a second before we made eye contact. He signaled a two on his chest with two fingers. As kids he talked me into running two football plays with him, and he wanted me to run play two. Without another second passing, I took advantage of Junior's terror and dove across the room,

tackling Betsy around the knees. We both hit the black and
white checkered tile hard. Evelyn screamed as several loud
pops cracked through the air. Sam leapt over the counter
and tackled Junior to the floor right in front of us. Betsy
screamed as the knife came dangerously close to my face.
We scrambled to the corner as Sam wrestled the knife from
Junior's hand.

I scanned my loved ones as Alex slapped the cuffs on
Junior, who stopped fighting and lay there, weeping, with
red blooming through the pants on his left thigh. Blood
welled up on my brother's arm.

"Mama! I'm hurt!" Junior wailed.

"It's okay, baby. Mama is going to take care of everything." Mrs. Gentry's voice had lost its steadiness. But she
still had possession of the gun. Why Eddie hadn't managed
to make it around the counter and apprehend the woman
concerned me. Was he hurt? He didn't appear to be.

"Sam, are you okay?" Eddie asked in a calm tone, his
backup weapon now in hand.

"Yeah, it's just my shoulder." Sam kept his hand over
the wound as he slumped against the back wall.

Mama appeared in front of Mrs. Gentry. Her presence
seemed to stir up more rage in the room. "You want a confession, Eddie? Fine." Mrs. Gentry's words came out
through gritted teeth. Her gaze held a wild glint.

"What are you talking about?" Mayor Bill's face held
the paleness of shock. "Evelyn, put the damned gun down.
Our son or Sam could have been killed. This has gone far
enough. If you need a doctor, we'll get you some help."

"Ma . . . Mama, I'm sorry." Junior continued to sob.

Mrs. Gentry's facial expression softened slightly, but
she didn't budge from her place behind her human shield.
"Shut up, Bill. Eddie, I'll give you a confession if you have
Alex call for an ambulance and take my baby out of here.
Junior, honey, it's going to be okay."

Alex glanced at Eddie.

"Why don't we let everyone else go too?" Eddie reasoned. "Then we can sit and talk this out. My son could use an ambulance too."

She laughed. "Nice try. I'm no fool. Your son can go, but everyone else stays."

Reluctantly Eddie agreed and we all watched the two of them hobble out the door. Sam hadn't wanted to go, but Eddie's face held no room for negotiations. Sam smiled at me and I whispered as he passed, "You did real good, Sam."

Mama moved to Mrs. Gentry's side. I hoped she knew what she was doing because the old woman seemed to shake with fury the closer Mama got.

"I wanted a baby so desperately. That's all I ever wanted." She sounded completely sober now as she glowered at her husband. "But I couldn't have one. Then I found out Bill had been fooling around with Pamela again and she'd gotten pregnant. First, I wanted to kill them both, but then I saw it as my only chance to have a child that could be my own. I faked a pregnancy. We went to Savannah to take Pam to the doctor. She agreed to give us the baby for fifteen thousand plus doctor's fees. Then she promised to leave. Swore she'd leave us alone. She lied to us. When Junior was only five months old, she came back and wanted him back. He *was* my baby! I was already upset because the pediatrician said Junior was delayed and asked if the birth mother had taken drugs. Stupid Pam. My boy had to suffer because of her lack of self-control."

Eddie inched closer to her as she continued to confess. Bill had slumped forward, his face in his hands. A wave of panic overtook me as I saw Mama start to fade. Her facial expression terrified me the most. It was happening again. She was being pulled away without any control. We were going to have to finish this without her. This was our fight, not hers.

"I invited the twins to the house. Picked them up at the market and drove them to our house. Bill didn't know about it, and when he called to say he was coming home for lunch, I made them wait in the cellar. I told them they could see the baby one last time and then I'd give them enough money to start a new life in California." She shrugged. "I'd forgotten about an event Bill and I were supposed to attend over the weekend. I'd locked them down there just to be safe but still thought they'd be fine. When I went down there when Bill went to work the Monday after, the girls were already dead. The pilot light on the furnace had gone out and the gas had killed them. It must have gone out sometime during the night because I hadn't noticed a smell on the main floor." She shrugged. "We got lucky."

Mayor Bill's head jerked back. "Oh my God! Evelyn! You knew where they were for all these years? Tell me this is some sick fabrication."

Her face creased in what could only be described as an evil grin. "You're a fool, Bill. I had to call my brother to help clean up the mess and repair the problem. I saw it as providence. I got to keep my boy and the twins were no longer a problem."

Bill craned his neck to face her. The fear in his face seemed to be replaced with fury. "I had Eddie drop the case, as a friend, because you said you'd given them money to move. I compromised my integrity for you!"

"Wow, we should have known it was that demon-possessed hag," Betsy whispered beside me.

The pieces fell into place perfectly. Poor Ms. Brooks had suspected her old friend. Mrs. Gentry was the wolf in sheep's clothing she'd referenced. She also knew Junior wasn't her biological child. She'd mentioned Pam giving away her precious jewels.

"Bill"—she rubbed the barrel of the gun against his neck—"your beautiful Pamela and her sister were stuffed into a chest freezer and moved with us throughout the years. Why did you think I insisted on having my brother move the freezer instead of the moving company? You never once questioned it. My brother is the only one I confided in. He stood by me, God rest his soul. We hid the freezer deep in the old cellar. You never bothered to even go down there. Always so preoccupied with everything other than *our* life. Did you even notice the new freezer I bought to replace the old one?" She snorted and shook her head. "Whatever. Over time I forgot about them."

"You're a monster! And you pulled my son into all of this. I gave you everything." He raised his hands in defeat. "Just shoot me." His deflated tone hurt my heart.

She waved her gun around. "Everything, my ass. You never loved me like you loved her. I should have stuffed you in there with them. In hindsight, I should have considered the age of the freezer. Nothing lasts forever. You never even noticed the smell. Junior did. But like he said, I told him it was rotten meat. How was I to know he'd look inside the bags?"

"What about Candi?" I couldn't help but ask.

"She's long gone." Evelyn cackled. "What luck to find out I had a kindred spirit on the island. Once we worked through the kinks of pricing, she agreed to do anything necessary. Candi had no problem breaking into the funeral home and stealing the embalming fluid. In fact it was her idea." This woman was truly evil and so was Candi. "I see you, Eddie."

Smooth Eddie was almost close enough to restrain the woman without chancing Mayor Bill's life. Mrs. Gentry aimed her gun at me. Betsy gripped my hand as I sucked in a sharp breath and pondered my next move.

"If you don't want to lose a child, you better keep your distance. I can get a shot off before you even—"

Eddie fired before I could blink. Mrs. Gentry dropped the gun and it went off. A stray bullet hit several feet above our heads. Blood bloomed from the front of her blouse and she slumped over on top of Mayor Bill.

"'Ding, dong, the witch is dead,'" Betsy sang, sounding nervous.

We giggled together for a second and then both began to cry.

CHAPTER 37

Tara Reynolds opened the French doors of Beach Daze Cottage. We'd seen so many cottages over the last several weeks that they all started to run together. This one, however, stood out, with its high ceilings and exposed beams and an abundance of square footage. It also needed the most work. At first, I'd ruled it out. It would need a complete gut of the interior, and Zach informed me that before he got into the walls, we wouldn't know the exact extent of the work that needed to be done. Not that it wasn't doable, he'd rushed to say to thwart further concerns.

This Sunday, I'd called in the big guns. Everyone was here to give their opinion. Zach and Eddie talked about what was and wasn't possible to change without ruining the original feel of the home.

"Try to envision it, Marygene." Yvonne had brought swatches and a few design plans along to help me see past the run-down interior. She held them up to the shabby walls of what would be my kitchen.

"You're so much better at that than I am. If you tell me it can be done and that it will be magnificent, then I'll take your word for it." I chewed on my bottom lip. This purchase would be the first major purchase of my life. I'd never owned a home I hadn't inherited.

Betsy had the champagne ready to pop as she waited for me to make the decision and sign the papers the Realtor had for me. The offer we'd discussed would be accepted. I had my Realtor's word on that. The current owner was extremely motivated and told her he wouldn't balk at my low-ball offer. Which I felt extremely grateful for. I could put the remainder of the settlement into renovations and furnishings.

Yvonne came up next to me and looped her arm through mine. "I promise you I can help you make this place your dream home. Zach and I have gone over the plans that you and I discussed and, even if we hit a few snags, it will all work out beautifully. This is my area of expertise. Trust me."

"Oh, I do." I smiled at my friend.

Her face glowed. Things were smoothing out for her. The new meds Doc Tatum prescribed kept her mama lucid the majority of the time. The marked improvement made it possible for Yvonne to move her back home. She'd hired a full-time nurse to help out. It thrilled me to see how much happier the two of them were.

Tara clasped her hands in front of her. "Then there's only one question left. Can you see this as your home? Do you feel it when you walk through the doors? Is this the view you want to wake up to every morning? Remember the master suite opens up to this sundeck as well."

"Imagine the wall-to-wall window pocket doors here." Yvonne motioned to where the small set of French doors were.

Jena Lynn came rushing back into the room. "Sorry. I have to pee every five minutes it seems. I don't know what I'm going to do if I get any bigger." She was adorable. Her little abdomen had started to show a pooch.

Zach came up behind her and wrapped his arms around her. She lifted her head and he planted a kiss on her nose.

I grinned as I walked past them and went outside. What the home currently lacked on the inside, the outside was a dream. A gorgeous deck had been added by the previous owner before he'd decided to abandon the project. Herbs grew in pots all around the perimeter. A grill station had been built. It lacked the grill, but that'd be easy to remedy.

"If it's privacy you're after, you certainly have that here," Tara, my ever-patient Realtor said. Her lined pants flapped in the breeze.

This property came with three lots attached. No one would ever be able to build close to me. Aunt Vi waved as she walked up the deck, arm in arm with her beau of the week. She'd closed on the Pelican, located down the beach from this one, last week. Close enough to be neighbors. Far enough apart we'd both be happy. Betsy, Meemaw, and I were thrilled to have her home where she belonged.

"Is this the one?" Aunt Vi crossed her fingers. She tried to be kind, but I knew she was ready to get rid of me. Or at least to see an end in sight. She'd been so accommodating and welcoming, despite my presence cramping her style.

"It's such a gorgeous view. Can you see us out here sunbathing and having cocktails?" Betsy took in a lungful of salty sea air.

I could. I really could.

"It's a good house, pumpkin." Eddie patted the wall.

Doc Tatum, who'd joined him, gave him one of her doe-eyed smiles. "It's got good bones."

He and I had made amends and sort of come to terms on my little intuition.

I recalled the fear that'd gripped me when Eddie asked about my *ability*: his word, not mine. He'd told me there wasn't any way those shots fired at such a close range would all go wild. I thought back to the night we'd sat on the beach. Junior had just been sentenced. Mayor Bill, well, Mr. Gentry since he'd stepped down from office, had talked him into accepting a plea deal. He'd been given twelve months in a good psychiatric rehabilitation center. One that Doc Tatum gave her stamp of approval on. His mother, who'd only sustained a flesh wound by Eddie's hand, however, still had yet to stand trial. From what we heard, she was hoping for an insanity defense. She hadn't much choice on another defense. A month ago, Candi had been picked up by a state trooper in Atlanta and agreed to testify against the old woman in exchange for leniency on her murder and attempted murder charges.

I explained it as I had with Yvonne, referencing Nanny and her gifts.

That seemed to satisfy him and piqued his curiosity further. "Are you able to get these feelings"—he slowed—"with all crimes, or just murders?"

"Honestly, Eddie, I haven't a clue. Most of the time it feels as if I have no control over what senses I get. Or not that I've figured out yet." All true statements.

"Will you forgive your old man for being a stubborn mule? Perhaps keep me in the loop as you figure this all out. I'd like to run interference, if at all possible. Help you when I can."

I leaned my head on his shoulder. "If you'll forgive me for lashing out."

He kissed the top of my head. "There's nothing to forgive."

Doc Tatum was right. We were so much alike.

I planned to do a bit of research about island spirits in the coming weeks. A quick search at my local library had proved useful. Old lore books were easy to come by. How much actual knowledge they contained remained a mystery at this point. Mama only knew her part to play. The rules she must adhere to in order to make amends and cross. I no longer faulted her for her role. Truthfully, other than the deaths and near-death experiences, this gave Mama and me a second chance for a relationship. We regretted the tumultuous relationship we'd had while she'd been living. And I felt grateful.

I'd promised Teddy I'd speak on his father's behalf at his sentencing. I wasn't doing it for Mr. Gaskin, although I did believe he never intended to truly harm me. But still, what he'd done was wrong in the worst sort of way. I didn't believe anyone would ever find out about the part he played in the body disposal. Mama said he suffered from the guilt. How she knew, she couldn't say. Still, I would speak on the man's behalf for Teddy. Because he was my friend and that was what friends did. They stuck together.

"Well, don't keep us in suspense!" Betsy brought me back to the present.

I glanced around at the house full of wonderful friends and family. Then gazed down the long stretch of private beachfront. Sam fished at the shore. He had three poles going. Farther down the beach I caught sight of Mama, her dress flowing in the breeze as the waves lapped at her shins. At first a wave of panic struck me, but when she waved her hand in a greeting manner, relief washed over me that she'd only shown up for moral support. I could sense her emotions now. The new development needed to be studied. Later.

With a big sigh and a smile, I said, "Pop the cork, Betsy! I'm home."

Cheese Biscuits

2 cups self-rising flour
1 teaspoon salt
½ cup cold butter, diced
1 cup buttermilk
1½ cups grated sharp cheddar cheese
½ stick butter, melted
¼ teaspoon garlic powder
Sprinkle of parsley flakes

Preheat the oven to 425°F.

Add the flour, salt, and cold butter to the bowl of an electric mixer fitted with a paddle attachment and blend on low until the flour resembles cornmeal.

Add in the buttermilk and cheese. Mix until just combined. If the dough is a little stiff, add an additional splash or two of buttermilk.

Turn the dough out onto a lightly floured surface and sprinkle the top of the dough with flour. With a rolling pin, gently roll the dough ½-inch thick. With a floured biscuit cutter, cut out rounds and arrange ½ inch apart on a baking sheet lined with a baking mat or parchment paper.

Bake on the top rack position until nicely browned, about 15 to 20 minutes.

Combine melted butter with garlic powder and parsley flakes. Brush the tops of hot biscuits with melted butter and serve.

Broccoli and Cheese Soup

2 tablespoons extra virgin olive oil
2 tablespoons unsalted butter
1 large yellow onion, diced
2 cloves garlic, finely chopped
1 carrot, peeled and chopped
4 steam-in-bag broccoli florets, steamed
⅓ cup flour
7 cups chicken stock (two 32-ounce cartons if using
    store-bought)
2½ cups grated sharp cheddar cheese
1 cup heavy cream
½ teaspoon garlic powder
1 teaspoon thyme leaves, chopped
Salt and pepper to taste

Heat oil and butter in a large pot over medium heat. Add onion, garlic, and carrots. Sprinkle with a little salt and pepper. Reduce the heat to low and sauté, stirring frequently until the onions are translucent, about 5 to 7 minutes.

Add the steamed broccoli and flour. Stir until all the vegetables are coated. Add stock and stir. Increase heat to medium, stirring frequently.

Once the stock has reduced slightly, place cheese in a bowl and ladle a little hot stock over the cheese. Stir with a wooden spoon until cheese is melted.

Reduce heat to medium and pour melted cheese into pot and stir until evenly distributed. Add garlic powder, thyme, and heavy cream. Season to taste.

Serve with an extra sprinkling of cheese and sourdough croutons.

Sourdough Croutons

3 tablespoons olive oil
2 tablespoon melted butter
2 teaspoons parmesan cheese
2 cups ½-inch sourdough bread cubes
½ teaspoon garlic powder
Salt and pepper

Preheat the oven to 300°F.

In a bowl combine olive oil, butter, parmesan cheese, and bread cubes. Toss to coat cubes. Spread on a baking sheet and sprinkle the sourdough with a little salt, pepper, and garlic powder. Bake until nicely browned, about 15 to 20 minutes, stirring occasionally.

Roadkill

1½ pounds ground beef sirloin
1 small onion, diced
1 egg, beaten
2 cloves garlic, finely chopped
2 tablespoons Worcestershire sauce
3 tablespoons chopped thyme leaves, 1 tablespoon if
   using dried
½ teaspoon ground mustard
¼ cup panko bread crumbs
½ cup flour
1 tablespoon butter
About a tablespoon of olive oil for frying
Salt and pepper to taste

For Gravy

2 tablespoons butter
8 ounces baby portobello mushrooms, also known as
   cremini mushrooms, well cleaned and sliced
1 onion, sliced thin
1 teaspoon thyme leaves, chopped, half a teaspoon if
   using dried
¼ cup all-purpose flour
1 can beef consommé
1 can beef broth
½ cup heavy cream
Salt and pepper to taste

Preheat oven to 350°F
Combine ground beef, egg, Worcestershire, onions, garlic, thyme, ground mustard, bread crumbs, flour, and a sprinkle of salt and pepper in a large bowl. Shape the mixture into 6 equal-sized patties.

Heat oil and butter in a large frying pan. Fry patties until brown on both sides. About 5 minutes. Place browned patties in a baking dish. Drain all fat but a tablespoon from the frying pan.

In the frying pan, over medium heat, melt butter for the gravy. Add the mushrooms, onions, thyme and season with salt and pepper. Sauté until onions are translucent and mushrooms are tender. Sprinkle with flour and stir until vegetables are fully coated. Slowly pour in consommé and stock and mix until smooth. Let the mixture come to a boil and cook until reduced and thickened. Pour in heavy cream and taste for seasonings.

Pour sauce over patties and cover with foil. Bake for approximately 20 minutes or until patties are medium well, at 150 degrees.

Serve over mashed potatoes with lots of creamy gravy.

Chicken and Dumplings

1 large 3- to 5-pound whole chicken
1 large yellow onion, cut in half
4 whole cloves garlic
Two stalks celery
2 bay leaves
2 steam-in-bag mixed vegetables
Water
2 cups all-purpose flour
1 stick diced butter, cold
1 cup whole buttermilk
½ teaspoon garlic powder
Salt and pepper to taste

Place whole chicken in a large stock pot with onion, bay leaves, celery, and garlic. Add 2 teaspoons salt and 1 teaspoon pepper. Cover with water. Bring to a boil, then reduce heat to medium-low and simmer for about an hour. Remove chicken, onions, celery, bay leaves, and garlic from the broth. Let chicken cool until easy to handle. Remove skin and shred chicken. Set aside.

Bring broth to a boil; steam mixed vegetables in the microwave and set aside.

Add the flour, a couple of pinches of salt, and cold butter to a bowl of an electric mixer fitted with a paddle attachment and blend on low until the flour resembles cornmeal. Add the garlic powder and sprinkle in a little salt and pepper. Add in buttermilk and blend until dough forms.

On a floured surface, roll out dough to ¼-inch thickness. With a knife, slice 3-inch squares and drop into the boiling broth. Reduce heat to medium-low and simmer, stirring occasionally until the dumplings are done; about 8 to 10 minutes.

Sprinkle the shredded chicken with a little flour and stir into the pot along with the steamed vegetables. Serve.

<u>Note</u>: When reheating leftovers you'll need to add a little water to achieve original consistency.

Peach Muffins

3 cups all-purpose flour
1 tablespoon cinnamon
½ teaspoon allspice
1 teaspoon baking soda
½ teaspoon salt
1 cup vegetable oil
½ cup buttermilk
1 teaspoon vanilla extract
3 eggs, lightly beaten
1½ cups brown sugar
3 cups chopped peaches, fresh or canned

Preheat the oven to 350°F and line muffin tins with 16 muffins cups.

In a large bowl, mix flour, cinnamon, allspice, baking soda, and salt. In a separate bowl, mix oil, vanilla, buttermilk, eggs, and brown sugar. Pour wet mixture into dry and mix gently until combined. Fold in peaches.

With a large ice cream scoop, spoon batter into muffin cups.

Bake 20 minutes or until toothpick inserted into the center comes out clean. Cool 10 to 15 minutes before turning out on a wire rack to cool.

Yvonne's Lime Cream Puffs

1 cup water
1 stick unsalted butter
1 teaspoon sugar
1 cup all-purpose flour
4 large eggs

For lime pastry cream

2¼ cups whole milk
6 large egg yolks
⅔ cups sugar
⅓ cup cornstarch
1 tablespoon vanilla extract
Zest of 3 limes
Half a stick of butter

Preheat oven to 425°F.

Line 2 rimmed baking sheets with parchment paper. In a small saucepan, bring water, butter, and sugar to a boil over high heat. Immediately remove from heat. With a wooden spoon, stir in all-purpose flour until mixture pulls away from the sides of the pan and forms a ball. Allow to cool for 2 to 3 minutes.

Add eggs one at a time, mixing after each addition. You should have a lovely pate a choux dough. Transfer dough to a pastry bag fitted with a half-inch round tip. Pipe batter into small mounds (about the size of Hershey's Kisses) 1 inch apart. Use a little water on the tip of your finger to smooth out pointy tips.

Bake 10 minutes, then reduce heat to 350°F and bake until puffs are light, airy, and golden brown, about 20 to 30 minutes. Let cool on sheets while you make the filling.

In a medium bowl, whisk together ½ cup milk, egg yolks, ⅓ cup sugar, lime zest, and cornstarch. In a heavy saucepan over medium heat, add 1¾ cups milk, vanilla, and remaining sugar. Bring to a simmer without stirring.

Whisk hot mixture into egg yolks and return to the saucepan. Whisk constantly over heat until lime pastry cream thickens, about a minute or so. Remove from heat and transfer to a bowl. Cover with plastic wrap, placing wrap directly on cream to prevent a skin from forming. Chill 4 hours.

Fill a pastry bag fitted with a medium round tip and pipe cream into each puff from the bottom.

Serve.

Note: Pastry cream can be made up to 3 days in advance.

Note: Leftovers can be kept in the refrigerator up to a week in an airtight container.

Connect with Us

Visit us online at
KensingtonBooks.com
to read more from your favorite authors, see books
by series, view reading group guides, and more.

Join us on social media

for sneak peeks, chances to win books and prize packs,
and to share your thoughts with other readers.

facebook.com/kensingtonpublishing
twitter.com/kensingtonbooks

Tell us what you think!

To share your thoughts, submit a review,
or sign up for our eNewsletters, please visit:
KensingtonBooks.com/TellUs.

Grab These Cozy Mysteries from
Kensington Books

Forget Me Knot   978-0-7582-9205-6 $7.99US/$8.99CAN
Mary Marks

Death of a Chocoholic   978-0-7582-9449-4 $7.99US/$8.99CAN
Lee Hollis

Green Living Can Be   978-0-7582-7502-8 $7.99US/$8.99CAN
   Deadly
Staci McLaughlin

Death of an Irish Diva   978-0-7582-6633-0 $7.99US/$8.99CAN
Mollie Cox Bryan

Board Stiff   978-0-7582-7276-8 $7.99US/$8.99CAN
Annelise Ryan

A Biscuit, A Casket   978-0-7582-8480-8 $7.99US/$8.99CAN
Liz Mugavero

Boiled Over   978-0-7582-8687-1 $7.99US/$8.99CAN
Barbara Ross

Scene of the Climb   978-0-7582-9531-6 $7.99US/$8.99CAN
Kate Dyer-Seeley

Deadly Decor   978-0-7582-8486-0 $7.99US/$8.99CAN
Karen Rose Smith

To Kill a Matzo Ball   978-0-7582-8201-9 $7.99US/$8.99CAN
Delia Rosen

Available Wherever Books Are Sold!

All available as e-books, too!

Visit our website at **www.kensingtonbooks.com**